**Also by Debra Webb**

**SHADES OF DEATH**

*The Blackest Crimson* (prequel)
*No Darker Place*
*A Deeper Grave*
*The Coldest Fear*
*The Longest Silence*

Look for Debra Webb's next novel,

*The Secrets We Bury,*

available soon from MIRA Books.

For additional books by
*USA TODAY* bestselling author Debra Webb,
visit her website at www.debrawebb.com.

# DEBRA WEBB

# THE LONGEST SILENCE

mira

**mira**

ISBN-13: 978-0-7783-0854-6

Recycling programs
for this product may
not exist in your area.

The Longest Silence

For questions and comments about the quality of this book, please contact us at CustomerService@Harlequin.com.

www.Harlequin.com

**Printed in U.S.A.**

# CONTENTS

This book is dedicated to my sister and my two brothers. Growing up on a farm in small-town Alabama, we didn't have video games or iPads or cell phones. We had one television for the family that received three local channels. So we spent a lot of time reading books and creating our own entertainment. My sister, Mary Ann, was the caretaker when my parents were out working the farm. She was like a second mother and is a very talented singer and songwriter. She kept us entertained with her beautiful voice and her happy laughter, and our bellies full with her good cooking. My elder brother, Eddie, was the artist and the storyteller. His stories were always Hitchcockian and kept my younger brother and me scared of our own shadows. Johnny, my younger brother by two years, was my true partner in crime. We explored the farm and beyond, climbed trees and turned towels into superhero capes to see if we could fly off the smokehouse roof. We pretended to be superheroes and cops and robbers. Despite the ups and downs that came later in life, I am so lucky to have such a wonderful family. I love you all, and thank you so very much for inspiring me.

# THE LONGEST SILENCE

## Acknowledgments

Writing a fiction novel is hard work. An author puts her heart and soul into the task. It's extremely important to love the characters in your story. If you don't, it will show. In fact, for me, the characters are the most important element of the story. No matter how amazing and exciting the plot is, if you just can't connect to the characters, then what good is it? I love the characters in this story. They are real to me in so many ways. In particular, Joanna Guthrie's character is close to my heart. A tragic life event caused her to lose touch with her family. Eighteen years passed before they found each other again. This element of the story was deeply personal to me because the same thing happened between my elder brother and me. Seventeen long years passed without me seeing him or hearing his voice. I am immensely thankful to have him back in my life.

Another important aspect of creating a fiction novel is research. Since the work is fiction, I sometimes take liberties. For instance, the Aubri Lane Restaurant doesn't serve lunch, but for the purposes of this story it does. Milledgeville, Georgia, is a beautiful town. I so enjoyed visiting. The people are welcoming and charming. I felt completely at home and plan to return in the future. There are many folks I need to thank for their help in my research. First I must thank my assistant for the trip, Donna Boyd. She was a wonderful asset for taking photos and notes and just being good company. The wonderful folks at the Antebellum Inn Bed & Breakfast were incredible. The best place to stay in Georgia! I so enjoyed the delicious breakfasts with the other guests. From the local tour guides to the folks on the street, it was a treasured experience. Thanks to Wayne Crenshaw, Mike Couch, Dr. Bob Wilson and Nancy Davis Bray for providing direction and advice on the old asylum. I must thank Jamaal Hicks of Georgia College security. I was quite impressed with the highly trained and caring folks who take care of the students. There are too many other sources to name them all!

As always, please know that any liberties taken or mistakes made are mine and mine alone. Happy reading!

deep conversation with the officer. For Pete's sake, you would think she was some sort of criminal. This was what she got for attempting to obey the speed limit. Everyone else, including the old fart who'd hit her, wanted to fly like they were in a race against time.

The officer peered suspiciously in her direction once more.

This was ridiculous! Her hair was damp from the rain that continued to sprinkle just enough to be ignored by every single person except her standing on the side of this godforsaken road. On top of that she was freezing and no one appeared to care. The officers who were so kind at first now appeared too busy taking the old bastard's statement and shooting those wary looks in her direction. He sure as hell had no right to cry whiplash. He was the one who hit her, for God's sake!

Neither of the cops had offered to have her wait in one of the police cruisers or in her car. She groaned as she considered the ugly way the tailgate of her Mercedes was crushed. That old pickup had done a number on her SUV.

Where the hell was Art? The officer who'd taken her report had called him. Her husband would be livid. The Mercedes was barely a year old. God, this was all she needed. Ellen closed her eyes and tried to keep her body from swaying. The spinning eased a bit and she hugged her arms around herself to try and control the shivering. The rain made the cool morning air feel even colder.

"Ma'am."

Reluctantly she opened her eyes, grateful for the vehicle at her back since the whole world seemed to have joined the spinning in her head. "What now, Officer…?"

"Do not tell secrets to those whose faith and silence you have not already tested."
—Queen Elizabeth I

# One

*Westwood, Kansas*
*Friday, March 4, 8:30 a.m.*

Ellen Schrader only wanted a gallon of milk.

How was she supposed to feed her children break-fast without milk? Now her son was late for school. All because she'd needed that damned milk. What she got instead was rear-ended by an old man who couldn't see his hand in front of his face and suddenly somehow it was all her fault. No one had said as much but why else would that young officer be sending her so many sus-picious glances? He and the old man had been huddled together talking for far too long.

Probably whispering about her.

Ellen braced her hip against the police cruiser. T officer had told her to wait right here next to his cru All those flashing lights from not one but two p cruisers as well as the ambulance were making he swim. She'd already told the paramedic that she hurt. She was fine. Perfectly fine. Now he, too.

She frowned. What was his name? She blinked to clear her vision and stared at his chest. The two blurry name tags finally blended to become one. "Officer Edwards?"

"I'm afraid I'll need you to take a Breathalyzer test, ma'am."

His words hit her square in the stomach, making her sway again. "Are you suggesting I've been drinking?" She made a scoffing sound. "It's not even nine o'clock on a school day. Please."

For some unexplainable reason her knees began to shake.

"Ma'am," he said a bit more firmly, "you have the right to refuse, but then I'll have no choice but to arrest you."

The rain was coming down harder now. Ellen hugged herself more tightly. This could not be happening. Thank God Art's minivan pulled up behind the cruiser. As if the officer had only then realized they were all standing in the rain, he asked, "Mrs. Schrader, would you like to sit in the squad car?"

What difference did it make now? She was soaking wet already. Before she could say as much, Art shouted, "Ellen! Jesus Christ, are you all right?"

She tried her best to summon a smile for her husband but somehow her lips wouldn't make the transition. There was something she should remember but whatever it was her mind refused to cooperate. Her head automatically moved up and down in a nod that she was okay. Her knees tried to buckle. The officer— Officer Edwards—steadied her.

What was wrong with her?

Before she could explain to her husband that she really was perfectly fine except for the fact that the careless old man hunkered under his little umbrella with its one broken rib had ruined her car, Officer Edwards pulled him aside. Art would be very upset that Alton was late for school and that their daughter hadn't had her breakfast yet. It didn't help that Ellen wasn't feeling so well. She swayed again. She really needed to sit down.

Art looked from the officer to Ellen, fear or dismay claiming his handsome face. As if he'd only just realized that his wife could have been seriously injured in the accident, he rushed over to her and took her by the shoulders. Rather than pull her into his arms to comfort her, he shook her hard and for the first time in their ten years of marriage Ellen felt afraid.

"Where are the children?" he demanded, his voice an icy roar.

Ellen frowned. What did he mean where were the children? The two officers were back at her SUV, searching around inside. This made no sense.

Art shook her again. "Ellen, where are the children?"

"I…" She licked her lips. Her mouth felt so dry. "They're at home, of course. I wouldn't take them to the store with me when…" The rest of what she needed to say eluded her. Why hadn't she brought the children with her?

"Who's watching them?" he shouted.

"Art, please." She pulled free of his punishing grip and bumped against the cruiser. "The children are fine. I just had to run to the store for milk. I would have been home already if not for—"

He didn't wait for her to finish.

Her husband rushed back to his minivan and drove away, tires squealing. One of the officers followed in the second cruiser.

Officer Edwards took Ellen by the arm, his grasp firm. "Why don't we take that test now, and then we can drive to your home and make sure the children are okay?"

At this point the entire situation felt surreal, like a very bad dream. This couldn't be happening. She didn't understand all the fuss. Of course the children were okay. She would never allow them to ride with her when—when she'd been drinking.

*Drinking.* That was the thing she'd forgotten. She'd been drinking all morning. Something she'd seen on the news had upset her but she couldn't remember what it was. Ellen shook off the idea; she didn't want to think about that or the vodka she'd chugged as if her life depended on it.

Disappointment and hurt twisted inside her. Art would be so angry with her. The children would be upset she'd left them for so long. The accident wasn't supposed to happen. She was only going five miles to the store and then right back home.

Resigned to her fate, Ellen took the silly Breathalyzer test. Officer Edwards stared at her funny, and then he announced that she was under arrest. Focused on preventing herself from vomiting, she scarcely paid attention to the rights he read her. The spinning was completely out of control now.

This whole shitty morning had been blown way out of proportion. She hadn't done anything wrong. The entire ridiculous episode was the old man's fault. As the officer closed the cruiser door, imprisoning her in the back seat, she watched through the window as the asshole old man drove away free as a bird. The milk she'd bought was spoiling in her SUV and Alton was late for school. How many times could a child be late for kindergarten and still be promoted to first grade?

This was silly. They were all worried for nothing. The children were fine. Ellen loved her children more than anything else in this world. She would never, ever put them in danger. She was a good mother. Always careful. Like this morning, to ensure they were fine until she returned with the milk she had blockaded them in the coat closet before leaving the house. She'd made a game of it by telling them to stay hidden while Mommy went in search of the breakfast fairy. There was no reason for all this fuss or for Art to panic.

Fear knotted in her belly. Then again, she'd never expected to be gone so long.

How long had it been? Minutes? Hours? She tried to focus on the digital clock on the dash of the cruiser. Her vision wouldn't clear enough to read the blurry numbers. Didn't matter. When they got to her house everyone would see. The entire episode was nothing more than a series of unfortunate events. The children were fine.

Except the children weren't fine.

Ellen saw the flames the moment the cruiser turned onto her street. Her heart launched into her throat. People were crowded into the street—*her street*—watching the burning house—*her house*.

In time she would learn that the children had gotten out of the closet. Hours, instead of minutes, had passed since their mother left them and they were hungry. Fearless and protective, five-year-old Alton had tried to scramble eggs for his little sister.

The fire had started in the kitchen. The smoke alarms didn't send an alert to the monitoring service since Ellen had forgotten to pay the bills the past three months. Though her little boy had successfully wiggled the chair out of the way to open the closet door to freedom, he wasn't big enough or strong enough to get past the doors she had locked to keep them in the house.

# Two

The phone wouldn't stop ringing.

The annoying sound echoed off the dingy walls of the tiny one-room apartment.

Joanna Guthrie chewed her thumbnail as she stared at the damned cell phone. Three people had this number: her boss, a research analyst she occasionally worked with and *Ellen*. If it was work, the caller would simply leave a message, but it wasn't work—it was Ellen.

Jo's foot started to tap so she stood and paced the floor. "Not answering."

Why should she answer? The calls came about three or four times a year and they were always the same. Ellen would complain about her life and her husband and her kids. She would bemoan the hand fate had dealt her. She would never be whole. Nothing she attempted fixed her. Not the shrinks or the meditation or the yoga or any of the other crazier shit she'd tried, like cocaine, and certainly not the alcohol.

The ringing stopped.

Jo stared at the phone. Two minutes tops and it would start that fucking ringing again. She closed her eyes and exhaled a measure of the frustration always generated by calls from Ellen. Guilt immediately took its place. No matter the reason, whenever Ellen called Jo always wound up feeling guilty whether she answered the damned phone or not. A voice mail carried the same guilt-generating effect.

"Not my fault." She paced the room like a freshly incarcerated criminal on the front end of a life sentence.

Ellen had chosen her own path. She'd made the decision to pretend to be normal. Dared to marry and to have children. Jo shook her head. How the hell could she do that after what they went through—*what they did*? Now the woman spent every minute of every day terrified that she would somehow disappoint her family or that something bad would happen to them because of her. Or, worse, that someone would discover her secret—*their* secret.

*Deep breath.* "Not my problem."

Jo had made the smarter choice. She'd cut ties with her family and friends. No boyfriends much less husbands. No kids for damned sure. If she wanted sexual release she either took care of it herself or she picked up a soldier from one of the clubs in Killeen. She didn't go to church; she didn't live in the same town for more than a year. She never shared her history with anyone. Not that there was anything in her past that would give anyone reason to suspect the truth, but she hated the looks of sympathy, the questions.

The past was over and done. Dragging it into the present would not change what was done.

She had boundaries. Boundaries to protect herself. She never wasted time making small talk much less friends. Besides, she wasn't in one place long enough for anyone to notice or to care. Since her employer was an online newspaper, she rarely had to interact face-to-face with anyone. In fact, she and the boss had never met in person and he was the closest thing to a friend she had.

Whatever that made her, Jo didn't care.

Hysterical laughter bubbled into her throat. Even the IRS didn't have her address. She used the newspaper's address for anything permanent. Her boss faxed her whatever official-looking mail she received, and then shredded it. He never asked why. Jo supposed he understood somehow.

She recognized her behavior for what it was—paranoia. Plain and simple. Six years back she'd noticed one of those health fairs in the town where she'd lived. Probably not the most scientific or advanced technology since it was held in a school cafeteria. Still, she'd been desperate to ensure nothing had been implanted in her body—like some sort of tracking device—so she'd scraped up enough money to pay for a full-body scan. Actually she'd been short fifty bucks but the tech had accepted a quick fuck in exchange. After all that trouble he'd found nothing. Ultimately that was a good thing but it had pissed her off at the time.

A ring vibrated the air in the room.

Enough. Jo snatched up the phone. "What do you want, Ellen?"

The silence on the other end sent a surge of oily black uncertainty snaking around her heart. When she would have ended the call, words tumbled across the dead air.

"This is Ellen's husband."

A new level of doubt nudged at Jo. "Art?"

She had no idea how she remembered the man's name. Personal details were something else she had obliterated from her life. Distance and anonymity were her only real friends now.

*Now?* She almost laughed out loud at her vast under-statement. Eighteen years. She'd left any semblance of a normal life behind eighteen years ago. Jesus Christ, had it only been eighteen?

*Felt like forever.*

"Yours was the only name in Ellen's phone I didn't recognize." He chuckled but the sound held no humor. "Her mom and dad's number is there. Her little sister's. The number for Alton's school, my mom's and the pedi-atrician. Mine, of course. But yours was the only other one." He made a sound of surprise. "I never realized there was no one else. No friends. Not even any of the other mothers from Alton's class or from our neighbor-hood are in her contacts. I just assumed she lunched and shopped with the other mothers. Set up playdates, but Alton said no playdates." He sighed. "Doesn't re-ally matter now, I guess."

That inky blackness spread through Jo's chest like icy water rushing over a cliff. "Where's Ellen?"

Another of those humorless chuckles. "I wish I could tell you she's at home with Elle—that's our three-year-old. But Elle's with my mom. My wife isn't here at the hospital with me and Alton either."

Jo held back her questions through another long, weary sigh. A steady beep, beep, beep echoed in the background. He'd said he and Alton were in the hospital. "Is Ellen sick?"

Wait, he'd said Ellen wasn't there. *Doesn't matter. Doesn't matter. Doesn't matter.* Jo repeated those two words to herself during the silence that followed. Ellen's problems weren't hers.

Ellen made her own choices.

"No," Art finally said, his voice cracking on the single syllable. He cleared his throat. "Alton is having his second surgery, by the way. They weren't able to finish all the skin grafts with the first one. He'll be okay. Maybe one more surgery after this." Silence filled the air between them once more. "The fire wasn't her fault, you know. She didn't mean for any of this to happen. She tried. She really did. I should have given her more credit for trying."

*Fire?* As hard as she tried to ignore it, worry gnawed at Jo.

"In case you didn't know, Ellen had a serious problem."

*Had?* More of that tension twisted in Jo's gut.

Art drew in a shaky breath. "I tried to help her but nothing ever seemed to work. Don't worry though, Alton will be okay. The burns on his hands and arms will heal. I tried to tell her he'd be fine, but I guess I was so angry I waited too long to reassure her. At first I was too upset to think rationally. Any father would have done the same. I was so scared and so damned furious. I told her she had to leave. That I couldn't trust her to take care of the children anymore. So, you see, it's really my fault. I shouldn't have said so many hurtful things. I wasn't thinking... I was so upset by what she'd done." Pause. "I guess I should have called you sooner, but I—"

"Art," Jo snapped, "where is Ellen?"

He cleared his throat. "Ellen killed herself three weeks ago today. Last night I finally worked up the courage to go through some of her things and I thought—since you were the only friend listed in her contacts—that you might want to know. And maybe you could tell me what she meant by the note she left. Three words and I don't have a clue what they mean. *She knows everything.* Do you know what she meant by that?"

Jo ended the call.

Ellen had tried to call her three weeks ago and Jo had ignored the incessant ringing. No voice mail was left. If a caller didn't leave a voice mail, you weren't actually obligated to call back, right? It had been a Saturday. Must have been the day before...

Jo sank onto the floor and hugged her knees to her chest. She should have answered. She should have tried to be the friend Ellen's husband thought she was. And Ellen was right. She did know everything—Jo had lived it with her. Now the only other person who knew what really happened eighteen years ago was dead.

Jo wondered why in all this time she'd never considered taking that avenue out of this pretend life she muddled through?

Maybe because she was a coward—or maybe because if she did then the bad guys won.

She looked around the place she called home for now. Her entire apartment was this one ten-by-twelve room. Even the bathroom was nothing more than a small corner hidden behind a makeshift partition wall. The wood floors were worn and creaked with every step she made. The plaster on the walls was cracked, the blue paint faded. The only window was covered with a cheap, nicotine-stained paper blind, the sort made for temporary use. There was a tired sofa that served as a bed, along with a rickety metal and Formica table accompanied by two well-worn chairs. Along the shared wall between this room and the neighbor's the kitchenette looked like something out of a 1950s Airstream.

Jo blinked. None of it really mattered. There was a roof over her head and four walls to protect her from the weather and whatever other threat showed up. No leaks in the roof and the plumbing worked most of the time. She pushed to her feet and shoved her cell into the back pocket of her jeans. Uncertainty and disappointment and all the other weaknesses she rarely allowed herself to feel suddenly assaulted her.

Memories from her former life poured through the emptiness inside her before she could stop them. She'd had a family. She'd had a scholarship. The future had been hers for the taking. Now, Jo turned all the way around in the middle of the room; she was thirty-six years old and *this* was her life—all because she'd made a terrible, terrible mistake eighteen years ago.

Poor Ellen had tried as best she could to salvage some semblance of a life and look how that turned out.

Bottom line, they had both allowed persons whose names they hadn't known—whose faces they couldn't be certain they had ever seen—to get away with destroying their lives.

Determination surged in Jo's veins. Ellen was dead. The *other* girl was dead. Jo suspected the bastards who had orchestrated all of this were responsible for numerous other devastated lives and deaths, as well. Was she going to do nothing and allow them to never have to face responsibility for what they'd done?

Jo had been silent far too long.

Besides, what did she have to lose?

Not one damned thing that wasn't already gone.

# *Three*

The god-awful sound wouldn't go away. Like an earthquake shaking the whole damned townhouse, the noise splitting his skull.

Former Special Agent Anthony LeDoux cracked one eye open. Sunlight poured in through the slits in the blinds and he snapped his eyes shut once more. What idiot designed bedrooms facing east? Better question, what idiot rented a townhouse with a bedroom facing east?

A rusty groan growled out of him. *You did, Tony. Special agent... Yeah right.*

He should probably get up. Maybe eat something so he wouldn't lose any more weight. Maybe even do something worthwhile like look for a job. His brain ached with the weight of the thought.

What the hell time was it? One hand tunneled from under the sheet and pawed across the bedside table until he found his cell phone. Once his fingers wrapped around it, he dared to raise his head from the pillow. Pain abruptly throbbed in his skull like a series of IED blasts.

"Shit." Despite the agony, he forced his eyes open and peered at the cell phone—*11:20 a.m.* "Christ."

Before he could drop the phone back onto the table it vibrated. So that was the infernal noise that had awakened him. Even with the phone in his hand the noise was like a blender full of rocks roaring on high speed. He stared at the screen until the caller's identity came into focus.

*Angie.*

Oh hell. Tony cleared his throat and said hello aloud a couple of times just to make sure he sounded normal and not hungover before answering. "Hey, sis. What's up?" Didn't help. His voice sounded rusty and cracked twice.

"It's Tiffany."

He sat upright, the room rocking like a boat about to capsize. Plowing a hand through his hair, he prayed his head wouldn't explode before he got through this conversation. "What'd she do? Drop out of school?"

His niece had been the perfect angel from the day she was born until high school. It was as if the day she turned sixteen she wanted to make up for lost time. The girl had given her conservative parents pure hell the past three years. As Angie's only sibling, Tony had been the sounding board for the worst of the awful episodes. Thankfully things had been mostly quiet since Tiffany left for college. He'd hoped she had grown out of her wild stage.

A sob echoed in his ear and his heart reacted. "Ang, what's going on?"

He stood. Swayed some more before he could steady himself. It wasn't until then that he noticed the blonde in his bed. Her bare ass and rumpled mane were the only parts not covered by the tangled sheet. What the hell was her name? Chelsea? Chanel? Fuck! He couldn't remember.

"She's missing, Tony," Ang said in his ear. "My girl is missing."

A hint of fear roiled in his belly. He turned away from the blonde, who hadn't moved. "Okay, sis. Take it from the top. Tell me what happened."

As Angie spoke, he put her on speaker and left his phone on the table while he searched for his jeans and shirt. When the blonde still didn't move, he leaned close and listened for any sign of breathing. She smelled of expensive perfume and high-octane vodka. Her soft purrs confirmed she had survived whatever the hell they'd done last night.

"We wanted her to come home for spring break," his sister went on, "but she had other plans. She wouldn't say what or with whom. Said it was none of our business and that we'd hear from her when she got back. So we thought maybe she had a boyfriend. Maybe a serious one. But ever since spring break she's been distant. I called her every day last week and she never answered or called me back." More of those heart-twisting sobs resonated in the room.

Tony hopped on one foot and then the other to tug on his jeans. "Is she showing up for class?"

"She was in class on Friday, but she didn't show up for any of her classes yesterday or this morning."

"Whoa, whoa, wait a minute." The room spun a little so Tony sat down on the bed. The blonde moaned but didn't move. He picked up the phone and took it off speaker. "Let's not get ahead of ourselves. It's not even noon, Ang. Maybe she's just late. She could be on her way back from a weekend trip right now." His niece had hardly been out of pocket long enough to overreact. Ang did that sometimes. She was particularly emotional when it came to her only child.

"No. No, I spoke to her roommate. Tiffany didn't—"

"Ang, listen." He rubbed at the back of his skull. Damn, his head hurt. The taste of bile and vodka climbed up his throat. He swallowed it back. "She's nineteen and trying out her wings. Wait and see... She'll show up sometime today. Just try to stay calm."

"You don't understand!"

His sister's raised voice was like a bullet to his brain; he flinched. He needed something for this headache. Angie was older—only by fifteen months—and she never let Tony forget it. As calmly as he could, he said, "Explain it to me then."

"None of her clothes are missing. Nothing. If she went on a weekend trip, wouldn't she take something? A change of clothes? Her purse?"

That drop of fear he'd felt earlier widened into a distinct trickle. "She didn't take her purse? What about her driver's license and cell phone?"

"No. Nothing. Tony," Ang said somberly, "she didn't even take her makeup or her Jeep."

A flood of uncertainty crowded into his chest now,

making his next breath difficult. "Okay. Have you alerted campus security?"

His niece was a beautiful girl and certainly didn't need cosmetics to enhance her natural beauty but she refused to step out the door without the works. If she didn't take her makeup, she hadn't left willingly. Not to mention her cell phone and driver's license. If they possessed one or both, no teenager left without them.

"Yes, of course. We're headed to Milledgeville now. I need you, Tony. I don't care what's going on with you and the Bureau—I need you. *Tiffany* needs you."

With Ang and Steve in Dahlonega, the drive down to Milledgeville would take between two and three hours. They would arrive well ahead of Tony, which meant he had to get moving.

He leaned forward, fighting back the urge to vomit, and gathered his sneakers. "Call the Dean and ask him to put campus security on high alert. As soon as you get to Milledgeville, go straight to the security office. I'll call the Milledgeville chief of police and explain our concerns so he'll see the urgency in the situation."

"Thank you." His sister made a keening sound. "What if—"

"Ang, stop. Don't even go there right now." She started to cry and the sound was like daggers twisting in his chest. In the background her husband, Steve, offered quiet reassurances. When silence filled the air between them, Tony said, "Listen to me, sis, we'll find her."

"Promise me, Tony. Promise me you'll find our baby."

"I promise."

The call dropped off. Tony blew out a heavy breath. Now sure as hell wasn't the time to tell his sister that he wasn't simply having trouble with the Bureau—he had resigned from his position at BAU-2. He'd been keeping that secret from his ex-wife and his sister for more than a month. He glanced back at the blonde. He'd filled his nights with booze and women whose names he couldn't remember the next morning. Like a vampire, he spent his days sleeping.

He grabbed his shirt and headed for the bathroom. A better man would shave and shower before hitting the road, but Tony wasn't a better man anymore. He'd stopped being that man more than a year ago.

Bitter bile rushed into his throat and he barely made it to the toilet. He heaved until there was nothing left to exorcise from his gut.

*The path of self-destruction.* His new boss had said those words to him in the final weeks before Tony gave the hard-nosed asshole and the Bureau the middle finger. He flushed the toilet and, with effort, pushed to his feet. He ducked his head under the faucet and rinsed his mouth. Swiping his face with his forearm, he stared at his reflection. He definitely needed to shave. Needed a haircut. Looked like death warmed over.

No time to fix his broken image.

He bumped into the wall on his way to the walk-in closet. The idea that his blood alcohol level might still be lingering above the legal limit filtered through his mind. No time to fix that either. He'd take food and water with him and work on that particular issue en route. He grabbed the leather overnight bag he'd used for the eleven years of service he'd given the Federal Bureau of Investigation.

He ignored the row of suits and crisply pressed shirts and stuffed a couple of polo shirts and another pair of jeans, socks and underwear into the bag. A pair of loafers went in next. Should have gone in first. Before his fall from grace he'd packed this damned bag so meticulously that even his shirts came out as smooth as when they'd gone in. Not anymore. On second thought he shoved a suit jacket into the bag. If he halfway looked the part maybe Angie wouldn't have too many questions.

At the door to the bedroom he remembered his Dopp kit. He might not want to shave now but he'd have to eventually if he expected the local cops to listen to what he had to say. He added the toiletry kit to his bag.

As a profiler for the Bureau he'd spent a lot of years learning how to manipulate the locals to accomplish his goal. In fact, he'd become a master manipulator. Maybe all that bad Karma he'd left in his wake had finally caught up to him.

He glanced at the blonde in his bed. This was the part he always dreaded.

Chelsea or Chanel wasn't happy about being roused. She called him every foul name in her vast repertoire while he helped her dress. When he'd called a cab, he gave her a bottle of water and maneuvered her out of the building. As the car pulled away from the curb she shouted *asshole* and flipped her middle finger at him.

Nothing he didn't deserve. He climbed into his BMW and collapsed against the seat. *Anthony LeDoux, this is your life.*

Somehow, until he figured out where the hell Tiffany was, he'd have to find a way to pull himself together and at least pretend his world hadn't gone to shit and that he could help rescue his niece from whatever trouble she had gotten herself into.

Too bad he'd lost his hero credentials months ago.

# *Four*

It was late, but the tension in the chief of police's office was motivated by far more than the hour. Tony sensed the animosity the moment he walked through the entrance doors of the Public Safety building. Obviously, the man already had Tony's number. Not surprising. Any cop worth his salt would do his homework.

There was a time when Tony had been damned good at prompting all the right reactions. Not anymore.

Since it was well past business hours, a uniformed officer had been waiting to allow him into the one-story building and then to escort him to the office of the town's top cop. A tall, fit man, Chief Arlan Phelps had no doubt spent the last thirty or so years in law enforcement and possessed no tolerance for those who used evasion and innuendo to manipulate events.

Not so good for Tony since these days those were his most valuable assets.

"Make yourself comfortable, Agent LeDoux." Phelps gestured to the chair in front of his desk.

"Thanks." Tony settled into the offered seat, careful to keep his gaze on the chief. He'd pulled over at a truck stop outside Atlanta. After topping off the gas tank, he'd spent some time in the bathroom shaving and changing clothes. Then he'd forced himself to eat a hot meal. He'd used some Visine to tone down his bloodshot eyes and popped a couple of Advil. By the time he made the exit for Milledgeville some ninety miles later he felt reasonably human.

Phelps hadn't stopped staring at him since he came into the room. The older man smoothed a palm over his slick head. "There is nothing in this world I hate more than having my time wasted, and you, *Mr.* LeDoux, wasted a good deal of my time this afternoon."

So, he knew Tony's secret. Great. Might as well play this out and see if there was anything salvageable. "How do you mean, Chief? When a young woman—anyone for that matter—goes missing, I take it very seriously, and time is not an asset that should ever be wasted in a situation such as this one."

"The FBI tells me you're no longer in their service." Phelps leaned back in his chair and rested his hands on its worn, smooth wooden arms. "I don't know what to make of that, *Mr.* LeDoux. Isn't it against the law to impersonate a federal agent?"

Now he was just being an asshole.

Tony nodded. "You're right. I used the position I once held to prompt you to action. The truth is Tiffany is my niece—my only niece, daughter of my only sister. My goal is to ensure everything possible is done to find her." He held up a hand when Phelps would have spoken. "I no longer serve the Bureau, that's true, but I did and I was very good at my job. I can help—I *want*—to help."

Phelps smiled. "I figured as much after I spoke with the girl's parents. Here's the problem." He leaned forward, eliciting a groan from his chair. "We have no real proof at this time that Tiffany Durand is missing. She's nineteen years old and even her roommate said she might just have decided to take a little vacation with the new guy she's seeing and hasn't made it back to class in time. It happens. It's too early to get worried just yet."

Tony prepared to list the litany of reasons that assessment was inaccurate except this time Phelps was the one holding up his hand. So Tony grabbed onto his last shred of patience and heard the man out.

"I make my decision based on facts and the facts simply don't indicate foul play just yet. I don't know how well you keep up with your niece, but this isn't the first time she's disappeared. Campus security is lead on any case that involves the students and they've questioned her roommate and several of her friends—just because her parents called. I spoke with the chief over there—for no other reason than you asked me to do so. As you know, without some indication of foul play or suggestion of imminent danger, Tiffany is not technically missing. She's a nineteen-year-old woman who didn't show up for class and who has a record of doing so. The good news is she always comes back. Never misses more than a day or two."

When the chief paused to take a breath, Tony argued, "We believe this time is different. Tiffany's mother knows her better than anyone and she has reason—"

"Mr. and Mrs. Durand explained their feelings very clearly and we all completely understand their misgivings. Hell, I have two daughters and raising them about put me six feet under. Girls, no matter how smart and how sweet, can break your heart and scare you half to death."

Tony took a moment as if he were weighing the chief's sage words. "So, you're choosing to impose a waiting period?"

Federal law left the decision in the hands of local law enforcement, but few opted to hold out and be the reason a missing child or young adult became a homicide case. Tony held the older man's gaze. Men like Phelps didn't like veering outside the lines. They chose a path in their careers and they never deviated, kept it simple. But life wasn't simple. Tony had seen up close what a psychopathic serial killer could do to a victim in a couple of hours. Time was always the enemy.

"Tiffany's done this before," Phelps reminded him. "The security folks over at the college are an outstanding team. They go through the same training as our state police so we're not talking about a group of rent-a-cops. They've performed their due diligence. Frankly, they've already gone above and beyond—questioning other students, talking to her professors. They haven't been twiddling their thumbs over there. In fact, I've spoken to the chief several times today. Based on Tiffany's previous activities, he feels she'll show up in the next twenty-four hours."

"Her previous activities?" The headache had resurrected and started to throb behind Tony's eyes. "You keep insinuating she's done this before but I'm not hearing any actual dates or firm accounts."

Phelps heaved an impatient sigh. "Twice last semester and a third time back in February, she disappeared for a couple of days. Her confidential contact confirmed that she left of her own volition after her final class last Friday. Bottom line, at this time we have no credible reason to consider her missing. If she does not show up or contact her family or confidential contact by tomorrow morning, we'll move forward with a missing person report."

"Confidential contact?"

"Each student has the option of designating a confidential contact that isn't necessarily a parent or other next of kin. Typically, a confidential contact is close to the student and would be aware of his or her whereabouts."

"Well." Tony stood. He closed the button of his jacket. "I'll see you first thing in the morning, Chief."

Before Tony reached the door, Phelps said, "You're that convinced she's not going to show up."

Tony thought of all Angie had told him. "I wouldn't be here otherwise."

He reached for the door once more, and Phelps said, "Sit back down, Agent LeDoux."

Tony hesitated for a couple of seconds, mostly to annoy the man. Finally, he turned and took the three steps back to his chair. There was only one reason to continue this discussion after such a lengthy discourse of reasons not be concerned. "You know something you haven't shared with the family."

"I'm speaking to you in a professional capacity."

*Could have fooled me.* "I appreciate that, Chief."

"This goes no further than this room. We have to consider the welfare of our students and the last thing we want is to have them unnecessarily unsettled."

What he really meant was he didn't want parents calling to demand answers. "I understand."

"There's another freshman who didn't show up for class yesterday."

The rising tide of fear Tony had been holding back for the past nine hours threatened to push past his defenses. He needed a drink. "Any similarities?"

Phelps nodded. "Her purse, other personal belongings as well as her cell phone are still in her room. Her car is still in student parking, just like Tiffany's. Unlike your niece's, this girl's confidential contact insists that something is wrong. Since this student has no history of failure to show up for class or of disappearing for a couple of days without telling anyone, her parents have already been contacted. The chief over at campus security, Ed Buckley, has started the missing person protocol."

"Are my niece and this other student friends? Classmates?"

Phelps reached for a manila file on his desk. He opened it and pushed it toward Tony. "As far as we can tell, they don't know each other. Had no classes together and look nothing alike. No friends in common. About the only trait the two share is that they're both students who maintain a steady four point oh."

Tony studied the file. Vickie Parton was eighteen. Her black hair was one of those feathery short cuts and her eyes were hazel. Other than being model thin, Par-

ton and his niece had nothing whatsoever in common—
on the outside.

Phelps scrubbed a hand over his somber face. "No
one has seen or heard from her since her final class on
Friday afternoon."

Tony pushed the folder back toward him. "I'll see
you in the morning."

Phelps nodded.

"You know," the chief said, stopping Tony at the
door once more, "I can already tell I'm not going to
like you, LeDoux."

Tony shifted to face him. "If it makes you feel any
better, I was just thinking the same thing."

One corner of the older man's mouth quirked. "But
if you can help, I'll pretend for as long as it takes."

Tony gave a nod. "Sounds like a plan."

As he moved along the corridor, Tony gave himself
a mental pat on the back. He might be out of the game
but he hadn't lost his touch. He would find Tiffany. If
his niece had been harmed in any way, whoever did the
deed better hope the locals found him before Tony did.

*Antebellum Inn, 11:00 p.m.*

"I wanted you close."

Tony dredged up a smile for his sister. "Saved me
the trouble of looking for a place."

Angela LeDoux Durand looked so damned much
like their mother with her fair skin and dark hair and
those oddly pale eyes, more gold than brown. Sometimes even her voice made him have to look twice to
ensure their mom wasn't talking to him. Tony had in-

herited his lighter hair and darker eyes from their father. Right now, his sister's eyes were filled with worry and fear—the same worry and fear he felt churning in his gut.

"I was afraid you'd be angry."

Tony tossed his bag on the floor of the room. "Why would I be angry?"

Ang had been to Milledgeville several times to see Tiffany. She'd stayed at this historic inn every time, which was why she'd automatically called in a reservation on the way here. Only this time she'd reserved a room for him, as well. Not a problem. Really. He and Ang had always been close. As kids they'd been inseparable. Even as teenagers they'd shared many of the same friends. Adulthood hadn't changed that—at least not until recently. Sharing the news of his divorce with his sister had been relatively easy; the career crash and burn, however, was a whole different ball game. He didn't want to see the disappointment in her eyes. She'd always looked at him as if he was a hero, starting the day he'd kicked nine-year-old Lacon Turner's butt for putting gum in her hair.

He did not want to fail her or Tiffany now.

Ignoring his question, she gestured to the room at large. "I knew you'd need some privacy. I hope this works."

The pool cottage was behind the main house with its four guest rooms. A narrow rear yard, small parking lot and the pool stood between the cottage and the back steps of the hundred-plus-year-old home. The cottage accommodation was bigger than the rooms in the house and had its own kitchen. His sister had been right about the need for privacy. The last thing he wanted right now was for her to start worrying about his personal issues.

He gave her a nod. "It's perfect."

She summoned a weary smile. "Good. I'll see you in the morning."

She'd insisted he replay verbatim his meeting with the chief of police. To prevent the hysteria he noted beneath the surface of her carefully controlled expression, he'd done as she asked—except for the news about the other girl. He loved his sister and he would do anything to find Tiffany, but there were some things civilians didn't need to know.

Civilians? He almost laughed at himself. *You're a civilian now, dumb ass.*

Maybe so, but he'd seen things. There were things he couldn't erase from his brain—things that haunted him every single hour of every day of his life. Those things were what really scared him where Tiffany was concerned.

*Don't go there yet.*

Before his sister could go, he pulled her close and hugged her tight. "We'll find her, Ang. I promise."

She cried for a minute. He squeezed his eyes shut to hold back his own emotion. He had to be strong for her and for Tiffany.

Tony stood at the door and watched as she crossed the property, returning to the main house. The night air had a chill to it. Once Ang was inside, he closed and locked the door. He plugged in the laptop Ang had carried in for him. The damned thing had been in the trunk of his car since the day he walked out of his office. The box of personal possessions from his office was still in his trunk, too. He hadn't cared about looking at any of it. The few scattered personal items he'd kept on his desk were just a reminder that he'd screwed up. The photo of his ex-wife he'd shoved into a drawer months ago. The bag of peppermints he'd recently started using to conceal the alcohol on his breath. The keys to the house that was no longer his. His ex got the house and the dog and his best friend—who hadn't really been a friend at all as it turned out. Tony had gotten nothing. Didn't matter. He didn't need anything. The townhouse he moved to suited his needs and friends were overrated.

Enough about the past. His new motto was to live in the moment.

He closed the blinds and dug into his bag where he'd stashed the pint of bourbon he'd found in the trunk— ironically in the box of personal effects from his office.

He opened cabinet doors until he found the mugs. A mug in hand, he made himself comfortable at the table. He fired up the laptop. While it loaded, he poured himself a healthy serving of bourbon. He'd been dying for a drink all evening.

The first sip burned like hell. But the promise of that burn allowed him to begin to relax. He downed another swallow and focused his attention on the laptop screen. Time to see what his niece had been up to on social media. He may have walked away from his career with the Bureau's Behavioral Analysis Unit but he still had a few valuable contacts.

Even when the police had officially listed her as missing, it would take time to unlock all the barriers that prevented law enforcement from seeing what Tiffany had been doing online and on her cell phone the final days and hours before she disappeared.

Tony intended to know as much of that as possible before he closed his eyes tonight.

The chief had made a reasonable point when he mentioned Tiffany's occasional disappearing acts. Tony got that. But this time was different. He trusted his sister's instincts far more than he did those of Chief Phelps.

There were necessary steps that had to be taken before determining Tiffany's status. As with unlocking her phone and social media accounts, each step required time.

If she was in trouble, time represented one of the biggest threats to her staying alive.

# *Five*

Jo reached for her coffee but curled her shaking hand into a fist rather than risk picking up the mug.

She wasn't supposed to come back here. *Ever.* In fact, she hadn't set foot in the state of Georgia since she left eighteen years ago. *Never coming back. Never, never coming back.* She shouldn't be here now. Deep breath. No choice.

*Keep your head on straight, Jo.*

From what she could see last night not that much had changed other than the old asylum had closed down. She'd read about the closure a few years ago.

*Not soon enough.*

Images flickered through her brain. She pushed them away. Don't look. Don't look. *Have to look.*

They should burn the whole place down. Every decaying building.

A complete contrast to the old asylum, Milledgeville

was a quaint place that exuded small-town charm and promised parents of potential students that it was a safe and wholesome setting. In truth, it was, for the most part, despite the college campus and endless assortment of official and unofficial sorority and frat houses. Bars, clubs, restaurants, boutiques. All the things every college student needed handy for the launch into adulthood.

Jo went for her coffee again. This time she managed to lift the mug without the risk of spilling the hot brew. She downed a couple of swallows as she stared out the window toward Hancock Street. The first day of her freshman year she'd been so excited. No one in her family had ever gone to college. She was the first. Her parents had been so proud. Even her brother—a man who was far more contented with his head under a hood than in a book—seemed genuinely happy for her.

She'd arrived with big dreams and fully determined to prove she deserved the opportunity. She hadn't bothered with friends the first semester. Her academic work had been her singular focus. Christmas had arrived and she'd stayed on campus to volunteer with local Christmas charities and to earn some extra cash. She'd gotten a job through the holiday season so she could afford a couple of new outfits and presents to send back home.

Every day had been a new adventure. She was so happy. Then winter started to fade and the promise of spring in the air had her hoping for more.

*Her first mistake.*

Ray had come to Milledgeville to help with the search on the ninth of March eighteen years ago. Her mother hadn't been able to come. Their father had been too ill to travel. Cancer. He'd died a year later. She doubted her brother or her mother would ever forgive her for not coming to the funeral.

They didn't understand.

How could they? She had never told anyone what really happened. She and Ellen had made a pact never to tell. Would it have changed anything if they had told the truth? Would Ellen and the others be alive? Probably not.

Jo shouldn't have come back here. *Had to*. Two weeks, one day and six hours had been required for her to work up her nerve to begin the journey from Texas to Georgia. She'd rolled into town in the middle of the night last night. Slept in her twelve-year-old Celica. Nothing like traveling in style.

She was here. That alone was a freaking miracle. Eighteen years. Seventeen years, ten months and twenty-five days to be exact since she left this place.

Jo watched the cars on Hancock Street cruise by. This time of year prospective students were visiting the campus with their parents. Two young girls sat on the bench outside the Blackbird right now. Faces all smiles. Hearts full of excitement. Probably freshmen with that first awkward year nearly behind them or high school seniors hoping to start in the fall. Their futures were just beginning. Others rushed along the sidewalk. Most of the students lived on campus or in one of the sorority or frat houses and used bicycles to get around. Milledgeville was that sort of town. She'd had a bike eighteen years ago. But then she'd sold it when she decided to leave. A single backpack with a couple of changes of clothes was all she'd carried with her when she boarded that bus to anywhere but here.

At the front of the café the door opened and new voices filled the coffee shop. Jo scrutinized the group. So young. They had no idea how important the decisions they made today would be to their futures.

She'd made the wrong decisions and she'd paid the price. Every single night of her life she woke up at least once with her heart racing and her skin clammy with fear that someone was coming for her—that someone knew what she had done, that *they* would show up at her door.

No one ever came. After nearly eighteen years it was obvious that the only evil she or Ellen or any of the others had to face was their own reflections—the fear, the secrets. *The truth.* And the years of silence.

Jo started to push the memories away but stopped. She had come back to this place to confront the past. No more pushing it away. No more running. She picked up her cell phone and studied the screen. On the drive here she'd considered calling her mom. She'd only spoken to her once or twice since she left, but she did send her a card on her birthday every year. Disappearing without letting her mother know from time to time that she was okay had been something she couldn't do.

Her hometown of Madison was less than an hour north of here. She turned her phone screen down on the table. Not yet. She had to take care of this first. When this was done, she would call her mother and maybe even drop by for a short visit. Ray probably wouldn't speak to her and certainly wouldn't want to see her. He was married now and had two kids. She didn't know

Tracey, the woman he married. According to Facebook, she was a nurse. Ray was still a mechanic at the same garage he'd worked at when Jo was in high school and then in college, only he owned the place now.

Sometimes she felt like a stalker following his wife's social media activities but it made her feel better knowing they were all okay. Her mom had wanted grandchildren. She looked happy in the photos Tracey posted. Jo didn't have any social media accounts of her own. Instead she used her neighbor's. Wherever she lived there was always at least one neighbor who was careless. Leaving a door unlocked, drinking or drugging too much. Using the apps on their phones was easy. She could look at whatever she wanted, and then delete the history.

"You sure you don't want something to eat, hon?"

Jo looked up at the server who'd asked that question about half an hour ago. She'd been here too long. Time to move. "No, thanks. I'm good."

The server—Regina—frowned. "All right then." She placed the check for the coffee facedown on the table.

Grabbing the check, Jo stood and headed for the register. She made it a point to avoid eye contact with those she passed. Not meeting people's gazes had become automatic, like dressing nondescriptly and keeping her hair short so she didn't call attention to herself.

Two customers were in front of her at the register so she waited.

"No," a girl behind her insisted, "I'm telling you this is for real. I heard my father talking to the chief of police this morning. That girl is missing. She left class on Friday and never came back. I think," she added in an attempt at a whisper that failed miserably, "there might be two missing."

Jo pulled her compact from her bag and pretended to check her teeth. She scrutinized the girl seated in the booth across the aisle directly behind her. Young. Likely a student. She was huddled in the booth with a guy, maybe her boyfriend or a study partner.

The guy said, "Well, your dad's the sheriff. I guess he would know."

The girl looked around again before saying, "It'll be all over the news by this afternoon. It's cray cray. The one who's for sure missing is a freshman so I don't know her. Poor thing, she probably went home with the wrong guy. It happens, you know."

"You're gonna have to hand me that check, hon, if you want me to ring you up."

Jo jerked her attention forward and passed the check to the server behind the register. "Sorry." She dug for a bill from her purse and handed it to the woman. "Keep the change."

"Are you sure?"

Jo was already headed for the door. She didn't look back.

"This is a twenty! You only had coffee," followed her out the door.

Jo forced her feet to slow. Running would only draw attention to herself. *Deep breath. Another.* She climbed into her Celica and locked the doors. More slow deep breaths. She needed to calm down.

At least one freshman was missing.

Didn't mean the abduction was relevant to why Jo was here. Hundreds of people went missing every day all over the country. That would be way too big of a co-incidence. Not possible. Her fingers tightened around the steering wheel.

*Think.*

If by some bizarre twist of fate it was *him*, the girl had potentially been unaccounted for at least four days. That left another ten days—if she was like Jo, like Ellen—until it was too late.

*Stop borrowing trouble, Jo-Jo.* She had no idea the circumstances of the girls' disappearances.

"Stay focused."

She drew in a deep breath. *Stick to the plan.* Going to the cops at this stage would be premature—a mistake. She couldn't help if she was detained for questioning or worse, arrested.

Can't tell the whole truth yet. *Can't tell.* Gotta keep quiet for now.

But if those two girls were taken by the same person who took Ellen and her, Jo had at best ten days to find the truth before someone died.

Only what the police didn't know was that there wouldn't be just two victims—no one knew about the other girl yet.

# Six

Tony moved slowly through the shared space where Tiffany had lived for the past nine months. The suite was reasonably sized. On her side of the room was a typical twin-size bed with nightstand, a desk and chair, bookshelf, chest of drawers and lockable closet. The closet had been unlocked when he arrived. The roommate, Riley Fallon, stated that Tiffany never locked her closet. He snapped photos as he went along to review later. This might be his only opportunity for access to the room.

The roommate and Angie had been allowed to view the closet before their official questioning for the purpose of attempting to determine if anything was missing. Both had confirmed that Tiffany's belongings, as best either one could tell, were all there. Tony was amazed at Angie's ability to remain so strong during the questioning that followed. She explained how Tiffany would never leave without her makeup, purse and cell phone. No one challenged that assessment. The birth control pills found in the nightstand drawer added yet another check to the *missing* column. Angie hadn't known Tiffany was on birth control but didn't appear upset about it. The date of the prescription and the number of missing pills indicated Tiffany had taken one every day until the day she was last seen in this room— four days and eighteen hours ago. Tony snapped a photo of the prescription just in case. Never knew what would turn out to be important.

In his opinion there was more than enough evidence to confirm the status of missing. Phelps as well as Chief Buckley of campus security were now equally convinced. A press conference was held at eight this morning and the alerts were issued. The Georgia Bureau of Investigation as well as the Federal Bureau of Investigation had been notified. Setting up a joint task force with Chief Buckley as lead was the next order of business for the local authorities. Something else that would burn valuable time they didn't have to spare, but it was a necessary step. The more eyes they had on the case, the more boots on the ground, the better.

Tony sat down in the chair on Tiffany's side of the room and waited for Riley Fallon, the roommate, to return to the dorm. In this morning's interview she had stated that she came back to the room for lunch Monday through Friday. She used the break in her schedule for relaxing and studying. According to Riley, Tiffany often did the same thing. Only Angie didn't think so. Not that Tiffany's mother called the other girl a liar or even countered her statement, it was the expression on Angie's face that alerted Tony to her feelings on the matter. Later he'd asked her and she'd mentioned that Tiffany talked about the quad and the many wonderful places provided by the college for students to chill. He'd noticed the benches and tables. Lots of places for students to hang out besides trudging back to the dorm.

Riley Fallon hadn't been completely honest. Even without Angie's thoughts on the matter, Tony had watched the young woman's gaze avert when asked a direct question and the way she fidgeted. Fingers tugging at cuticles, then clasping and unclasping. Reaching up and adjusting her hair repeatedly. Chewing her bottom lip. Clearing her throat again and again. Looking anywhere as she spoke except at the person who'd asked the question. Classic signs of deception.

The question now was whether what she was hiding was relevant to the investigation into Tiffany's disappearance.

Residue from the search for fingerprints still littered surfaces in the room. Since the roommate needed to use this room and no indication of foul play had actually occurred in this space, the forensic techs had made quick work of going over the room and clearing out so as not to disrupt the resident. Extensive photos had been taken as well as the sheets from Tiffany's bed and the few items from her laundry bag.

Coming back for a second round of questions was motivated by more than the idea that Tony thought Riley Fallon was lying, it was the lack of sincere concern for her roommate that bothered him most. It was the way that, when the interview was over, she looked directly at the person asking the questions and presented a worried face without the first drop of moisture appearing in her eyes and insisted she hoped Tiffany was okay.

The key turned in the door lock but the door only partly opened. "I need the money before we go in."

Riley's voice.

"Sure."

Male voice.

After a few seconds, Riley said, "Okay. Ten minutes. That's all you get for twenty bucks."

"That's all I need."

Well, well. The roommate had decided to try her hand at entrepreneurship while she was still a freshman. And right here in the dorm. How ambitious of her. Tony sat back and waited.

The two came into the room and Riley closed the door and locked it. The impatient young man was already unfastening his fly when Riley turned and spotted Tony. Her eyes rounded behind her nerdy glasses and he saw the first hint of genuine emotion there.

"Give him his money back and send him on his way and we'll pretend this—" Tony gestured to the two of them "—never happened."

"Holy shit, is that your dad?" the guy asked, hands going up in front of his chest as if to protect himself from a coming attack.

"Just go." Riley shoved the twenty at him. He almost fell over his own feet trying to reach the door while fumbling with his fly. Another half a minute elapsed with him struggling with the lock before escaping.

Once he was gone, Riley said, "I told you all I know about Tiffany."

"Sit." Tony indicated the other chair. No matter how much psychology he forced into his brain, the idea of how mankind survived, considering survival required the species to go through puberty and adolescence, remained a mystery to him.

Riley sidled over to the chair on her side of the room and collapsed into it. "Are you going to tell on me and ruin my college career? I'll lose my scholarship, you know."

*Gee, so nice to see more of that overwhelming concern for her roommate.*

"That depends on how cooperative you are in the next five minutes."

The girl glanced at his crotch.

Tony rolled his eyes. "Really?"

She cleared her throat. "What do I have to do?"

Leaning forward, he braced his forearms on his thighs and looked her straight in the eyes. "You have to tell me the truth. You and Tiffany weren't getting along, were you?"

For one long moment she didn't answer. She drew in a deep breath and released it. "We hate each other."

Tony concluded as much. "Why?"

"She came into the room and caught me with…a guy."

It happened. Guys loved it when other guys caught them getting laid by most any means. Apparently girls didn't feel the same way. "Why was that such a big deal?"

Another exaggerated sigh huffed from her gloss-shined lips as she glanced to the bare mattress behind Tony. "Because we were in her bed."

Now that was dirty. "So you were conducting your little business in this room in *Tiffany's* bed?"

Riley nodded.

"I can see why she would be angry. When did this happen?" He opened his phone to his notepad.

She gasped. He showed her the screen to confirm he wasn't calling anyone.

"Right after the semester break. She's barely spoken to me since."

"Have you been using your own bed?" He held up a hand. "Before you answer that question, keep in mind that the forensic folks will find all DNA on Tiffany's bed linens."

She nodded adamantly. "I don't go near her side of the room anymore."

Tony decided she was telling the truth. "We'll keep this between us, if you tell me what you believe happened to Tiffany."

She blinked, her eyes still wide behind the oversize eyewear. "I already said what I think in my statement."

"I want everything you have, Riley, even if you aren't completely sure it's important. Any suspicions you have or rumors you've heard might be important, too." He shrugged. "The goal here is to make sure Tiffany comes back home safely, right? Unless, of course, you have some reason to hope she doesn't come back."

The missing tears showed up then. "I don't want Tiffany to be hurt. I mean, we're not friends or anything, but I wouldn't wish anything bad on anyone."

Tony rolled his hand in a go-on motion.

"So there was this guy…" She shrugged. "I saw Tiffany with him once and she kept talking to someone on her cell. I think it was the same guy. That's why I told the chief she had a new boyfriend. That's what I figured."

Frustration lit in Tony's veins. "Did you recognize him or hear her say his name?"

Riley shook her head. "No. She's very private. Not that she would have shared any of her business with me anyway."

"Something made you think this guy was different," Tony suggested. "Something more than just a study friend or a friend-friend?"

"Oh yeah for sure," she agreed. "He was older. Maybe closer to forty. Like thirty-five or something." She frowned as if trying to recall. "Dark hair. Black-ish, you know. Taller than Tiffany. About your height, I guess. She acted all swoony around him like she was with some rock star."

Now they were getting somewhere. "Heavy? Thin? Muscular?"

"Kinda lean and muscular. Not the overdone body-builder type. I remember thinking he looked like a con-struction worker but better dressed."

Tony added those details to his notes. "When did you first notice Tiffany with this man?"

"Early last month. I remember because I'm a leap-year baby. When I was a kid, every year that wasn't a leap year we always celebrated my birthday on March first. This year I was at a club in Macon with a friend. For my *birthday*." She put the word in air quotes. "I saw Tiffany with this guy but I never got a good look at his face. It was dark and I was a little—"

"I get the picture. What was the name of the club?"

"Wild Things. Fair warning, it's not exactly one of the better establishments."

Obviously. If they served alcohol to minors the place fell far below that mark. "Is that the only time you saw Tiffany with this man?"

She shook her head. "Friday I saw her getting into her Jeep with him."

"Her Jeep?" Tony pushed to his feet. He refrained from demanding why the hell she hadn't told anyone this already. He needed her cooperative. "You're certain it was hers?"

"Positive. The black Jeep Wrangler she drives has one of the pink breast cancer ribbons on the tailgate. I think she said her mom survived breast cancer."

An ache pierced his gut. His sister had gone through a rough time four years ago. She'd been cancer free since. He hoped like hell she stayed that way. He did not want to lose her. This kind of stress was not good for her, or anyone for that matter.

"You're certain it was Friday—the same Friday she disappeared?"

The girl nodded. "Positive. I told the chief I saw them together but I might have forgotten to mention the part about the Jeep. I really just remembered that part."

"Thanks, Riley." Tony moved toward the door, but hesitated before opening it. "I may have other questions about Tiffany. As long as you stay truthful with me, no one will hear about your secret from me." He handed her a card with his name and number. Something else he'd dragged out of the box in the trunk of his BMW. "Call me if you think of anything else or hear anything. For now, I'll talk to Chief Phelps about getting a sketch artist in touch with you. If we can locate the man you saw Tiffany with, he might be able to help."

She accepted his card, then nodded. "Okay."

Tony had Phelps on the line before he reached the first floor. He explained about the potential suspect perhaps being far more than just a new boyfriend, considering his age. "If you haven't already lined up a sketch artist to meet with the roommate, I think you need to make that happen."

"This is exactly why eyewitnesses are so blasted unreliable," Phelps complained. "Fallon insisted she didn't know the guy's name and barely caught a glimpse of him on one occasion."

Tony wasn't surprised. Fallon had no desire to mention the club in Macon. She was more concerned with protecting herself than helping the investigation.

"I'll get a sketch artist lined up ASAP," Phelps assured him.

"We also need a complete forensic examination of Tiffany's Jeep." Tony exited the building and dragged a chestful of air into his lungs. He prayed this was the lead they needed to find his niece.

"Her vehicle is still in the parking lot at the college. You know something else I don't, LeDoux?"

"Fallon saw Tiffany in the Jeep with an older man as recently as a few hours before she disappeared. The same older man she spotted her with at the club in Macon. This man may very well be the unsub we're looking for. He may have driven the Jeep back to campus to confuse the investigation. At any rate, it's a lead and I'm headed to the club now to follow up on it."

Phelps hesitated for a moment. "I'm curious as to

why the roommate was so forthcoming with you when she gave us diddly-squat."

Tony had made a promise to keep Fallon's secret and he would do that as long as she didn't hold out on him. "She had some time to think about it. Realized what she'd seen might be important. I'll let you know what I find in Macon."

Tony ended the call before Phelps could ask any more questions or suggest he let the task force handle the lead in Macon. As he climbed into his car, he Googled Wild Things. If he was lucky, they had video surveillance.

If he was even luckier, they kept it as far back as a couple of months.

He hadn't been lucky in a long time. He hoped like hell that unfortunate streak was about to change.

# *Seven*

Tony fought to restrain his temper as he waited for the manager to pick through the wad of keys he'd dug from his pocket for the one that would unlock the door. No matter that he had called the club manager en route to Macon, he'd still waited an hour in the goddamned parking lot. According to the owner, who lived in Atlanta and was the contact Tony had called first, a new security system, including video surveillance, had been installed three years ago. The owner couldn't confirm whether the recorded data from a month or more ago would still be available. The manager handled the day-to-day operations and such decisions were at his discretion.

While Tony had waited for the manager to show up he had walked around the building. There was a camera at the front entrance, the emergency side exit as well as the rear employee entrance. No cameras focused on the parking lot. No windows in the building. He'd glanced in the Dumpster noting the discarded condoms and drug paraphernalia which spoke to the establishment's general clientele or, at least, those who hung out in the parking area.

His phone vibrated again. *Angie*. He let the call go to voice mail as he had the previous two. He wasn't ready to talk to her. Anything he told her now would only get her hopes up. Until he had confirmed the roommate's new story he wouldn't share the information with his sister.

"You got a warrant?" Sean, the manager, asked as he finally unlocked the door. Then he leaned against it rather than opening it and waited for Tony to answer.

Sean Waldrop. Twenty-five. Shoulder-length hair badly in need of a wash. A few curly hairs that looked more like they belonged somewhere in the vicinity of his balls sprouted from his chin. Tony felt reasonably confident the tight, ripped jeans were cutting off the blood supply to his upper body and, more important, his brain. With the heavy metal band T-shirt, worn leather jacket and combat boots, he had the 90s grunge look down. So not the kind of joint he would have wanted his niece to patronize. Something else his sister didn't need to know.

Apparently Tony didn't respond quickly enough since Waldrop lifted his skinny shoulders in a shrug and warned, "No warrant, no entrance, man."

If he didn't have one hell of an ongoing hangover from the past week—maybe month—Tony would have taken that punk-ass attitude down a notch or two. Instead, he smiled and said, "I showed you my credentials already." What was one more flash of his invalid creds? "The owner, Kenneth Jonas—you might recognize the name from your paychecks—gave me permission to look to my heart's desire. You want to call him?" Tony offered his cell. "I'm certain he'd be interested in learning why your bartenders are selling alcohol to minors."

Waldrop stared at him a moment before relenting. He opened the door. "Make yourself at home, Mr. Fed. I got shit to do."

Tony waited for Waldrop to go inside first. The stench of nicotine had infused the air, the dark paneled walls as well as the worn upholstery, all of which was underscored by the smell of countless spilled beers emanating from the cheap carpet. Waldrop flipped on the lights, which only confirmed Tony's assessment. Tables filled most of the space. A small tiled dance floor butted up to an even smaller stage while a long bar stretched across the far side of the space. A door behind the bar probably led to the kitchen and/or the office. Between the bar and the stage, a narrow hall disappeared into the darkness. A sign directing patrons to the bathrooms pointed in that direction.

"What's the lighting like during business hours?" Tony asked.

Waldrop plopped a rack of glasses on the counter. "We keep the lights you see now on behind the bar and the stage." He gestured to the stage. "The rest that stay on during opening hours are along the baseboards and under the tables—ambience lighting, they call it."

In other words it was basically dark in the place during operating hours. The one camera Tony had spotted was above the mirrored wall behind the bar. "Is this the only camera inside?"

Waldrop picked up a rag and set his hands on his hips. "That's it. Old man Jonas is a cheap motherfucker. I see that when I look at my paycheck, too."

Tony decided it wasn't worth the effort to point out that the owner was likely getting exactly what he paid for. The rows of liquor bottles behind the bar had his mouth watering. "Is the video recorder in the office?"

The manager hitched his head. "Follow me."

The door behind the bar led into a small kitchen, as Tony suspected. The grill was blackened with use and the sink was stacked high with beer glasses and mugs. The rest of the counter space was cluttered with cans, boxes and utensils.

"Told you I had shit to do," Waldrop said.

Tony doubted the regulars showed up every night for the health department rating. "Hopefully this won't take long," he offered. "I have shit to do, too."

Waldrop opened the office door and gestured for Tony to go on in. "The system's set up in that coat closet."

The office had the same tired, dingy decorating scheme as the rest of the place. Papers were stacked in reasonably tidy piles on the desk. Part of a calculator stuck out from under one of the piles. An ashtray full of cigarette butts was jammed amid the stacks as if the smoker hoped it would all go up in flames so he wouldn't have to file it. An oscillating fan sat on one of three file cabinets. Judging by the dust on the blades it hadn't been turned on in years.

He opened the closet door. The VCR sat on top of

a safe. The machine was off and covered with about as much dust as the fan blades. Frustration ground in Tony's gut. He turned back to the asshole watching him. "When was the last time this thing worked?"

"Mmm." He pursed his lips as if in deep thought. "About two months after they put it in. I think that was three years ago."

Tony grabbed him by his shitty T-shirt. "Listen to me, asshole." He put his face close to Waldrop's. "I'm in a really bad mood. Someone I care deeply about is missing. I drove all this way hoping you were going to be my big lead. Turns out, you're just a piece of shit with an attitude. Now I got no choice but to call in backup and show you just how unhappy you've made me."

Shit-for-brains shook his head. "I don't want any trouble. Tell me how I can help you, man. Seriously. Anything."

Tony released him. He reached into his pocket for his cell and the man's eyes widened. He held up his phone to relieve his tension and then showed him a photo of Tiffany. "Have you seen her? She was here with a dark-haired, older man about a month ago."

Waldrop squinted at the pic. "She's been here a few times. I don't know the guy you're talking about though. The chick's usually with Hailey."

"Hailey? Who's Hailey?"

Waldrop snickered. "I don't know her last name. She's this older chick who comes around sometimes. I think she digs on younger girls. Know what I mean?"

Tony grabbed him by the throat. "I know what you mean. Now, how do I find this Hailey?"

He held up his hands, fear back in his eyes. "I don't know, man."

Tony tightened his grip on the scrawny bastard's throat.

"Kayla knows her," he squeaked. "She works here. She…she can tell you all about Hailey."

Tony shoved him loose. "Take me to Kayla. Now."

*Clinton Road, 5:50 p.m.*

Kayla Maples opened the door of her shabby duplex and immediately tried to close it. Tony used Waldrop as a doorstop.

Waldrop squealed. "Goddamn, man, you trying to kill me?"

Kayla screamed and ran for the kitchen. Tony shoved Waldrop aside and rushed after her.

"He's a fucking fed!" Waldrop shouted from where he'd landed on the floor.

Kayla stopped and held up her hands. "I swear to God, I didn't do whatever you think I did."

*Almost as good as a confession.* Tony ordered, "Sit down."

She inched her way back toward him but didn't sit. Kayla was maybe twenty. She had short, curly red hair. She might be five feet tall and weigh all of a hundred pounds. Her face was clear; her skin looked healthy. Not the first visible tattoo. Since she wore shorts and a tee, he spotted no visible needle tracks either. But then there were a million ways to get high that didn't show.

"I swear to God the pot's not mine. It's my brother's. He lives here, too." She turned big round eyes up to

Tony. "Please, I'm a nursing student. Any trouble could get me tossed out of the program."

"I don't care about your brother or his pot." Tony pointed to the sofa. "Sit. Tell me about Hailey."

The girl frowned. "Why do you want to know about Hailey?"

"That girl she's been hanging out with," Waldrop piped up, "is missing."

Kayla's eyes rounded. "Tiffany? Tiffany Durand?"

Tony nodded. "You a friend of hers?"

"Not really." Kayla shrugged. "I've seen her around the campus. I'm a sophomore at the same college. She started coming to the club last month." She frowned. "I thought she was going to the beach or something for the weekend."

"She's missing."

"Oh my God." Kayla clasped her hand over her mouth.

Tony followed her gaze to the silenced television screen. The alert for Tiffany and Vickie Parton flashed on the screen.

"Tell me about Hailey," Tony repeated. "Tiffany was hanging out with her?"

Kayla took a moment to compose herself. Waldrop collapsed on the sofa next to her and complained, "This guy is seriously fucking with my schedule."

Kayla waved him off. "Shut up. I'll help you open." She lifted her attention to Tony. "Hailey Martin. She's like thirty something. She comes to Wild Things a couple times a week. She's a big tipper. She's usually with someone younger and female, like Tiffany."

"Did you ever see Vickie Parton, the other missing freshman, with Hailey?"

Kayla shook her head. "I've never seen Vickie before."

"Are you and Hailey friends?"

"Not really." Kayla glanced at Waldrop. Waldrop shrugged.

"What?" Tony demanded.

"They say," Waldrop said, "she always has X handy."

Son of a bitch. "Was Tiffany getting Ecstasy from her?"

Kayla shook her head adamantly. "I'm pretty sure Tiffany doesn't do drugs. I didn't get that vibe from her at all. She's more like me—about getting her education."

Tony looked to Waldrop. He shrugged again. "Who the fuck knows? I try my best *not* to see shit."

This was getting him nowhere. "Where can I find Hailey Martin?"

"I don't know where she lives," Kayla said, her eyes relaying the honesty in her words.

"Cell number?"

Kayla shook her head. "She acknowledges my existence but that's about all. I'm not her type."

"Hell, man," Waldrop wailed, "you're a fed. Just ask your po-po friends to get the 411 on the bitch. I got shit to do."

"Did you ever see Tiffany with an older man? Dark hair?"

Kayla did some more of that frowning as if she were searching her memory banks. "Are you talking about

Miles? Hailey has a friend named Miles who hangs out with her sometimes."

"You have any other details on Miles? A last name?"

She made a face. "Sorry. I don't. He's tall, dark hair, late thirties maybe."

"You talking about that guy who drives the Ferrari?" Waldrop asked.

"That's him," Kayla said. "I just figured he's some older rich dude who likes to go after younger women."

Tony had a bad feeling she was closer to being right than she knew.

Waldrop stood. "I gotta go, man. I do not want to get fired."

"I appreciate your help." Tony headed for the door.

"Wait!" Waldrop called. "You brought me here, man."

"Kayla said she'd help you open," Tony tossed over his shoulder. "Ride with her to the club."

He walked out the door and scanned the neighborhood. At least he had a lead. It might not pan out but it was better than the nothing he had a few hours ago.

# *Eight*

Hailey Martin was forty and lived in a Mediterranean-style home on a good-sized lot overlooking the lake. Her income last year was listed as 41k. The house was at least a half-million-dollar estate. The same property in Atlanta would be worth four or five times that much. The Jag coupe parked out front was not only new but also registered in her name. The damned car alone cost more than she made in two years.

Either the lady was earning extra income off the books or she'd married well. Tony's resource hadn't found any information on her marital status. He climbed out of the BMW and walked toward the front steps. The sun was dropping behind the trees. He had hoped to get back to Milledgeville before dark but that wasn't going to happen. He checked his cell. Ang had left two voice mails. Phelps had left one. None of the messages included an update. They only wanted to know where Tony was and what he was doing.

At the moment he wasn't entirely certain, but he would continue to follow his instincts until he felt he'd found all he was going to or his need for alcohol lured him to his room.

He pressed the doorbell. The chime echoed through the house. The double doors were more glass than wood. No curtains or blinds obscured the view into the entry hall and to the staircase that stood in the middle of it. He saw a woman's bare feet first, then her lean calves as she descended the stairs. The sides of the white robe she wore came together but not before he got a glimpse of toned thighs. Martin tightened the sash as she walked runway style toward the door. She didn't look forty, more like thirty. Long blond hair hung in thick waves around her silk-clad shoulders. Her eyes were pale. Gray, he decided as she neared. But it was her mouth that gave him pause. Wide with full, lush lips. The kind women paid the big bucks to have and men paid even more to taste.

"You lost, honey?" she asked through the glass.

A sleek black Doberman pinscher trotted up beside her. Black eyes scrutinized Tony.

"Hailey Martin?" Tony showed his official ID—the one he'd lost years ago and had to replace, then found in his glove box just this morning when he'd dug around for a pair of sunglasses.

Her face registered surprise. "Well, alrighty then." She opened the door. "Come on in."

Tony glanced at the dog.

"Brutus, go."

Perfect name for the animal that stared suspiciously at his owner's visitor. With one last glower at Tony the dog walked away, toenails clicking on the gleaming hardwood.

Martin cocked her head, scrutinizing Tony much as the dog had done. "You staying or am I going? I'll need to get dressed if we're going somewhere." She pushed the door closed, the move causing the robe to show even more of her generous cleavage.

Tony ignored the instinctive stir of desire. "I have a few questions for you, Ms. Martin. As long as you're cooperative, I don't see why we can't take care of what I need right here."

"Follow me." She turned and started in the same direction her pet had taken. The last of the sun filtering in through the windows highlighted the curve of her bare ass beneath that thin layer of silk.

Tony watched the sway of her hips for a moment before following. "Nice house."

"Compliments of my first and only husband."

The entry hall flowed around the staircase on both sides and then into the center of the home where an enormous kitchen sat to the left. On the right was the great room. A leather sofa flanked by upholstered chairs were nestled around the fireplace, the stacked stone soaring upward to collide with the vaulted ceiling. The rear wall of the house was mostly glass and showed the view of the lake. Behind the stairs a dining room separated the kitchen from the great room.

Tony asked, "Divorce?" The sun was just settling down against the water. The view was breathtaking—the one out the window and the one inside.

She smiled. "Heart attack. Seventy-year-old men shouldn't take Viagra but his fondest wish was to make me happy."

Tony acknowledged the comment with a nod. "I'm sorry for your loss."

She reached for a pack of cigarettes and a lighter. "Thank you."

He waited until she'd lit up before moving to the next question. "How long have you lived in Macon?"

"I moved here when I was eighteen to attend Mercer University." She took a long drag from her cigarette and blew out a plume of smoke. "Would you like a drink, Agent LeDoux?"

His throat ached at the offer. "No, thanks. I'd like to get to those questions I mentioned, if you don't mind."

"Of course. Please, sit." She sashayed over to the bar and poured herself a Scotch on the rocks.

Tony's mouth watered. He looked away and made himself comfortable on the sofa. "Do you know Tiffany Durand?"

Martin curled up on a chair near the wall of glass. The white silk slid all the way to the tops of her thighs. "I don't really know her, but I see her at a club I visit occasionally."

"Are you aware she's missing?"

She gasped. "Are you serious?"

"You haven't seen the news?"

She made a scoffing sound. "Honey, I haven't been up long enough to watch the news. I was in a dead sleep until you showed up at my door."

"She and another freshman from Georgia College,

Vickie Parton, haven't been seen since Friday afternoon."

Realization dawned in her gray eyes. "I don't know the Parton girl, but I saw Tiffany at Wild Things a few days ago. Maybe on Wednesday or Thursday."

"Did she mention a new boyfriend or any plans to go out of town?"

Martin shook her head. "No. She did seem excited though." She sighed. "Oh dear. I feel terrible about this. Tiffany is such a sweet girl."

"Do you know a man named Miles?"

"Miles Conway?"

"Does he frequent Wild Things?"

"Occasionally. He's—" she shrugged "—a little reclusive. He doesn't get out much."

"How can I get in touch with Mr. Conway?"

"I think I have his number." She finished off her Scotch and got up. The brief glimpse of the Brazilian wax job between her legs had Tony glancing at the floor. Martin went back to the bar. She left her glass and returned to her chair with her cell phone. For a half a minute she scanned her contacts. "Here he is. What's your number and I'll send you his contact info?"

Tony gave her his number. A fleeting vibration announced he'd received the number. "What does Mr. Conway do for a living?"

She seemed to consider his question. "I really don't have any idea. I see him from time to time but we're not really friends, more acquaintances who share an appreciation for the same things."

Tony didn't have to ask what those *things* were. "So

Tiffany never mentioned a boyfriend or anyone new in her life?"

Martin moved her head side to side. "Never. She was a little shy when it came to men. Smart girl but very sheltered. I think she came to Wild Things just to prove she had the nerve to step outside her comfort zone."

Tony could see Tiffany stretching her boundaries exactly that way. She loved life and wanted to experience it to the fullest. *Please don't let that free spirit attitude have gotten her into something dangerous.*

"Do you recall anyone at the lounge watching her? Anyone odd who was new to the crowd who hangs out there?"

Again Martin appeared to consider the question. "I'm afraid not. It's most always the same crowd. I go once or twice a week just to check on things. The owner is a friend of mine."

"The owner?" Tony asked as if he didn't know.

"Kenneth. He lives in Atlanta. He and I had a thing back in college." She smiled as if remembering. "Back then he was too poor for me. I had my sights set on finding a rich old man with one foot in the grave and the other on a banana peel, as the saying goes."

Apparently she'd found one.

"You have my number." Tony stood. "I hope you'll call me if you remember anything at all that might help with the search for Tiffany."

"I will, yes." She stood. "I'll check with some of the others who frequent the club. If I learn anything at all I'll be sure to call it in."

"Call me. You have my number," Tony countered. "I

don't want any information you find lost in the storm of calls coming into the hotlines."

"All right. I'll call you." Her lips slid into a smile. "Maybe we can have dinner or something."

He decided not to touch that one. "Thank you, Ms. Martin."

"Hailey," she insisted as she walked back to the front door with him. "The pleasure was all mine."

Tony felt her eyes on his back as he walked through the dusk to his car. A woman as hot and wealthy as Martin wouldn't generally be caught dead in a place like Wild Things. Drugs? Maybe. Disposable fresh meat? Probably.

His phone vibrated against the console.

*Angie.*

Maybe if he gave her an update now she wouldn't be waiting at his door when he got back to his room.

He would call her, and then he intended to find Miles Conway.

*Antebellum Inn, Milledgeville*
*10:30 p.m.*

He'd meant to call Angie but he'd gotten distracted and frustrated with trying to find Miles Conway.

As Tony walked past the pool and through the gate his entire body sagged with dread. His sister waited for him on the covered patio that served as a porch for the cottage. The lamp on the table next to her provided all the illumination necessary to get a good look at the devastation on her face.

He exhaled a big breath. "I'm a jerk."

Funny how he regressed to their teen years whenever he was with his sister. No matter what he'd done in his life—good or bad—she was still the big sister who was older, smarter and cooler than him. And prettier, no matter that she was an emotional wreck right now.

"You couldn't call? Your phone is dead?"

That her voice rose and then wobbled tore him apart inside. He sat down in the other chair flanking the table. "I'm sorry, Ang. I've been tracking down leads from here to Macon. I was so absorbed in my work, I lost all track of time."

Her lips trembled before they twisted into a sneer. "I can smell how absorbed you were."

"Do you want to hear what I've found or do you want to argue about my bad habits?"

She looked away, swiped the back of her hand across her cheek. When she glared at him once more she said, "Fine. Let's hear it."

"First, this part is for yours and Steve's ears only. I had a friend do some digging into Tiffany's social media accounts. There are only two and she hasn't posted anything in the last couple of weeks. No private messages, no email. Nothing. Before that, she posted frequently, mostly about school. So something definitely changed recently. I haven't been able to get to her cell phone records yet."

"The police say the call and text histories were deleted on both girls' phones," his sister pointed out.

"True, but the carriers will have records of their communications. It just takes time to get them."

Angie looked at him as if she'd expected more. "It took you all day to find that out?"

"I spoke to Tiffany's roommate again."

Angie's eyes widened in surprise. "Why?"

"She wasn't completely forthcoming in her official statement." Few her age were. "In my second interview with her she mentioned that Tiffany was dating some guy with dark hair—a guy Riley didn't know."

Angie frowned. "Tiffany never said anything about a new boyfriend to me. I assumed the boyfriend her roommate mentioned was only a friend. I can't believe Tif would keep a new boy in her life a secret from me."

"Well, there's probably a good reason for that. This guy is older. Mid- to late thirties."

"Oh God." Angie hugged herself, a fresh wave of tears gathering in her eyes. "Does she know his name or where he lives?"

"No, she didn't know, but I do."

Angie covered her mouth with her hands.

"The roommate also told me she'd seen Tiffany at a club in Macon with this guy. I went to the club." No need to tell his sister how sleazy the place was.

"Tiffany went to a club?"

Tony raised his eyebrows. "Like you didn't when you were in college."

Angie squeezed her eyes shut. "Right." She drew in a deep breath. "Keep going."

"The roommate saw her with this guy. According to a friend of the manager the guy is one Miles Conway. I spent the past few hours trying to track him down. He's not at home. I interviewed a couple of his neighbors who say he's employed in some capacity in Milledgeville but no one knew where. I've got someone working on tracking down his place of employment."

"You think this guy may have seen her before she… disappeared, or do you think he's involved somehow?"

Tony opted not to mention the roommate's statement about seeing Tif with the dark-haired man on Friday. He needed to know more before he gave Ang something else to worry about. So he shrugged. "Until I find him, I can't say, but if the two were involved he may have seen her or know where she planned to go for the weekend."

The truth was he couldn't say the guy was involved. Until Tony looked him in the eyes and questioned him, it would be best to keep his thoughts to himself. At this point he felt confident that Tiffany was taken by someone she knew. Her disappearance was far too clean to think otherwise. Generally, with an abduction by a stranger there were signs of a struggle or something left undone. The victim's car might be left in an unexpected place. The vic's home or room would be left unlocked or show signs of breaking and entering. Some little something would be off. A neighbor would have heard a noise. There was always some unexpected element, small though it might be.

But this was clean. This was planned. And Tiffany cooperated without realizing she was doing so.

"Did you share this information with the police?"

"I called Chief Phelps on my way back here. He'll pass the information along to the task force. Tomorrow morning I'm hoping to catch Vickie Parton's roommate or one of her friends to see if I can connect this Miles Conway to her. Beyond that, I'll continue trying to find him."

Angie swiped at her eyes again. "I'm sorry I was so hard on you."

Tony reached across the table and took his sister's hand. "I won't let you down, Ang." He looked away a moment. "I know I screwed up with the Bureau. I let down my wife and myself. But I won't let you or Tiffany down."

She squeezed his hand. "Giselle's a bitch. She didn't deserve you."

Tony laughed. "Yeah, well, maybe I made her that way."

They shared a good laugh before Angie hugged him hard and hurried back to the inn.

Tony dropped back into the chair. He didn't know how the hell he would keep the promise he'd made his sister, but he would die trying.

# Nine

Angie Durand hugged her husband closer. As hard as she tried she could not go to sleep. How could her beautiful daughter get involved with an older man? She knew better. Angie had taught her better. Tif was so much more mature and responsible than most girls her age.

Anger and hurt twisted inside Angie. She closed her eyes tight to hold back the tears. Dear God, how could she feel anger right now? Her baby was missing. She could be hurt badly or, oh God, dying. *Please, please, just let me find my baby alive.*

Didn't matter how old Tif was, she would always be her baby.

Tif had her entire future ahead of her. Angie closed her eyes and prayed. *Please, God, don't let my sweet girl be taken from me.*

Maybe Tif did make a terrible mistake, but she was only human and so very young.

"I'm so scared."

Steve turned onto his side, facing her. He stroked her hair gently. "I know. I am, too. But we have to trust Tony and the police. They will find her. I refuse to believe otherwise."

"I don't know about Tony." More of that ridiculous anger fired inside her. "He'd been drinking tonight." Tears choked her for a moment. "Maybe..." Her voice broke. She cleared her throat, fought back the tears. "Maybe he can't help. I know he wants to, but maybe he just can't. Between the divorce and all the drinking and now his career is tanked." She pressed her hand to her mouth for a moment. "Maybe he just can't help the way he wants to...the way we need him to."

Steve pulled her close against his chest. "Please don't cry. We have to be strong right now. For Tiffany and for Tony. We have to believe."

Angie nodded, unable to speak for fear of breaking down completely.

She believed. *She believed.* Tiffany was coming home. Tony would find her.

Angie believed this with all her heart.

# Ten

Jo sipped her beer slowly. She'd been nursing this same one for two hours. Keeping her head clear was far too important to risk a second one. Tonight's objective required her to play her part perfectly. He would see through anything less and this one step could make all the difference.

The prelude was the hardest part. Blend in. Be cool. Pay close attention. Don't say too much or too little. Listen carefully. Be the part.

"To tell you the truth," Wes Cline, an up-and-coming assistant producer at CNN, said as he leaned closer, "I don't trust anyone at the FBI or the GBI, for that matter."

Jo rested her elbows on the table and put her forehead closer to his. "I'm with you. I'm not certain we can be confident that anyone will give us the down and dirty on a hot case like this one—not until they're ready to anyway."

"You said it." He knocked back his third shot of tequila, then leaned forward again, placing his forearms on the table as she had. "I was a newly hired intern six months ago when that serial killer psychiatrist, Randolph Weller, was on the loose. I followed our top investigative journalist, Chase Whitt, all over Savannah. Turned out the FBI was not only keeping secrets; they were deeply involved in Weller's escape. One of the former top dogs at Quantico is still under investigation. My guess is he's going up the river."

That was the thing about young men. They always needed to prove themselves. Wes, twenty-three and barely a year postgrad from Georgia Southern University, was kissing every available ass on this assignment in hopes of scoring brownie points. Jo singled him out in a flash. The first time she caught him alone, she introduced herself. He'd spent the initial couple minutes of that conversation immersed in a study of her cleavage. After she mentioned she was close to the Durand family, he'd stuck to her like glue.

"I'm with you on that one." She sipped her beer. "You're going places, Wes. I can feel it."

He grinned before waving at the server to bring him another. "You ready for a fresh beer?"

She shook her head. "I'm good. A girl's gotta watch those carbs."

"I know all kinds of ways to burn off extra carbs."

She bet he did.

Cowboy Bill's was a nice place. The corrugated metal walls and wood floors provided that country-chic atmosphere. A big bar and plenty of pool tables kept those not interested in the dance floor occupied.

The crowd was rowdy but in a happy way. Servers were efficient and the drinks were a decent price. She didn't remember the place from before, but then she'd done all in her power to block that year from her memory banks. Not that she'd ever really been the party girl type.

Maybe that was where she'd gone wrong. If she'd learned the ins and outs of partying before she found herself immersed in the college culture she might have handled things better.

Too late for what-ifs now. She'd made the decisions she made. So had Ellen.

Now it was time to make the people responsible pay.

"Berman is convinced we won't be finding these two girls alive." Wes shook his head somberly.

"Why's he so sure?" Jo ordered her heart to slow. David Berman was one of CNN's hotshot journalists. Evidently good old Wes knew how to get assignments with the top guns.

"He ran some statistics," Wes explained. "Based on the number of women who've gone missing over the past two decades and the percentage of those found alive, we're due a couple murders."

"Wow." She sipped her beer. "That's depressing. I'm guessing his headline won't read that way."

Wes chuckled. "Certainly not."

Jo glanced toward the bar. Special Agent Anthony LeDoux had been seated on a stool there for the past forty minutes. The bourbon on the rocks the bartender set in front of him was his third. Apparently he was no lightweight since he hadn't slid off that stool yet. Still, he should be feeling plenty relaxed.

"Well." Jo reached for her purse. "I see an old friend

I need to catch up with before calling it a night." She reached across the table and squeezed Wes's hand. "You have my number. We should do this again. *Soon*."

He grinned, clearly enamored with the idea of getting into an older woman's pants. "Count on it."

She gave him a wink and headed for the bar. With a dramatic sigh, she dropped her purse on the counter. "Vodka martini, please."

She didn't have to look to know LeDoux was checking her out. She could feel his eyes on her. Good. She'd selected this dress for that reason. Tight, short and the cream color looked good with her olive skin tone. She worked hard to stay in shape but it had nothing to do with luring the male species.

If anyone ever tried to hurt her again he would be in for one hell of a surprise. Jo could kick the shit out of guys three times her size, including the one sizing her up right now. She had experienced things—things that changed her view of the world and of people. Long ago she had decided that she would never again be caught off guard or unable to defend herself or to take care of herself. Mostly she preferred living in her small one-room world without ever having to deal with people.

*This has to be done. It has to be over. No more silence. No more pretending.*

She'd done her homework on the man seated next to her. He'd built a stellar career as a profiler with the FBI. More than one article had called him the Bureau's Top Gun. He was a year older than Jo and the victim, Tiffany Durand, was his niece. LeDoux, she decided, was the perfect person to help her. He was just desperate enough to buy her story.

At least, she hoped he was. Time to cast a line and see if she nabbed herself a bite. If she was wrong about LeDoux… *No.* Being wrong wasn't an option. He was her best and possibly her only hope.

The bartender placed the drink in front of her.

"Thank you." She lifted the glass to her lips and closed her eyes. "Hmm." She lowered the glass back to the counter. "If it weren't for martinis I'd never survive assignments like this."

She turned to the man still staring at her. "Please tell me you're not another reporter. The last one almost talked my ear off."

LeDoux looked away. "Not a reporter."

His voice was deeper than she'd expected. Sandy blond hair looked a little scruffy for an FBI agent. She'd yet to see one sporting a two-days' beard growth. The outfit—polo shirt and jeans—was not exactly what she'd expected either. The slightly wrinkled suit jacket looked more like an afterthought. Above all else it was the don't-give-a-shit look in his eyes that told her Special Agent Anthony LeDoux was not on duty. Maybe he was only here to support his sister.

Jo had done all the research on the family she could from her iPad. Whether LeDoux was here on official business or not, some of the more recent articles she'd read about him suggested his illustrious career was also on the rocks.

That last part was irrelevant as far as Jo was concerned. He would have the connections she needed.

"I guess it's my lucky night then." She ate the olive and downed the rest of her drink. "Now, that hits the spot." A nod to the bartender had him preparing another. Jo thanked him and took a deep breath. *Play the part*.

"You're a local then?" She turned on the stool to face LeDoux, the hem of her dress stretched tight across the tops of her thighs as she crossed her legs. "Do you believe those two missing freshmen were taken by someone who lives in Milledgeville?"

He twisted to face her, his knee bumping into hers. "Sorry." He shook his head. "I'm not a local."

"I get it now." She sipped her martini. "You're a cop."

He finished off the bourbon but didn't ask for another. Oh hell, she'd waited too long for the approach.

"Not a cop either." He pushed the glass forward and gave the bartender a nod. "Not even close."

He was staying, at least for a little while longer. Her heart rate leveled off. She set her glass aside and leaned forward. His eyes were brown but there were these little gold flecks. "Don't tell me, you're a fed."

He looked away. "In another life."

So much yearning and defeat were packed into those three words that Jo was caught off guard for a moment. So the rumors of his fall from grace were true.

"Well—" she smiled "—I've been many things, the worst of which might very well be a reporter."

He didn't look at her.

"I know. Scum of the earth."

The slightest hint of a smile made his lips twitch.

"I had bigger plans but you know how it goes, shit happens."

"Yeah." He picked up his fresh bourbon. "Shit definitely happens."

"So why are you here?"

For five seconds she was certain he wouldn't answer or he'd just get up and walk away. Instead, he turned to her and said, "I'm here to find my niece."

"Is she…?" Jo put a hand to her throat. "One of the missing girls is your niece? I'm so sorry. I didn't mean to intrude. You probably need to be alone."

She opened her clutch and reached for a couple of bills. "I swear, I'm usually better than this at reading people." She left the cash on the counter as she scooted off the stool. "Really, I'm so sorry."

He caught her by the wrist when she would have walked away. "Maybe you'd like a private interview."

Jo's pulse bumped into a faster rhythm. "Your place or mine?"

The drive to his hotel, which turned out to be the Antebellum Inn, took all of four minutes. Jo had time to change her mind. She could just turn around and drive in the opposite direction. But she didn't. She parked her Celica behind his BMW and got out. The real question now was whether or not *he* would change his mind.

Heart thumping, she met him in front of his car. He reached for her hand and led her through the darkness. Rather than climb the steps to the front door they walked around the house. Trepidation slithered over her. The low lighting around the pool lit their path as he guided her to what looked like a pool house. He reached into his pocket for a key and unlocked the door. She glanced back at the dark house, nerves jangling. *No backing out now.*

Inside, the room was cool and dark. He turned on a lamp. The place was considerably larger than the dump where she lived in Copperas Cove. She heard the lock turn behind her. *Play the part.*

She needed to know who she could trust before she told her story. He could be the one. Having a fed related to a victim was a truly lucky break—maybe, possibly. Not so lucky for the victim or the family. Jo closed her eyes and blocked what she knew from experience was probably happening to the victims at that very moment.

He came up behind her and moved her hair aside to kiss her neck. She shivered. His fingers tugged her zipper slowly down her back while he trailed kisses along her spine. By the time the dress hit the floor she was trembling with need.

Usually her lovers were sloppy and in a rush. Usually she was, too.

LeDoux might be legally inebriated but he was in no hurry. He turned her around and kissed her long and deep. She pushed his jacket off his shoulders. He flung it aside. Together they pulled his polo free of his jeans.

Somehow they managed to finish unclothing each other before he dragged her onto the bed and buried himself inside her.

Jo stopped analyzing the situation and lost herself to the moment she would regret in the morning.

The story of her life.

# *Eleven*

Miles Conway was one hell of a lucky bastard. He grinned as he pushed the bedroom door open and she walked in. His dick thumped against his fly just watching her move. He couldn't remember when he'd had one this fresh.

As she crossed the room she tossed her big bag—the massive ass kind chicks loved to tote around these days—on the floor and reached for the hem of her skin-tight dress. He closed the door and leaned against it, watched her reach beneath the sleek fabric and tug the lacy thong down her thighs.

A chick after his own heart—straight to the point. Oh yeah, he was one lucky bastard.

Maybe turning forty hadn't fucked with his ability to draw in the younger chicks as badly as he'd thought. And this one was all his. No strings. No leveling of the playing field with a little compliant cocktail. He pushed off the door and strode to where she stood, her arms twisted behind her, fingers tugging at the zipper tracing her spine. She licked her lips and he thought he'd have to fuck her with the dress on.

*Patience.* If he played this right he might get an hour of magic on video.

He pushed her hands away and dragged the zipper slowly down to that perfect little dimple where her ass began. Damn he couldn't wait to tap this bitch. She was so fucking hot.

The dress fell to the floor and she stepped out of it, racy stilettoes all that was left of her fashionista outfit. She glanced over her shoulder, eyes hooded as if she, too, was already burning up. "Take off your clothes and get on the bed."

Miles laughed. "Yes, ma'am."

He grabbed the hem of his V-necked tee and pulled it over his head, tossed it aside. He was usually the one who gave the orders. He liked being in control. But he could see the fun in being the submissive one from time to time. Especially with this chick. This one was special, he could tell. Jeans went next and that was it. Underwear and socks were two things he never bothered to wear. *Ready* was his middle name.

While she watched, he climbed onto the bed and stretched out. He didn't mind her staring. His body was his temple and he took very good care of it. Like a movie star or a rock star, the way he looked was part of the job. He had used his looks and his charm to lure so many pretty girls into his sweet trap he'd lost count. Young things were his specialty. There was money to be made with the tender ones. Young, usually innocent, girls showed up for college with wide eyes and big dreams. Then, after a while, they got lonely. So lonely. And ripe for the picking. All they wanted was someone to care about them—to love them and touch them in just the right ways.

It was so freakin' easy to spot the neediest ones. The ones who would never dare tell. College campuses were the perfect hunting ground.

Not this time though. This time, she had spotted him outside the club. She came to him, wanted him. Tempted him. He liked it.

A change of pace could be a good thing.

By God, he was about to give her every hard inch of what he had. "Come on, baby. I'm ready."

She bent down and picked up her bag, carried it to the bed and placed it next to him.

He grinned. "Got some tricks in there, huh?"

She smiled as she straddled his hips. "And they're all just for you."

"I don't do handcuffs," he warned. He'd made that mistake once and ended up having to take the bed apart to get out of the motel after the bitch left him that way.

She reached into her bag and brought out a condom. "Don't worry. I don't do handcuffs either."

He growled, "Hurry up." His dick was already nudging the slit in that sweet naked cunt of hers. He hated hairy pussy. Bare was the way to go. *Good girl.*

She tore the package open with her mouth, then licked her lips. When she'd smoothed the slick rubber onto him, he shuddered. He was so fucking ready. She guided him deep inside her. He groaned. Jesus, she was hot and snug.

He reached for her tits, barely a handful but enough. He took one in each hand as she started to rock. She did this little maneuver with her thighs, tightening them against him at the same time her pussy cinched like a vise. Man, he was ready to explode. He closed his eyes and lifted his hips. He wanted more.

"Go, baby, go," he murmured.

While she rocked, she reached into her bag again and brought out silk scarves. She leaned forward, leaving nothing but his tip throbbing inside her. He almost lost it as she tied his right hand to the headboard with the scarf.

"You're okay with this, aren't you?"

He nodded and arched his hips to get back inside her. Right now he would have agreed to most anything. "Oh yeah."

She did the same with his left hand, and then she smiled down at him. For one instant he was caught off guard—his gut clenched. There was something familiar about her eyes. Did he know her?

"Relax," she urged as she executed another of those vise-like moves, and then pressed harder down onto him.

His eyes closed as those hot, mind-blowing contractions started deep in his belly. The world could come to an end right now and he wouldn't care… All that mattered was that freakin' awesome pressure building, making his dick throb and swell, ready to explode.

Something hit him hard in the chest.

His eyes shot open.

Red oozed from a narrow slit in his chest. What the hell? His chest hurt like a son of a bitch. "Motherfucker!" He gasped. Coughed. Tried to yank his hands loose.

The big ass knife she held came down again, stabbing deep into his gut, and then twisting. Blood spurted. He gasped, a terrible seal-like sound. He couldn't get enough air inside his chest.

Where the hell was all that blood coming from?

Another blaze of pain seared through his chest. He couldn't breathe...

He couldn't get loose.

*Air.* He needed air. He gagged. Gasped.

She leaned down closer, driving the knife deeper with her weight. He grunted the strangest sound. She pressed her cheek to his, hot blood squirting between them, and then she whispered to him.

Smiling, she rose up and started rocking slowly against him once more.

His mind wouldn't work, wouldn't wrap around the words she said. He tried to speak. Couldn't. Blood was no longer spurting from his gut—it only oozed. He felt his heart stutter, then stop.

Was he supposed to feel it stop like that?

He'd always thought if your heart stopped you were dead, but he wasn't dead yet, just helpless. He could still see... Could still hear and even feel...

Moving faster now, she cried out, head flung back in orgasm.

He groaned... Sick, sick bitch.

His vision narrowed and just before the darkness engulfed him, he came.

Those awful words she'd said followed him into the nothingness.

# Twelve

Tony jerked awake. He blinked. What the hell?

Memories of the woman he'd picked up at the bar flashed one after the other in his brain. He checked the other side of the bed. Empty. The sheets on that side were cold. She'd been gone for a while.

He ran a hand through his hair and prayed the throbbing would go away. What the hell had he been thinking? He was supposed to keep himself together. Angie and Steve were counting on him. Tiffany was counting on all three of them.

A bang on the door jerked his attention there. Angie? Not likely. Even if his sister was thoroughly pissed she wouldn't try and break down the door. He swept aside the sheets and dropped his feet to the floor. Grabbing his jeans, he tugged them on. Hopefully nothing worse had happened while he was going stupid last night.

"Open up, LeDoux!"

Tony blinked and swayed. Shit. He staggered toward the door but it burst open before he reached it. Sunlight poured in around the two suits who stepped inside as if they owned the place.

"Who the hell are you?" The throb in his head increased with the pounding in his chest. If something had happened to Angie… What if Tiffany's body had been found? His gut clenched.

The first and older of the two suits flashed his credentials. "Special Agent Jerry Richards. This is my colleague, Special Agent Liam Johnson. We need to have a talk with you if you're not too busy this morning."

Tony dragged on his shirt. "Make yourselves at home."

The two agents pulled out chairs around the table and settled there. The younger of the two held up a paper cup. "We brought you coffee. Thought you might need it."

"Thanks." What he needed was to take a piss. His need to hear what these two pricks had to say overwhelmed the other urge so he reached for the cup and sat down on the foot of the bed. "How long have you had someone watching me?"

Richards and Johnson glanced at each other as if they had expected their appearance to be a total surprise. He wasn't surprised at all. Annoyed, pissed even, but not surprised. He turned up the cup. The coffee was hot and black. He flinched at the welcome burn. Caffeine was something else he needed badly right now.

Richards spoke first. His years of experience showed on his face in deep lines and around his middle in a spare tire. The suit was a little less perfect than his partner's, the shoes a little less shiny. "That girl you harassed, Riley Fallon, filed a complaint with campus security. But everyone understands that you're upset about your niece so they're willing to overlook that one misstep as long as it doesn't happen again."

Tony was on the same page now, though he doubted Fallon had worked up her nerve to file a complaint. Most likely they'd encouraged her to do so. These two knuckleheads had likely questioned her right after he did for no other reason than to find out what he was up to. "Surely you understand." He played along. "I'm only trying to find my niece."

"We get that," Richards said, "but we need you to stay out of the way on this investigation, LeDoux. You no longer serve or represent the Bureau. Unless you want a shit storm raining down on you, you need to cease representing yourself that way."

Tony downed more of the coffee in hopes of relaxing the tense muscles around his skull. "You got a younger sister or a daughter, Richards?" He glanced at the other man. "Johnson?"

Johnson shook his head. He looked to be about thirty. Medium height, lean. Black hair, high and tight. Freshly laundered, off-the-rack suit, shoes polished to a high sheen. "Not me."

"You know the law, LeDoux," Richards said. "Let's not play games here. Chief Phelps passed along the information you gave him and we appreciate it. From this moment forward, you need to stay on the outside of the investigation with your sister and her husband. We're happy to get your input but we can't have you poking around in the investigation."

"If it happens again," Johnson spoke up, "they'll

make us bring you in. We don't want to do that. I'm certain your sister would be very upset if that happened."

"Point taken." Tony finished off the coffee and stood. "Now, if you fellows will let yourselves out I need a shower."

Johnson's mouth quirked. "Be careful, LeDoux, a chick that hot might be more trouble than you need right now."

Richards laughed. "Sounds like you've had enough trouble with hot chicks lately."

Tony ignored their smart-ass remarks and followed the two to the door. "Anything new on the case?"

Richards hesitated on the porch. "Not a damned thing."

Just once he'd like to hear that his instincts were wrong. Tony watched until the two agents had loaded up in their nondescript sedan and driven away. Going forward he would be on the lookout for a tail. He closed the door and turned back to the bed. His cute reporter had sneaked out on him. Funny, he was the one who usually played that role.

A note on the bedside table drew him there. He picked up the folded piece of bed-and-breakfast letterhead.

Call me. I have a few ideas on these abductions. I added my number to your contacts. Carrie

At least now he knew her name. He shoved the note into the pocket of his jeans. She wouldn't be interested in hearing from him when she found out he had no intention of sharing anything he learned with a reporter.

He surveyed the floor in search of his shoes, then hesitated. Yesterday was the first time his current status had really bothered him. When his sister and niece needed him most he wasn't in the position to help them the way he wanted.

*You fucked up, Tony.*

Funny how doing the right thing sometimes cost you everything. He forced the idea away. Time for that shower and a shave and then he would get back on the trail of Miles Conway. He grabbed his overnight bag and started for the bathroom. A soft knock on the door stopped him.

"Damn it." He tossed the bag on the bed and strode to the door expecting to see Angie with a breakfast tray or maybe his Bureau buddies had forgotten something. Instead he found the mystery woman from last night. *Carrie.*

"I thought you might be hungry. I woke up starving." She shoved a bag and a tray with two paper cups toward him.

She wore the same body-hugging cream-colored dress she'd had on last night, the enormous leather bag still draped over one shoulder.

"Sorry." Her gaze lingered on the coffee cup he'd abandoned on the table. "Looks like you already had something." She shrugged. "I guess I should have just kept going when I left." She drew the bag and tray away from him. "I meant to, but I just kept thinking—"

He took her by the arm and pulled her inside, cutting off whatever else she would have said. When he'd closed the door, he stared at her for long enough to have her squirming. "Carrie? That's your name?"

She nodded. "Look, if you don't want breakfast, I can leave now."

What he wanted was not in the bag she carried. "I'm starving."

She relaxed. "Great."

Before he could say more she ducked around him and went to the table. Every time she reached across the table the dress slid upward giving a fleeting glimpse of her lacy panties. Tony drew in a deep breath and ran his fingers through his hair. For all he knew she could be the someone the Bureau had watching him.

At this point he trusted no one.

"Ham or sausage?" She held up the wrapped sandwiches from the bag.

"Sausage."

"Good. I hate sausage." She put the sandwich on the table, pulled out a chair and sat down. "Excuse me if I don't wait for you."

He walked toward her, watching her every move. She tore the wrapper from the sandwich and bit into it. She closed her eyes and moaned. He pulled out the chair across from her just as she licked her lips.

"I know it's not good for my body, but fast food tastes so good."

He reached for his own sandwich. "Something's gotta kill you."

She laughed. "True."

The conversation lulled as they ate. The way she devoured the sandwich, licked her lips and seemed to make love to the coffee cup with her mouth fascinated him. The idea that he got hard just watching her was seriously fucked-up, particularly under the circumstances.

She balled the paper and her napkin and tossed it in

the bag. "There's something I want to show you—*if* I can really trust you."

He wadded his napkin and dumped it in the bag with hers. "I thought we played that game last night."

"Haha." She took a breath. "I almost lost my nerve. That's why I left without saying goodbye, but then—" she moistened her lips "—I realized that if I couldn't trust you, maybe I couldn't trust anyone and that won't work. I can't do this alone."

"I'm listening."

She pushed the breakfast remains aside, reached into her bag and removed what looked like a photo album. She placed it on the table. "This is a scrapbook I've been keeping for a while. Have a look at it while I use your shower."

Bag in hand, she disappeared into the bathroom but didn't close the door. He opened the scrapbook to the first page.

The article was dated the twentieth of March, eighteen years ago. Milledgeville, Georgia. College Freshmen Found Alive was the first headline. His pulse reacted. The page taken from the newspaper was yellowed with age. His gaze moved over the typeset words. The water in the bathroom turned on and he glanced that way. With the door open, he watched as she stepped into the shower, the water gliding over her smooth skin. As much as he would enjoy watching, the headline drew his attention back to the article.

The two freshmen were last seen the Friday before spring break, and then found fourteen days later. Dehydrated, bruised and battered, but alive. He turned to the next page. A year later, two students went missing. Different colleges that time. Different dates. But both were found alive fourteen days after their abduction. Dehydrated, bruised and battered. He turned to the next page. Another year passed. Two more women, a nurse and a brand-new mother this time. Both turned up fourteen days later. Same condition as the others. Yet another page showed a similar scenario. The ages of the victims varied slightly; the location of the abductions included Georgia, Alabama and Florida. The time frame the victims were missing was always the same—fourteen days. The condition of the victims upon release was always the same as well.

Not a single one could identify her abductor or the place where she'd been kept.

Carrie returned to the table. This time she wore jeans and a sweatshirt proclaiming her love of rock and roll. Her short blond hair was as untamed as the woman who'd brought him to his knees twice last night. At the bar she'd looked petite and thin but that was far from true. Though she was maybe five-two or -three, she was lean and strong.

"So, what do you think?" She stared at him with those inquisitive blue eyes.

"You've been following these abductions all this time? When the first abductions took place—" he turned back to page one "—you had to be what, twelve or fifteen?"

She laughed. "Not quite. I was in college myself. I guess I wanted to be a reporter even then."

He closed the scrapbook. "What's your theory on how all these are related? Apparently the Bureau and the local cops have never found any dots to connect."

"I thought you might be able to tell me. After all, you're the profiler."

So she'd done a little checking up on him. He should have expected as much. She was a reporter. "I'm afraid it doesn't work that way. I need to read the police reports and crime scene reports. I need to meet and interview the victims."

"What would you like to know?"

"Are you saying you know one of these victims?"

"May I?" She gestured to the scrapbook.

"Of course." He pushed it across the table.

She turned to the first page. "Joanna Guthrie." She exhaled a big breath. "That's me."

Her answer wasn't the one he'd expected. He thought about the note in his pocket. "So your name isn't Carrie."

"I had a moment of doubt. I needed some distance to get right with the decision to trust you."

He laughed a strained sound. "You made that decision while you went for Egg McMuffins and coffee?"

She hesitated, and then nodded. "I did."

"Well, all right. So tell me this, your collection stops thirteen years ago. What happened thirteen years ago?"

She shook her head. "The abductions continued for five years and then nothing. I don't know why—they just stopped or the MO changed so drastically I couldn't connect any new abductions to the old ones—until yesterday."

Tony exhaled a weary breath. This wasn't the first time he'd been approached by a crime junkie. The woman could be a fiction writer looking for inspiration for her next novel. He was doubtful that she was actually the victim from the eighteen-year-old abductions. "I see. What is it you think I can do for you, Ms. Guthrie?"

Her pale eyebrows went up in surprise but she didn't relent. "Help me find the persons who did this. If we find them, we'll find your niece."

Tony nodded slowly. His instincts were telling him not to set aside her theory so quickly. "How can you be so sure about that?"

She put her hand on his arm. "I wish I could explain this feeling." She shook her head. "I just know. I've kept quiet about this for eighteen years. If I wasn't as certain as I can be I sure as hell wouldn't be talking to you now."

As much as he wanted to believe her story, how could he risk the distraction from his niece's case? "I'd like to help you, Carrie—Joanna, but my first priority has to be finding my niece."

"We have the same goal, Tony. If my calculations are correct, your niece has at most ten days before one of the three of them dies."

He held up a hand. "Wait a minute. My niece and one other girl are missing. According to your collection of articles, two girls go missing and two girls come back *alive*. Where is this new theory coming from?"

Joanna or Carrie or whoever the hell she was took another breath and said, "There's always one who doesn't come back."

He held her gaze for a moment. She didn't flinch. "Not one of these victims—including you—mentioned a third victim or a murder."

She squared her shoulders as if bracing for what she had to say next. "We were afraid to tell…but, believe me, someone always dies."

# *Thirteen*

Hailey stood in the center of Miles's bedroom and stared at all the blood. So much for warning him about the fed asking questions.

Motherfucker!

What kind of crazy bitch did he bring home with him? His naked body was stretched out on the bed, hands tied to the iron headboard. He'd been stabbed or halfway gutted, something. She groaned and put her hand over her mouth. There was blood all over the rug by the bed. She hadn't seen any in the hall but there could be traces there. She'd watched enough cop shows to know there was likely evidence all over the goddamned apartment.

"Holy shit."

She walked around the apartment. Checked the other bedroom. She shook her head when she saw the computer monitors. "You stupid fuck."

If he had been videotaping the work they did together he was in seriously deep shit.

She laughed out loud. He was dead. How much deeper could the shit get?

"Holy fuck." She dug in her bag for a pair of latex gloves. She had learned a long time ago that a pair of gloves to cover her tracks was the most important accessory she could carry in her purse. When she'd tugged them on she awakened the monitors. After several login attempts she threw up her hands.

Okay, what was the worst that could happen? The police would decide that Miles had abducted the women he'd videotaped. She doubted she was in any of the videos. The chances that he would have mentioned names was highly unlikely. This was, after all, his own little side venture.

She shook her head. But she couldn't trust that he hadn't named names any more than she could trust him not to fuck anything that would hold still long enough. The man was obviously a stupider fuck than she'd known.

Wait, wait—there was that one time. Shit. Shit. Shit. She'd walked in and he'd been recording. He'd promised to destroy all the videos. Obviously he hadn't done that any more than he'd stopped his side business.

"Idiot." There had to be a way to resolve this quickly. Every minute she was in this apartment was another one she risked being remembered by a neighbor or a passerby. She would be damned if she would go down with this worthless piece of shit.

Okay. *Think*. She drew her cell from her bag and went to Google. A couple of minutes later, she had a plan. She went to the bathroom and set the water to running in the tub. The traces of blood there told her whoever had taken the knife to him had showered before leaving the apartment.

She was damned glad she had a gun with her. The crazy bitch could come back.

Water was running. Now she needed something without a ground fault interrupter. A hair dryer wouldn't work. She hurried to the kitchen and searched the cabinets. Nothing. She moved around the junk on top of the washing machine and found an iron.

"Perfect." According to Google, an appliance that heated up—the hotter the better—was best. She placed the iron on the vanity in the bathroom.

Taking care to avoid the blood on the floor as she moved back down the hall, she left her bag next to the door of the bedroom with all the computers. One by one she unhooked the hard drives and carried them to the bathroom. On the second trip she shut off the water. She sure as hell didn't want it to get high enough to splash onto the floor. When all the hard drives were in the bathroom, she immersed each one in the tub of water, holding it down until it stayed submerged.

She needed to hurry. The smell of blood and shit was making her heave. She dried her gloved hands on her skirt, checked again to ensure there was no water on the floor or on her shoes. Then she plugged in the iron. Wait, the outlet in the bathroom would be a ground fault, too.

"Fuck."

It took her a few minutes but she found an extension

cord. She plugged it into an outlet in the hall, and then plugged the iron into it.

She took a breath. "You get one shot at this."

Backing as far away from the tub as she dared, she turned on the iron and waited for it to heat up. A minute later when it was hot to the touch, she tossed it into the tub.

The explosion or flash of fire she'd expected didn't happen but she wasn't getting any closer to check and see if her plan had worked. On the way out she grabbed her purse and his cell. On second thought, she executed a quick search of the place. She moved carefully from room to room, watching where she stepped.

She found no photos or stacks of DVDs as she'd feared. Whatever he'd done, he'd kept it on his computer or he had some other storage facility.

She glanced at him once last time. "Dumb ass."

Once she'd ensured none of the neighbors were on the landing outside, she tucked on her sunglasses and got the hell out. It wasn't until she was on the street headed away from the scene that she made the necessary call.

Her partner was not going to be happy.

# *Fourteen*

Tony glanced at the woman in the passenger seat. "Don't mention being a reporter. Just observe. If you recognize her, don't say a word until we're done."

Joanna scrutinized him for a long moment. "You're still undecided about trusting me."

"I'm not taking chances with my niece's life." He reached for the door but hesitated. "Fair warning, if you're wasting my time you will wish you'd latched onto some other player in this case."

Still angry that the chief of police had called to warn him about crossing any lines in his jurisdiction, Tony's options were sorely limited. He'd expected the Bureau to put up roadblocks to his involvement in the case, but he'd held out hope the chief would keep a back door open. No such luck. He climbed out of the BMW. If his suspicions were on the money Miss Hailey Martin would still be in bed. She struck him as a full-time night person, not just the occasional stay-out-late kind of gal. The Jag in the driveway was a good indication she was home.

Joanna walked around the hood and joined him. "I'm sure you have contacts you can use to confirm what I've told you is the truth."

He considered her for a long moment. "You were abducted eighteen years ago. You and another freshman were missing for fourteen days. You survived, got away somehow and returned to finish the semester, and then you vanished. At some point over the years you cut your hair and went blond. You move frequently. Never been married. No long-term relationships. Your mother hasn't seen you in nearly two decades. The only trail you leave is your work for an online newspaper. Otherwise you're a ghost. That's what I confirmed. That's what I believe. Until you show me proof, that's all I believe."

She had refused to discuss her time in captivity. The chief's call had interrupted the shouting match over her refusal, and then she'd given him the silent treatment on the way here. He'd decided to give it a rest for now. When the time was right, he would have his answers.

"You called my mother?" The shock on her face quickly dissolved into anger. "You shouldn't have called my family."

"You want me to trust you, then I need to know you're not some nutcase off her meds."

She set her hands on her hips and glared at him. "Fuck you, LeDoux."

He decided not to mention that she had already or that he had done a bang-up job of fucking himself the past few months. "Just keep quiet and let me do the talking."

When they'd climbed the steps, he crossed the porch and pressed the doorbell. The chime echoed through the house. A minute later Hailey Martin's toned legs came into view. By the time she reached the bottom of the staircase he glimpsed a full frontal view of Martin's naked body before she bothered to cinch the robe closed.

"Jesus." Joanna rolled her eyes.

The door opened. Martin was all smiles; the dog on her heels eyed her unexpected guests warily. "Agent LeDoux, aren't I the lucky one? A visit two days in a row." She opened the door wider. "Please, come in. Did you locate Miles?"

"Actually, we hoped you might be able to help with that."

She glanced at Joanna. "Is this your partner?"

"We're working together on this case," Joanna said before Tony could. She thrust out her hand. "Carrie Cole."

The lie slid right off her tongue without the slightest hesitation. *She's almost as good as you, Tony.*

"As you know," Tony moved on, "we have two missing freshmen from Georgia College. You appear to be one of the last people to have seen Tiffany Durand."

"Would you like to come in and sit?" Martin glanced at Joanna again and smiled. "I'm dying for a cup of coffee."

"Actually," Tony said, "we don't have a lot of time. Any additional information you could provide that might help us locate Conway would be helpful."

"I wish I could do something more." Martin lifted

one silk-clad shoulder. "I gave you his number. I really don't know him that well."

"If you hear from him or recall anything else, call me." He drew another card from his pocket and passed it to her. "Just in case you lost my number."

Hailey took the card and flashed him a flirty smile. "More than happy to."

Before she could reach for the door once more, Joanna snatched the card from her hand. She dug in her bag for a pen and jotted her cell number right under Tony's, then offered it back to the woman. "Now you have my number also."

Hailey didn't smile this time. She opened the door once more and Joanna hesitated again. "Do you know Professor Orson Blume?"

Hailey frowned but not before Tony spotted the surprise in her eyes. "I don't think so. The name doesn't sound familiar. I'm sorry, do you and I know each other?"

Joanna shook her head. "I probably have you confused with someone else. I remember now. I was thinking of Madelyn. She had red hair. You're a natural blonde, aren't you?"

Hailey's lips curved into a smug expression. "I am." She reached out and touched Joanna's hair. "And you are not."

Joanna drew away from her and flashed a fake smile. "No, I'm not."

When they were in the car driving away, Tony said, "You recognized her."

"I did." Joanna stared forward, the fingers of her right hand clenching the armrest. "Eighteen years ago she was Madelyn. She had red hair and she worked as an assistant to Professor Orson Blume."

"Blume?"

"He was a psych professor when I was a freshman. He was also a much-loved advisor. All the freshmen I knew went to him. After the abduction Professor Blume went out of his way to try and help with our recovery. He was convinced Ellen and I needed additional therapy. I blew him off but I think Ellen went to see someone a few times."

"You didn't feel you needed counseling?" Tony kept his eyes on the road but he felt hers burning a hole through him.

"No. Words weren't going to make what happened go away. Nothing anyone could say would change what we lived through."

Tony only had a general overview of the case file. His one remaining contact at the Bureau who was still speaking to him hadn't been able to provide more than a cursory briefing. "Tell me about you."

"Didn't my mother do that already?"

The anger was gone but there was something else—defeat, disappointment maybe. "We only spoke for a couple of minutes. She was happy to know you were well. I hope I wasn't wrong about that part."

Five miles zipped past the windows before she decided to respond. "I grew up in a small town where everybody knew everybody else. My folks were strict. Went to church every time the doors opened. My brother was the captain of the football team, class president, you name it. When my father had his first heart attack, Ray stepped right into his shoes as breadwinner instead of going to college. He always did the right thing. The leader. Model student and son. Married the right girl. Had the perfect kids. Everybody loves Ray."

More of that silence lapsed. While he waited for her to go on, Tony headed for the only address he'd been able to find for Miles Conway.

"I was the quiet one. The wallflower. Didn't belong to any clubs, didn't play sports. No friends. Stayed holed up in my room. A loner."

"No boyfriends?" He made a left.

"I was fat and kept my nose in a book all through high school. No one noticed me and those who did only wanted to get a laugh at my expense."

"Kids can be cruel." He'd never had any trouble in school but his sister had been bullied—at least until Tony found out. The resulting expulsion was the only black mark on his high school record. It cost him three games that basketball season but he would have kicked the shit out of the guy making fun of her if it had cost him his spot on the team. "You came into your own in college?"

"I tried. The extra weight disappeared the summer before. I think I was so nervous I couldn't eat. Working out was my new best friend when I didn't have my head in the World Wide Web. Suddenly I was enthralled with what was going on in the world when I couldn't have cared less in high school." She shifted in her seat so she could look at him. "My father always said it was the quiet ones who changed the world."

Tony noticed that she glossed over the part about her father dying the year after her abduction. The brother had eventually taken over the shop where he'd worked. "You met someone in college?"

"No. I just hung out in the places my roommate told me I should if I wanted to have a life."

"Did that work?" He parked in front of the Cherry Tree Apartments. Decided the car sporting the fancy cover was Conway's Ferrari. Hadn't been here the last time he stopped by.

Joanna looked away. "Do the math and you'll have your answer."

Eight months into her freshman year Joanna was abducted and her life changed forever. She'd been a ghost ever since.

"You know, if my niece is going through what you went through—" he offered a different approach "—it would help if I had a better understanding of what happened during those fourteen days."

She stared out the window at the Dumpster that sat next to the line of trees separating this property from the next. "They made us fight. You know, like gladiators or something. If you lost you didn't eat."

The idea that Tif might be in that same position ripped at his gut. "Do you know if this fighting was recorded?"

She shrugged. "I don't know. I think so, but the room was either completely dark or blindingly light. All I wanted to do was survive. Everything else was pretty much irrelevant."

He would take that for now. "So who's Carrie Cole?"

"My make-believe friend."

Rather than delve into an analysis of that statement, they got out and Tony led the way up the exterior staircase to the second floor. Conway's apartment was the fourth door along the row of six on the right. A crying baby behind door number one and a barking dog behind number three were the only sounds. Tony took a position to the right of the hinged side of number four. He gestured for Joanna to get behind him. He knocked. No television or other noise. The second time he raised his fist he pounded harder.

Still nothing.

He turned to the woman behind him. "You should wait in the car."

She held his gaze a moment. "No way. I'll know if he's the one."

"The one?" Tony's instincts went on point.

"The one who made me believe I was going to be a star in a video he was making. The one who drugged me and delivered me to that place where my life ended."

She hadn't mentioned that part before but she had a damned good point. "Just don't touch anything."

He pulled a credit card from his wallet and reached for the doorknob. There didn't appear to be any dead bolt. The knob turned freely. Not locked. Which still didn't give him justification for going in without a warrant, but that didn't stop him. As he crossed the threshold, he reached under his jacket for the .22 at the small of his back. Living room was clear. Typical single guy decor. Large sectional sofa, ottoman that served as a coffee table. Even bigger television hanging on the wall. Kitchen and dining area were to the right. *Clear.*

He ordered, "Close the door with your elbow."

Joanna elbowed the door closed. "It stinks in here."

She was right. Smelled like cigarettes and leftover pizza.

The pizza remains were still in the open box on the counter. Dirty dishes were stacked in the sink. Ashtray on an end table was overflowing.

A cramped hall led to a row of three doors, two on the right, one on the left. First door on the right was a spare bedroom that served as what appeared to be a home office. Something of that order. Tony surveyed the three desks crammed into the room. Large monitors stood on each one but there was only one chair. Tony dragged a pair of gloves from his pocket and pulled them on. One by one he tried to awaken the screens. Nothing happened. Then he noticed why—the hard drive towers were missing.

As much as he wanted to go through the contents of the desk drawers, a new odor emanating from this end of the apartment told him the real trouble was behind door number two or three.

At the door on the left an extension cord had been plugged into an outlet in the hall and run under the door. He opened the door to what turned out to be a bathroom. No Miles Conway, but the answer to where the missing hard drives were became painfully clear.

Before moving into the bathroom, he kicked the extension cord free of the outlet that had blackened, probably from burning out. He then eased into the room. An iron had been thrown into the water with the three hard drives.

"Son of a bitch."

Beyond the piss stains on the toilet seat and the scum

circling the sink basin, there was definitely nothing left to see. Dirty towels lay in a pile in the floor.

He moved on to the final door.

Tony listened at the door for several seconds before opening it. The smell had him holding his breath. A male victim lay in the bed amid the tousled and bloody sheets. His head was stationed on the pillow, eyes and mouth open wide. In the center of his chest a wound had puckered angrily. The one lower on his abdomen had done the same but it was a bigger gash. Blood had spurted and oozed over his torso, soaking into the sheets.

"Stay right here at the door and for God's sake don't touch anything," he reminded the woman standing behind him.

Tony moved to the side of the bed, careful of the bloody rug on the floor. He touched the vic's neck. No pulse. The body was cold, the blood coagulated. Lividity confirmed that he'd died right where he lay. Judging by the stage of rigor Tony estimated he'd been dead eight to ten hours, which put time of death between 3:00 and 5:00 a.m. The lack of blood in the area of his pelvis, as well as the mess on the bedside rug, suggested someone had been straddling him when he was stabbed, and then cleaned their feet or hands on the rug.

Arms were stretched toward the headboard, colorful silk scarves secured his wrists there. All signs indicated the victim had sex just before his death.

Surveying the floor carefully before each step, Tony moved around the room. The killer had apparently taken the murder weapon with her—or him.

"It's him."

Joanna took a step toward the bed.

Tony held up a hand. "I told you not to move."

She pointed at the victim's face. "He's the man who talked me into meeting him at that bar." She shook her head. "We had a drink, and then I don't remember anything else. *It's him.*"

Tony backed up a couple of steps, pulled out his cell and took a pic of the victim. "It's been eighteen years. How can you be sure? You told the police you went to a bar alone." He studied her face for tells. "You said you didn't know who drugged you."

"I lied. I didn't want my family to know what I'd done." She lifted her gaze to his. "I was afraid to tell anyone the truth about what happened." She stared at the dead man in the bed. "It's him."

"Go back outside. Get in the car and stay there. I have to call this in."

When she'd done as he asked, he moved back into the hall. Only a couple of droplets of blood but those few indicated the unknown subject was headed for the bathroom.

Had his murderer also attempted to destroy any evidence that might have been on those hard drives?

Tony stared back into the bedroom at the dead man on the bed. "Fuck."

His cell vibrated. He heaved a weary breath, dragged it from his pocket and checked the screen. The text message from Chief Phelps was a pic of the sketch artist's rendering of the man Riley Fallon had seen with Tiffany. Tony looked from the screen to the dead man on the bed.

Damn, he had needed this guy alive.

# *Fifteen*

I made a terrible, terrible mistake.

I only wanted to be like everyone else. To fit in. What was so wrong with that?

*I made a mistake.*

The room is dark. I can't see a thing. It's so cold. I can't stop shivering. I don't understand what happened. Beer and wine tastes awful to me so I rarely drink. I didn't overindulge last night. No way. I remember the one drink, a cosmopolitan. I shouldn't have a hangover like this. I feel disoriented. My mouth is dry and I feel so sick. There was something wrong with that drink.

This is wrong—a mistake. I shouldn't be here.

*Don't fall apart, Jo.*

I feel my way around the dark, cold space on my hands and knees. My clothes are missing and so is my virginity. I hurt inside and down there between my legs.

There's something dried on my thighs. Don't know if it's semen or blood. Maybe both.

I made a terrible, terrible mistake.

I crawl over the dark place, back and forth, back and forth, until I'm as sure as I can possibly be that there are no holes or traps to step into, so I stand. My father taught me this. He's always working on that old house we call home. The leaky roof or the sagging floors. I remember him moving slow and cautious over the place he needed to repair to make sure there were no surprises before he set to the task. He laughed and said, "I fell through a floor once. Don't have no desire to repeat the indignity."

*I'm so sorry, Daddy. I really screwed up.*

I have to find a way out of here. I can do this. I'm smart. *Just focus, Jo.* The walls feel smooth and cold like the floor. I walk around and around the black space. It's completely black. Not even a hint of light. Strange.

There is no one or nothing else in the room or whatever it is. Only me. *Me.* Not the same me who stupidly flirted with an older guy I didn't even know but a bruised and damaged me.

*Joanna Guthrie, you are in deep trouble.*

My family will be so disappointed.

I made a terrible, terrible mistake.

That's when I start to scream for help.

# Sixteen

*2:00 p.m.*

Cops were everywhere.

LeDoux had told Jo to stay in the car. She had for a while, but curiosity had gotten the better of her. Digging her sunglasses from her bag to shield as much of her face as possible, she walked the length of the car to stretch her legs. Impatience and frustration had her nerves jumping. She needed to walk off the tension.

*Stay close to the car, Jo.* Too many reporters way too close for her comfort. If they thought there was a story—and clearly they did—they'd be going long for any shot they could get. She knew the drill. Though she had never worked a live crime scene, her research assistant had told her plenty of war stories.

Uniformed cops moved from door to door canvassing the neighbors. Apartment 216 was blocked off as best as possible considering the residents of the one occupied apartment beyond it needed to be able to come and go via the same stairs and corridor. A uniformed officer was posted on either side of the door to the victim's apartment. A strategically placed patrol car and two more officers prevented anyone other than residents from entering the parking lot.

While Jo studied the fray the coroner's van turned in from the street running parallel to the building. She leaned against the car and watched the coroner and his assistant hop out of the van. They pulled the gurney from the van, placed a medical case and body bag atop it and headed for the stairs. Neither was wearing a white lab coat or scrubs or even uniforms for that matter. The two men, one midfifties and black, the other early twenties and white, were dressed in everyday clothes. Wash-and-wear trousers, dark in color, and polos. She couldn't say for sure but a small logo might have been embroidered on the left front panel of their shirts where a pocket would have been.

A forensic unit as well as two suits, no doubt feds or maybe GBI, had joined the party. The chief, Ed Buckley, from Georgia College security, had arrived. Jo had seen his picture on the website. She figured the two other guys with him were from Milledgeville PD. So far none had questioned her or really even noticed her for that matter.

Suited Jo. She had what she wanted.

Miles Conway was dead.

She had wished him dead a million times. She'd learned his identity and kept tabs on him via the internet all these years the same way she had Madelyn Houser until she seemingly dropped off the face of the earth. Now Jo knew why. She had become Hailey Martin.

The one issue with Conway's death was the unfortunate detail that Jo didn't get the name she needed.

There was still Madelyn. She wasn't innocent in this. She knew things. Jo had seen it in her eyes when she realized Jo recognized her from back in the day.

Oh yes, she was as guilty as sin.

Jo should have come back here and done this ten years ago or even five like she wanted. For the first few years after their escape, release—whatever it had been—she hadn't wanted to think about it much less talk about it. Neither she nor Ellen then had been mentally capable of breaking their silence. Jo had hidden from life, burrowed deep into nowhere. Eventually though, the guilt had started to gnaw at her. How could she let the people who did this over and over get away with it?

So she'd started with what she had: a cute guy who was a couple or three years older than her. His name had been Miles, but she hadn't known his last name. The redhead named Madelyn she'd run into once at a club—with Miles—but mostly she'd seen her at Professor Blume's office. After repeatedly coming up with nothing, Jo had pushed aside the whole idea of finding the truth. Maybe she and Ellen were the only ones— maybe the whole thing had been one really bad drug trip. Maybe it never even happened.

Then, five years ago, after a decade of making excellent connections in the cyber world, she was able to do the kind of research that had in the past been available only to law enforcement. Jo started to dig again. Their abductions had been cleanly executed. Their treatment during captivity had been organized, structured. Maybe for some sort of bizarre experiment or simply a new type of reality show to sell to exclusive clients on the internet. Who knew? But Jo damned well intended to find out.

But she'd waited too long. She had tracked down four other sets of abductions very similar to hers and Ellen's. Time and persistence had been required, but the other victims—at least the ones who were still alive—had eventually confided in Jo.

All those victims—she closed her eyes and dropped her head. Maybe if she and Ellen had told the truth eighteen years ago the others would still be alive—maybe no one else would have had to go through that hell. But Jo had been weak. Ellen had begged her to let sleeping dogs lie. She had gotten married and had a child with another on the way. She insisted resurrecting what happened would tear her life apart all over again. Jo shouldn't have listened. She should have followed her instincts. She'd let Ellen dissuade her.

Yeah, that's right. Blame your dead friend.

*Friend.* Had she and Ellen ever really been friends?

No. Not in the true definition of the word. They had been forced to share the same space and endure the same hell for two weeks. Before that, they hadn't known each other at all. But that status had changed quickly. They had watched each other suffer, come apart at the seams, and then rise up from the ashes and fight back.

All except for the other girl—the one who didn't survive.

Jo pushed away the memories.

The bottom line was she should have done this a long time ago. That was on her and no one else. Conway, Houser—or whoever she was—should have been stopped eighteen years ago.

The abductions appeared to have stopped four years after Jo and Ellen were taken. She supposed it was possible the bastards had only changed their MO. If that was the case, why take Tiffany Durand and Vickie Parton using the old MO? So far, every step was exactly the same, including Conway and Houser's involvement. Didn't make sense.

Whether it made sense or not, she had to find them before it was too late.

Two young women just disappear one day. All their worldly possessions are left behind. No one has a clue where they went and no one really saw a thing. No ransom demands. No notes left behind. No real prior problems or clues that would have indicated trouble. Just gone. Vanished.

The police were just as stumped today as they had been eighteen years ago. But Jo had some idea where they might be. She'd already been scouting the area. She should tell LeDoux. Could she really trust him with the whole truth?

The coroner and his assistant descended the stairs drawing Jo back to the here and now. The body of Miles Conway had been tucked into a body bag and laid out on a gurney between the two men. No one deserved to be murdered more than the bastard now shoved into a bag like yesterday's trash.

The rear doors of the coroner's van were opened and the gurney was pushed inside. When the doors closed and the men in the embroidered polo shirts had loaded up, they rolled back out onto the street, squeezing past the blockade of spectators. The piece of shit in the body bag would endure one final atrocity before being planted or burned.

Every inch of Miles Conway's naked body would be photographed. Next came the X-rays to see if all was as it should be inside. Fluid samples would be drawn from his eyes and his body. His penis would be thoroughly examined as would every orifice of his body. Then the real fun would begin. The typical Y-incision would be cut into his torso. Shears would peel the skin and muscle back to uncover the rib cage. A bone saw would aid in removing the ribs and sternum so that the organs could be examined, weighed and tissue samples taken. The top of the skull would be sawed off next, allowing the brain to be removed and examined. Once the testing was complete, all the organs would be bagged up and stuffed back inside. By the time he landed in a coffin he would look more like the lead character in a Frankenstein movie than the ladies' man he'd passed himself off as in life.

"See you in hell, you bastard."

LeDoux and two of the suits descended the steps. All three looked pissed. At the bottom of the stairs LeDoux broke away from the other two and moved toward his car. Jo climbed into the passenger seat and waited. He dropped behind the wheel, started the car and drove away.

Jo kept her head down until they'd passed the flock of reporters. Then she asked, "What happened?"

"Murder weapon wasn't found. Coroner said it was likely a broad blade knife, like a butcher knife. Estimated time of death between two and six this morning."

Uneasiness stiffened her spine. "Are you in trouble for going into the apartment?"

"Not yet. But it's coming. I've already been warned to stay clear."

She moistened her lips. "Did they ask about me?"

He glanced at her. "I told them my girlfriend waited in the car."

She dredged up a smile. "Girlfriend, eh?"

"No one questioned it so I guess it worked."

"Maybe." The air in the car suddenly seemed to vanish. She was too close to this, to him. She wasn't supposed to get this close. Too late now.

"Miles Conway is the man who drugged you and passed you off to whoever held you, is that what happened?"

"What makes you think he passed us off to anyone?" She believed that to be the case, but she had no proof.

"Because he was still here doing the same thing." LeDoux slowed for a turn. "Like a drug dealer who hasn't gotten caught."

"I don't know. Maybe. You're the profiler." Jo couldn't be sure. She would bet money he was the one who raped her and Ellen, but did he hang around after that? Just another question without an answer.

"You're certain about Martin?"

"As certain as I can be." She stared out the window at the passing houses and trees. "I saw her with Conway. They seemed like a couple or intimates of some sort."

And she'd been stupid enough to think he wanted her. He'd flirted, teased and charmed her until she'd come to what he called his favorite place. Only she'd been nervous so she'd gone early. He'd been there already, too. With *Madelyn*.

Jo had been devastated, ashamed. She'd wanted to go home but he'd begged her to stay. She'd surrendered to his vast charm.

The biggest mistake of her life.

# *Seventeen*

"**S**he's not home."

Tony ignored Joanna's statement. He would keep looking for Martin or Houser or whatever the hell her name was until he was ready to call it a night. He pounded on the door again. The dog, Brutus, sat directly on the other side staring at them. Wouldn't he bark if his master wasn't home? Then again he hadn't barked the last two times Tony dropped by. What kind of guard dog didn't bark?

What if Martin was already dead the same way Conway had been?

"I'm going in."

Joanna stepped back, arms folded over her chest. "Breaking and entering will get you arrested and it would be a waste of time. She. Is. Not. Home."

Irritation burrowed deep into the back of his neck. He rubbed at the tension. "You don't know that."

"She has a security system. I saw it blink when we were here last time. Her car isn't here."

"Her car could be in the garage." Tony turned on the woman staring at him then. "Why are you so fucking calm?" He shrugged. "I mean how often do you see a dead man with blood all over the place? Aren't you the slightest bit upset?"

Maybe that was why he was so worked up. Her reaction to the scene had been bugging the shit out of him since they found Conway's body. She'd seemed surprised when they discovered the bastard sprawled naked in a pool of his own blood. Surprised but not shaken and she'd recovered in record time. Tony might have fucked up his personal life and his career, but he did read people accurately more often than not.

Doubt poked at him. He ignored it. Joanna Guthrie was hiding something besides her tragic story from eighteen years ago and that scrapbook she'd been keeping for years.

"What time did you leave my room this morning?"

Her jaw dropped. "Seriously? We're going to have that conversation right now? Here, on another person of interest's porch?"

"You're so certain she's not home, what difference does it make?"

He had her there. She glared right back at him, her stance defiant, but he saw the way her throat worked as she struggled for a comeback.

He shook his head. "Let's go."

With a final glance at the statue-still dog, he headed back to the car. He waited until she was seated on the passenger side and he slid behind the wheel. Dusk had eaten up the last of the daylight as he rolled away from Martin's home.

Goddamn it! He needed a break here.

Right now, the woman in the passenger seat was the only one he had. "What time did you go for breakfast?"

She exhaled a big breath. "It was before seven. I didn't exactly check the time before I walked out the door."

"So you left before seven and you went where? Exactly?"

"I drove to the McDonald's over on South Wayne Street. It shouldn't have taken long, but traffic was backed up at the Hancock intersection. There was something wrong with the traffic light." She shoved the sun visor up. "I had to wait forever. Once I could make that turn, it took me maybe five minutes to get to Mickey D's. I probably waited another ten or fifteen minutes in the drive-through line. Then I drove straight back to the inn. I didn't go via Macon and kill anyone if that's what you're asking."

Tony wished he hadn't drunk so much last night. Maybe he would have roused when she left the room, and then he wouldn't have to wonder. It was in his nature to be suspicious.

*Do you really believe she did what you saw in Conway's apartment?*

If she had driven all the way to Macon, had sex with and murdered Conway, and then drove back those thirty miles that would have taken at least two hours. The scenario was unreasonable.

She'd left Tony a note, which confirmed she hadn't

expected to come back. Maybe the note was just in case she didn't make it back before he woke up.

"Are you still weighing the idea?" she demanded. She shook her head and stared out the window. "Remember, I'm the one who shared who I really am with you. *You*. No one else. Why would I do that if I planned to commit murder? Why would I even connect with you? I would have stayed anonymous. You wouldn't have even known I was here."

He stopped for a traffic light. Stared directly at her. "To tell the truth, I don't care if you killed him. My single goal is finding my niece and Vickie Parton alive. The rest—your tragic story included—doesn't matter to me at all."

"Wow." She looked away. "Thanks. Of all the cops and feds involved in this case I'm really glad I picked you out of the herd."

The idea that he felt guilty for saying what he'd just said made him even angrier. His phone vibrated and he fished it from his pocket. A local number. He was grateful it wasn't Angie. She'd called him twice already. He wanted a better handle on how Conway's murder connected to Tiffany's disappearance—if it did at all—before he spoke to her.

"LeDoux."

"We need to talk, Mr. LeDoux."

*Phelps.* "I'm headed your way now, Chief."

Joanna didn't say another word during the thirty minutes that followed the call from the chief. She was pissed and maybe he didn't blame her. He'd basically accused her of murder and told her he didn't give a shit about her painful past. But he'd needed to know if she was telling the truth. Pushing her into a corner—hitting her where he suspected it hurt most—was the only way to get an organic reaction.

Was she lying to him? Frankly, the jury was still out on that.

Once they arrived at the Milledgeville Public Safety office he added insult to injury when he ordered her to wait in the lobby outside the chief's office and not to move. He'd even gone so far as to inform the officer who'd let him into the building not to allow her to leave. Now she was really pissed. Fire sparked in her eyes but to her credit she didn't say a word.

Tony kept his cool and let the chief kick off the conversation. After all, he was the one who demanded the meeting. Before getting around to whatever it was he really had to say, Phelps brought him up to speed on the investigation so far; that much Tony appreciated.

The Macon Police Department was all too willing to turn Conway's murder over to Milledgeville. Phelps as well as Chief Buckley from campus security had sent lieutenants representing their departments to the crime scene. The two had introduced themselves to Tony. If he'd been smart he would have left after that, but old habits died hard. He was accustomed to taking his time and absorbing the scene as well as all the activities involved. He wanted to hear what the neighbors had to say about the vic, et cetera. Hanging around had ensured he was still there when the Bureau and the GBI had shown. The two agents who'd paid him a visit that morning had put him through the paces, and then issued another warning.

Milledgeville's coroner had taken the body. Again,

Macon PD had been only too happy to pass off the drain on tax dollars. Tony had been ready to go at that point. He hoped the chief would fill him in on anything he missed. Phelps, however, had other ideas on where this conversation was going.

"Walk me through one more time how you ended up at Conway's door," the chief said as he leaned back in his chair. "I'm having trouble wrapping my head around your story."

Tony was well aware of the routine. Phelps wasn't entirely sure Tony was telling the truth so he asked the same questions repeatedly in hopes of garnering a different answer.

"A club, Wild Things in Macon, was one of the last places my niece, Tiffany, was seen by any of her friends. The manager said that this Conway guy had been talking to her. Riley Fallon saw him in Tiffany's Jeep with her just days before she disappeared. The first time I visited Mr. Conway's apartment—yesterday—he wasn't home. I decided to try again today. I knocked on the door and it swung open. I asked my girlfriend to wait in the car and I went inside to have a look."

"You know, Mr. LeDoux," Phelps said, his tone sounding somewhere between annoyed and resigned, "that would all be fine and good *if* you were an officer of the law. We could have justified your actions by pointing out some vague notion of exigent circumstances. But you are not an officer of the law. You are no longer a special agent for the FBI. You are a civilian. A civilian who trespassed on a murder scene. A civilian—" he pointed at Tony "—who has a potential motive for wanting Mr. Conway dead. This does not bode well, Mr. LeDoux. Not well at all."

Tony hated the way he repeated *Mr. LeDoux*. "Agreed. But I'm human, Chief. What would you do if one of your daughters was missing? If you were lucky enough to find a guy who may have been the last person to see her, wouldn't you do whatever necessary to speak with him?"

Phelps heaved a big breath. "Get out of my office, LeDoux. If I find you at another of my scenes, I will arrest you. Go take care of your sister and her husband and let us do what we need to do here."

"Any update from the coroner's office?"

Phelps glared at him, but he answered the question. "Murder weapon was definitely a broad blade knife—an old-fashioned butcher knife. They found the knife, by the way, in the second of the two Dumpsters belonging to the complex. It was in the one behind the apartment building. We think the killer parked there and came around the building. Nobody saw anyone and the building has no video surveillance." He shook his head. "Anyway, the stab wound to the chest missed the heart. Too bad for the vic, it punctured a lung. But it was the second thrust of the knife that killed him. The blade went in just shy of the center and sliced right through the aorta. It was like our perp knew this and twisted the knife to open things up even more. Doc says he bled out in a minute or two."

"Did the unsub leave any evidence behind?" No matter that Tony was leaning toward believing Joanna, he didn't completely trust his instincts right now.

Phelps shook his head. "Not that they've found so far.

She—and we're assuming it was a she—was extremely careful. Your friends from the Bureau took the computer hard drives. They're assuming some sort of internet crime considering the setup in the apartment. We found half a dozen hidden cameras in that bedroom."

Tony expected that the Bureau would take exactly that action. He stood. "I appreciate the update."

Phelps bobbed his chin. "Stay out of the way, LeDoux, and we'll continue to be friends."

Tony thanked him and headed for the lobby. Joanna still looked just as pissed as she had twenty minutes ago. "We can go now."

She pushed to her feet. "Anything from the coroner?"

Tony shook his head. "Nothing we didn't already know."

She followed him outside and to the car. "Where to now?"

"We're going to work." He looked over the top of the BMW at her. "Before this night is done, I'm going to know everything about you, Miss Guthrie."

"What about Martin?"

"Tomorrow. And after we find her and rattle that cage, we're going to visit this Professor Blume you mentioned."

"You found him?"

When they'd settled in the car he said, "I did. He's retired now but he still lives in Milledgeville. Until recently he was still involved in a project at the old Central State Hospital."

Joanna didn't ask anything else. Instead, she stared straight ahead.

Before he did anything else, he had to talk to Angie. She would be walking the floors and cursing him.

"When we're done for the day," Joanna announced, "I'm heading back to my place."

Oh yeah. She was not happy with him. Well, her displeasure was about to get worse.

"I think it's best if you stay close to me for now."

She scoffed. "I'll bet you do. Not happening, LeDoux."

Oh, it was happening all right. Somehow this woman was connected to whoever had taken Tiffany and he damned sure intended to find out how before he allowed her out of his sight again.

# Eighteen

*"I don't want to die."*

Tiffany pulled the younger girl into her arms. "We're not going to die."

They had been in this hellhole for days, at least four, maybe five. Why wasn't anyone coming to find them? Surely her mom and dad knew by now that she was missing. Tiffany bit back the tears. She should have been smarter and she wouldn't be in this mess.

Her mom would be so hurt. Tiffany should have called her back, but she had been so angry with her. Her mom just didn't get that she was an adult now. She needed to make her own decisions and plan her own life.

*And just look where that got you...*

Tiffany steadied herself. She had to be strong. Vickie needed her. The girl in her arms shook with her sobs. The other girl—Lexy—sulked in the corner on the opposite side of the room. Lexy had beaten Vickie badly today. Her arm might be broken. There were a lot of bruises and some swelling. Tomorrow if she couldn't perform...

Not going there.

They would get through this. Whatever that bastard wanted, they would do it until they figured out a way to escape. Then she could make it up to her mom for being such a bitch.

The box-style cage was about the same size as their dorm rooms. The room was white and totally empty. Well except for the three naked, bruised and battered women seated on the floor. Blood was smeared on the walls from where they'd leaned against them and steadied themselves when they felt too tired to keep their balance. There was puke on the floor, some urine, too. They tried to make it to the hole in the floor they'd been instructed to use but it wasn't always possible.

Tiffany closed her eyes. The light was so bright. It burned her eyes. At first the box had been totally black and so damned cold. She was certain they would freeze to death, but then suddenly everything turned white and the lights came on so bright. And it felt like the temperature was rising.

She was so hungry. He'd cut their food down to next to nothing. At least he still left water. Would he cut that down next?

She was so tired but sleep wouldn't come. No matter how tightly she closed her eyes she could still see the bright light. It was like looking into the sun. She squinted her eyes open enough to check the other girl. She'd won today's battle—thank God there had been only one—but Lexy hadn't gotten off so light. Her face was bloody. Scratches on her body showed Vickie's desperation. She'd fought hard. Vickie shuddered in Tiffany's arms as if she'd said the words out loud.

Tiffany ached from the battle she'd fought and won against Lexy yesterday.

How much longer could they keep this up? Weakness was already clawing its way into her bones. Vickie was losing her mental fortitude as well as her physical strength. Tiffany wasn't so sure about the other girl. Lexy, her name was Lexy. Lexy stared at Tiffany as if she'd read her mind. Was she talking instead of thinking? Maybe she was the one losing her mind.

"They're going to make us kill each other," she said.

Lexy could very well be right. Tiffany worried that was the ultimate goal. She couldn't be sure but the place where they were forced to fight appeared to have cameras. Were they videotaping this insanity and selling it on the internet? What kind of sick fuck did this?

Probably a serial killer.

Uncle Tony and his FBI friends would find them. He was the best.

"I'm not killing anybody." Tiffany had made that decision yesterday. No matter what happened, she wasn't killing another human being.

Lexy said, "How did you end up here?"

The girl who'd refused to say more than a word here or there since they were thrown into this place was suddenly all questions. Tiffany was glad. Talking distracted her from the hunger gnawing at her belly.

"I went to this club to meet a friend." Tiffany frowned. "Someone put something in my drink, I think."

"I got picked up in an alley." Lexy straightened her battered legs. "It was the middle of the night. I was taking a nap when I heard a noise. I got up and someone grabbed me from behind. Put something over my mouth and nose and that was it. I went nighty night."

Now that there were lights Tiffany could see what the other girls looked like. Lexy had the biggest boobs of any of them. And dozens of tattoos. Tiffany tried not to form an opinion based on all that ink but she couldn't help it. She had Lexy figured for a druggie, maybe a prostitute. *Not fair, Tif.*

"Your friend needs to toughen up if she wants to survive this."

Lexy was right about Vickie, too. Tiffany didn't really know Vickie. They were both freshmen at Georgia College but they had no classes together. Tiffany had seen her around. At the club that last time, too.

Vickie's steady breathing told Tiffany she was asleep. She asked the other girl, "What makes you think any of us will survive?"

Would they make it out of here?

So far they had food and water. Not much but enough to survive.

Lexy didn't have an answer for the question.

Tiffany didn't either.

*Please, God, don't let us die here.*

She thought of her mom and dad and determination welled inside her. Hell no, they weren't going to die. They would get through this. Whatever the bastard who'd taken them wanted, they would do it until they figured out a way to escape.

*Come on, Uncle Tony, find us!*

Tiffany had no idea who had taken them. She'd gone to the bar but she'd had to leave early. She felt sick. By the time she got to her Jeep she couldn't keep her eyes open. The last thing she remembered was her vision fading to nothing.

A human trafficker had probably taken them. They were young. Those sick pieces of shit liked to find young women. Her uncle had warned her to be careful for that very reason.

Or maybe it was a serial killer.

Uncle Tony knew all about serial killers, too. He would find them.

# Nineteen

*Antebellum Inn*
*9:00 p.m.*

Jo paced the sidewalk along McIntosh Street. She hadn't smoked a cigarette in ten years. There was no way to describe how badly she'd needed one or how good it felt to draw the smoke into her lungs right now.

She'd coughed and choked a couple of times on the first one, but the second one was going far more smoothly.

LeDoux sat on the back steps of the inn watching her. He was determined to keep an eye on her. She wanted to leave and he was having no part of it. It wasn't that she had some luxurious hotel room of her own. She didn't. Her Celica had been her room on wheels until she'd ended up here with him. This was what she'd wanted—wasn't it? To hook up with someone involved in the investigation, determine if she could trust that someone, and then spill her guts.

And she'd hit pay dirt. Not only had she latched onto

a federal agent—okay, a former one—but also he was the uncle of one of the victims. He had the cop smarts and the emotional involvement. Was that not everything she could have hoped for and more? If she was completely honest with herself, she would admit that at some point over the past twelve or so hours she had decided she could trust him. It was all good, right? Serendipity or whatever?

Yet they were getting nowhere.

And LeDoux grew more suspicious of her by the hour. She might have spent the past eighteen years avoiding other humans but she could still read them pretty damned well.

The only good thing that had happened was Conway getting his. She paused, closed her eyes and drew deeply on the cigarette. She smiled as she released the smoke. Oh yes. The bastard had gotten his. Bled out like a stuck pig. Whoever killed him—still felt like LeDoux thought it was her—she had done it right. In the chest, probably got the heart or close anyway. And the gut. Oh yeah, he'd felt that one before he sucked in his last breath.

The problem was, with him dead she couldn't exactly interrogate him the way she'd planned. Jo had imagined all sorts of ways to torture him to extract the information she needed. Now that wouldn't happen.

Maybe Madelyn had killed him. She may have figured out who Jo was, the same as Jo had recognized her. Was she tying up loose ends for the man in charge? Maybe the blonde who'd dyed her hair red eighteen years ago *was* the man in charge.

Jo stopped her pacing for a minute. Chain-smoking those two cigarettes had given her a buzz. Damn. She stared up at the moon through the massive trees shading the street. When she'd reached college she had never smoked a cigarette in her life. Cancer sticks were for idiots. That had been her opinion. But the minute she was released from the hospital all those years ago, she had made her brother stop at a convenience store and buy her cigarettes. He'd argued, but he'd felt so sorry for her he hadn't been able to refuse her request.

She'd smoked for almost eight years. Smoked, drank and tried about a dozen other ways to erase the memories from her brain. None of it had worked.

Not one fucking thing she tried. So many times she'd wished she had died in that damned box. She and Ellen would both have been better off. Ellen would never have had kids and a husband to leave so devastated. All the others, too. Half the ones who'd survived had committed suicide within five years of being found.

Jo had only considered checking out two or three hundred times.

Finally, one day she'd decided the whole broken and grieving process was too fucking complicated and time consuming. She'd made up her mind to put the past behind her and never look back. Maybe she could have succeeded if Ellen had killed herself back then. But that didn't happen. Ellen had continued to intrude into her life whenever she found herself too close to the edge. She would cry and whine and plead and Jo would listen, occasionally make a sympathetic comment and feel a little guiltier about what happened.

Now Ellen was dead and Jo was back in this damned place.

The definition of insanity, of stupidity or maybe both.

Jo threw the cigarette butt into the drain and shoved the lighter and pack into her back pocket. Reclaiming a bad habit wasn't going to get her through this. Neither was all the alcohol she wanted so desperately to consume right now.

Conway was out of the way but Houser—Martin, she called herself now—was still out there. Obviously their partnership or whatever the hell it was had still been operational. Was Houser the one who ran the show or did she report to whoever orchestrated whatever the hell *this* was?

Apparently, they had changed their MO or extended their hunting ground out of the Southeast. There had to be a reason why no similar abductions occurred for all those years before Tiffany and Vickie were taken. And by God, Jo had searched for them. Not a single day passed without her scanning news feeds and other sites a good reporter learned to search. She hadn't found even one set of abductions that matched the MO of the ones like hers in the past thirteen years—until she came back to Milledgeville two days ago.

What had suddenly changed? For one reason or another, he or she or them had gone back into business. If they had merely changed their MO so completely during the past thirteen years that she couldn't spot it in her searching, why the sudden about-face?

The concept was unreasonable, illogical.

LeDoux was on his phone now. She couldn't hear enough of what he was saying to gauge who might be on the other end.

She'd answered all his questions. She'd told him everything—well, almost everything. She hadn't told him the one thing she had promised Ellen she would never tell anyone. And she hadn't gone into the explicit details on any of it. Only the basics. They had discussed various motives for the abductions. Potential perpetrators—unsubs or unknown subjects, he called them.

They both agreed the motive was likely one of two things: behavioral trials of some sort that involved drugs—though she couldn't say for sure they had been drugged other than for purposes of sleep—or maybe for sick gladiator-type games involving nudity and violence for the purposes of selling on the deep web.

She'd read plenty of articles about the bizarre things people did for money. The internet was loaded with people who wanted to watch violent sex, violence period. There were even people who would pay another person to do bad things to them. Seriously bad things. There were those who bought body parts to eat. Others who sold body parts on the black market.

The world was a sick, sick place with some seriously demented people hidden behind their masks of normalcy.

Like Miles Conway.

"Bastard."

She turned to the man still watching her. With only a couple of streetlamps and the ambient lighting around the inn she couldn't really tell what was on his mind but she felt confident there was about to be a battle. He was a former FBI agent—a big-time profiler. LeDoux would be accustomed to doing things his way.

*He knows what he's doing, Jo.*

Deep breath. Get it over with. Her Celica sat next

to the curb on the street. She could leave if she wanted to. No one could stop her from doing whatever the hell she wanted. If he tried, well then there would be a battle for damned sure.

She marched up the small parking lot, stalled a few yards away from the steps where he sat. She would just tell him how it was going to be and that would be that. He looked at her and she looked at him and the uncertainty and worry she saw there shifted something inside her. No. No. No. She would not let this get personal.

Dredging up her wavering resolve, she announced, "I'm through talking. I've told you everything you need to know. I need some sleep. I'll see you in the morning."

He stood and descended the three steps, tucked his hands into the pockets of his jeans. "Give me five minutes. I think you're going to want to hear what I have to say."

She'd seen him on the phone while she sucked down those two cigarettes. Had no idea who he'd been talking to. Didn't give a shit. And still, she said, "Five minutes and then I'm gone."

Maybe she owed him that. After all she'd used him to a degree. Planned to continue doing so as long as things didn't get too complicated. Hear him out and take it from there. Fine. Okay. She followed him around the pool and into the cottage where they'd had sex last night.

A means to an end? Desperation? Stupidity?

Who knew? What she did know was that she needed a change of clothes. His scent was all over these. But to change clothes she'd have to get her bag from the trunk, and then he'd know she didn't have a room. She'd slept in her car the first night after she arrived. Motels, no matter how low rent, typically wanted ID. It was another of those trust things. If no one knew where she was no one could find her. That's the way she liked it. She'd spent the last half of her life living that way. She imagined she'd spend whatever was left doing the same.

He closed the door behind her and gestured to the sofa. "Have a seat."

"I'll stand. I'm not staying long."

He scrubbed a hand over his jaw. "If—" he sat down at the table "—Martin and Conway were in this together, as you believe, then you may be in danger."

"Now that's a good one." She shook her head. "I'm not staying here—in this room—with you. I have my own place. I like my privacy."

"The chief called me while you were taking a smoke break. They've confirmed that Conway's killer was female."

Jo snorted. "Really. It took them all this time to figure that out? I took one look at his position on the bed and the silk scarves used to tie him to the bed and figured that out." If it had been a man, Conway would have been lying ass up so that his dominant partner could enter him from behind.

"They found a blond hair."

Jo stilled. Now she got it. "So you think it was me? Didn't we have this conversation already?" She shook her head. "So yeah, I drove over to Macon, fucked the guy, stabbed him a couple of times, took a shower, gave his hard drives a bath, and then drove to Mickey D's for *your* breakfast. I'm that cold and calculating. Couldn't you tell when we were screwing last night?"

"The chief wants you to submit a hair sample for comparison."

The first hint of fear slithered through some errant

crack in her defenses. "Not no, but hell no." She folded her arms across her chest. "No way."

"I shouldn't have let you go in there with me. This is my fault. He wouldn't say where they found the hair. Could've been on the carpet. When the cops first arrived, to protect you, I told them that you were my girlfriend and you stayed in the car. I doubt they're going to believe me when I tell them I lied."

*Shit.* "Tell him to get a warrant and he can have his hair."

"The bottom line," he offered, "is you're here. You're involved somehow and maybe someone is trying to set you up. Hailey Martin comes to mind. Think about it—you and Ellen were the first two abductions like Tiffany's and Vickie's. Maybe you were part of it all along or maybe you're reenacting what happened to you. These are the scenarios the task force will consider."

"First," she argued, "Martin-Houser—who knows what her real name is?—couldn't have known I was here before today. She didn't have time to set me up. Second, I can prove when I left Texas."

"Having proof when you left home helps," he said. "As for the trace evidence found at the Conway scene, Martin did touch your hair."

Jo's throat tightened as the memory flashed through her brain. "She was just being a bitch."

But she could have taken a hair. No way. She couldn't have put it all together that quickly. Not possible. That kind of premeditation took time. Besides, Conway was already dead when she and LeDoux visited Martin.

Jo's money was on the scenario that Martin killed Conway—*tying up loose ends.*

"Maybe the chief needs to ask Ms. Martin for a hair sample. Did you tell him that?" Jo's heart started to pound as she waited for his response.

"I did. I provided her address and her connection to Conway. He'll have someone at her door first thing in the morning."

So maybe LeDoux did have her back. "Thanks."

He ran his hand through his hair, exhaled a weary breath. "My niece is missing. As best we can estimate she's been missing six days now. I need to find her. Soon. I need to find her alive. To do that I need all the help I can get. My gut tells me the person who took her is somehow a part of or involved with what happened to you eighteen years ago. For that reason, I need you safe. I need you close."

He looked her in the eyes then. "I need your help."

The faces of all those other women who were dead because she had kept silent all these years floated in front of her eyes. How could she keep doing that? She couldn't. Jo nodded. "Okay. I'll stay, but you keep that chief off my ass."

"I can do that for a little while anyway."

"I need to get my bag from my car."

"I'll go with you."

She hesitated. "You worried I've got another body in the trunk?"

He smiled. "You have no idea the things I've seen."

Actually, she did. She doubted many people had spent as much time researching missing persons as she had. She had perused story after story and image after image. Whether it was for money or pure sadistic pleasure, it was never pretty.

He followed her to the street. She opened the trunk and grabbed her canvas overnighter. "See." She waved her hand. "No bodies. Just a spare tire and tire iron."

He took the bag from her. "Good. I was really hoping I hadn't slept with a killer."

His words, spoken offhandedly, echoed through her. She decided not to correct him on that one. Knowing that truth wouldn't help him find his niece.

When they were back inside the cottage, she set her hands on her hips and gave him the ground rules. "I'm not sleeping with you again. I'll take the couch."

"I'll take the couch." He tossed her bag onto the bed.

"Deal." She wasn't above taking the man's bed. How often did she get to sleep on such a luxurious bed complete with down comforter?

Never.

"Tomorrow we'll lay out a strategy."

"You have a plan?" She reached into her bag for the nightshirt she'd packed.

"No. But I will by morning."

"Is your sister doing okay?" She'd come outside and talked to him once while Jo was pacing the sidewalk.

"She's terrified. Tomorrow she and the other girl's mother are making a public plea at the task force press conference."

Jo's mother had done that. Her brother, too. So had all the other parents from all the other victims she'd tracked down. In this situation it wouldn't help. Probably never did. Really. "If your niece was taken by the same people who took me, she'll be back."

"How can you be sure? You said there's always one who dies. The other girl, you said."

"Yeah, well, you never heard about the other girls for a reason. They were never reported missing. They were nobody. Homeless or…just invisible."

Jo had concluded that it was planned that way. The one who died was always the one no one would miss, no one looked for. Did they take steps to ensure the other girl was always the ultimate victim?

"Why did you stay silent all this time?"

Jo blinked, shaking off the thoughts. She'd wondered when that question would be tossed at her. The edge in his voice told her he was thinking that if she and the others had come clean long ago they wouldn't be here now. His niece and the other freshman wouldn't be missing.

Maybe he was right. But things looked different from this side, especially eighteen years ago.

"We were scared. Brainwashed. We did as we were told."

"But something changed your mind."

"Ellen, the other girl who was with me, killed herself less than a month ago. She left two little kids and a younger sister behind. It's enough already. We shouldn't have waited so long…"

"What about the body of the other girl?"

She shrugged. "Don't know." She grabbed her bag and headed for the bathroom. "Good night."

She closed the door and stared at her reflection in the mirror. If she was lucky he hadn't heard the lie in her voice. She closed her eyes to block the images that flashed one in front of the other in her mind.

Of course the body wasn't found—they buried it where no one would ever look.

# Twenty

*Day Two*
*Eighteen years ago...*

I'm not alone anymore.

Two other girls were here when I woke up. Actually one of them woke me up. She thought I was dead.

One girl's name is Ellen. She's a freshman at Georgia College, too. I don't know her though. She hasn't stopped crying. She thinks she was raped the same way I was. Like me, she can't remember anything.

The other girl won't talk to us. She refuses to tell us her name or where she comes from or anything. She keeps to herself in one corner.

It's so dark. I wish I could see.

The one named Ellen crawls over to sit by me. "Why are we here?"

I wish I knew. "I guess we'll find out."

She whimpers. She's really scared. I don't mention it but I am scared shitless myself.

Every minute that passes amps up the anxiety twisting inside me. Okay, so we can sit here and wait to see what happens next or we can do something.

"Tell me what you remember," I say to Ellen.

"I went to a friend's birthday party. There were six of us. We'd been to that bar a bunch of times. They serve food, too. Sometimes we'd go and eat there instead of in the cafeteria."

I wonder if it's the same club I went to. "I was taken from Grayson's over in Macon."

"The Watering Hole outside Milledgeville," Ellen says. "I don't understand how this happened. It seemed like a nice place."

The other girl who wouldn't tell us her name laughs. "You're so stupid. Don't you know that if they want you, they get you no matter where you are?"

Anger stirs in me. "What does that even mean?"

Ellen scoots closer to me.

"It means we're fucked," the nameless girl announces. "When they're done with us, they'll kill us and no one will ever find the bodies."

Ellen starts to sob again.

# Twenty-One

"You do realize this is stalking," Joanna pointed out.

"Which is why I need you to talk to them." Tony shrugged. "You're a reporter. That's what reporters do, right?"

He'd located—stalked, if you wanted to define his methods that way—Vickie Parton's roommate, Sadie Hall, and her closest friend, Marla Franks. The two were seated in one of the many study niches in the Student Center, huddled over their notebooks, discarded food wrappers and empty coffee cups scattered over the table.

Joanna folded her arms over her chest. "What would you have me say to them?"

She'd basically avoided participating in any conversation with him since she rolled out of bed. As if she still didn't want to speak directly to him or didn't trust him to do it right, she'd even leaned over the console and shouted her order out the window at the drive-through where he'd stopped for breakfast. Beyond that she hadn't said a word. He'd kept his questions to himself but only for now. At some point he would know whatever it was she was hiding. This morning's priority was Tiffany. He needed to make some sort of progress on her case. At this point, unless the chief was holding out on him, they still had not one fucking thing. Completely unacceptable.

Annoyed at her lack of cooperation, he offered, "You can start with, was Vickie Parton seeing anyone before she disappeared? According to Phelps, she wasn't. Had she been ill? Was she on good terms with her family? Was there anything that made those close to her feel she might want to disappear?"

"I'm pretty sure you can rule out that last theory, *Agent* LeDoux."

Her sarcasm wasn't helping his patience this morning. "We both know this but we need to know if they know it. We need their opinions and theories. Did they know Tiffany Durand? Did Vickie and Tiffany have anything in common? Play the part of reporter. Most witnesses get excited by the prospect of having their fifteen minutes of fame."

"Got it." She stood. "Then you'll owe me one."

"I thought this was a mutually advantageous relationship?"

She didn't answer, just walked over to the group of freshmen, including Parton's roommate. If she helped find his niece alive he'd give her anything he possessed the power to give—which wasn't a hell of a lot at this point. His ex-wife had taken most of his negotiable assets.

Joanna wore dark pants and a lightweight sweater. The blue shade looked good with her olive skin and blond hair. Something had changed in their relationship—if you could even technically call it a relationship. More like an understanding. An understanding he wasn't entirely convinced he understood. Whatever it was, things had shifted after Conway was found.

He thought of the chief's call about the single blond hair found at the scene. Finding only a single hair always made Tony suspicious. If two people had rowdy sex the likelihood of shedding only one hair was not exactly overwhelming. It felt more like a piece of planted evidence.

Speaking of blond hair, today he and his pseudo partner would do all within their power to track down Hailey Martin wherever she was hiding. His primary concern was that whoever killed Conway would find Martin before they did. He needed Hailey Martin— Madelyn Houser. If she and Conway had abducted Tiffany and Vickie and stashed them away for some unknown purpose, the stakes went way, way up with Conway's murder. If Martin ended up dead, they might not be able to find the girls before it was too late.

His cell vibrated and he checked the screen. *Angie.*

"Hey." He kept an eye on Joanna as he listened to his sister.

"They've moved the press conference up to nine. I need you there, Tony."

His sister's voice sounded shaky. Understandable. She was terrified. Her only child was missing and now the powers that be wanted her to go on stage and perform for all the world to see. Plead with some unknown piece of shit for her daughter's life.

"You don't need me there. My presence will only distract the focus. We need every reporter in the room as well as every viewer watching focused on you and Mrs. Parton."

She drew in an unsteady breath. "I don't know if I can do this."

"Angie, you're the strongest woman I know." His errant gaze flicked back to the woman chatting with the two college girls. Joanna Guthrie was another strong woman. But she was also keeping secrets. "You can do this. You'll be strong for Tiffany."

"In a few hours it'll be a week—" Ang's voice cracked "—since anyone saw her. Don't tell me you're not worried she isn't coming back."

"I'm not worried," Tony lied. "She's alive and we're going to find her and bring her home."

Another deep shaky breath. "I'm sorry. I know you won't let me down. I'm just terrified I'll do something wrong and find out later I could have made a difference if I'd done things differently."

Normal reaction. "You're doing exactly what you should be doing. Trust yourself. Trust your instincts. You brought Tif into this world. You and Steve raised an amazing young woman. You'll do this part right, too."

"I know," she conceded. "You're right. You stay focused on the investigation. I'll take care of this press conference. Steve will be standing right beside me."

"Good. Love you."

"Love you. Wait. What about Joanna? You didn't tell me if you confirmed her story."

"I did. And if Tiffany was taken by the same people who took Joanna all those years ago that's another point on our side. She and the other girl survived. So did all the others in the cases she's followed all these years. We have every reason to be hopeful."

"I'm holding you to that, Tony."

"I've got this, Ang."

His sister let it go there. He tucked the phone into his jacket pocket and glanced back to the table where Joanna and the girls were talking.

They were gone.

He shot to his feet and surveyed the dozens of faces crowded into niches and around tables. How the hell had he allowed his attention to wander?

*Can't be on your A game, pal, if you drink yourself into oblivion every night.*

His cell vibrated. He dragged it out and glanced at the screen.

Headed to Parkhurst Hall. Room 207. Catch up.

*Joanna.* Tony didn't bother going for his BMW. He needed to burn off some of this tension anyway. He didn't break into an outright run but he walked faster than he had in he couldn't remember how long. Across the campus until he reached Greene Street, then a short stretch to the freshman dormitory. The entry door had been left propped open.

"Smart move, ladies." He imagined students left doors unsecured all too often. He remembered doing the same thing, especially if a party was planned, back in his college days. He hoped his niece was being a lot smarter than he had been.

Rather than wait for the elevator he barreled up the stairs.

Once in the corridor on the second floor he slowed to catch his breath. He smoothed a hand over his hair and straightened his jacket. The door to room 207 was open. He stood in the open doorway and waited to be noticed before entering.

Sadie Hall spotted him first. Her eyes rounded and she said, "Is this your friend?"

Joanna turned around. "Yes. He's a research analyst for my producer. He used to be a profiler for the FBI."

Both Sadie and Marla appeared duly impressed.

"Tony will have a look around while we finish the interview."

The girls were only too happy to ignore him in order to focus on their chance for the spotlight. The sound of Joanna's low, steady voice along with the higher-pitched excited tones of the students filled the room as he took his time examining the place.

Vickie Parton's closet looked much like Tiffany's. The clothes were considerably more conservative. There were far fewer shoes and only one handbag. He had a look in the drawers of the small chest, then moved on to the bed. On the night table the Bible sat front and center. Tony picked it up and fanned through the pages. No bookmark, no notes. He checked the drawers of the table. In the bottom one far in the back beneath a handful of chocolate candy was a packet of birth control pills.

Like Tiffany's, pills were missing through Friday of last week. The packaging looked the same. The drugstore they'd chosen was the same one. The address told him it was near the campus. The prescribing doctor's name looked vaguely familiar. Tony pulled out his cell and reviewed the photos he'd taken in Tiffany's room.

*Ima Alexander.*

Same doctor. At least it was a connection. Thin, but a place to look they hadn't had before.

"Question," he said to the two students still deep in conversation with Joanna.

All eyes shifted to him.

"Do either of you use this Dr. Alexander?"

Hall said, "She's at the clinic over on North Glynn Street. It's a walk-in clinic. A lot of the students go there because it's quick and easy—especially since most of us don't have a personal physician here. And they don't ask as many personal questions. Dr. Alexander is the only doctor there, I think. There's a nurse-practitioner on Mondays and Fridays. Most of the time there's a couple nurses and that's about it. They're seriously overworked but always nice."

"I've been," the other girl volunteered. "I twisted my ankle really badly and didn't want to go to the infirmary so I went over to the clinic. They x-rayed my ankle. Nothing was broken thankfully. They gave me a ten-day supply of pain meds and an Ace bandage."

Tony figured the pain meds were the nice part Sadie Hall meant. Pain meds for a sprained ankle sounded a little overboard to him, but then he knew the statistics on the rampant abuse of prescription painkillers.

"They are pretty nice there," Sadie confirmed. "More understanding."

"Thank you for your time, ladies," he said. With a knowing look toward Joanna, he headed for the door.

"Thanks, girls. I'll be back with follow-up questions and the air date."

Joanna walked out behind him.

When they were in the stairwell going down, he said, "I hate to ask what you promised them."

"Then don't."

*North Glynn Street, 9:00 a.m.*

The clinic had seen better days. The old brick building appeared to have once been a private residence. The front yard had been paved for patient parking. Across the street was a church. The clinic was only a few miles from the campus but far enough away to give some semblance of privacy, as the students noted. Tony parked in the lot and shut off the engine.

"You don't really expect them to tell you anything, do you?" Joanna stared at the clinic. "I hear doctors take the whole HIPAA thing rather seriously."

He wasn't entirely sure what he expected to learn. Mostly he wanted to watch reactions. He turned to his passenger. "You seem like a reasonably good actress. With your younger sister missing, it's only natural that you'd have a panic attack."

She reached for the door. "I've given a few award-winning performances in my time."

Before he'd rounded the hood she had started breathing shallow and fast. She put her hand to her chest and presented a credible expression of fear. With his hand resting at the small of her back he walked her to the door. By then she was full blown hyperventilating.

He opened the entry door and murmured as she went in ahead of him. "I think I might actually be worried."

She hiccuped. "Oh, I don't like this."

Tony led her to the registration desk where she did, in fact, put on an award-winning performance. So much so, they didn't even make her wait to fill out the usual paperwork. The receptionist thrust the clipboard at Tony since the patient had named him as her husband.

A nurse immediately hustled them to an exam room. As Tony filled in the patient's name as Rita Durand Gates along with a host of other fictitious info, the nurse determined that the patient's blood pressure was inordinately high. An EKG was in order since his lovely wife also complained of chest pains.

While the nurse rigged Joanna up for the EKG, the doctor arrived. Petite, dark hair and eyes, Asian features. "Why didn't you go to the ER?"

Clearly she was put out by the potential emergency. "We were headed that way," Tony explained, "but we saw the clinic and my wife insisted on stopping here. She's had panic attacks before so I wasn't all that worried."

"Who's your family physician, Mrs. Gates?"

"We're…from…out…of…town," Joanna said between gasps.

"We're here because her younger sister is missing. Tiffany Durand," Tony explained. "You probably heard about it on the news."

The doctor stared at Tony for a moment, then looked

back to the patient. "I'm so sorry to hear this. Can you breathe more slowly, Mrs. Gates? Deep and slow."

Alexander tucked the stethoscope earpieces into place and positioned the diaphragm on Joanna's chest. Joanna abruptly stopped breathing or at least stopped gasping. Tony leaned to see past the doctor. Joanna stared, wide-eyed and unmoving, at the other woman.

Was she purposely not gasping anymore?

Joanna bolted upright. "I feel fine now." She started to yank EKG wires off her chest. "I just need to get back to the hotel and lie down."

The doctor stared at her, surprise or shock or something on that order on her face.

Joanna hopped off the exam table and rushed from the room, yanking her sweater down as she went.

"I apologize for my wife," Tony said, hoping to salvage the moment. He had no idea what just happened. "As you can imagine she's very upset. It's been a week and her sister is still missing."

"It's a terrible situation." Alexander hung the stethoscope around her neck. "I'm afraid I don't really know much about it—other than what I've seen on the news."

"Tiffany was a patient of yours," Tony said. "You prescribed her birth control."

"I have other patients, Mr. Gates."

The doctor rushed from the room. The nurse shrugged. "It's been that kind of day. I was really sorry to hear about Tiffany and Vickie. They're both really nice girls." She smiled. "Nicer than most."

Tony smiled sadly. "Thank you for telling me that. We're so worried that Tiffany met some guy who's taken advantage of her."

The nurse, Renae, nodded. "They were both here at the beginning of the month for physicals. Neither was—" she lowered her voice "—sexually active. At least they insisted they weren't—but Dr. Alexander likes to urge the girls to take precautions."

Tony grabbed the nurse and hugged her. "Thank you." He dug in his pocket for one of his business cards. Plain white with only his name and cell number printed on the front. He placed it in her hand. "Please call me if you think of anything that might help us find the girls."

The nurse nodded. "Sure."

As Tony headed for the door, she said, "Didn't you say your name is Gates?"

Tony glanced back at her, pressing a finger to his lips. "That's my stage name. I'm an actor. Gates is my real name."

"Oh." Her eyes widened and she grinned. "I thought you looked familiar." She pressed a finger to her lips as if trying to place his face. She shook her head. "I can't think of the movie, but it'll come to me."

Tony flashed her a wink and hurried out of the building. Joanna was already in the car, seat belt fastened.

As soon as he dropped behind the wheel, she said, "I need to get away from this place."

"You recognized her." He backed out of the slot and put the BMW in Drive.

"More important—" Joanna blew out a breath and nodded toward the clinic where the slats of a blind abruptly fell back into place "—she recognized me."

...she tried to remember why
... What did she really expect to ac-
Ellen was dead. What difference did it make
...vered the name or names of the person or
...ponsible for what happened to them? It
...g Ellen back. Wouldn't give comfort to her
...hildren. Or her parents and little sister...
...really have a little sister.

...r eyes. She tore the unlit cigarette out
...tossed it into the trash can. The pack
...lowed. She didn't want to smoke; she
...e bastards who had damaged and
...pay.

...er cell phone and stared at the re-
...number.

...er what happened before Ellen
...hild. Right after the semes-
...went back to their respective
...ered that she was pregnant.
...n't surprised her consider-
...n, but when she missed the
...ing was wrong.

*10:00 a.m.*

Jo locked the bath…
basin and stared …
made it all of …
Tony she nee…

He'd sw…
tered an…

Vo…
her…
h…

Pill. Wh…
bag. Why n…

---

complisu…
if she unc…
persons res…
wouldn't brin…
husband and …
Ellen didn't…
Jo opened he…
of her mouth and …
and the lighter fol…
wanted to make th…
taken so many lives…
She dragged out h…
cent calls list—Ellen'…
It had been years a…
had told Jo about the …
ter ended and they both …
homes, Ellen had discov…
The first missed period had …
ing what they'd been throug…
second one she knew someth…

Several home pregnancy tests had confirmed her worst fears. She was pregnant. Since, like Jo, sh... ...en a virgin before the abduction, the baby unque... belonged to her rapist. For weeks she had toye... idea of an abortion. Her parents had steppe... sured Ellen that they would support whate... she made. A compromise of sorts was rea... parents offered to raise the child as their... the baby to believe it was Ellen's youn... would only have to miss the fall semes... then she could get on with her life. ... After all, she'd insisted, it wasn't the ... baby was innocent.

Jo hadn't been very kind about the news whe... told her. She'd made a remark about how she shou... have aborted it. The kid would probably grow up to be a monster just like her father.

Ellen hadn't called her again for a long time after that.

Jo had never apologized. She should have. Goddamn it, she should have.

She bit her lip and blinked repeatedly to hold back the tears.

*Who're you crying for? Your friend or yourself?*

Ellen had not really been her friend—just her partner in tragedy.

Later Ellen had told Jo that maybe she had been right after all. The girl had problems. She'd been diagnosed with some sort of severe mental disorder. Jo had felt like a total asshole.

The damned tears she'd tried to hold back slid down

Twenty-Two

The doctor had noticed her birthmark.
Jo lifted her sweatshirt and looked at
lar shape that was several shades light
of her skin. She'd always hated it. Wh
mark was shaped like the state of Ter
She walked over to the toilet, clo
down. She rummaged in her bag fo
lighter. She fished a smoke out of t
it between her lips, but didn't pos
to light it.
Squeezing her eyes shut
she had come here

her cheeks. It wasn't her fault Ellen got pregnant or that her baby was ill. Ellen had made her own choices.

Yet, somehow it felt like Jo's fault. She should have been a better friend. She should have answered when Ellen called that last time before she took her life…

But she hadn't. She'd been selfish and uncaring.

She swiped the dampness from her cheeks and pressed the number for Ellen's phone. Two rings later Ellen's husband answered.

The man was keeping his dead wife's phone charged and handy. How pathetic was that? Jo wouldn't know because she'd never had a man besides her father who cared enough about her to want to call her again much less hang on to any part of her.

"Hey, Art. This is Joanna. How's Alton?"

As Ellen's husband explained that they'd gotten to go home today, Jo unrolled enough toilet paper to dry up the damned flood of tears flowing down her cheeks.

"Good. I'm glad he's getting better. And Elle?"

He assured her that his little girl was fine. A moment of silence lapsed between them before Jo gathered her courage once more.

"Art, I just wanted you to know that Ellen did the best she could. Something really bad happened to her a long time ago and she just never could get over it."

Ellen had never discussed what happened with her husband. Having been from Kansas, he'd never even heard about it.

When he asked Jo what she meant, she cut him off, "It doesn't matter now. All that matters is that I'm going to make it right. You have my word. I promise I'm going to make it right."

Before she could get away he asked Jo did she know Ellen's sister. She said no. If Art now suspected that the girl was Ellen's, she wasn't going to give him another reason to think badly of his dead wife.

Apparently the girl had run away from home. Ellen's parents were worried sick.

Jo said goodbye and ended the call.

More of those damned tears came. She cursed herself and wadded up more toilet paper.

A knock on the door made her jump.

"You okay in there?"

LeDoux. "I'll be out in a minute."

She rolled her eyes at the raw, emotional sound of her voice.

"Open the door, Joanna, or I'll make a scene."

God. She glared at the door. "Go away. Give me just five fucking minutes, please."

"I'm getting the manager."

Jo reached across the tiny room and unlocked the door without even having to get up. His tall frame crowded into the room. He shut the door and leaned against it because there was no place else for him to be.

She warned, "Don't say a word."

He held up his hands and kept his mouth shut.

Jo threw the wad of paper into the trash can and stood. She squeezed between him and the sink and washed her face with cold water. Did nothing to chase away the redness or the puffy eyes.

She patted her face dry, tossed the paper and turned to him. "It's nothing. I'm okay."

He nodded. "Good."

When he started to turn around he stopped and grabbed her, pulled her into his arms and hugged her.

She tried not to… Damn it, but she couldn't help it.

She cried again and she hugged him back. Relished the warmth and strength of his arms. How long had it been since anyone had held her like this?

Maybe not since that day in the hospital when her folks were finally allowed into her room. Her dad had hugged her just like this.

At that moment she realized how tired she was. So very tired. Tired of pretending. Tired of running from the past. Tired of the secrets and the lies.

Tired of the silence.

# Twenty-Three

*10:15 a.m.*

She stared at the screen of her phone, tension immediately tightening the band already crushing her skull. What now?

Just a few more days and everything would be in place.

With an annoyed sigh she accepted the call but didn't speak. Until Ima's voice was confirmed she would not utter a word.

"We have a problem."

*Ima.* She suspected the actual issue was that her old friend had a problem.

"I'm certain you're aware of the deal we made long ago, Dr. Alexander. The home you live in, the car you drive, the college fund your children will enjoy. None of it would have been possible if not for our arrangement. If your activities have been uncovered, you will keep our secret out of the equation. Whatever sort of deal you are offered, however overwhelming the pressure, if you fail to uphold the vow you took, your husband and lovely children will pay the price. Now, do I have a problem or do *you* have a problem?"

She paid her select few associates well to handle their end of things. Time had not changed the terms of their long-ago contract. Yesterday's complication had been unfortunate but those potential issues had been resolved. Whoever had taken her asset out of play had done them both a favor. Miles Conway would have had to go shortly, in any event.

Soon this would be finished and she would be free to move on with her life. Until then, there could be no mistakes—no more complications.

"I was visited by a woman today who claimed to be the sister of the Durand girl."

A frown tugged at her. "The Durand girl doesn't have a sister." The backgrounds of both subjects had been thoroughly examined. "Your visitor was lying."

"I thought as much." Ima sighed. "After she left, my mind wouldn't let go of the visit. The more I pictured the woman's face, the more I realized I had seen her before. Between that and what I discovered about the man who pretended to be her husband, I am very concerned that the police may know something."

"What man?" The police knew nothing relevant. Her asset in the department would have warned her.

"He claimed his name was Gates, but he was actually Special Agent Anthony LeDoux from the FBI."

Not surprising. LeDoux was Durand's uncle. He was actually one of the reasons the girl had been chosen. He would find the trail of prepared evidence she had left for him.

"We have nothing to fear from the police. Every detail has been taken care of." She exhaled a breath of impatience. "I will ask you again, Dr. Alexander, since I despise having my time wasted. How does this problem involve me?" So far her old friend had told her nothing for which she had not prepared.

"The woman, she was test subject number one."

The news sent a quake through her. That was highly unlikely. Why would she come back after all these years? Clearly Ima's paranoia was overriding her reason. "You must be mistaken."

"No," Ima argued. "I am not mistaken. I remembered the birthmark on her abdomen. It was her. It was Joanna Guthrie."

A moment's hesitation was required. She closed her eyes and calmed herself. "If you recognized her, then she certainly recognized you. Perhaps she came to your clinic because she remembered *you*."

"I…I'm not sure," Ima stuttered.

Being unsure was not good enough. "If you believe she recognized you, then I suggest you stop wasting my time and do whatever is necessary to protect your family."

She ended the call.

*Joanna Guthrie.*

If not for the shortness of time she would almost be interested in that development.

But there was no time.

The grand finale was already in place.

# *Twenty-Four*

*Day Three*
*Eighteen years ago...*

I can't guess what time it is or even how long we have been in this dark place. They haven't given us any food but water is provided every day. A sixteen-ounce plastic bottle of water is there whenever we wake up.

I have to watch the other girl. She tries to grab more than her share. She's a bitch. All she does is laugh whenever Ellen cries.

It feels weird sitting here in the dark. No clothes. No nothing but the smooth feel of this box or cage or whatever it is. Occasionally we bump into each other if we move around. There are the cylinder bottles of water. Nothing else. No other texture—except the roughness of our skin. We need more water. And there is no sound except the noises we make.

*Nothing.*

I talk Ellen into walking around the dark place with

me. I keep one arm out to make sure we don't run into anything. The other girl refuses to walk with us.

"Your muscles will atrophy," I warn.

She ignores me.

Whatever. I can't save someone who doesn't want to be saved.

I laugh. I can't even save myself.

I have felt over every square inch of this place and I am unable to feel a seam or crack that would indicate a door. It has to be overhead. They—whoever they are—are getting water in here to us somehow.

I suddenly feel so sleepy I can hardly hold my eyes open. Ellen is leaning against me. "We need to sit down."

I barely manage to lower myself onto the floor before my thoughts disappear into the darkness.

It is still dark when I wake up but this darkness is different.

It smells different.

I reach out with my hand. Nothing.

I listen.

Wait. I hear someone else breathing.

"Fuck."

I jerk at the word. I am pretty sure the other person breathing is the no-name girl. Where is Ellen?

My heart starts to pound, I rise up on my hands and knees and move around the room. I bump into No-Name.

"Get the fuck off me."

"Where's Ellen?"

"Who gives a shit?"

"If you hurt her," I threaten.

"I just woke up," she snarls.

"Stand up."

*Man's voice.* Where the hell did that come from?

No-Name and I scramble to our feet.

"Where's that voice coming from?" she whispers.

Hell if I know. "Sounds like a man."

But it's kind of garbled. Like one of those machines that disguises the voice.

"If you want to eat today, you will fight. The winner gets to eat."

"What?" I instinctively back away from No-Name.

"You have ten minutes. The winner of the battle gets to eat."

No-Name rushes forward. She hits me hard in the face.

Blood spurts from my nose.

# Twenty-Five

Phelps had called and demanded Tony come to his office. No doubt someone at the Student Center or one of Parton's friends had reported his visit. Maybe Dr. Alexander had filed a complaint, but he doubted that scenario. The woman had been as rattled as Joanna over the visit.

Tony issued a final warning to her. "Do not walk out that door until I'm with you."

"You said that already." She dropped into a chair in the lobby. "I'll be right here waiting, *honey*." She plastered on a fake smile and dug out her cell phone. "I'll just play on Facebook. See what all my *friends* are up to."

The visit to Alexander had unsettled her. Besides the breakdown in the bathroom at the gas station, she had picked at her lunch. Seemed distracted and distant. She'd said it was only because she remembered going to the clinic and being given her first prescription of birth control pills about a month before she was abducted. Dr. Alexander had been Dr. Kato then. Milledgeville was a small town, made sense that victims would have been to some of the same places and met some of the same faces. His thoughts on the matter had done nothing to calm her. If anything he'd made her more upset.

As for Facebook, he had a feeling she had about as many friends as he did, all of whom could be counted on one hand.

When the receptionist buzzed him through to the chief's office, Tony glanced at her one last time. She never looked up from her phone.

The short walk to the chief's office gave him about ten seconds to consider what the hell he was going to do next. He was no closer to finding Tiffany than he had been when he arrived. Something had to give here.

As he'd suspected, Chief Buckley from campus security waited with Phelps.

Phelps said, "Have a seat, Mr. LeDoux."

"Where are we on the official investigation?" Tony settled into the chair next to Buckley. "I assume things are going well since the two of you are able to take valuable time and assets away from the search to speak with me."

"Don't be a smart-ass, LeDoux." Buckley looked to Phelps.

Phelps said, "You dropped by the walk-in clinic this morning and met with Dr. Alexander."

"Do you have someone following me?" He directed the question to Phelps. He didn't expect Buckley to have the assets to spare. After all, he had two students missing.

"Dr. Alexander was in a terrible accident about two hours ago," Phelps said. "She survived but she's in critical condition. They airlifted her to Macon."

"Will she make it?"

"Don't know yet."

"Do you suspect foul play?" Someone would have had to act fast to make that happen. They didn't leave the clinic before quarter of ten.

Phelps shook his head. "Actually we suspect she was trying to kill herself. The one witness to the accident says it looked as if she drove straight into that power pole." He shrugged. "Don't know yet."

"What does that have to do with me?" Whatever they wanted to know, he wasn't drawing them a map.

"The reason I called you," Phelps went on, "is that my detective just told me Dr. Alexander's nurse said she was very upset after meeting with you and your *wife*. The doctor said she needed to run home for a few minutes and left a clinic full of patients."

"We'd like to know what the two of you discussed." This from Buckley.

"The doctor and I didn't discuss anything relevant to the case," Tony clarified up front. He didn't see the harm in sharing what he had so far. "Both Tiffany and Vickie had recently been prescribed birth control pills by Dr. Alexander. In fact, the nurse mentioned that Alexander did a complete physical on Tiffany and Vickie. I don't know about Vickie, but my niece had a complete physical when she was home over Christmas break. I can't imagine she would have bothered with another this soon, which tells me Alexander requested it as a requirement for issuing the birth control prescription."

Phelps considered the response, and then shook his head. "Maybe Alexander has been milking insurance companies by scheduling unnecessary tests and such but that just doesn't feel like a reason to want to kill herself."

Tony shrugged. "You got me, Chief."

"We don't have you, LeDoux," Buckley spoke up. "That's the problem. It seems as though you're conducting your own, separate investigation and I, for one, don't feel that's conducive to finding these young women."

"Did you find Conway's or Alexander's cell phones?" Tony asked. He looked from one man to the other.

"Not Conway's," Phelps admitted, "but we do have Alexander's."

"If my visit and the mention of my niece upset her that much, I would suggest you find out who she called after we left. Maybe that call was the reason she aimed for the power pole."

"We'd do that right now," Phelps tossed back at him, "except her text and call history was deleted, but we'll get the records in a couple of days. Just like we got Tiffany's and Vickie's."

Frustration tied a big knot in his gut. Tony hadn't seen those records yet. "You didn't mention you'd received those records."

Phelps shook his head. "No point. The only unknown calls were to a burner phone, ironically the same one. So we know the girls were communicating with the same person. We just can't track the number to that person."

Damn it. Tony gritted his teeth. Another dead end.

"Who is this woman with you?" Buckley asked. "My students seem to believe she's some big shot Hollywood producer."

Some of Tony's tension eased at the idea that Joanna had pulled that one off.

"I will get a warrant if she doesn't voluntarily provide a hair sample," Phelps reminded him.

Tony barely stifled a smile. "She's my girlfriend who's helping with my search for Tiffany. Since she was with me during the time Conway was murdered, she has a firm alibi. Good luck with that warrant." He stood. "Unless you have an update for me, I'd like to get back out there. This is day eight, gentlemen. How many victims are found alive this late in the game?"

Since neither top cop seemed to have any news worth sharing, Tony walked out. In the lobby, Joanna wasn't in her chair. He spotted her staring out the plate glass window near the door. The tension around his chest relaxed a fraction. The urge for a couple of shots of bourbon roared through him.

*Gotta stay focused.*

Joanna didn't ask any questions until they were in his car. "What did he want?"

"To know who you are." He backed out of the slot. "A Hollywood producer?"

She grinned. "It worked, didn't it?"

"It did." He wondered how she would take the rest. "Alexander left the clinic and drove herself into a power pole. She's in critical condition."

"I guess she wasn't so happy to see me."

Tony glanced at her. "That's cold."

"Yeah, well. What's cold is being kidnapped, raped and treated like an animal for fourteen days."

That shut him up. If Tiffany had suffered that treatment, he would make whoever was responsible pay or die trying. If? He knew it was happening and he wasn't smart enough to find her much less to stop it. He slammed his palm against the steering wheel. "Goddamn it."

When a moment had passed, Joanna said, "We can still find her in time before the worst happens."

There was none of her usual smart-ass attitude or anger in the words. He glanced at her. Hoped to hell she was right.

"We need to find Martin," he said then. "We know she was connected to Conway. Maybe with his murder she might be willing to talk."

Joanna sent him a skeptical look. "If she's not dead already."

*Clinton Road, Macon, 3:30 p.m.*

Tony knocked on the door of the duplex and waited for Kayla Maples to answer. Another knock and then another and the dead bolt finally clicked. His frustration had maxed out by the time the door opened. Sean Waldrop, the Wild Things manager, stared out at him.

"What the—" Waldrop tried to close the door.

Tony easily forced it open. "We have a couple of questions for you and your friend Kayla."

Having just gotten out of the shower, hair wet and a towel wrapped precariously around his hips, Waldrop backed away as Tony and Joanna barged in. "She's not here. She has class. What the hell do you want now?" He gestured to his face. "If you keep fucking with me, I swear I'm reporting your ass."

Tony felt badly that the guy was sporting a shiner because of him. He should have been more careful about where he punched him.

Joanna moved close enough to stick her face in his. "I need to speak to Hailey. Now. But she's not home. Have you seen her?"

Waldrop backed up another step, his head moving adamantly from side to side. "I haven't seen her in a week. I heard she's all busted up over Miles's murder."

"What do you know about his murder?" Tony asked.

Another shake of his head. "I don't know shit. I hardly knew the guy. Hailey's the one you want to talk to about him."

Joanna took Waldrop by the arm and ushered him over to the sofa. "Why don't you call your friend Kayla and ask her where we should look for Hailey?"

Waldrop picked up his cell from the coffee table. "Sure. I got nothing else to do." He glared at Tony. "Except prep a club for opening."

Tony sat down on the other side of him. "I'm sure your boss will understand your need to do your civic duty."

The call to Kayla provided a list of nightspots. Joanna entered each into her phone. Tony thanked the little creep and they headed for the first club on the long list.

He glanced at Joanna. She hadn't said much since her meltdown in that gas station restroom. "You okay?"

"Just dandy."

"I know what happened to you and to Ellen was unthinkable." Now might not be the time, but what the hell. He'd spent more time stepping on his dick the past few days than not. "But it feels like there's something more. Like you're not being completely forthcoming on what really happened."

She stared out the window, her face turned as far from his as possible.

"Maybe there's something you haven't told me," he suggested. "Maybe about the girl who died."

"Carrie Cole." She glanced at him then. "That was her name." She exhaled a big breath. "I've never told anyone about her. Ellen and I made a pact never to talk about what happened."

Outrage shot through Tony and before he could stop the words, he hurled them at her. "She was murdered by the people who took you and you never told anyone? You just pretended she never existed. Was it because you didn't want to get involved with an even more complicated investigation? Or did you just not give a shit?"

The scenario didn't really fit with his perception of Joanna so far. What the hell was he thinking? He didn't know this woman. His fingers tightened on the wheel when what he wanted to do was pull over and shake the hell out of her.

"I guess you had to be there to understand. We were afraid to tell." She glared at his profile then. "Do you have any idea what that kind of fear is like?"

Actually he did. But he hadn't been eighteen at the time. "Sorry." He glanced at her, hoped she saw the truth in the word. "I shouldn't have said those things. I'm certain you did the best you could."

"Maybe, maybe not, but I did what I had to do."

It was quite possible he really had gone over the edge the way his former boss had suggested, but he believed her.

Sometimes what you had to do was the best a person could do.

*10:30 p.m.*

After hitting seven clubs, they had still found no sign of Martin. They'd driven back to her house. Her dog had peered through the door at them. Her Jag wasn't in the garage, so they'd driven to Wild Things. The club was the only place—according to Kayla—Martin frequented that they hadn't dropped in on tonight.

The music was way too loud. The crowd was way too young. Tony led the way, cutting through the throng. He corralled the manager in his office. Wouldn't you know, his friend Kayla Maples was there, too.

"It's Friday night," Waldrop warned as he stood from the desk. "I don't have time for any of your shit."

Tony waved him off and turned his attention to Kayla, perched on the cluttered desk. "You have her number, don't you?" He suspected that was exactly why they hadn't found Martin at any of the locations Kayla had given them hours ago.

She shrugged, avoiding eye contact. "Yeah. I guess I do."

"Text her. Tell her you got something really important to tell her. You can't talk about it on the phone." Tony leaned down, put his face close to hers. "Do it now."

Kayla crossed her arms over her chest. "Maybe we should call the police, Sean."

Waldrop glared at Tony. "Maybe so. I think this fed is overstepping his bounds."

Tony was on the guy before his words stopped echoing in the cluttered little room.

"Look." Joanna moved between them, pushing Tony back. "Miles was murdered. You two know this, but you don't even want to know how. It was totally gruesome. We're really worried about Hailey. We have reason to believe she's next on the killer's list."

The fury on the manager's face slipped. He and Kayla exchanged a look.

"How do I know you're telling the truth?" Kayla asked. "Maybe you just want to harass her the way you're harassing us?"

"If something happens to her and you could've helped," Joanna went on, "you'll feel like shit. Trust me."

Kayla heaved a sigh and plucked her cell from her back pocket. "Tell me what you want me to say."

Joanna repeated the message, watching over Kayla's shoulder while she typed. Once she'd hit Send, Tony held out his hand. "You won't mind if I hang on to your phone while we wait for her response."

She rolled her eyes and slapped it in his palm. "You leave with my phone or fuck with it somehow and I'm calling the police for real."

They followed the two back out into the fray. Waldrop immediately stormed behind the counter shouting orders at his two bartenders.

Joanna claimed the only stool at the end of the bar

and ordered vodka straight up. When the bartender looked at Tony, he declined. He leaned against the counter next to her. The music was too loud for conversation so they watched the mob of bodies moving on the dance floor. The place was full of college-age revelers. Tony wondered how many had fake IDs sporting birth dates that proved they were over twenty-one?

Had Tiffany done this?

Of course she had and lowlifes like Conway and Martin were just waiting to strike.

Joanna elbowed him and nodded to the entrance. Martin strode in as if she owned the place. Tony moved away from the bar and merged into the mass of bodies. He cut across the crowd and came up behind Martin.

She stalled a few feet from the bar. Joanna lifted her glass to her.

Tony moved up beside her, putting his hand at the small of her back to usher her toward Joanna.

Martin took one look at him and bolted.

He went after her.

She was out the door and headed for her car when Tony caught up with her.

"Do not touch me!" She yanked her arm from his grasp.

Joanna joined them.

"Your partner is dead," Tony warned. "I'm sure you've heard the details of how he died. The knife nicked a lung first. While he gasped for air, the second stab of the blade clipped the aorta. He probably lived two or three minutes. Long enough to feel the pain and watch the blood spurt out of his body...and to think about what he'd done to deserve being murdered."

"Stay the fuck away from me!" Martin backed a few more feet away, her backside bumping against her Jag.

Joanna moved in on her, pressing her body against the other woman's. Tony resisted the natural urge to pull her away.

"Do you know what your friend did to me?"

The words were filled with hatred.

"I don't know what you're talking about," Martin argued. She pushed at Joanna. "Back off!"

"You're running out of time, bitch," Joanna warned. "Watch your back or you'll end up like your friend."

A cruiser rolled into the parking lot. The driver's side window came down. "Do we have a problem here?"

Tony grabbed Joanna by the shoulders and pulled her away from the other woman. "We're fine, Officer. Just a little misunderstanding."

The cop's flashlight flicked from Tony's face to Joanna's and then to Martin's. "You okay, ma'am?"

Tony wanted to kick something. Of course he thought Martin was the victim.

"I just want to go home," she said, her voice wobbling and her eyes shining with tears.

"Go on, ma'am. I'll just stay put until you're on your way."

"Thank you, Officer." Martin shot Tony a knowing look and rounded the hood of her Jag.

True to his word, the officer didn't leave until Martin's taillights were out of sight.

Though Tony knew it would be pointless, they hit all the spots Martin frequented once more, and then drove back to her house.

They weren't going to find her again tonight.

Rather than drive away immediately, Tony parked and turned off the engine. "We can wait for a while. See if she shows up."

"Probably a waste of time."

The silence went on for a couple of minutes. She checked her phone. He checked his even though he knew for once he hadn't received a call or a text.

"What did Conway do to you?" Maybe he was an asshole for asking. She hadn't mentioned anything before except that Conway was the person who lured her into a trap. Apparently there was more…a lot more.

"He raped us, Ellen and me, while we were unconscious…before he handed us over or whatever. I mean—" she shrugged "—I suppose it's possible it was someone else, but he was the one who drugged us."

Tony closed his eyes and prayed Tiffany hadn't been raped.

"We were both so naive. Stupid little virgins trying to play with the big kids. Got ourselves into something we couldn't handle."

He reached across the console and put his hand on hers. "You didn't get yourselves into anything. I'm thinking you were selected. They were looking for a certain type. Not necessarily height or weight, hair color or eye color, but a certain background and intelligence. All the known victims were from nice families, doing well in school, never in trouble. There's a pattern—it's just not the usual pattern when looking for serial offenders."

"None of the victims were troublemakers," she agreed. "Perfect school records. Normal, middle-class families."

"There's your pattern," he said. "Tiffany and Vickie fit that same pattern."

"But not the other girl," Joanna said, her voice small in the darkness. "The third girl was hostile and lived on the street. She had tats and did drugs." She drew in a big breath. "Like I told you before, they made us fight for food."

Tony stared at her profile. The moonlight softly framing the outline of her nose and her chin. She'd pretty much glossed over the details when they'd talked about this before. "Fight as in hand to hand?"

She nodded. "Sometimes they provided rudimentary weapons, but mostly it was hand to hand. If you won, you ate. At least in the beginning."

Tony knew how difficult that would be for someone who'd never had to fight for their lives before—someone who'd been protected by a good, loving family.

His hand closed around hers. "I'm glad you survived."

Her fingers tightened against his. "Maybe one of these days I'll be glad, too."

# Twenty-Six

Angie and Steve were waiting when Tony and Joanna pulled into the drive behind the inn. A fist of fear punched Tony in the gut.

Every step he took felt like the wrong one. As hard as he tried he was getting nowhere. The police were getting nowhere. They would've been back sooner except they'd had to make a quick stop at a Walmart for clothes. Neither of them had come prepared for an extended stay.

How could he have been here four days and still be no closer to finding Tiffany than he was when he arrived?

"Is there a new development?" He moved past Joanna to where Ang sat in a chair on the small covered porch outside the cottage. Steve stood next to her. She'd been crying again. Her eyes were swollen, face red.

What if he'd been chasing bullshit leads, wasting his time?

Steve spoke first. "There's nothing new, Tony." He

sighed, a bone-tired sound. "I've been trying to get her to go in the house for an hour now. She needs to sleep. She's exhausted."

"I don't want to sleep," Ang snapped. "I'll sleep when we find our daughter."

Steve looked as if she'd slapped him. He also looked dead on his feet.

"Let's go inside." Tony unlocked the door. "We can have some coffee."

The innkeeper kept the cottage well stocked with everything save alcohol. At the moment Tony wished he had something far stronger. He thought about the way Joanna had downed the vodka. He supposed she needed fortifying worse than him. Maybe if he plied her with enough alcohol she would tell him the rest of the secrets she was keeping. There were at least a couple more.

Sharing the fact that she'd been raped was a big step. No one would fault her for wanting to keep that secret buried. She had opened up in the past twenty-four hours. Knowing what they'd been forced to do in captivity gave him some amount of insight into the sort of person who had abducted them. Maybe the same unsubs who had taken Tiffany and Vickie.

It was possible the unsubs were making the sort of fight-to-the-death films that sick creeps paid the big bucks for, but Tony had a feeling there was far more to this story than an internet moviemaking project.

Once they were inside, Joanna readied the coffee maker while Tony ushered his sister into a chair. He sat down next to her. Steve searched the cabinets for cups. Tony wished there was something he could say to set them at ease but he had nothing except a bunch of loose ends that wouldn't weave together.

"The press conference was a joke." Angie scrubbed her hands over her face. "All it did was elicit a storm of crazies calling in with sightings and eyewitness accounts of seeing the girls taken by aliens."

No surprise there. Tony reached for her hand, gave it a squeeze. "Unfortunately it goes with the territory, but if it makes the unsub view the girls in a different light, it could make a difference."

"Bullshit." Joanna turned around from the coffee maker. "This guy isn't watching the news. He's too busy creating creepy scenarios for his victims to act out."

Tony sent her a look he hoped relayed his message: *Shut the fuck up.*

"What're you talking about?" Angie looked from Joanna to Tony. "What does she mean?"

Joanna left Steve to deal with the coffee. "I believe the same people who abducted me eighteen years ago are the ones who took your daughter."

"We can't be certain about that," Tony said, shooting Joanna another warning look.

Joanna sat down on the small sofa across from Angie. "He's wrong. The cops are wrong. The same doctor who gave your daughter a physical and a prescription for birth control a month before she disappeared did the same for me eighteen years ago. The same man who lured me to a club before I disappeared was seen with your daughter at least twice before she disappeared. That man is dead. The doctor who prescribed the pills is in critical condition. Whatever these bastards have been doing for nearly two decades, it's falling apart now and everything's going to shit."

Tony closed his eyes. Wanted to shake the woman he'd been feeling so sorry for a few minutes ago.

"Tony."

His sister said his name the way she had when they were kids and she knew he'd been sneaking around in her room. He opened his eyes and met Angie's glower.

"Is she telling the truth?"

Before he could answer, Joanna made a sound of frustration and shot to her feet.

"No. I make up shit like this all the time. On day one your daughter and the others were stripped and tossed into a dark room. It's what, day eight? By now they're hungrier than they've ever been in their lives. They've gotten used to the darkness and the cold. If she's performed well enough she's probably gotten something to eat here and there. They make sure you have water—not much—but enough to keep functioning. They're naked, hungry, scared and completely alone."

"That's enough." Tony was on his feet before his words stopped ringing in the air.

"They can't cling to each other," Joanna continued defiantly. "Because they're enemies. If one of the others eats, you don't."

Tony stepped in toe-to-toe with her. "I said shut up."

Angie lunged out of her seat. She grabbed Joanna by the arms. "You must have some idea of where they kept you. What they looked like. Something!"

Joanna shook her head. "If I knew who was calling the shots, that person would be dying an agonizing death right now. But I don't know. What I do know is that by tomorrow the lights will come on. It'll be so bright they can barely stand to keep their eyes open. It feels like you're walking around in a tanning booth with no protection. Your skin burns, your eyes burn and your lips crack."

"What about the next day?" Steve moved into the small tension-filled circle they'd made. "And the day after that."

Tony couldn't stop Joanna now. He wanted to promise his sister that he'd find Tiffany before things escalated, but he couldn't make that promise.

"They'll be forced to perform—to fight, whatever they're told to do—anything to survive. By day ten, you're getting maybe a half a bottle of water a day... maybe a bite of food. He wants you completely helpless...totally desperate."

"Dear God, why?" Angie pressed her hands to her mouth.

Joanna closed her eyes a moment, remembering. "To see who survives."

"I...I thought..." Steve glanced at Tony. "I thought Tony said the girls always come back alive."

"They should." Joanna cleared her throat. "It's some sort of twisted game. The fear of dying keeps you playing."

Tony was grateful she hadn't mentioned the other girl. He needed Angie and her husband calm and rational.

"But you got away. Where did the police find you?"

"On the highway." She hugged her arms around herself. "We were in the woods and we found the highway. A trucker saw us and pulled over. We were too mentally rattled and scared to trust him so we ran but he called the police."

"What highway? Where?"

"Vinson Highway."

"So they didn't take you far away?" Angie's tone grew more agitated.

"We never knew where we were held or how we ended

up in those woods." Joanna shrugged. "The whole area was searched repeatedly. Nothing was ever found."

Angie grabbed her purse from the floor and reached inside. "After the press conference a man came up to us." She thrust some papers at Tony. "He says there have been strange happenings at the old asylum for more than a century. He said we should look there."

Tony took the papers and shuffled through the stack of reports about patient abuse and mysterious disappearances. Like most old insane asylums around the country heinous things were done to patients back in the day, that was true. The pages went on and on and the accusations grew more outrageous.

"He could be just a conspiracy theorist."

"It can't hurt to check it out," Angie argued.

Steve passed his phone to Tony. "Vinson Highway runs close to the asylum property."

"It's…" Joanna shook her head. "The old hospital sits on hundreds or thousands of acres. The whole town is near the place."

"Please, Tony," Angie urged. "We drove around out there today, but security wouldn't allow us to go into any of the buildings. But you can make them see it's worth looking into. This man was so certain. It can't hurt to look."

Tony held up his hands. "Okay. I'll check it out."

Angie hugged him hard. "We'll get out of your way." She grabbed her husband's hand and ushered him toward the door.

When goodnights were exchanged Tony closed and locked the door. "You shouldn't have told her."

"She's stronger than you think," Joanna said. "If her daughter is as strong as she is, she'll survive."

Tony hoped she was right about that part. But, he searched her face, her eyes, looking for those other secrets she kept. "You've maintained that there's always one who doesn't."

She nodded. "There's never any mention of the other girl in any of the articles. The other survivors I interviewed argued with me at first because that's what had been drilled into their heads, but the more we talked about it, the more I pushed, they finally came around. Only one refused to admit there was a third girl."

"You said there were two, three if you count the unknown girl, taken each year for five years. How many of the survivors are still alive?"

"Me and three others. Two died of natural causes, the other four committed suicide either accidentally or on purpose. Drug overdoses. Stuff like that."

"Of the four who are still alive, are they like you?"

She laughed. "You mean totally fucked-up? Reclusive? Tortured? Alone?"

He nodded. Damn. It sounded way worse when she said it out loud.

"Two are workaholics. They're alone but they're extremely successful. The other one is more reclusive than me. She lives in her mother's basement. I expect her to be the next to…" She stuck her finger to her head in the universal gesture of pulling a trigger.

Tony lowered onto the couch. No matter that the other women survived—they weren't able to keep living.

He didn't want Tiffany to be haunted that way for the rest of her life.

Yet, he was powerless to stop it.

# *Twenty-Seven*

Angie paced the room. Back and forth. Back and forth. The people in the room under theirs were likely wondering what was going on, but Angie didn't care. She didn't have the energy to care. If Joanna was right— she stalled midstep and closed her eyes. Please don't let her be right.

"We have to focus on the end result," Steve said.

Angie opened her eyes and glared at him. He sat on the end of the bed in his boxers. He'd come straight to the room and readied for bed. How could he do that after all the woman said? "What does that mean?"

Her husband scrubbed a hand over his jaw. "Joanna survived. Even if Tif has to play those awful games, even if she gets hurt, isn't finding her alive what really matters?"

Angie hugged her arms around herself. "Of course." She shook her head. "I don't know. I can't bear the idea of her going through those awful things. You heard what she said. They starve them, make them fight. Oh God."

She started to pace again. "I don't know if I can take much more of this."

All those reporters, all those people at the press conference, all the police. The lights, the questions—it was all too much. Flyers about the missing girls had been plastered all over Milledgeville and the surrounding communities. Their faces were all over the news. Still, she and the other girl's mother had stood in front of those cameras and given their statements. Pointless, the entire exercise had been utterly pointless. She'd torn her heart from her chest and laid it out for all to see and nothing had changed. No one who really knew anything had called the hotlines. The police were no closer to finding Tif and the other girl than they were this time yesterday.

Those people at the press conference—the ones at home watching on their televisions—they didn't really care; they only wanted to be entertained by someone else's tragedy. How much longer could she and Steve pretend that everything was going to be okay?

"If we lose her…" Angie couldn't stay the rest.

Steve stood. "I need to shower."

He went into the bathroom and closed the door. Angie stared after him. How could he not see that hope was waning? She thought of all the things Joanna had said. Their little girl could very well be going through those things—or worse. She could have been raped already; she could be dying at this very moment.

The agony rose so swiftly and so sharply that Angie swayed. She moaned. Everyone was trying to help, including Tony and Joanna. All she could do was complain. All she could do was make her husband miserable.

If she had been a better mother perhaps Tiffany wouldn't have been lured by the charm of that bastard. If she had done a better job teaching her to protect herself…

Angie stared at the closed bathroom door. If she were a better wife, she would not allow her pain to be all that mattered.

She rushed to the door and opened it. Steve stood beneath the spray of water, his whole body shuddering with his sobs. Water splashed on the floor where he'd forgotten to close the curtain.

Angie went to him. Clothes and all she climbed into the shower and held him, told him how very much she loved him. Assured him over and over that they would find their daughter.

They cried together. They would get through this. Somehow.

# *Twenty-Eight*

Tiffany picked herself up from the floor and swiped the blood from her lips. Her nose was pouring.

She couldn't see Lexy. They'd turned the lights out today. In the box and in here, the place they had to perform.

It was so damned dark.

She could hear Lexy breathing.

Tiffany worked hard to keep her breathing quiet. She moved around the room, hoping she didn't hit a wall or something else she hadn't encountered during this battle. The sound of Lexy's breathing was louder now. She was close.

*Hold your breath.*

If she could just get close enough to grab her.

A scream split the darkness.

Lexy's body slammed into Tiffany.

They hit the floor. Rolled.

Tiffany grabbed her hair and pounded her head against the floor.

Lexy punched her hard in the stomach. Tried to get a jab at her chin. By sheer luck Tiffany dodged.

She pounded Lexy's head into the floor a couple more times, and then punched her, aiming for her face but hitting her in the throat instead.

Lexy gagged and shoved her hard.

Tiffany landed on her back against the hard floor. She gulped in air, trying to feed her starving lungs.

Lexy coughed, choked and heaved.

Tiffany started to reach for her but stopped herself. Instead she scooted away and prepared to launch into battle again.

Lexy retched and puked.

Please let him call it.

Maybe... Tiffany moved toward the sound of her puking. She kicked her in the stomach, not hard at all but enough to make her grunt.

More puking and gagging.

"Back to your corners," the voice said.

Thank God. Tiffany moved to her right. She felt along the wall until she found the corner. Lexy was still coughing and gagging.

The door opened. She heard it. Couldn't see it.

"The loser leaves first."

Lexy's heavy breathing grew fainter and fainter until she was gone.

"The winner takes the spoils."

Tiffany felt her way to the door. She smelled the food before she found it with her hands. It was warm. The plastic plate was full. She picked it up and moved carefully along the short, narrow corridor that was just as dark as the other rooms. She held on to the plate terrified that she would drop it.

Once she was back in the white room that was now as black as pitch with the others, she moved to each of them, giving them part of the food on the plate, then she found her corner and she sat down to eat.

She closed her eyes and prayed she could do this again tomorrow. He'd started making them fight two and three times a day. She was so, so tired.

"You faked that last kick."

Tiffany jumped. Lexy was suddenly right next to her, whispering in her ear.

"Don't be stupid, bitch," Lexy muttered. "I won't do the same for you."

Tiffany bit off a piece of bread and didn't say anything. If she did she might just cry and she damn sure wasn't going to cry for this mean bitch.

She felt Lexy move away.

Tiffany didn't even taste the food. She ate. It was essential to survival.

Did anything else matter at this point?

# Twenty-Nine

*Day Four*
*Eighteen years ago...*

Ellen and No-Name are missing.

I woke up and they are gone. He must be using something to put us to sleep. My whole face hurts like a bitch. My nose and eyes are swollen. No-Name beat the shit out of me.

Next time I'll do better. I wasn't prepared yesterday. But I will be ready next time.

I don't want to hurt anyone but I don't want to die.

I'm so hungry. And afraid. I've never liked the dark. That doctor, Dr. Kato, said it was perfectly normal to have childhood fears spill over into adulthood.

No-Name isn't afraid of anything.

I sure hope she doesn't kill Ellen.

I honestly don't see how we can keep doing this. My body shivers. *My body*. Strange. It feels almost separate from me. I guess the lack of light is messing with my head. I ache all over. I'm pretty sure nothing is broken but what do I know? I could have internal bleeding for all I know.

How long have they been gone?

For some reason I can no longer judge time. I don't know if it's been a minute or an hour or a day. I just want to go home. I don't understand why the police can't find us. Are they even looking?

My parents are probably so worried. Ray would be, too. He would be ready to kick the shit out of whoever did this. A smile tugs at my busted lip.

I close my eyes and go someplace else. I let my mind wander to the bedroom I've slept in my whole life. The pink walls and the big old bed with its white lacy canopy. The bed was secondhand but I never cared. I loved it then and I love it now. When I went home for Christmas I remember lying there thinking how even though I was a college girl I didn't really feel any different.

I feel different now.

*Please don't let me die here, God. Please.*

I must have drifted off. The smell of food wakes me. My stomach rumbles.

No-Name is eating. She sounds like a fucking pig, grunting and slopping.

Of course she doesn't offer to share.

Where is Ellen?

I crawl all around the room, rove my hand over every square inch. "Where's Ellen?"

"Dead maybe."

Her words ignite something inside me. I feel ready to explode. Like hot lava rushing through my veins. I want to kill No-Name.

I lunge at the sound of her nasty lips smacking.

Her plastic plate clatters to the floor.

I am on top of her, my hands around her throat. "If she's dead, you're next."

For all the times I sat in church and listened to the preacher warn about obeying the ten commandments—do not kill—I want to kill her. I want it so bad. When I finally release her, she gasps for air.

I scrape up her food and start to eat. Just let her try and take it from me.

She doesn't dare. She doesn't come anywhere near me.

I save some for Ellen. I refuse to believe she's dead.

I close my eyes and picture her breathing, sitting right next to me.

I will not let her be dead.

# *Thirty*

Barnett Griffin served as the head groundskeeper of Georgia's Central State Hospital until 2013 when it officially shut down. Tony had promised his sister he would talk to the man. Griffin was eighty if he was a day but far from feeble. He informed Tony that he walked five miles every day and ate *clean*. No drinking, no smoking. He could be the poster boy for healthy living.

"It opened in 1842." Griffin nodded. "A sad day in our history. 'Course I suppose it was a necessary evil. Taking care of the mentally ill was a learning process and Central State Hospital was part of the curve.

"Folks back then had good intentions, I suppose," he went on, "Just not enough money or the right kinds of doctors. It was the biggest asylum in the country, you know. Sitting on about two thousand acres. Hundreds of buildings. Had around thirteen thousand patients at any given time. The things they did to patients." He shook his head. "From lobotomies to forced sterilization, they did it all. Worst of all, they buried their dead in graves with nothing but old iron markers with numbers on them. Why, most folks bury their dogs better than that. God only knows who all's buried out there. The state sure don't have a clue. Makes it the perfect dumping ground, don't you think?" He shrugged. "Shoot, a person could bury anything out there and no one would ever find it."

Next to Tony, Joanna shifted. She had not wanted to come. They sat on the sofa in Griffin's living room. Griffin sat in his easy chair facing the picture window. He claimed he never watched television or listened to the radio. He preferred the peace and quiet. His only social media was the newspaper.

The elderly man said, "Let me show you something."

Griffin stood and led the way from the living room down a short side hall to a bedroom turned office of sorts. Images of deteriorating buildings, wooded grounds and sad-looking patients covered every square inch of wall on all four sides.

"These old buildings—" he gestured to the once-grand brick architecture that was now covered in vines with boarded-up windows and padlocked doors "—they all look deserted. They look good for nothing." He directed their attention to another set of images. "These are surrounded by twelve-foot fences and the kind of wire you see around prisons. And that's what they became. Some of the buildings were turned into prisons for a while back in the day." He studied the grim images a moment. "Once the hospital shut down, they sent all the patients elsewhere, except a couple hundred mentally ill patients who were deemed too violent for prison.

So they set up a forensic hospital out there. That's where they keep the ones nobody else was willing to take." He waved his arm around the room. "Most of the buildings look deserted and empty, like rotting corpses. But like a rotting corpse, you always got your flies and maggots and other critters who want to pluck the bones clean."

Tony asked, "Are you saying there are still activities on the property?"

"Oh yeah. Pockets of all sorts of activities. Rumor has it that a security software company has some of their geniuses stashed out there. There's a film group who has actually lured a couple of moviemakers to the area. But, the most interesting rumor I've heard is about a pharmaceutical company who tests drugs on participants—not necessarily volunteers is what I heard. And at least a couple of clinical studies on the mentally ill. You gotta believe me when I say there's all sorts of things going on out there that nobody knows about. Security is as thick as fleas all over the place. There's no gate so anybody who wants can go on the property but the security guards are always watching—24-7. With their cameras and their little electric cars buzzing around like bees. Lots of activity."

"But you don't have any proof these activities are actually going on," Tony countered.

Griffin shook his head. "The production company has an office in the old administrator's house. The software company and forensic hospital are legitimate operations. The others, no I can't prove they exist but folks know there's stuff going on out there. There's always been bad things happening in that evil place."

Tony moved closer to the images, studying each one.

Joanna stayed near the door. He sensed her discomfort. Maybe this guy was crazy or paranoid or both, but Tony had a feeling there was some basis to his theories.

"What makes you so certain any of these rumors are true?" He turned back to their conspiracy theorist. "I've yet to visit a town with a deteriorating asylum who didn't have lots of tales to tell."

Griffin nodded. "I'm sure. But I worked there until five years ago when the state moved out the last of the noncriminal patients and closed the doors. I heard things. Got glimpses of *things*. I can give you a map. I'll mark the spots I think might be hiding something. You can investigate at your own risk. Some of the buildings are falling in on themselves. Others are inhabited by squatters but they're likely more scared of you than you would be of them. Then there's the ghosts."

Tony scanned the images again. He had to admit that the property posed the perfect setting for imprisoning victims. The kind of place no one would bother to look. Too dilapidated, surrounded by too much security. Some buildings were being torn down. "All the buildings are padlocked and marked no trespassing."

"Yep. But people roam around out there all the time. It's a felony if you get caught in one of the buildings. For a while that didn't stop people but they've cracked down lately. To tell you the truth, it's a big tourist attraction. You can go anywhere you want but security will be watching. If you try to go into one of the buildings, they'll show up."

"Let's have a look at that map."

Griffin opened up the folded layers and spread across the desk a hand-drawn map. He circled what he called hot spots. "I'm pretty sure this is where you'll find those software geniuses. Note the towering antenna and a couple of satellite dishes." He touched another of his marked spots. "This is one of the prisons that came later. If I was operating a pharmaceutical trial, I would like the security offered by the fence and the steel wire on the windows. I've been in all these places—the ones I've marked—they're in decent shape. It would be easy to whip them up to par for use on the inside and leave the outside looking abandoned."

"The local police aren't suspicious of the activities going on out there?" Tony supposed there was really no reason for them to be interested. The state owned the property. It was their jurisdiction. Their problem.

"Maybe there are legitimate licenses or what have you for these pockets of activity," Griffin offered, "but that don't mean they're doing what the powers that be think they're doing."

"You were the head groundskeeper. Did you ever notice any *new* graves?"

He pointed to another spot on the map. "There's more than twenty-five thousand patients buried right around in here. You can see the memorial they set up a few years back right here." He pointed to another spot. "There's a gazebo and a little arrangement of some of the markers that got moved from the original grave sites. The bodies were buried all around in this wooded area. You'll stumble over the tops of markers if you're not careful. The area is a big slope. Time and water rushing over the ground there have all but swallowed them up. All the pine trees keep plenty of needles covering the ground. Like I said before, it would be easy as hell to lose a body in there, and then just rake pine needles over the freshly turned dirt. No one would notice. You'll see what I mean."

Tony thanked the man. Joanna was out the door and in the car before the door had closed behind Tony.

When they'd driven away from Griffin's home, he asked, "What's going on with you? You were agitated last night and you're—I don't know—more so today."

"I need to get out of the car."

"What?" He shot her a look.

"Now!" She reached for the door handle.

Tony hit the brakes and whipped off to the side of the road. Her door was open before the car had jerked to a complete stop.

She stumbled into the grassy ditch and fell to her hands and knees. Tony turned on the hazards and shoved the gearshift into Park. He got out and sat down next to her. She heaved and gagged. He dug around in his jacket pocket, found a cocktail napkin from the other night at that bar and offered it to her.

When she'd stopped heaving and sat back in the grass, he spoke, "Tell me what's going on, Joanna."

She wiped her mouth with the napkin. "I don't know what you're talking about."

As frustrated as her refusal to come completely clean about the past made him, he took a breath and tried to speak calmly. "You came to me because you want help. You want to make sure whoever took my niece—whoever took you and Ellen—is stopped. I can't help make that happen if you aren't completely honest with me." He glanced around, considered how many days he'd been in Milledgeville already and the fact that he had basically nothing so far. "To tell you the truth, I'm beginning to think you don't want to find the people responsible for what happened then or now."

"I think Griffin is right. Where we…woke up in the woods wasn't more than a mile or so from the hospital, I always thought deep in my gut that we were held there somewhere. At the time the hospital was still operational so I couldn't be sure. My brother told me the cops had searched the whole place. He talked about how creepy it was so maybe I'm way off base." She drew in a big, steadying breath. "All I know is that when Angie started to talk about it I couldn't listen. It was like hot coals raking over my skin. That's why I was so mean to her." She shook her head. "I shouldn't have said those things to her. Anyway—" she inhaled a big breath "—when we were at Griffin's house and he kept going on and on, my head started spinning and I felt like I needed to puke."

"What they talked about nudged a memory you've repressed." Tony saw it on a regular basis when interrogating witnesses. "That's why you're reacting this way."

She glared at him. "So you're a shrink now?"

Tony shook his head. "No but I've walked enough victims through the horrors they suffered to know what PTSD looks like and the things that can make it flare up."

"Yeah, yeah." She shoved the napkin into her pocket and stood. "What else is new?"

Tony followed her to the car, stood at her door as she slid into the passenger seat. "If you want to help me find Tiffany and Vickie and whoever else this bastard took, stop fighting me. Don't hold back. Let the memories come. We need all the help we can get."

"Easy for you to say," she grumbled.

# *Thirty-One*

*Day Five*
*Eighteen years ago...*

Ellen is alive.

I am so grateful. I can't even articulate the words I want to say to her. I hug her gently because she is hurt really bad. Then I feed her. She can't eat much but I make sure she eats at least a little.

No-Name stays out of the way.

I don't know how long Ellen was gone but I had time to think. If we don't try to escape, we are going to die here. No question.

There has to be a way out. It can only be overhead.

If only I could reach it.

After she eats, Ellen goes to sleep. I decide it's time to take a chance. I crawl over to No-Name. She scoots away but I grab her hair and hold her still.

I put my face next to her ear and whisper, "We need to find a way out."

"No shit," she snarls.

I whisper again, "No seams or irregularities in the walls or floor except for the hole we use for a toilet. The way they're getting us in and out has to be overhead."

She shrugs.

"We need to find it."

I stand up.

As if she suddenly understands what I need, she stands up, too. I feel for her shoulders, then climb onto her back. She holds my legs so I can let go of her neck. I reach up and start to smooth my hands over the ceiling.

It takes forever. We have to take frequent breaks because No-Name is like the rest of us—she is weak and injured.

Finally, my hand hits air.

I touch her face—a sign for her to stop. My heart is pounding. There is an opening. I don't know how deep it is or where it goes or anything but it's a void above our heads. I get down and pull her close.

"If I pat you on the head, go forward. On the left cheek, left. Right cheek, right."

No-Name nods.

When I'm on her back once more, I press my hand against the ceiling until I find the void. I pat her on the head and she walks forward. Three or four feet. I tap her left cheek. We go three or four feet that way. Then left again.

I slip back down to the floor and draw her close. "The opening is like three to four feet square. I can't reach the top. I may have to try and climb up your back."

She nods.

So we try again. I can feel another edge maybe ten inches above our ceiling. All I have to do is get there.

I stretch upward. I can feel a floor or flat surface of some sort. I flatten both palms on the surface and push hard as my feet work their way up her back. To her credit, No-Name grabs my right foot in her hands. For a second I'm dangling from my hands. Then she grabs my left foot and pushes up on both.

I scramble up onto the floor or whatever it is.

My heart is pounding. Air is sawing in and out of my lungs. It's dark up here, too.

When my breathing slows and my heart calms, I begin to crawl, keeping my hands well ahead of my knees. I don't want to accidentally fall into the void.

I hit a wall.

I stand and feel my way down the wall, hugging close to it.

My fingers hit a different surface.

*A door!*

I feel over the surface, find it and wrap my fingers around the knob. A wild mixture of fear and relief sears through my veins. I turn the knob.

The door bursts inward, knocking me on my ass.

Before I can scramble away, a figure I can't see drapes something over me, like a heavy blanket.

I'm suddenly swaddled by the blanket and strong arms. I scream for the good it will do.

He or she or they are dragging me. I try to fight my way out of the trap. Can't get free.

Abruptly we stop. The floor starts to move.

I jerk with the feel of it.

Then it turns upright and I tumble off. Land on a hard surface. The air whooshes out of my lungs.

My sore body screams in protest.

I kick the blanket off me. Feel more hands on my skin.

"Get away!" I scream.

"It's me."

*No-Name.*

I'm back where I started.

# *Thirty-Two*

Madelyn roused. She sighed.

Last night had been amazing—considering she'd had another run-in with LeDoux and that bitch Guthrie.

Madelyn dismissed the nuisance as she opened her eyes and stared at the beauty on the pillow next to her.

So young—her skin was perfect. So smooth. No signs of aging like Hailey suffered. God, when had she gotten so old? Young or old, the truth was she'd always preferred women to men.

But age was inevitable. Her true love told her that often. Madelyn smiled at the thought of her dear, dear love. How had she been so lucky to find her all those years ago? They had been secret lovers for almost twenty years now and finally it was their turn. Finally they would have all they'd dreamed of far away from this place where no one could touch them. Where alternative lifestyles were embraced.

And the money—so much money.

All the years of waiting and serving had been worth it. Now they would both live the lives of queens.

Madelyn peered at the sweet young thing lying next to her. What was one more fling before she began the rest of her life? Her true love didn't care. She liked it when Madelyn made love to other women. She even liked to watch sometimes. Madelyn got wet just thinking about the adventures they were going to have in such an exotic country. All they had worked for was finally achieving the results they deserved.

Sleeping Beauty's long-lashed lids fluttered open and dark eyes stared at her. Such big eyes. A soft wide mouth and sleek blond hair. Not naturally blond but well-done.

Madelyn smiled. "Breakfast?"

She rolled Madelyn onto her back and straddled her waist. Then she leaned down and kissed her so hard that Madelyn lost her breath.

Just as abruptly she stopped and climbed out of the bed.

Madelyn watched her lithe body as she moved toward the bathroom. So perfect. Not an ounce of fat and all that smooth, unmarred skin.

When she'd disappeared into the bathroom, Madelyn sat up. She needed coffee. The sound of the water running in the tub had her smiling. A bath would be nice first.

She padded toward the bathroom, Brutus followed. Madelyn turned to him. "Back in your bed."

Her guest wasn't a fan of dogs.

Brutus whined but he traipsed over to his bed and

curled up. Madelyn walked into the bathroom, her toes curling against the heated marble floors.

Her guest was already in the huge soaking tub, the water pouring in from the Roman-style spout. Madelyn closed the door and walked slowly toward her.

The young girl's eyes greedily drank in her body. Madelyn remembered clearly being that age and that hungry. She saw all the things she wanted when she looked at Madelyn. Beautiful clothes, jewelry, the freedom to be with whomever she desired without a husband to rule her life. Without children to get in the way.

Madelyn stepped into the tub and lowered her body down next to her young guest's. Her hands immediately moved to Madelyn's breasts and then lower to her crotch. The girl might be young but she was good with her hands.

Within a minute she had worked Madelyn's body into a frenzy. She closed her eyes and leaned her head against the sleek tub. She cried out as orgasm claimed her. Before the final waves had receded, those magic fingers were moving up her body, massaging her breasts, tracing her throat.

Madelyn's head suddenly slammed under the water.

She fought. Tried to get loose from those steel fingers wrapped around her throat, keeping her head pressed against the bottom of the tub. The other woman's weight was on Madelyn's chest, her thighs holding her arms against her torso like a vise.

She couldn't move.

Couldn't get loose.

When she could hold her breath no more, she surrendered, gasped for relief.

Water rushed into her lungs.

# Get Up To 4 Free Books!

Dear Reader,

**IT'S A FACT:** if you answer 4 quick questions, we'll send you 4 FREE REWARDS from each series you try!

Try **Essential Suspense** featuring spine-tingling suspense and psychological thrillers with many written by today's best-selling authors.

Try **Essential Romance** featuring compelling romance stories with many written by today's best-selling authors.

## Or **TRY BOTH!**

I'm not kidding you. As a leading publisher of women's fiction, we value your opinions… and your time. That's why we are prepared to reward you handsomely for completing our mini-survey. In fact, we have 4 Free Rewards for you, including 2 free books and 2 free gifts from each series you try!

Thank you for participating in our survey,

*Pam Powers*

## To get your 4 FREE REWARDS:
### Complete the survey below and return the insert today to receive up to 4 FREE BOOKS and FREE GIFTS guaranteed!

## "4 for 4" MINI-SURVEY

**1** Is reading one of your favorite hobbies?
☐ YES ☐ NO

**2** Do you prefer to read instead of watch TV?
☐ YES ☐ NO

**3** Do you read newspapers and magazines?
☐ YES ☐ NO

**4** Do you enjoy trying new book series with FREE BOOKS?
☐ YES ☐ NO

Please send me my Free Rewards, consisting of **2 Free Books from each series I select** and **Free Mystery Gifts**. I understand that I am under no obligation to buy anything, as explained on the back of this card.

❏ **Essential Suspense** (191/391 MDL GNQK)
❏ **Essential Romance** (194/394 MDL GNQK)
❏ **Try Both** (191/391/194/394 MDL GNQV)

| | |
|---|---|
| FIRST NAME | LAST NAME |

ADDRESS

| | |
|---|---|
| APT.# | CITY |

| | |
|---|---|
| STATE/PROV. | ZIP/POSTAL CODE |

## READER SERVICE—Here's how it works:

Accepting your 2 free books and 2 free gifts (gifts valued at approximately $10.00 retail) places you under no obligation to buy anything. You may keep the books and gifts and return the shipping statement marked "cancel." If you do not cancel, approximately one month later we'll send you four more books from each series you have chosen, and bill you at our low, subscribers-only discount price. Essential Romance and Essential Suspense books consist of 4 books each month and cost just $6.74 each in the U.S. or $7.24 each in Canada. That is a savings of at least 16% off the cover price. It's quite a bargain! Shipping and handling is just 50¢ per book in the U.S. and 75¢ per book in Canada*. You may return any shipment at our expense and cancel at any time — or you may continue to receive monthly shipments at our low, subscribers-only discount price plus shipping and handling. *Terms and prices subject to change without notice. Prices do not include sales taxes which will be charged (if applicable) based on your state or country of residence. Canadian residents will be charged applicable taxes. Offer not valid in Quebec. Books received may not be as shown. All orders subject to approval. Credit or debit balances in a customer's account(s) may be offset by any other outstanding balance owed by or to the customer. Please allow 3 to 4 weeks for delivery. Offer available while quantities last.

▲ If offer card is missing write to: Reader Service, P.O. Box 1341, Buffalo, NY 14240-8531 or visit www.ReaderService.com ▲

## BUSINESS REPLY MAIL
FIRST-CLASS MAIL PERMIT NO. 717 BUFFALO, NY

POSTAGE WILL BE PAID BY ADDRESSEE

**READER SERVICE**
PO BOX 1341
BUFFALO NY 14240-8571

NO POSTAGE
NECESSARY
IF MAILED
IN THE
UNITED STATES

# Thirty-Three

Jo stared up at the Jones Building. Vines had crept over the brick, like evil arms stretching up to draw this place into the ground, into the depths of hell where it belonged. On the dome two black crows sat staring at those who dared to pass.

Just like eighteen years ago. She remembered thinking that those black crows were surely signs that evil lurked here. Griffin's stories had reminded her of her early days as a freshman at Georgia College. On several occasions she had tagged along with a group of other freshmen who'd heard about the old asylum and wanted to poke around. Parts of the asylum had still been in operation at the time so they'd had to be on their best behavior—or at least pretend to be until no one was watching.

Voices whispered through her. Giggles and whispers. Young girls with nothing better to do on a Saturday morning than explore the local ghost stories. They had found a room filled with old patient files in one of the buildings. The others had laughed as they read the notes but Jo hadn't laughed. She'd read, absorbing the horrific details, the anguish generated by the words creating a sort of movie in her brain. The words, some written by doctors and others posted by nurses, spoke of fear and desperation, hopelessness and coldheartedness.

> Without enough staff for a pediatric ward, the children were often placed in cages to protect them from the older patients. Their fear is palpable, but so is that of the few remaining nurses. The children are small but they are violent and cannot be trusted.

How had anyone left a child in this place? She closed her eyes and tried to block the images, like scenes from a horror movie, her mind automatically created.

"I'll keep driving," Tony said, his voice startling her. "You tell me when something looks familiar."

"I came here a few times that first semester," she said. "Exploring with some other students, but I know what you mean." He wanted her to look for anything that looked familiar during or after the abduction.

She focused on the buildings and the landscape as he drove. He moved so slowly she wanted to jump out of the car and push to make it go faster. It all looked vaguely familiar. Something dark and foreboding pulsed in her blood, made her heart beat too fast. She had come with those girls and a couple of guys from her orientation class several times. It was part of the freshman ritual. You explored all the spooky old shit.

How was she supposed to remember if any aspect of this shithole felt familiar in any way that related to the fourteen days she had spent in the pits of hell? For the past eighteen years she had worked diligently to block those memories from her brain.

*Stop, Jo. Just stop.* He was desperate to find his niece. She wanted to finish this as much as he did. She wanted it to end and she wanted the people involved to pay.

She also recognized the other aspect of what drove him, perhaps better than he did. He wanted to find his niece alive before she was turned into what Jo and Ellen had become. She could understand wanting to save someone he loved. He needed her help to do that and she wanted to help. The problem was she didn't know how to help! She had told him all she could that might somehow make a difference. So many of the events that led up to what happened eighteen years ago were hardly more than theories. She was positive that Conway and Martin or whatever her name was were involved, but she couldn't actually prove it. She couldn't point to a place here or near the highway and say this is it—which was what he wanted. She had no idea how she and Ellen ended up where they did. They had awakened in those woods with no one and nothing around them but trees.

The car in the side mirror caught her attention. *Security.*

She dropped her head back against the headrest. "And it begins."

Tony had spotted them, as well. He probably noticed them before she did. She stared at his profile and wondered how much longer he would permit her evasion and lies on the parts she didn't want to share. Lying wasn't right, not really. She'd told him the truth—at least everything she'd told him had been the truth. But he knew she was holding back. He'd been some big-deal profiler with the FBI. He probably knew her better just by watching her than she knew herself. She could say the same about him. Maybe she should have been a profiler.

Like her, he was desperate on a number of levels. His life had hit a place almost as low as her long-term situation. His career was in the toilet and, from what she'd seen so far, so was his personal life. The two of them were a pair for sure. How the hell were they supposed to figure this out when they couldn't even figure out their own lives? Maybe he just didn't want to do this alone. Maybe he needed a friend.

Was that what they were? Friends?

Her boss was a friend, sort of, maybe.

He liked her. She liked him. To some degree they counted on each other. What was the definition of a friend anyway? She'd considered the same about Ellen and decided they weren't really friends, but maybe she was wrong.

But LeDoux? The two of them were acquaintances, she decided. She had a number of those, though she rarely exchanged body fluids with an acquaintance. Getting close to LeDoux had required the extra effort. Her occasional sexual encounter was never with anyone she'd met before and the chosen partner never knew her real name. Telling LeDoux was necessary, wasn't it?

Did he see the real Joanna Guthrie? The empty shell?

Maybe she was borrowing trouble. She almost smiled at the phrase. Her mother had used that phrase all the time. Yes, Jo was borrowing trouble. Easy to do, spending so much time with a man like LeDoux. *Not true,*

*Jo*. He wasn't the problem. She was the problem. This part she knew with complete certainty. She spent 99 percent of her time completely alone and had since she was eighteen years old. How was she supposed to know the intricacies of carrying on a normal conversation much less being a friend? Concern for his niece likely had him off his game or he would have seen through her completely already.

She had a niece and a nephew. She'd never met either one. The boy was twelve, his sister ten. Without question, Ray was a good father. He'd always taken really good care of Jo—until she moved away to college. He'd tried then. He would show up on weekends. Her roommates would get all giddy because a cute older guy smiled at them. Jo had teased her brother relentlessly about it. Eventually, he stopped coming so often. Their mom had told him to let Jo be. She could just hear her. *She needs to be making friends, not hanging out with her brother.*

Jo had a family. Once. A good one. But then she'd tossed away the life she had known. Why had she thrown them away, too?

She pushed the painful thoughts away and stared out the window at one of the ugliest parts of humanity's past. The screams and wails of patients echoed through her soul. One of the freshmen had read aloud newspaper articles about the old asylum when they toured the place the second time. The notes from the patient files they had found were right. Children were often kept in cages among the adults. Experimental treatments were the norm.

What sort of desperation did it take to prompt a person to bring a loved one to a place like this and leave him or her? *As if you have the right to judge.* Hell, she didn't even trust herself to take care of a cat much less another human. The neighbor at the last place where she lived had offered her a kitten from the unexpected litter her cat had dropped on her. Jo had insisted she traveled too much for a pet. Funny how the lies came so easy after so many years.

She ordered her brain to stay on track. *Focus on those fourteen days.* If she was held here surely something would feel more deeply familiar. She powered the window down and inhaled the scents of the place. Listened to the sounds.

She remembered the crunch of leaves under their feet as they ran through the woods after they escaped. They'd done what they had to do; the other girl hadn't made it. It was just the two of them.

*They'd done what they had to do.*

Jo closed her eyes and silently repeated the words, then she opened them again and stared forward. Bile churned in her stomach. She tried to swallow, to keep the bitterness at bay.

She cleared her throat. "Tell me, Agent LeDoux, is a victim still a victim even when she does whatever it takes to survive?"

He slowed for an intersection at a maze of buildings. Thankfully the security vehicle had turned onto another street. Tony scrutinized her for a moment. "Did you do what you had to do, Joanna?"

"It's a hypothetical question." She looked away from him, stared forward. "I think a friend of mine did."

"Victims do what they have to do to survive," he

agreed. "The survival instinct is strong in most people, unless it has been drummed out by previous bumps in the road."

"Like drugs or hard luck?"

"That can do it, yes. Abusive parents or spouses can do it, too."

They rode in silence for half a minute before he said more. Maybe he was considering whether or not he was driving around with a person who'd done something really bad.

"With some people, their will to survive isn't as strong because they have much less to live for. Maybe they've suffered tragic loss. I have a friend, a homicide detective. She lives in Montgomery, Alabama. A serial killer murdered her husband and was responsible for the deaths of her little boy, her partner and a dear friend. She was one of those people who decided she didn't have anything worth surviving for."

Jo understood that feeling so damned well. "Did she die?"

He shook his head. "No. She survived so she could find the killer and make sure he paid for what he'd done."

"Did she?"

Tony braked for another stop. He nodded. "She did. She picked up the pieces and now she's married again."

"She's happy?"

"She is."

Jo didn't see how that was possible. "With those kinds of scars to her psyche I don't see how she could put it behind her and ever be normal."

"What's normal?"

She rolled her eyes. "You know what I mean. Go on living life as if nothing happened."

"You'd have to ask her about that." He focused on driving.

Jo studied his profile again. "You have a few scars of your own."

"I spent a lot of years profiling killers. Yeah. I have a few."

Maybe more than a few. "You tell me your secrets. I've told you mine."

His jaw tightened. Ah, so he was good at telling others how to do it but he couldn't do it himself.

"What a hypocrite." She stared out the window once more.

The high fences with their concertina wire tops made her insides tighten. She remembered the buildings that later had been turned to small prisons. At some point in the past half century or so treatment for the mentally ill had changed and so the need for places like this one had waned. Some parts of the property had been re-purposed, so to speak. Eventually, even those new purposes became obsolete and were abandoned. The side roads that went off into the woods made her shudder. She hated this place.

"I was very good at my job."

His voice startled her. She'd thought he wasn't going to answer.

"So good that the idea of defeat was unthinkable. I made a decision to do whatever necessary to make sure I never failed. There was this one serial killer who remained elusive after years of tracking him. I wanted him so badly I could taste it."

She waited for him to go on, the sound of his voice making her relax. Or maybe it was the idea that he was admitting his flaws that made her feel more at ease.

"He dropped a body in Montgomery so I rushed there and I met Detective Bobbie Gentry. When I looked at her I was stunned. She was the perfect example of all that this killer craved in a victim."

Jo watched his throat work in an effort to swallow. His fingers tightened on the steering wheel.

"I used her to bait him. And he came back. He murdered her husband, took her… The things he did to her…" He drew in a deep breath. "Unimaginable torture. He raped her over and over for weeks. Beat her so badly. Broke her leg and carved up her body. Starved her to the point that she was so weak she could hardly walk. But somehow she got away. Despite the broken bones she walked for miles through the freezing cold."

Another of those long lapses of silence.

"But she made it," Jo offered, foolishly needing to hear a happy ending.

"She did, but *I* did that to her. All I cared about was my career. I lost my marriage and eventually my career because I lost sight of what really mattered. When I realized what I had done, I made it my life's goal to do whatever necessary to make it right."

He was preaching to the choir and the sermon was one she knew all too well.

Jo shook her head. "I can't be like you."

He stopped the car and turned to her. "You are like me. You're like Bobbie. You're a survivor. That's why you came back to this place. To stop the persons who did this to you and to all the others."

"Yeah well, that's not really working out so far. Your niece is still missing. By now she believes no one is coming, including her super cool uncle the FBI profiler."

"Does it make you feel better to throw that at me?" She refused to look at him.

He rolled back onto the road. "Maybe you don't care how this turns out. You survived. You can just walk away like you did before. You don't need anyone or anything. Is that how you feel?"

"You don't know me."

Her cell vibrated. The text was from her boss.

You still alive?

She almost laughed out loud. She hadn't been alive in nearly two decades. To avoid more of her boss's questions, she sent him a yes in response along with a happy face. That should really freak him out.

"Tell me the part you haven't told anyone else, Joanna. I don't care if it was right or wrong. I only care that it might help me find my niece alive."

"That building." She pointed to the upcoming one on the right. "It looks more familiar than all the others."

It didn't but she was tired of his questions. He'd hit too close to home. The only reason she pointed the building out was because the gate was open. The twelve-foot fence would have kept them out otherwise. Beyond the open gate, one of the entry doors stood open, too. Seemed like a good place to change the subject.

He pulled over and turned off the car.

"You're sure?"

"I'm not sure of anything." She opened the car door and got out.

He rounded the hood and followed her through the gate.

The whirr of something moving jerked her attention upward. A camera was focused on them as they approached the entry door. Old man Griffin had said there were cameras everywhere.

Why was that?

If there was nothing here, why all the cameras? Maybe the old man was right about the *pockets* of activities.

Tony came up beside her. "Let me go in first."

She should be ashamed of herself for sending him on a wild-goose chase like this. He really was trying to help her. Had she grown so coldhearted that she didn't care about him or his niece? Was Ellen's death for nothing? "Wait."

He turned back to her.

"I—"

He held up a hand for her to give him a minute, and then he reached for his cell. "LeDoux."

He listened for a few seconds, glanced at her, and then listened some more.

"I'll be right there."

He shoved his phone into his pocket and she asked, "What's going on?"

"That was Phelps. Hailey Martin—Madelyn Houser—is dead."

*It's coming down to you, Jo.*

Everyone else who knew what really happened was dying.

*What're you going to do now?*

# *Thirty-Four*

*Day Six*
*Eighteen years ago...*

No food today.

Nothing.

No sound.

Everyone is too tired to make any noise.

A bottle of water was left next to each of us while we slept.

That's something. At least we have water.

My body is sore. I feel every scrape, every bruise as if it goes all the way to the bone. Ellen lies beside me. She is withdrawing more into herself every day.

No-Name is… I don't know where she is.

I pray there will be no battles today. I feel too weak. Too tired. Too depressed.

A flicker on the wall snaps my attention. Another. Like an old movie reel that takes a moment to reach the full frame of an image—only there are dozens.

More flickers. Faster. Blurry images moving frantically across the wall.

Next to me Ellen sits up.

"What's happening?"

I don't know. I'm not sure whether I answered her or if I only thought the words.

"What the fuck?"

No-Name is suddenly on the other side of me.

It must be bad if she's scared.

Then the blurry images become clear.

People.

*Blood.*

Lots of blood.

So many images, as if multiple movies are playing all around us. Slasher movies. Blood and guts. Knives and axes.

My eyes hurt looking at them.

My brain hurts thinking about the images.

"Don't look," I murmur.

Then I close my eyes.

# *Thirty-Five*

The forensic techs were finishing up by the time Tony and Joanna arrived on the scene. She stayed in the car. Her idea, not his. As long as she didn't disappear on him he was okay with that. He suspected she wanted to avoid Phelps. On the other hand, the past two days had been hard on her. He had a feeling she spent a lot of her quiet time reliving the horrors of eighteen years ago.

He couldn't afford for her to bail on him anytime soon…not until this was done. On some level he trusted her. They shared a common goal and she wanted it as badly as he did even if she didn't admit it.

"No forced entry," Chief Buckley was saying as they moved through the entry hall. "We had to call animal control to come get her dog. Between the lack of forced entry and the dog I'd say whoever she was entertaining was a familiar or at least an invited guest."

A reasonable conclusion. Brutus had appeared more

than a little protective of his master. Then again, knowing Martin's lifestyle, maybe not. Tony kept the comment to himself. He hadn't been asked for his opinion as of yet. The security system hadn't been breached, which also appeared to confirm the chief's conclusion. But then there were people who knew how to get around a security system.

Was the person who hired Martin and Conway to do their dirty work tying up loose ends? They were the only two people Joanna remembered being close when she was abducted. Both had been seen with Tiffany. At this point they were running out of suspects and they already didn't have a damned lead.

As he and Buckley started up the stairs, Tony noticed Chief Phelps in the dining room with another detective. They were huddled over a laptop.

"Ultimately," Buckley said, "the coroner thinks Martin drowned in that big old tub. But there are marks that indicate someone's fingers were around her throat. Someone strong enough to hold her down."

Forensic techs were covering every square inch of the place. Tony had seen two uniforms and another tech moving back and forth in the yard. Milledgeville PD was on top of the situation. They wanted this case solved almost as badly as Tony did.

At the top of the stairs, Buckley gestured to the right, and then headed that way.

"No video with her surveillance system?" The system was high-end. Tony had spotted a couple of cameras on his first visit.

"There is video," Buckley answered. "Chief Phelps and one of his detectives is reviewing it now."

So that was what they were doing in the dining room with the laptop.

"Don't take this the wrong way, Chief," Tony said, "but how did you and Phelps end up here? This is way out of your jurisdiction. As I recall, when I mentioned that Miles Conway might have an accomplice named Hailey Martin, you two didn't want to hear about it."

"Chief Phelps had been trying to catch Martin at home for a hair sample, considering she was blond and that blond hair was found in Conway's apartment. I believe you suggested Martin as a person of interest."

For the good it had done, Tony mused.

"The detectives made a couple of attempts to find her with no luck so they sort of let it go," Buckley admitted. "But that was before the FBI called us about the hard drives found in Conway's bathtub."

Now there was some news Tony hadn't heard. Maybe his Bureau contact had gotten his hand slapped for giving Tony a heads-up now and then. "The Bureau was able to pull something from the hard drives?"

"At first we thought they would be damaged beyond recovery but whoever put them in the tub made a mistake. He or she didn't take the parts that counted out of the casings so they were protected to some degree. They couldn't recover everything but they got enough to show that Martin and Conway were working together in some capacity."

"Meaning," Tony pressed.

"We have footage of Tiffany Durand, Vickie Parton and an unidentified female restrained in the back of a van. Conway was taunting them."

Shock sucker punched Tony. "Are you able to see the license plate of the vehicle?"

Buckley shook his head. "We found another clip that wasn't more than thirty or forty seconds of Conway having sex with Parton. She's tied to a bed—looks like the one in his apartment—and she's unconscious."

Son of a bitch. "What about Tiffany?"

"We weren't able to recover any footage of a sexual nature involving her."

Tony somehow managed to drag air back into his lungs. He was glad that bastard had gotten his in such a fucked-up way.

Buckley led the way to Martin's master suite. Like the downstairs, the rear wall of the room was all glass, the view overlooking the lake. The massive bed was front and center. Tangled sheets. Lingerie on the floor. The earthy smell of sex lingered in the air.

"How does Martin tie into what Conway was doing?" Tony asked, since the man hadn't mentioned her in relation to the video footage they'd found on the hard drives.

"You're gonna love this." Buckley stepped back, allowing the gurney to be pulled from the bathroom.

"May I?" Tony asked with a gesture to the body bag. It wasn't that he didn't believe Buckley and Phelps fully capable of doing their jobs, but he didn't trust Hailey Martin—aka Madelyn Houser—not to have another identity up her sleeve.

Buckley gestured to the gurney. "Of course. Her real name is Madelyn Houser. She has a criminal record from fifteen years ago when the college fired her for stealing from some of the students. She was a professor's assistant. Anyway, the driver's license in her purse lists her as Hailey Martin. I'm guessing that was her way of escaping her criminal record."

Joanna had mentioned some connection to a professor at the university. "The professor she worked with, was that Professor Blume?"

"That's the one."

The attendant drew back the zipper and revealed Martin's pale, bloated face. Tony really had hoped she would lead them to Tiffany and the others. Son of a bitch. He nodded and the bag was closed once more.

As they continued toward the en suite bath, he said to Buckley, "You were saying that I was going to love something."

"Martin—Houser—whoever the hell she was, walked in on Conway while he was raping Parton. That's why the video ended abruptly. She pulled him off the girl and started screaming at him. Stuff like: *I'm going to fucking kill you!* and *These girls are not your playthings, they're goddamned merchandise.*"

"Merchandise." Tony felt sick to his stomach.

Buckley nodded. "I'm thinking human traffickers?"

Tony stared at the massive soaking tub that had been the death of the bitch partially responsible for his niece's kidnapping. "I'm guessing we're looking at something far bigger than two local thugs like Martin and Conway."

Buckley made an agreeable sound. "We haven't found her cell phone. Never found Conway's. Car's in the garage. My money's on the same perp. This kill was cleaner than the other."

Tony nodded. "Conway's murder was far more emotional. His killer knew him. Hated him."

Buckley nodded. "That's my thinking."

"Chief Buckley!"

Tony and the chief turned as the officer rushed into the bedroom. "Chief Phelps needs to see you, sir." He looked to Tony. "You, too, Agent LeDoux."

*Agent.* What do you know? Tony was apparently back on the right side of this cluster fuck with the local cops. Whatever he had to do. Bringing Tiffany and Vickie home safely was all that mattered.

Joanna, too. Maybe she was still waiting for this to be over so she could go back home.

Downstairs, Phelps gestured to the computer screen. "Have a look at this."

Tony and Buckley moved around behind where the chief was seated at the table. The screen was frozen on the front door of Martin's home.

"There's no video in the bedroom," Phelps explained. "Only at the entrances to the home. This is the last person to come into this house last night just after midnight and the first and only person to leave at ten forty-five this morning."

A young woman, nineteen or twenty at most; short, tight blue dress; mega high heels; big tote bag–style purse arrived in the middle of the night. Martin met her at the door, gave her a big hug, and then invited her inside.

"She looks really young," Buckley noted. "Like one of the students at the college."

"Another freshman," Tony agreed. *Like Tiffany.*

"She's blonde," Phelps said. "What you want to bet if we search that bedroom upstairs closely enough we'll find a match for the hair we found at Conway's apartment."

Tony said, "There's someone else who needs to see this video."

Both Phelps and Buckley swung their attention to him. Phelps was the one to demand, "Who?"

"One of Martin's and Conway's first victims."

Before they could demand any more answers, Tony walked outside, the idea that Conway had raped Parton twisting in his gut. Had Martin interrupted before he could do the same to Tif or had he already finished with her? The entire concept made him sick to his stomach. He suddenly wished the son of a bitch was still alive so he could kill him.

Joanna watched him approach the car. When he reached her door her eyes widened in question. She opened the passenger side door and got out. "What's going on?"

"There's video."

She blinked. "What do you mean?"

"The Bureau's forensic team was able to pull some video off the hard drives in Conway's apartment. They now have proof he and Martin-Houser-Whoever took my niece and the other girl." He held her gaze. "As well as a third girl. Just like you said."

The pulse at the base of her throat fluttered wildly. "Was there anything about the other person or persons involved?"

"Not yet. But we may also have the unsub who murdered Conway and Martin on the home security video. I want you to have a look to see if you recognize her.

She may be connected to someone else involved. Maybe one of the other victims you interviewed."

Joanna nodded. "All right."

He felt her tension mounting as they entered the house. The walk along the hall to the dining room felt like miles. When they reached the huddle around the laptop Joanna moved closer to him.

"This is Joanna Guthrie."

Buckley frowned. "I thought your name was Carrie Cole."

She shrugged. "I made that up."

"What's this about?" Phelps demanded. "I thought she was your girlfriend."

Tony looked at her, urging her to tell them the truth.

"I was lured into a trap by Miles Conway and Hailey Martin—she was Madelyn Houser back then. Eighteen years ago. Ellen Schrader, too. Carson. Ellen Carson. Carson was her maiden name. We were taken the Friday before spring break. We were found fourteen days later."

"Wait, wait," Buckley said. "I pulled some old files and found this case—your case. It's the only one I found that was anything like this one."

Joanna took a breath. "There were others. One each year after we were taken for another four years. Different colleges, different times of the year. Of the ten victims, only four are still alive. They all described a blonde woman and a dark-haired man as flirting with them or associating with them in some way before they disappeared. The descriptions fit Conway and Martin."

"She's done extensive research," Tony said. "It wasn't until today—when you told me about the recovered video footage that we had evidence to back up what she's been telling me all week."

Phelps stood and offered Joanna his seat. "Have a look at this video and tell me if you recognize this woman."

As Joanna moved around the desk, Tony brought her up to speed. "She's the only person besides Martin who came into the house last night and she was the only one to leave this morning."

Phelps cued up the video.

Joanna stared at the video for five seconds before speaking. "Oh my God."

"You recognize her?" Tension coiled tighter in Tony's gut.

"I've only seen a photo of her once when she was about thirteen, but this…" She glanced up at Tony, then stared at the screen once more. "I'm as positive as I can be that this is Sylvia Carson, Ellen's daughter."

For the benefit of the chiefs, Tony explained, "Ellen Carson was raped when she was abducted—the same way Vickie Parton was. She realized weeks after the nightmare was over that she was pregnant. She had the child and her parents raised her so the child grew up thinking she was Ellen's younger sister." He shifted his attention back to Joanna. "She'd be what? Seventeen?"

Joanna nodded. "She must have learned that Ellen was her real mother and what happened to us all those years ago. It's the only way she could possibly have known to come after Conway and Houser." Joanna put her hand to her mouth, then let it fall away. "That's what Ellen's husband meant." She lifted her gaze to Tony.

"She left him a note before she killed herself. All it said was 'She knows everything.'"

"First thing we need to do," Phelps said, "is to find this Sylvia Carson. I'm not releasing anything about this murder for the next twenty-four hours, maybe more. We want Carson to think she's gotten away with it so she doesn't go to ground." He surveyed those gathered around the laptop. "The cell phone belonging to Martin… Houser—whatever the hell her name—isn't the only thing around here missing. There's an empty leather gun case in her nightstand. We couldn't find anything registered to her, but whatever kind of gun she had is missing, too."

Joanna stared at the frozen image on the screen as she recited Ellen's husband's name and address as well as the names and address of Ellen's parents. "Sylvia has antisocial personality disorder. When I spoke to Ellen's husband, he mentioned that Sylvia had run away from home." She shrugged. "A few days ago, maybe." She shook her head. "Oh my God, I can't believe she did this."

Buckley said, "We'll need a full statement from you, Ms. Guthrie."

Tony reached for her. "We'll come into your office tomorrow. Right now Ms. Guthrie needs some time to deal with this."

Tony pulled her to her feet and ushered her toward the door.

"We'll be expecting you first thing in the morning," Buckley called behind them.

"Your friends from the Bureau will likely be there, too," Phelps warned.

Tony gave a wave of acknowledgment before walking out the door. When they were in the car, Joanna stared at him as he buckled first her seat belt and then his own. He started the car and drove away. They were two blocks away before she spoke.

"What're we doing now?"

"We're going to find the only other lead connected to our dead players that we know of."

"What lead?"

He braked for a traffic light. "You said Madelyn Houser worked for a Professor Blume?"

She nodded. "I think that's how she chose Ellen and me. She worked at the college so she had access to the students, maybe their records."

His thoughts exactly. "Madelyn Houser was fired from the university for stealing from students. Maybe Blume had her checking out potential victims and their extracurricular activities. She may have gotten greedy and decided to take a little something on the side and got caught. But she was very good at what Blume needed her to do so he hired her back—after hours, of course."

Considering how Houser had lived, she'd earned a great deal of money over the years, particularly in contrast to Miles Conway. Then again, maybe the man only cared about cars. Besides the Ferrari, he could have a whole stash of high-end sports cars in a rented garage somewhere. On the other hand, Houser had mentioned that she'd married well.

"Blume could be the person in charge." Joanna glanced at Tony, then turned her attention back to the passing landscape. "As a psychologist and advisor he would've known everything about the students. Their weaknesses, their strengths. He worked most hands-on with the freshman class. He was the go-to guy for freshmen in need of advisement." She rubbed at her eyes. "I don't know why I never thought of that. He was always so nice and caring. I wouldn't have considered him capable of being that kind of monster. He...he was part of the school staff. He made us feel safe."

"Sometimes monsters are the nicest people." Tony reached for her hand and gave it a squeeze. "That's why so many go unnoticed for years."

His source had confirmed that Blume was involved with some sort of work at the old Central State Hospital until very recently. Just maybe, all the pieces were finally beginning to come together.

"No one will ever believe he did this." Joanna shook her head. "I'm not sure I can believe it."

"At the moment, he's our only known connection between you and Houser. Which is why we're going to find him."

Hopefully before he ended up as dead as Houser and Conway.

# *Thirty-Six*

*Day Seven*
*Eighteen years ago...*

The movies won't stop.

They play over and over and my eyes and brain can't take it anymore.

We all lie on our sides on the floor curled into balls. Our knees pulled to our faces, our eyes squeezed shut.

Why doesn't it stop?

I'm so hungry. No water today.

Is it another day?

I don't know how long the movies have been playing. I can't remember when they started. An hour ago? A day? Weeks—it feels like weeks. No. Couldn't be weeks. I haven't been in this place a week—have I?

Then the screaming starts.

I sit up. Who's screaming? The three of us—Ellen, me and No-Name—are huddled close on the floor looking around at the insane images. The screams match the images. Women screaming. Children screaming. Men wailing—so much shrieking.

I just want it to stop. I put my hands over my ears and close my eyes.

Don't look, don't listen.

But I can see the images through my weary eyelids. I can hear the screams no matter how hard I press my hands against my ears.

My head is spinning.

Please make it stop.

# Thirty-Seven

*8:00 p.m.*

"You should eat."

Jo plucked a fry from the bag and stuffed it into her mouth. She didn't want to eat. She had no appetite. The fry was like chewing wax. "Satisfied?"

By the time they found Blume's house it was too dark to see anything and no one was home. Disgusted, LeDoux opted to call it a night. She hadn't argued. They'd hit a drive-through as soon as they reached Milledgeville city limits. He'd wanted to stop and have a decent meal but she'd wanted to go straight back to the inn. A drive-through was the compromise. She needed quiet. Spending this much time with other people was not the norm for her. After all that had happened, she needed her solitude as badly as she needed the air to breathe.

She had to think.

She closed her eyes and wished LeDoux would drive

faster. Jesus, how could this be? How could a child have done these things?

*Just look at what you did when you were hardly a year older than her.*

Jesus Christ, no wonder Ellen couldn't take it anymore. She'd lived with what they'd done, assuaging her conscience with alcohol all these years. Why had she suddenly told her daughter the truth? Had Sylvia learned Ellen was really her mother and demanded to know why she hadn't claimed her as more than her sister?

Why else would she tell her after all these years?

What a screwed-up mess. Jo could only imagine what Ellen's parents were going through right now.

*What about your own family? Look what you've put them through.*

Guilt stabbed her to the bone. This was why she stayed deep in her own little world. She didn't have to think about these things, didn't have to feel. Except she had started to feel. She turned to study the man behind the wheel. He had helped her to dare to feel again, to want more. Damn it. Where the hell did she go from here?

"At least the investigation is moving in some sort of forward direction now." LeDoux glanced at her. "Having the locals on the same sheet of music is always a good thing."

"Guess so."

A BOLO had been issued for Ellen's daughter, Sylvia Carson. Mr. and Mrs. Carson had last seen her three nights ago when she'd left in her Honda Civic headed to a friend's house to spend the night. She never showed at the friend's house but they didn't know until the next afternoon when she failed to come home from school. Frantic for some sort of explanation of why she'd suddenly run away, Mr. and Mrs. Carson discovered Sylvia had stopped taking her meds at least a month ago and started sampling a number of illegal drugs. On top of that, Ellen had committed suicide.

Jo could almost see how, in Ellen's mind, she had ruined one child and was on the road to harming two others. No wonder she ended it all.

"She's seventeen," Jo said, her chest aching so hard she could barely breathe. "She planned those murders like a pro. Still, I don't see how she knew who to look for unless Ellen told her." She dropped her head against the headrest. "The few times we talked about it, Ellen said she never wanted Sylvia to know any of it. But there's no other way she could have known. No one knew the things that really happened except the two of us."

LeDoux asked, "What about her husband?"

"No. He had no idea." She thought about the dismay she'd heard in his voice when he realized his wife had only one friend—not that Jo had been a true friend. She should have been. She dragged in a shaky breath. "Art is one of those hardworking, dedicated husbands who believes all is right and good in the world. He kisses his wife on the cheek every morning and goes off to work his twelve-hour day, assuming that she will take care of their neat little world while he's gone."

"Yeah." LeDoux studied the traffic in front of him. "I know the type, maybe a little too well. He has no clue his personal life is falling apart until one day he comes home and all his clothes are waiting on the porch."

Jo turned to stare at him. "Your wife did that?"

He nodded. "She liked the home we had built together—she just didn't want me in it anymore. I was too disconnected from her and our marriage. I only cared about work."

"That's what she thought?"

He laughed. "That's what I was. She was sick of my drinking. And she wanted kids. I couldn't go there… not after all the sickos I've seen."

"You didn't try to fix it?" Wasn't that what normal people did? Maybe former Special Agent LeDoux was broken, too.

He shook his head. "I waited too late. She'd already turned to someone else. My fault. Not hers."

That was a first. How often did you hear a guy claim responsibility? Maybe he really was the nice guy she'd pegged him for the first time they met. Jo closed her eyes. Distraction was not going to help her get to the person responsible for what happened to her and Ellen and all the others.

Another unimaginable thought occurred to her. "How could Sylvia do…what she did to Conway if Ellen told her everything?"

"She may not have told her that she suspected Conway was her father," he suggested.

Jo hoped he was right about that part. The idea that she'd lured the man with sex made that option seriously sick. But then, desperate people did desperate things. Jo knew that all too well. And Sylvia was ill. Without her medication, her mind wasn't working right. Besides, Jo had done her share of sick shit. Maybe the whole world was broken.

"I don't know," she admitted.

"Eat," LeDoux urged as he pulled into the parking area behind the inn.

"The fries are cold." She crumpled the bag as they climbed out of the vehicle. Of course the fact that the food was cold was her fault. "I'll get something from the snack bar."

"Jo-Jo."

Jo felt as if someone had stepped on her grave. She turned toward the male voice—the voice of her *brother*. No matter that it had been seventeen years since she'd seen him or heard his voice, she would know him anywhere. He rounded the hood of a pickup truck parked on the street and walked toward her.

"Ray?" Was her mind playing tricks on her? He couldn't be here. Why would he come, after she'd deserted them? "What're you doing here?" The only real possibility slammed into her gut. "Is Mom okay?"

Ray nodded. "Mom's fine. I saw what's happening on the news. She told me you were here and I..." He shrugged. "I wanted to see you. The chief of police told me where you were staying."

Jo wasn't surprised by that last part. LeDoux had said Phelps was watching them. Didn't matter. But this— this was surreal. Ray was standing right in front of her. Her knees started to shake. Her eyes burned. Her big brother was here.

As Ray walked toward her, Jo couldn't move. She told herself to move, to meet him halfway, but her legs wouldn't cooperate. Told herself to say something but she couldn't. Her brother walked all the way up to her and hugged her. So many emotions whirled inside her, spinning out of control. Somehow she managed to put her arms around his broad shoulders.

When he drew back, he said, "You look good."

She swiped at her eyes with the back of her hand, hoping he wouldn't notice. "You, too."

"Why don't we go inside?" LeDoux suggested.

Jo tried to pull herself together; it didn't work as well as she'd hoped. She stepped away from Ray, wrapped her arms around her waist to prevent anyone from seeing how her hands were shaking. "Good idea." She gestured to Tony. "This is Tony LeDoux. He's—" Her gaze collided with his. "He's a friend of mine with the FBI. We're working together to find the people behind the abductions."

Ray looked from one to the other and nodded, then thrust out his hand. "Ray Guthrie. Nice to meet you, LeDoux."

LeDoux gave his hand a shake. "Same here."

They all stood around and stared at each other for a moment before LeDoux gestured toward the cottage and Jo headed that way.

Once they were inside, she indicated the sofa. "Sit. How's Mom?"

Should she have asked about his children first? God, she was so bad at this. What kind of aunt ignored her niece and nephew their whole lives? Jesus! She collapsed into a chair before her knees gave out completely and she embarrassed herself further.

Ray just kept looking at her. Maybe he didn't know what to say either.

"How about I make some coffee," LeDoux offered.

"I'd like coffee, thank you," Ray said.

While LeDoux readied the coffee maker, Ray said, "She's good. She officially retired last year. She's involved in all these community activities." He laughed wearily. "She takes the kids to Disney World every summer."

"That's nice. She always talked about grandkids."

Ray nodded. "They're good kids, too. David Colton—we named him after Dad—wants to play football. If he can keep his grades up, I'll probably let him. Heather Frances is a straight-A student. She doesn't care about anything except books."

"Frances?" Jo managed to push a smile into place. Her middle name was Frances. Someone on his wife's side of the family must be named Frances. Why would he name his child after the sister who had abandoned them?

He nodded. "We named her after you."

Her lips started to tremble and holding her smile in place proved impossible. She blinked a couple of times to stem the burn of emotion. "Wow. That's…that's really nice."

The conversation lulled with nothing more than the sound of cups landing on the counter and water bubbling from the coffee maker to fill the lull.

Ray broke the silence first. "Mom really misses you."

LeDoux placed a cup of coffee on the table in front of Jo. To Ray he said, "Cream? Sugar?"

"Black is fine."

Before going for the next cup of coffee, he sent Jo a reassuring smile. Her lips struggled to return the gesture. This visit from her brother was unexpected, to say the least. Unwanted, not so much. And yet she wasn't sure how to feel or to proceed without dissolving into a blubbering mass of emotion.

Finally, she moistened her lips and spoke the truth. "I miss her, too. Miss both of you."

"We talk about you every day," he said, a tremor in his voice. "My kids think you're some kind of secret agent hero. We tell them your work keeps you away."

A new tremor started in her hands and worked its way through her whole body. "I'm glad."

LeDoux placed a cup for Ray on the table next to the sofa. "I have some calls to make. I'll be right outside."

Jo nodded. Wishing like hell he'd stay but, on some level, glad he wasn't.

When the door closed behind him, more of that heavy silence settled around the two of them. Jo and Ray. How long had it been since she'd sat alone with him? Almost eighteen years.

"Jo, I don't know what's happening here," Ray began, "other than what I've seen on the news. I guess with you being here, it's like before. The case of these two missing girls is like your case?"

"It is. We're pretty sure the same people who took me took these girls, too. One of the missing girls is his niece." She gestured to the door to indicate the man who'd stepped outside. "We're working hard to find them."

"You look really good," he said. "Strong and healthy."

He'd said that before. She smiled. "I've seen the kids on Facebook, your wife's page. They're beautiful, Ray, and so's your wife. And you own the garage now. I'm really happy for you."

"What do you do now?" he asked. He picked up his coffee and sipped. "Did you go back to school?"

She was the first one in the family to go to college. They'd all had high hopes. "I never went back to school. No. But I have a job I enjoy with an online newspaper. My boss is great and the environment suits me." Code for she never had to leave the apartment.

"That's good." He smiled. "I remember you worked on the high school newspaper. You enjoyed trying to dig up interesting stories."

More of that thick silence lapsed around them like a heavy fog. Ray focused on his coffee. Jo wished LeDoux would come back inside.

Finally, her brother stood. "I should head back home."

Jo stood. The trembling still plaguing her limbs. "I'm glad you came."

After nearly eighteen years was that the best she could do? She should say something more. Hug him again—something.

Instead, he moved to the door and opened it and she followed him outside. LeDoux sat on the steps at the back of the main house. Ray was halfway to his truck— she trailed two steps behind him—when he stopped and turned around to face her.

"I just want you to know that no matter how much time has passed not a day goes by without one of us mentioning you. Something always reminds us of you." He laughed and blinked furiously as if holding back tears.

Jo tried to speak. Wanted to say that she thought of them every day, too, but she couldn't bring herself to speak the words. She'd worked so hard to block the past, to cut all ties with the people she loved so she wouldn't ruin their lives the way she had her own.

He started to turn away again, but hesitated. "We've never stopped loving you, Jo-Jo. And we never will. You're part of our family and if you ever choose to come home for an hour or a day or forever, we'll be there waiting for you."

Tears flowed down her cheeks. Jo watched him walk to his truck. He'd reached for the door when she realized she could not just stand there and let him drive away.

"Ray!" She ran to him and hugged him hard. "I love you, too." She drew back. "All of you. When this is done, I'm coming home." She shrugged. "For an hour or a day... I don't know, but I will be there. I promise."

He hugged her again before climbing into his truck and driving away.

LeDoux walked up behind her, placed a hand at the small of her back. "You okay?"

She nodded. "I will be. As soon as I get these damned tears under control." She couldn't remember the last time she'd cried before coming back here. She'd locked away her feelings and focused solely on survival.

"What I did wasn't just for me," she confessed. "I walked away from my family to protect them from what happened...from what I became because of what happened." She hugged her arms around herself. "I wasn't the daughter and sister they lost. I couldn't be that person anymore and I didn't want to hurt them even more than they'd already been hurt. I did what I thought was the right thing to do."

"That's the only thing any of us can ever do."

Jo inhaled a deep breath. She had to finish this. For her family. She still had a family and by God she wanted to be part of it again. "We have to find Blume or whoever is behind this. We have to stop him."

"I called someone who might be able to help." LeDoux guided her back toward the cottage. "Nick Shade and Bobbie Gentry are as good as you can get when it comes to finding monsters. They'll be here tomorrow afternoon. They can help us."

"Thank you."

Maybe when this was over she could finally put the past behind her. Whether she could truly ever be a part of her family again, she couldn't say. But for the first time in nearly two decades she wanted desperately to try.

Once her family knew the whole truth, they might change their minds about wanting her back in their lives.

She was no secret agent and she damned sure was no hero.

# Thirty-Eight

*Day Eight*
*Eighteen years ago...*

The images are gone.

Ellen is gone.

No-Name and I are in a different place. We woke up here.

My heart is pounding. I am so hungry. I need water. My lips are so dry and cracked. My throat feels like I swallowed sandpaper.

No-Name and I sit next to each other. Our bodies are bruised and scratched. Bones maybe fractured. I have a couple of cuts that feel infected.

I wish I knew where Ellen is.

I wish I could go home.

"Stand up."

*The voice.* I take No-Name's hand in mine. For once she doesn't pull away.

"Stand up!"

Afraid not to obey, we get to our feet. Not so easy because we're so tired and weak.

"Step away from each other."

I hold tighter to her hand. He's going to make us fight again. I know it.

"Step apart!"

Her fingers slip from my grasp and I back up a few steps.

The lights come on.

Bright, blinding light.

I put my arm up to shield my eyes.

"Choose your weapon!"

I look around. Spot the pole—kind of like a pool stick except the same size on each end. There's also a whiplike leather thing.

"Choose your weapon!"

No-Name scrambles forward. I do the same.

I manage to take the pole away from her. She grabs the whip.

My eyes are burning like fire.

The lights go out.

I am at once grateful and terrified.

"You have ten minutes. Fail to fight and you lose by default."

Ten minutes—how would we ever hold out ten minutes?

The whip cracks and leather stings the skin across my chest.

I charge forward with the stick held lengthways in front of me. I knock No-Name to the floor.

Now if I can just keep her down for the next nine or so minutes, we both might make it.

# Thirty-Nine

*Lands Drive*
*Sunday, April 15, 10:00 a.m.*

Professor Orson Blume was sixty-eight years old. Based on the rundown Tony had received from one of his few remaining friends in the Bureau, the man inherited well, which explained his million-dollar estate on Lake Sinclair. He had a wife who had recently retired, as well. No children. None of his former colleagues at the college knew what he'd been doing since he retired. Not a single one was aware of his involvement in any project connected to the old asylum. A neighbor they had questioned this morning said that Blume and his wife were out of the country on a tour of Europe for their anniversary.

If that was true, then Blume was another dead end. Joanna insisted the voice that had given the orders while they were in captivity was male. There was a remote possibility it was Conway, but Tony didn't think so. Someone higher up the food chain would have been in control of the subjects, merchandise, whatever. Conway wasn't nearly smart enough to hold together this complicated maze of abductions, much less conduct any sort of organized operation. His haphazardness had been evident in his home movies.

Martin/Houser? Maybe. She'd appeared far smarter than Conway, but her lifestyle had been too risky. The person behind these abductions, and whatever the hell he or she accomplished with the results, was smart. Tony was sticking with the scenario that the abductions were related to some sort of research or were episodes to be sold on the internet. His money was on the former. Those taken for making snuff flicks or fight-to-the-death gladiator-type videos didn't typically survive. But none of the victims in question had ever popped up in known cases involving those types of abominable behavior.

It was as if the college girls were taken, used, and then released. No harm, no foul. Except for the *other girls*. The ones no one knew about who didn't survive.

Tony pressed the doorbell again. The chime echoed through the house. No barking dog. No television. Like last night, there was no one home. But at least it was daylight and they could have a look around.

As if she'd read his mind, Joanna said, "I'm taking a walk around the property." She headed down the front steps.

"Hold on. We'll do it together."

With the front windows blocked by plantation shutters there was no way to see inside. Maybe they'd have better luck around back. If they were caught it would be easy enough to say they'd thought the property was on the market. The one next door was for sale. So far he hadn't seen any nosy neighbors out and about other than the ones with whom they'd spoken. Tony had flashed his invalid credentials so the neighbors shouldn't give them any trouble.

He caught up with Joanna in the backyard. The view over the lake was peaceful, serene. He wondered how often the couple had sat on the back deck with a beer or a glass of wine and contemplated their life's work. When he reached that age would he have a body of good work on which to reflect? Or someone with whom to celebrate and travel? *Not at this rate, pal.*

A dock and boat garage along with a small private beach were among the amenities that went along with the lakefront property.

If Blume was involved with this—how many young women had suffered while the bastard sat in this elegant home?

Anger roared through Tony. His niece was out there, enduring God only knew what. *Shake it off. Stay on track.*

There was no time to waste. What they needed to determine as quickly as possible was if Blume's work included abducting and using young women for his own sick self-interests? Did his wife know? Was she involved, too? She was some sort of scientist. She apparently had retired from a reasonably prestigious career in the field of Cognitive Science at the University of Georgia in Athens, some seventy-five miles north of Milledgeville. With the husband's specialization in psychology, it almost made sense that the two were in this together—if they were involved at all.

*Grasping at slim leads, Tony.*

Maybe he was, but it was the only lead they had left. Joanna walked up onto the deck and peered through the towering windows that allowed the lake view into the back of the home. No shutters or drapes obstructed the key feature of the home. Since the rear of the house faced east, sunlight poured into the hearth and breakfast rooms as well as the kitchen.

She said, "The neighbor might be right about the Blumes being out of the country. It looks like they haven't been here for a while."

Tony picked up on the same details. The sun highlighted the fine layer of dust on the black granite counters and rich wood table. He ran his hand over the thickly cushioned back of one of the deck chairs. Dust- or pollen-coated, as well.

"Feels like no one's been around for a couple of weeks." Had they taken the girls, and then disappeared? Were they with the girls? Conducting their bizarre studies or orchestrating movieworthy scenes?

"I guess that rules out finding the victims in the basement," Joanna offered. "I was really hoping it was almost over."

Tony shrugged. "Maybe the victims aren't here but, if the Blumes are involved, there could be useful information in the house."

"The problem is, as Phelps will see it," she offered, "there's no true probable cause to go after a warrant."

He nodded wearily. "That's right."

Joanna stared at him for a long moment. The sun highlighted the weariness in her eyes and on her face. No matter how tired she was, she still looked far younger than her thirty-six years. Especially with the T-shirt and skinny jeans she'd grabbed at Walmart. She could be one of the college seniors visiting her professor. Looking at her made Tony feel old, though he was only a year older. And exhausted.

"I'm desperate," she said. "Am I in this alone, Agent LeDoux?"

"*Former* agent," he reminded her. "And no, you're not alone."

She lifted her chin in challenge. "Does that mean you're willing to break the law?"

They'd already bent it considerably. To be clear, he said, "Willing, ready and able."

She smiled. "Let's do this then."

He checked the rear door. Locked. Then he checked each of the windows. The third one from the door that looked into the hearth room moved.

"There could be a security system," she reminded him.

"Give me a minute."

He hustled down the steps and back to the end of the house where he'd noted the electrical meter as well as other typical utilities. The power had been turned off to the house. No power, no security system. Strange though. If the Blumes were on a vacation in Europe surely they intended to return. Why turn the power off? Wouldn't that present an issue with the insurance company?

He hustled back to the deck where Joanna waited. "Oddly enough, the power is off."

"That's weird, right?" She frowned. "People don't turn the power off to go on vacation."

"They don't," he agreed.

Tony raised the window and ducked inside. Joanna eased in behind him.

They moved through the downstairs rooms. Other than the recent layer of dust the home was tidy. Shelves were lined with books and photos. Artwork still hung on the walls. Drawers and cabinets contained the usual household items. But there was the distinct hint of that closed-up smell that went along with the idea that the owners had been gone for a while. Upstairs the bedrooms were in order. Clothes in the closets. Jewelry in the jewelry box. The house was stuffy without the circulation of the heating and cooling system.

Once back downstairs they headed for the basement. He'd spotted a flashlight in one of the kitchen drawers so he grabbed it en route. The door to the basement was in the hall off the kitchen. He clicked on the light and moved down the stairs. The basement was quite large. Thankfully four hopper windows lined the wall near the ceiling, allowing morning light to fill the room. He switched off the flashlight.

"Looks like they used this space as a shared office."

"Looks that way," she agreed.

Two large desks sat in the center of the space facing each other. Shelves lined with books covered most of the wall space. A couple of dead plants sat on the top shelf below the windows. A large, vault-style door stood at the end of the space. The digital lock was dark. No getting in there.

A file cabinet stood on either side of the door. Tony said, "Start going through the file cabinets and see if you spot any familiar names."

Since she had kept up with all those who'd gone missing over the years it would be easier for her to pick up on any familiar names. Though he doubted Blume would be careless enough to leave important files out in the open in file cabinets without locks. He figured the vault door was for those sorts of files.

While Joanna went through the drawers crammed with file folders, Tony went through the desks. The first, the wife's desk, was well organized. The top was neatly arranged with only a photo of the two from what appeared to be an awards ceremony. The wife held a plaque. The print was too small for him to read. The blotter pad was a crisp expanse of unmarked white. The desk drawers were uncluttered. Pens, pads, pencils and other office supplies were carefully arranged.

The husband's desk was completely opposite the wife's. The blotter was barely visible beneath the stacks of notepads and printed articles. He skimmed the notepads. Lecture notes. He moved to the desk drawers. More notepads, pencils, pens and other supplies—not so neatly arranged. In the bottom drawer he discovered two files. Tony sat down in the man's chair and opened the first of the two. The notes were recent. The files were not college students but those of patients at the forensic hospital for the violent, criminally insane still operating on the old asylum property. Apparently Blume had consulted on the two cases. So maybe this was the involvement his resource had meant.

Tony read over the notes related to a number of private sessions Blume conducted with the two inmates. Using his cell phone, he snapped a photo of the next of kin information for the two patients. Questioning the patients wouldn't be easily accomplished but talking to family would be simple enough. He might not have bothered at all except the patients were a part of the pockets of activities Griffin had mentioned still taking place on the property.

"I may have something," Joanna said.

Tony put the two files back into the drawer and joined her at the file cabinet on the right side of the vault door. She pointed to a heading on one of the folders. *Test Subjects 1-10.*

All the files that would have been behind that heading were missing.

"So he's either taken the files someplace else or he's destroyed them," Joanna offered.

"We can't be sure he's the one. These files may be his wife's. And they might not have anything to do with what we're searching for."

She looked at him. "Videos. We should search the whole house for videos."

"You make a good partner, Jo," he confessed.

She looked away, closed the file drawer. "Thanks."

"You don't mind if I call you Jo?"

She shook her head, met his gaze. "I guess, if we're partners, I should call you Tony."

He smiled. As tired as he was, it felt good to smile. "You should."

They went through the office first. They checked each shelf, each book. No hidden files. No hidden videos. Room by room, the first floor, then the second, they moved through the house. Not one file or video was tucked away. The search stole more than an hour.

"What we do have," Tony offered when she looked crestfallen, "are the names of family members for two patients Professor Blume was treating or consulting on at the forensic hospital still operating at the asylum.

Maybe we can get some idea of the kind of work he's doing from the families."

Jo countered, "Or maybe the neighbor is right and the Blumes are over in Europe seeing the sights. Or maybe they took a detour and are in Barbados soaking up the sun."

She looked ready to pull out her hair.

He cocked his head and pretended to ponder their dilemma. "As soon as I find my niece, I'm thinking I'm way overdue for a vacation. Barbados sounds perfect."

"Just promise you'll take me with you."

Before he could tell her that he had already considered extending the invitation, she walked out of the house and down to the car. From the front door Tony watched her settle into the passenger seat. He hoped like hell for his niece's sake—for Jo's sake—that he had one more hero card left in him.

As they drove away from the Blume residence, she said, "Tell me about this Nick Shade you called. I know Gentry is a detective. You told me what happened to her."

Tony wasn't sure a week would be enough time to explain to her who Nick Shade was. He had single-handedly turned the Bureau on its ear. They'd watched him for years, primarily because of his connection to Dr. Randolph Weller—a serial killer and the man who raised Nick. Tony and Nick had become allies of sorts when the Storyteller returned to Montgomery for the one that got away—Bobbie Gentry.

"Nick is a whole different kind of animal." Tony made the turn onto the highway. "He was raised by Dr. Randolph Weller, a renowned psychiatrist and a serial killer, one of the most heinous and prolific in recent history. He murdered more than forty people, including his own wife, and orchestrated the murders of numerous others. Nick was the one to discover his secret life and to turn him over to the cops."

"Good for Nick, but that had to be tough for him to get past."

"He had it rough for a while, that's true. What he did was dedicate his life to finding monsters like Weller, particularly the ones no one else can find. He's saved a lot of lives and brought countless serial killers to justice."

"Do you think he can help us find Blume or whoever is orchestrating these abductions?"

"I believe he can help. He's like a natural-born profiler. He can instinctively feel what the rest of us struggled for years to learn." Tony had concluded that truth had been part of the problem with him and Nick in the beginning. Tony had felt threatened by him. He was human. He'd worked long and hard to reach a high point in his career and Nick came into it with nothing more than his instincts. He was one of the few people Tony counted as a friend.

"I hope he can help."

Tony nodded. He was counting on Nick. Time was running out way too fast.

*Merry Drive, 11:45 a.m.*

Virginia Ruley was more than happy to talk. She invited Tony and Jo into her home and promptly proceeded to let it all out.

"My brother Eli was a sick man, there's no denying that fact," she said. "But what someone in that place did to him was just wrong."

"Who is it you believe did these things?" Tony asked since she didn't mention Blume by name.

She shrugged. "That's the sixty-four-thousand-dollar question."

Beside him, Jo sagged with defeat. They needed a connection to Blume, not another going-nowhere lead.

Tony asked, "Can you tell us what sort of things you mean?"

"Damn straight I can," Ruley piped up. "It's not like I can't talk about it. The lawsuit was dismissed. Since I'm not getting nothing for what that place put him through, I might as well tell anyone who asks what they're doing out there."

Tony exchanged a look with Jo.

"They were bombarding Eli with videos. No one was supposed to know. The hospital claimed Eli signed, giving permission to do all this experimental stuff, but I don't believe he would ever have imagined that it would be videos of people hurting each other. Murdering and maiming. It was sickening."

"You saw these videos?"

"No." She shook her head. "Eli told me about them. He said they worked him up something fierce but then they made him calmer. Said he didn't have no desire no more to hurt nobody, just wanted to watch other people doing it. I was glad for him but I found it disgusting."

"Did he say if it was men or women in the videos?" Jo asked, her voice hollow.

"Women. Young ones. He said it looked as real as anything he'd ever seen."

"So you confronted his doctor about this?" Tony asked.

"Sure did. He said I must have misunderstood. But I knew Eli wouldn't lie to me. Why would he make up such a thing? Didn't make a lick of sense."

"Who was your brother's primary physician at the hospital?" Tony needed a name.

"Dr. Lance McLarty." She shook her head. "He had a car accident right after I filed the lawsuit. Killed the bastard."

McLarty. Tony hadn't noticed the name in any of Blume's notes. Interesting that, like Dr. Alexander, he died in an automobile accident. "The lawsuit was dismissed despite your brother's statements?"

She nodded resignedly. "He had a heart attack right after I went to see a lawyer. So I didn't have no evidence except my word and that was considered hearsay since the person who said it was dead."

"Did any other doctors work with your brother?" Jo asked. "Do you know a Dr. Blume?"

Tony wished she hadn't mentioned Blume's name. They needed the facts, not supposition. If Blume had been involved with what this woman—a potential witness—knew, she would have said so. Leading her to what they wanted to hear was the wrong move.

The older woman perked up. "Do you mean Professor Blume from out at the college?"

Jo nodded as if she had realized her mistake.

"Oh yes, he was so kind. A friend of mine who works over at the college suggested I talk to him. He went over to talk to my brother about two months ago. He wanted to help. But my brother died pretty quick after that so I was too late. Professor Blume told me how sorry he was and that he'd see what he could find out anyway, but I never heard from him again."

Tony's hopes hit rock bottom again. Ruley certainly wanted to see Blume as the angel of mercy or hero of sorts, but was he the reason her brother had the heart attack? Didn't help the investigation that the persons of interest kept dying on them.

Jo asked, "Were there any other patients that you're aware of who had a similar experience at the hospital?"

"I talked to another woman, Geneva Corliss," Ruley said. "She was a patient in the hospital for a while. She claimed they did stuff to her but she couldn't remember much. She was seventy and never had any problems with her memory until her stay at that hospital. She was bedridden and dying of cancer. That's why she got out. But she refused to talk to the lawyer about it. Then she died. As you can see I didn't have no choice but to let it go."

"You've been through a terrible ordeal," Tony offered. "Did you ever speak with Professor Blume outside the hospital? In a private office perhaps?"

So far they hadn't found one, past or present.

"No. He hadn't seen patients for years, spent all his time helping the kids at the college. What he did for me was mostly a favor."

"Did you know his wife?" Tony asked.

Orson Blume wasn't the only Dr. Blume. Tony might be grasping at straws but he wasn't about to overlook any aspect of this flimsy lead. It was the only one they had at this point.

Ruley shook her head. "Can't say that I do. He wore a wedding ring so I presumed he had a wife but he never mentioned her and I never asked. I only met with him once but he spoke to Eli twice."

Had Dr. Blume, the professor, walked blindly into a situation that sent he and his wife fleeing to Europe? Maybe their vacation had been about escaping the trouble he'd unknowingly stepped into. Or this could simply be another dead end.

"Mrs. Ruley," Jo said, "were you aware of any other unusual treatments conducted in the area? Maybe in another of the buildings on the old asylum property?"

"I'm seventy-five years old," Ruley said, "and I've known people who were patients out there back in the late sixties and early seventies. I even talked to a few who had kin who was sent to that place way before that. What I can tell you is that nothing good ever comes outta that place. The patients suffered unimaginable horrors. From little kids on up to old people, it was like a mad scientist was running the place, trying to create his own versions of monsters like in the old movies."

"That's all closed down now though," Tony offered, trying to wrap his head around looking at the Blume situation from an entirely different angle. "There's not much happening out there anymore."

Ruley made a harrumphing sound. "So they say, but I hear rumors about all the secrets still buzzing around out there, like black flies after a rotting carcass. If I was you, I'd stay away from that place."

"I heard those missing girls were being held there somewhere," Jo suggested.

"I wouldn't doubt it a bit." Ruley bobbed her chin. "This town, for all its Old South, genteel ways, has that awful place right in the middle of it. Like a cancer sprouting right up from the heart. I don't think we'll be free of that nightmare until they tear down the last building and leave the dead to rest in peace."

Tony stood. "Thank you for your time, Ms. Ruley."

Jo followed suit, thanking the lady again.

The elderly woman saw them to the door and wished them luck. Tony had a feeling they were going to need it. Worry that he wouldn't be able to find his niece in time nagged at him.

"They did that to us." Jo stared at him across the top of the car.

"They did what to you?" Tony braced for more news about what his niece might be enduring to haunt him.

"The movies—images of people murdering other people. It was crazy and intense and all around us like the very walls, even the floor and ceiling, were one big movie screen." She shuddered. "It went on for days. But it was the screaming and moaning that was the worst. It was as if they wanted to desensitize us to the images and sounds."

Tony absorbed the information and filed it with the rest for later dissection. "Thank you for telling me. Anything you remember could be useful. Any connection to what happened to you could be relevant."

She nodded. "There's so much I buried. I hadn't thought of that until today."

As they loaded into the BMW, she asked, "What now?"

"I think it's time to go to Phelps and give him our theories and see if he's willing to follow up on what Blume was looking into and how the hospital ties into it. At this point, we might get more done working with the locals rather than around them."

Tony had thought he could come in here, work his magic and all would turn out the way he wanted, but that wasn't happening. The unsub—presumably Blume or someone he knew—hadn't made a new move since Tiffany and Vickie went missing. He was lying low and biding his time. What did that mean for the victims— like his niece? Had they simply been left to die? Fear coiled like a hissing snake in his gut. Tiffany and Vickie could be tucked away somewhere with no water or food while this sick son of a bitch waited for the heat to pass.

Tony had to find him.

There appeared to be three certainties in all this— the college, the clinic and the tie to the old asylum. The victims were plucked from the college. Jo had admitted that it was possible they were held on the old Central State asylum property. Blume was a logical connection. His work at the college and then his investigation of patient treatment issues at the hospital on the Central State property. It had to be him.

He'd had the file on both patients Mrs. Ruley mentioned in his desk, her brother and the Corliss woman. Had Professor Blume accidentally stumbled across the person behind the abductions who also abused patients at the hospital?

How the hell would they lure the bastard out of hiding?

It was damned hard to find a monster whose tracks ended at the edge of the forest.

# *Forty*

*Day Nine*
*Eighteen years ago...*

It's dark again.

I awoke on fire. My skin burns as if I've been scorched by flames.

The slashes where the leather whip bit into my flesh. My legs and arms feel so weak and limp. My body aches.

The only good news is that today there is water.

I'm grateful for the darkness. My eyes are still stinging from the movie images.

Ellen and No-Name are not here. I'm certain they've been taken to the other room to battle. Since No-Name beat the hell out of me, today is her day to show she is stronger than both Ellen and me.

Ellen was quiet after we were dumped back in this place. She still favors her right arm. But she seemed as strong as the rest of us. I wondered if maybe she got food while we were in the other place. She needed it. I was really worried about her. I hope she's strong enough to endure whatever happens today.

I haven't gotten any food. But then losers don't get fed.

I wonder what my mother and father are doing. They must be so worried. I wish I could spare them this nightmare. But I cannot. There's nothing I can do but try to survive.

And then what? I can't foolishly pretend I'll be set free no matter how strong I am.

My family will likely never see me again. I wonder if the police will figure out what was done to us. I suppose that depends on whether they find our bodies. My poor parents will be devastated. My brother, Ray, will be hurt, too.

No-Name never mentions her family. Ellen and I talk about ours often. Maybe No-Name has no family.

I think of the stupid mistake I made that caused me to end up here. How could I have been so blind and foolish?

If I make it out of here I wonder if I will ever see those people again. I'm sure it was that red-haired woman and the man I thought was so sexy.

My body shudders at the idea that he raped me. I want to ask Ellen and No-Name if he raped them but it's not exactly the kind of question you just pop up and say, "Oh, by the way did that handsome guy who helped land us here rape you while you were unconscious?"

What difference does it make?

God only knows if we are getting out of here. *Don't be stupid, Jo.*

Most likely we are dead even if we survive.

I force myself to stand and walk around the dark room. I need to keep my strength up by whatever means possible. I hate it when I'm in here alone. When Ellen is with me I can focus on helping her. Even No-Name gives me something else to focus on besides what's probably going to happen.

They've done terrible things to us already.

I can't even imagine what is coming next.

# Forty-One

Chiefs Buckley and Phelps took seats at the table, along with Agents Richards and Johnson and Special Agent George Wagner from the Georgia Bureau of Investigation. Jo got the impression Tony had met everyone except the GBI guy.

She'd started to itch as soon as they entered the campus security building. She'd been here before—seventeen years, eleven months and eighteen or nineteen days ago. She honestly couldn't remember the exact day. Right before she walked away from her life and never looked back.

How was it that nearly eighteen years later she was no better off? It felt as though nothing had changed. No one had been made to pay for what she and the others had lost, for the murders of those who didn't make it out alive. Instead, other girls were missing, other lives were in danger. And no one knew where to look or what to do.

She refused to count Madelyn and Miles as the only villains in this. There was someone else, she felt certain.

The GBI man spoke first, "Mr. LeDoux has explained how you came to him for help, Ms. Guthrie."

Her mouth felt so dry she didn't dare speak. She nodded, then reached for the bottle of water next to her. When they'd first arrived another uniformed member of campus security had placed bottles of water at each of their places at the table. Images of all those days in captivity and hoping for just one bottle of water flickered through her brain. He'd known exactly how far to go with the withholding of food and water. Take them to the brink, and then bring them back.

"At this time our full attention must be on finding Miss Durand and Miss Parton." Chief Buckley spoke next. He looked to Jo and said, "When we've brought them safely home, I hope you'll sit down with us and help us to understand where we went wrong protecting you and what we could have done differently."

Big breath. She found her voice. "I'm not sure there was or is anything you could do differently. The mistake was mine," she confessed. "The others would tell you the same if they could. We didn't protect ourselves and we paid a heavy price."

The men around the table glanced at each other.

"You have no idea where you were kept?" Agent Richards asked.

She had known it would be like this. She'd lived through the questions and the sometimes sympathetic, sometimes suspicious looks several times the weeks and months after she and Ellen were found alive. She couldn't give them what they wanted and for that she would always be guilty on some level in their eyes.

*Just answer the question, Jo.* "I believe it was some-where on the old Central State Hospital property."

Phelps and Buckley exchanged another look. "It's true you and Ellen Carson were found near the area. But, according to your statements after you escaped, neither of you could be certain of where you were held. Is that correct?"

"You asked me where I believed we were held and I answered. But, you're correct in that I can't be cer-tain." She cleared her throat and struggled to keep her voice steady. "Wherever we were, it wasn't just some thrown-together prison, not just a simple room. There were several rooms. All connected. The walls weren't drywall or paneling or block. They were like television screens, massive monitors. They could be completely black or blindingly white and they could display im-ages…videos. It could be freezing cold or burning up hot."

"I believe," Tony spoke up, "they were held in spe-cialized lab environments made for a particular set of testing procedures. Someone at the state level must have an accounting of any and all activities taking place on the old Central State Hospital property. It still belongs to the state—there has to be a paper trail." He looked from one man to the next. "Have there been, in the past or at present, researchers conducting activities that might require similar environments to what Ms. Guth-rie experienced?"

"Based on Chief Phelps's previous conversations

with you and what he has relayed to me—" Agent Wagner spoke first "—I've been doing some digging. There are twenty-three contractors who utilize space at the facility. The research activities of each, as you can imagine, are highly classified. We're going through one by one and requesting authorization to have a look around. Those who refuse will complicate matters, but we'll do our best."

"Which takes time," Tony argued. To the room at large, he said, "I understand what you're doing is necessary, but I would ask that you divide your assets into two teams. One working with the known contractors, and the other picking through the numerous supposedly vacant areas of the property. The unsub or unsubs we're looking for may not be operating legitimately. This may be a completely dark operation by someone who knows the place better than any of us. There's always the chance they are completely off the books."

"You're thinking this Professor Blume is somehow connected to the abductions," Chief Phelps said.

"The sister of one of his former patients/prisoners at the forensic hospital filed a lawsuit for treatment trials conducted on him and Professor—Dr. Blume looked into it. Then suddenly he and his wife go out of the country for an extended vacation. The electricity to their home has been disconnected. Would you turn off the power while you were away? What about security? Homeowner's insurance? We need to know if they left the country. What flights they took. We need to speak with Professor Orson Blume. The fact that there is a connection between Hailey Martin—Madelyn Houser—and him from two decades ago only solidifies my concern that there's more to his part in this than we can see."

"Houser was the professor's assistant for a good number of years," Buckley pointed out for anyone who didn't know.

"Ms. Guthrie," Tony went on, "has already told us of Houser's connection to her abduction and we have video taken from Conway's apartment proving a connection to the current abductions. Blume is a lead that needs to be followed quickly and thoroughly."

The room was quiet for ten or so seconds. Jo's pulse pounded with each one.

"We've been looking into Professor Blume," Buckley said. "He has no family beyond his wife, but most of his friends are current or former faculty members so it was relatively simple to get some recent background on him. According to those who know him best, the professor and his wife decided to take an extended vacation for their anniversary. Most got the impression they would be gone for several months. Agents Richards and Johnson have just this morning put into works an investigation into their whereabouts."

"What about Sylvia Carson?" Jo spoke up. "Has she been located?" For God's sake Ellen's parents were going through the horrors of having a missing child all over again. It was bad enough to live through it once. No family should have to go through that nightmare twice.

"We've had several tips come in on our BOLO for Sylvia Carson," Phelps said. "She used her debit card so we were able to confirm a stop at a gas station in Macon three days ago. The attendant confirmed she was driving a white Honda Civic."

"No sightings since?" Tony asked.

"She's taken to ground," Phelps said, "the best we can tell."

"Or she's driving something else," Tony argued.

"It's possible," Jo countered, "whoever gave Houser and Conway their orders has Sylvia."

Nods and grunts of agreement went around the table.

"Since we haven't discovered her car abandoned," Phelps said, "we're going with the scenario that she's in hiding, but we'll keep an eye on any vehicles reported missing, as well. She may very well have taken another vehicle."

"What about the missing weapon in Houser's home?" This from Tony.

"Since the weapon wasn't registered, it's hard to say." Phelps shook his head. "We believe it was a .38 based on the case she kept it in. Whatever it was, Carson likely took it with her."

"Where are the boots on the ground focused?" Tony wanted to know.

"We have people on Central State Hospital property," Buckley advised. "We have a committee of students who are helping with the questioning of other students. Every student on campus is being asked if they knew Tiffany or Vickie. We're hitting all the clubs, bars and restaurants suggested by those who knew the two best with flyers and pleas for help. Every detective and deputy in the county is shaking his or her sources. We have hundreds of volunteers working with us. The entire county is being turned upside down."

"Tip lines are still ringing off the hook," Phelps added.

More search options were suggested and discussed. Jo couldn't slow the pounding in her chest as the men went back and forth about the best way to find the unfindable. This—this meeting felt like a waste of time. They all—everyone at this table—should be out there searching.

"What about Dr. Alexander?" she blurted. No one had mentioned her and Jo was certain she was involved on some level with this.

All eyes shifted to her.

"She's still in guarded condition," Phelps said. "Her doctor has assured me that my detectives should be able to question her by tomorrow. We didn't find anything on her cell phone. She'd obviously deleted her call and text history. We've subpoenaed her phone records. We'll have those in a couple of days. Her husband was out of the country but he's back now. We've talked to him and he has no idea about her being involved with anything outside the clinic."

Jo nodded. She appreciated their efforts but they were getting nowhere faster and faster.

Tony said, "Ms. Guthrie and I would like the authority to continue our own search on the Central State Hospital campus. I'm hoping she might see something that triggers a memory."

An argument about the legalities of the proposition broke out among the members of law enforcement. Jo could hardly catch her breath as they went back and forth and back and forth. Didn't they understand that they were wasting precious time?

Phelps held up his hands for the others to quiet. "LeDoux is a former highly trained federal agent. He is fully aware of evidentiary procedures. I'm certain—" Phelps stared straight at Tony "—that if he stumbles upon possible evidence that he will immediately call me or Chief Buckley."

"Absolutely," Tony confirmed. "The only thing worse than not finding your unsub is screwing up the evidence and losing him in the courtroom. Do not forget for a moment that this is my niece we're talking about. No one wants to find her and to see that justice is served more than I do."

Buckley nodded. "It's in the best interest of these two missing students to do all within our power to find them. They've been missing far too long. If unorthodox measures are necessary, then so be it. I, for one, don't want to be the person who looks back at this time with regret."

Agent Wagner leaned back in his chair. "You'll get no argument from me."

Richards shook his head. "I'll need to speak with my superiors before I agree to having a disenfranchised federal agent stumbling around a potential crime scene."

Phelps crossed his arms over his chest. "Well, I tell you what, Agent Richards. You go ahead and speak to whomever you feel you need to, but since this is my jurisdiction, this is how we're going to do it." He turned to LeDoux. "As of right now, Mr. LeDoux, you're working as a special consultant to me and this department. You do everything you know to do to find these young ladies, but don't cross that line we talked about or your friends here will be the least of your worries."

"Thank you, Chief."

The meeting adjourned and Jo couldn't get out of the

building fast enough. She hurried down the steps and into the shaded yard. The security building was actually a historic home that had been renovated years ago. She scanned the neighborhood, the sorority houses, the buildings of the main campus where she'd started the rest of her life eighteen years ago.

One mistake had stolen that future from her and so many others, like poor Ellen.

Someone was going to pay for all the futures they'd stolen.

Whatever Tony had promised Phelps, she hadn't made the same promise. The bastards who did this didn't deserve their day in court.

Conway and Houser were already in hell where they belonged. If Jo had her way, the others would go straight there, too.

# *Forty-Two*

*Day Ten*
*Eighteen years ago...*

Ellen is back. She is seriously injured.

She keeps vomiting.

I demand to know what happened, but No-Name won't talk. She's hiding in the farthest, darkest corner of this place.

I hate No-Name. She isn't like us. She doesn't care if we all make it out alive. She only cares if she makes it.

Bitch!

I stroke Ellen's tangled hair. I whisper softly to her, promising her that she's okay now. I caress her skin. My fingers come away wet. I smell the sticky stuff and recognize the metallic odor of blood.

I search her body in the darkness for the origin of the blood and find a wound on her chest. A slash.

Dear God—had they been given knives?

Rage detonates inside me.

I shoot up and rush around the blackness until I find the fucking bitch who won't even tell us her name.

I launch onto her, straddling her skinny body before she can scramble away. I grab handfuls of her stringy black hair. "What did you do to her?"

I'm screaming, I know. I don't care who hears me.

She doesn't answer. Only whimpers.

I bang her head against the floor. "What did you do?"

"They gave us spears. We had to fight."

Her body starts to shudder and she sobs like a child. My fingers loosen in her hair.

This isn't her fault. She is like us. A victim. She's only doing what they make her do. What she must do to survive.

I get off her and pull her across the darkness until we find Ellen, and then we all lie there in a sobbing huddle.

The world we were snatched from no longer exists. There is only this place, this moment and our fears.

We now know the truth.

We're all going to die.

# Forty-Three

Before hellos or introductions, Tony hugged Bobbie Gentry. Nearly overwhelmed with emotion, it took him a moment to find his voice. She looked great and he was damned glad she was here.

"I'm grateful you were able to come."

"Nothing could have stopped us." She smiled. The darkness they had shared was an unspoken knowing between them. It was a bond that could never be broken.

He turned to Nick Shade and shook his hand. "Thank you for coming."

"You would do the same."

Yes, he would. Tony shared something intense with these two people and he was immensely grateful for their friendship.

Nick looked relaxed, at peace. Tony was glad. The sadistic serial killer who had posed as his father for most of his life was rotting in prison where he belonged.

Dying would have been too good for him. He deserved to live his final years having to mull over and over what he'd done to Nick and all his other victims. The bastard was in solitary confinement. All the benefits he'd once enjoyed for cooperating with the Bureau had been taken from him. He was merely an old man serving multiple life sentences.

He was nothing—no one—dying a slow, meaningless death.

"Joanna Guthrie," Tony said, "this is Sergeant Bobbie Gentry." He grinned at Bobbie. She'd received the promotion she deserved. She and Lieutenant Lynette Holt, the newly promoted unit commander, had rebuilt their homicide team. The former commander of homicide, Eudora Owens, was now the Montgomery chief of police and had married Bobbie's uncle. Life was good in Montgomery.

The two women exchanged a quick embrace.

"Nick Shade," Tony said.

Nick extended a hand to Joanna. "Tony filled me in on your situation. I hope we can help."

"Thank you." Jo shook his hand. "We need all the help we can get."

"Let's sit." Tony gestured to the booth he and Jo had claimed to wait for Bobbie's and Nick's arrival. "I've ordered pizza and a pitcher of beer."

As they settled into the booth Nick and Bobbie exchanged a glance. Then Bobbie said, "I'll have water."

Tony's jaw dropped. He laughed. "The two of you have news?"

Bobbie smiled. "I'm pregnant. We found out a few

weeks ago but haven't made the official announcement yet."

"Wow." Tony was so damned happy for them. "I'll bet Amelia is thrilled."

Amelia Potter was Nick's mother. He'd always assumed the woman married to Weller was his mother but that turned out to be a lie. Nick had been stolen from his mother when he was three years old. Amelia had spent a lifetime praying her son would one day come home to her, and he had. The investigation had concluded with that rare happy ending.

Nick nodded. "She's moving to Montgomery to take care of the baby after Bobbie returns to work."

"We've been trying to lure her from Savannah for months," Bobbie added. "It took a baby to draw her away from all she knows. We've promised to take her to Savannah often to see her friends."

The pizza arrived, Tony ordered water for Bobbie, and then brought the two of them up to speed on what he and Jo had learned since he called Nick last night. He'd never been more thankful for backup. The idea that he could be allowing his personal attachment to his niece to get in the way of what needed to be done wasn't lost on him.

After they'd polished off the pizza, Bobbie was the first to speak. "No ransom demands, no contact whatsoever. The victims simply disappear." She turned to Jo. "Frankly, if I didn't know your story and the story of the other victims you've followed, I would be leaning toward the human trafficking scenario."

"Unless this is an entirely different perpetrator," Nick said, "we can assume for the moment that this guy—

perhaps Blume or someone he's associated with—is gaining something else for his trouble."

Bobbie looked to Tony. "Have you considered the most likely motives?"

"I have. After hearing Jo's story, my first assessment was that our unsub was creating snuff films or gladiator-type videos for deep internet consumers. Then we found the sister of a very violent, mentally ill prisoner who was exposed to movies similar to the ones Jo and the others were forced to watch and I considered another possibility. Drug trials or unorthodox testing of some sort. We all know it happens. Usually in some foreign country where the laws are less stringent."

"They exposed us to extremely violent images," Jo explained. "Mrs. Ruley talked about her brother being exposed to the same sort of images. He told her that watching eventually relaxed him and depressed his violent urges, so to speak. But it also made him want to see more."

"Soothing the beast," Nick suggested. "I read a paper on research trials performed twelve or so years ago that suggested violent patients could be controlled if their urges were met with something that satisfied their cravings—like movies depicting the sorts of activities they desired to participate in. Exactly the opposite of what we've believed for decades about the impact of violence on the human psyche."

"That's the time frame of the abductions like mine," Jo pointed out. "They took place over a five-year period starting eighteen years ago."

"If I can locate the articles on those trials I might be able to find a name associated with the work. I believe the work was considered bogus and charges of misconduct were filed. Numerous studies have proven the theory wrong time and again."

"Which begs the question," Tony spoke up, "why repeat the trial? If the unsub who took Jo and the others nearly two decades ago is the one we're dealing with today, why reenact the same scenario? Unless, he's hoping for a different ending."

"Maybe he's using subtle differences or maybe this latest abduction has nothing to do with the previous study," Jo offered. "Maybe his colleagues discovered a more lucrative option for the same work."

"The film clips found on Conway's hard drives may be just the beginning," Tony interjected. "The little bit they were able to recover may only have been his secret cut. We could be looking at a much larger operation that is in no way related to the health or drug industry."

The server headed toward their booth and Tony waved her away. "Let's assume the new wave of abductions is not related to Blume or anything he's involved with, but only to Conway and Houser. What if the two of them picked up where their former boss left off? What if there have been numerous other abductions we're not considering? Hundreds of young women go missing in the Southeast every year. Many are never heard from again. This taking of two college students in the same manner as the older abductions may have been coincidence or a stupid mistake."

"You're right. We can't assume," Nick picked up from there, "that we're dealing with the same scenario as eighteen years ago. This may be a whole different game."

The realization shook Tony. Why hadn't he seen that sooner? He'd grabbed on to the first feasible scenario and hung there for days. He knew better but he'd allowed his emotions to blind him. He'd wanted Tiffany's abduction to be like Jo's. He'd wanted to believe she was alive and would be coming back, battered and bruised but alive. How selfish was that?

He took a breath. "Tiffany and Vickie may not have any time left." He looked to Jo. "They could be dead already."

"No bodies have been found," Bobbie argued. "We should still operate under the assumption they're alive."

Tony rode out the wave of knots twisting in his gut. "Right. The Bureau is working on the hard drives found in Conway's apartment to see if they can pull off anything else. Houser had a laptop for her security system but there was little else on it. Her cell phone hasn't been recovered. Conway's either for that matter. In all probability both were taken by Sylvia Carson, their murderer."

"What about Blume?" Nick wanted to know. "Has his office been checked? His home?"

"He cleared out his office at the college when he retired," Tony explained. "Moved everything to his home." He glanced at Jo. "We had a look around inside the house and didn't find anything useful."

"We couldn't get into the safe room," Jo reminded him.

"Safe room?" Bobbie asked.

"Yeah." Tony nodded. "A part of his basement office was portioned off and the door was like one you would see on a bank vault. I'm working on local law enforcement to seek a warrant to have a look inside, but, as you know, that can be problematic when you don't have probable cause or strong evidence."

"Let's put it all on the table," Nick said. "We have two people—Conway and Houser—involved in abductions between fifteen and eighteen years ago. Their involvement was confirmed by multiple witnesses. Those same two people have been confirmed by eyewitnesses as a part of the most recent abductions. Our problem is, both are dead. So, we're left with a single thread that ties to both sets of abductions."

"Professor Blume," Jo said.

Nick nodded. "We need inside that safe room. Today."

*Lands Drive, 7:30 p.m.*

Tony's insistence that Blume's involvement could not be overlooked had paid off. No sooner than Nick had made the statement about needing to see in the safe room back at the pizza joint, Phelps had called. He had decided it wouldn't hurt to take a look inside the Blume home.

Time was required for Phelps to assemble the necessary personnel. Finding a judge willing to sign the warrant ran even more time off the clock. While Phelps had taken care of the official steps, Tony had tracked down the company who installed the safe room.

As it turned out, the safe room was actually like a room within a room in the basement. Concrete walls eight inches thick with a web of rebar snaking around inside all that concrete. Ten feet by fifteen feet in size with the standard eight-foot ceiling height. Emergency lighting in case the power went off and hidden air intakes—not large enough for anyone to climb through. The thickness of the walls had been the sticking point for Tony. Cutting through it would take hours. Blowing a hole in it might damage any potential evidence inside. That left one option—use the keys. The vault-style door required either a combination or a set of two keys. A whirlwind search of the house had not revealed the keys or the combination.

Fortunately, the owner of the company, Dennis Horton, who designed and installed the safe room had master keys to all the safe rooms he installed. The safe room as well as the installer was registered with the county. In the event of a disaster, tornado, fire, or whatever, if those inside were unable to get out of the safe room for any reason, the installer would be called to open the door.

By the time Phelps and his team were on-site, Tony had Horton standing by.

"This is costing the city a small fortune," Phelps said. "I hope your hunch is right, LeDoux."

"I guess we'll see in a minute."

Though Tony had explained that Bobbie was a detective from Montgomery and Nick was a special advisor for the Alabama Bureau of Investigation, Phelps insisted they stay outside the house with Jo.

In a strictly legal sense, Tony understood his reasons, but it was difficult to accept that edict when coming from a personal place. This was deeply personal for him and for Jo.

His sister and her husband were doing their part.

Continuing to speak to the community through the media. They were working with the Partons and the students at the college in hopes of finding someone who saw something they didn't know about yet. In Tony's opinion Buckley was a genius for putting the parents in positions of responsibility working with students who wanted to help.

He hoped like hell he'd have something significant to share with Angie after this. He'd been here five days without making any measurable progress in finding Tiffany. This case had to start moving forward soon.

The locks clicked and Horton stepped back. "It's ready to open. I'll wait outside with the others."

Smart man. There could be anything inside, including a booby trap. Not exactly what he would hope to discover in the home of a psychology professor and a scientist, but one never knew.

Tony and Phelps stayed behind a protective portable wall that had been prepared at the other end of the basement while the bomb squad checked out the situation.

Tony held his breath. No explosions. No orders to mask up due to a released potentially toxic gas. Bomb squad came out; two detectives went in. The door was left open this time and what did waft from beyond those thick concrete walls was a horrendous stench Tony knew all too well—that of at least one rotting corpse. His heart dropped somewhere in the vicinity of his shoes.

The chief and a two-man forensic team went in next. The chief didn't much more than poke his head inside before moving away from the door and calling for the coroner.

"Suit up and have a look-see," Phelps said to Tony. "Can't say if it's Blume in there, but based on the clothes should be male. Since he's lived in Milledgeville his whole life, we should be able to round up dental and medical records and get an ID fairly quickly. Meanwhile, I'll try to run down the wife. Obviously the two aren't in Europe as their friends and neighbors believe."

"Thanks. I appreciate you trusting my instincts, Chief."

He gave a nod and started for the stairs, his cell already attached to his ear once more. Tony pulled on shoe covers and gloves and headed into the fray.

Inside the safe room were a small sofa, a desk, five four-drawer file cabinets and a couple of tall storage locker-type cabinets. At the desk the rotting corpse sat in the upholstered swivel chair. A pair of dark trousers and a man's button-down shirt had collapsed against bone as the flesh and tissue beneath it dissolved. Body fluids had seeped into the upholstery and slid off onto the faux wood floor, forming a slimy puddle. A ring that had once been on a finger stuck up in the yellow, gooey mass. Tony recognized a Rolex watch still on the victim's wrist.

"The Rolex will have a serial number," he said to the detective.

The detective nodded his understanding. "Coroner's on the way. We'll be sure to take the watch into evidence as soon as he gives us the okay."

"Thanks." Tony put his forearm over his nose to help block the smell and used his cell to take a photo of the ring and the Rolex.

Amid the muck on the floor below the wrist with

the Rolex was a Ruger 9mm. The right side of the skull was shattered, rotting tissue still hanging around the broken bone.

It was entirely possible the professor had shot himself in the head just as the scene would suggest. The question was, who locked him inside this room after the deed was done?

Tony moved on to the file cabinets. Most of the files were of students from the college. Blume had kept copious notes on the students with whom he worked. Tony flipped through the hundreds of names. When he'd gone through the cabinets without finding a suspiciously marked file or a name related to the case, he moved to the first of the two upright storage type cabinets. The cabinets were wood with two doors and a single lock. The second cabinet was not locked.

A detective joined Tony at the cabinet. "I'll get this one open if you want to move on to the next one."

"Thanks." Tony sidestepped to the next cabinet and considered the three-inch binders stored there. He reached for the first one on the highest shelf. Test Subject #2 Ellen Carson.

The find sent a shot of adrenaline firing through his chest. He moved on to the next and the next. Files dating back eighteen years, including the other women in Jo's scrapbook were there. There were a couple dozen files—women and men. Ages varied from late teens to midtwenties. Each was labeled with a Test Subject # whatever.

They were all here—except Jo's.

Tony moved to the other cabinet the detective had opened. No binders in there. This one contained supplies. Reams of paper. Ink cartridges. Pad, pens. The usual.

Where the hell was Jo's file?

Tony walked back to the desk and looked around. He picked through the papers until he found one with Jo's name. He crouched down to look under the desk. He had to lean just so to see beyond what was left of the professor draped in the chair.

And there it was. Another three-inch binder on the floor far beneath the desk. Blume must have removed the contents and tossed the binder out of his way. Judging by the pages on the desk he'd been reading Jo's file when he shot himself or someone else did the honors.

"LeDoux," the second detective called from the other side of the room. "You'll want to see this."

What looked like a copy machine or printer sat on the table where the detective waited. He held two sheets of paper he'd pulled from the paper tray. The pages had been faxed from Dr. Ima Alexander's office. Examination conclusions on Vickie Parton and Tiffany Durand.

Son of a bitch. One or both of the Blumes were involved. "Thanks."

The detective nodded. "This is what we've been looking for."

The detective was right. Tony turned back to the decomposing professor. Unless his wife was involved, how the hell would they find Tiffany now?

A forensic tech found Blume's wallet in his trousers. Amid the mass of papers on the desk they also found what appeared to a suicide note.

I cannot live with what I've allowed to happen.

It was signed Orson Blume.

A handwriting expert would be required to determine if the signature was Blume's. Jesus Christ. Why couldn't they have found this days ago?

Tony thanked the forensic techs and the detectives and exited the safe room. He peeled off the shoe covers in case he'd picked up something that might be scattered to other parts of the house, but he kept the gloves on. He headed upstairs, moving from room to room until he found what he was looking for. A photo that showed Blume's left hand and right wrist.

The ring currently trapped in the goo and the Rolex on the skeleton's wrist were the same. Had to be Blume. Despite the jewelry and the wallet, an official ID confirmation would be necessary.

Hopefully the coroner could confirm tonight.

From the conditions of the cool, dark room, maybe sixty degrees, and the decomp of the body, Blume had likely been dead three or so weeks.

Whatever happened in this house, one thing was abundantly clear: Orson Blume couldn't have taken Tiffany and Vickie… He had an unshakable alibi.

He was dead.

# Forty-Four

*Day Eleven*
*Eighteen years ago...*

The lights are on—the walls are no longer black, they're white. There's a cage-like door with a big lock over the opening between this space and the one above us. I don't know what this means.

It's so bright we can't bear to open our eyes for long. It burns.

Ellen is better. No more vomiting. The bleeding has stopped.

No water today.

No food.

I'm so hungry and thirsty. I tell myself not to think about it but it's so hard.

I have come to realize that no one is coming to save us.

We will die here.

"My name is Carrie."

I try to open my eyes and look at No-Name. "Carrie?" My lips split further even as I say her name.

Her knees are pulled to her chest. She lowers her face to her arms to shield her eyes from the light. "Carrie Cole."

I shelter my eyes the same way. "Joanna Guthrie. My friends call me Jo." She already knows my first name but she doesn't know my last.

"Ellen Carson."

Ellen is lying on her side, curled into the fetal position. She sounds so tired. So weak.

The light feels so hot, like the blaring bulbs in a tanning bed. My skin feels as if it's blistering, too.

Don't think about it. I say, "I have a brother named Ray."

"I only have my mother," Carrie says. "She doesn't even know where I am. I got mixed up with drugs when I was sixteen. She threw me out. I don't blame her. I was one crazy bitch."

"I want to go home," Ellen whispers so softly I can hardly hear the words.

I sigh. "Me, too."

Carrie says, "We can't let them win. No matter what."

"No matter what," I agree.

"I don't know if I can fight again," Ellen whimpers.

I reach out and squeeze her arm.

There's nothing else to say.

"Let's make a deal," Carrie says.

"Okay," I murmur.

"If just one of us gets out of here, promise to find the families of the others and tell them we love them.

I mean, I don't have anyone but my mom but I'd like her to know since I've been such a shit to her. I wish I could do my life over."

"I like that deal," I tell her.

"Me, too," Ellen whispers.

For the next few minutes we talk about home and who our parents are. Then more of that silence closes around us.

"But we won't have to worry about doing any of that," I say with renewed determination, "because we're all getting out of here together."

*Alive, I pray.*

# Forty-Five

Tiffany wasn't sure which of them was hurt the worst.

Vickie just lay on the floor saying nothing. Lexy was curled up in a corner. They should close their eyes but the two of them just stared unblinking at the images.

At first it felt like the people in the movies or whatever it was were real. Even now, Tiffany reached out and tried to touch the moving images.

"Not real," she murmured.

Maybe she wasn't even real anymore.

Maybe they were all dead—zombies or something.

She had thought she preferred the darkness to the light but now she didn't care which came as long as the pictures stopped.

The people in the movie or whatever it was were slashing and stabbing each other. Limbs were chopped off. Heads severed. Eyeballs poked out.

It didn't stop. She couldn't say for sure but it felt like the movie had been playing for days. The words *murder, murder, murder* kept floating across the images.

Then it would change to *kill, kill, kill*. And then *survive, survive, survive*.

Tiffany closed her eyes and put her head down. She didn't want to watch.

She wanted to think of home. Of her mom and dad and her uncle Tony.

They were looking for her, she was certain.

The others didn't believe. They were sure there was no surviving because no one was coming. But Tiffany refused to give up.

She couldn't estimate how long it had been since they ate. Two or three days. No water today either. Her lips were so dry and cracked. Every bone and muscle in her body seemed to ache.

She had dried blood all over her. It hurt to pee. She wasn't sure why, maybe because she wasn't getting enough water.

Her coordination was off.

And she was so tired. She just wanted to close her eyes and sleep but her body refused to shut down enough to allow sleep to come.

The movie suddenly stopped and the screaming began. So loud, so many different people screaming.

Tiffany covered her ears.

She scrambled to her feet and tried to remember where Vickie and Lexy were lying.

A body slammed into her and knocked her on the floor.

Tiffany tried to scramble away.

"They told me what you said!"

Lexy's voice.

Tiffany tried to fend off her blows. "What are you talking about?"

"You said you were going to kill me in my sleep!"

What the hell was she talking about?

Lexy suddenly flew off her.

Tiffany scrambled away.

"You're the one!"

Vickie's voice.

"You told them you want to kill *me* because I'm weak." Vickie screamed the words. At Lexy, apparently, since she wasn't close to Tiffany.

The screaming stopped. Tiffany's ears rang but she could still hear the smacks and punches coming from the other two.

She felt her way to them and pulled Vickie off Lexy.

"Stop it! This is what they want us to do!"

Vickie tried to break loose. Tiffany kept her arms locked around Vickie's skinny body.

"I don't trust either one of you," Lexy snarled.

"That makes two of us!" Vickie shouted as she jerked away from Tiffany. "I don't trust anybody!"

Tiffany drew as far into a corner as possible. Any hope she had clung to that they might survive faded.

They were never getting out of here.

# *Forty-Six*

*10:00 p.m.*

If Madelyn hadn't answered her text when she did, there would have been hell to pay. She'd said she would arrive within the next five minutes. Madelyn was the only other person who knew the location of the testing facility.

She was also the only person in this world that Pamela trusted.

Pamela Blume was not a patient person, nor did she trust easily. Despite turning sixty-two next month, age had not mellowed her. Orson should have understood her need to reach beyond his wildest dreams.

Men were never really satisfied. Pamela had lived in Orson's shadow in this Podunk town for more than thirty years—since she lost the grant for her first research endeavor. Losing that one wasn't so bad, but every subsequent application was overlooked or turned down. Her work had been pushed aside repeatedly for that of her male peers. Eventually she had realized what she needed to do. Her adoring husband had gladly turned over large chunks of his inheritance without question to make her happy. Five years of risky studies had been required to reap the attention she deserved. Her published works were now considered some of the most respected in the field of Cognitive Science.

The results of the secret work she had done all those years ago had garnered the attention of the military. They wanted soldiers who would kill without thought. Insurgents who would go in killing without blinking, no matter the target. Pamela had chosen the least likely of humans to turn into killers, and then she'd chosen targets who wouldn't be missed. The homeless and the destitute—the parasites of society. That research had made her career.

But the real return on her investment had come from those whose salacious desires could only be sated by watching the most heinous of acts. With Madelyn's help, Pamela had found a market deep in the darkest parts of the World Wide Web that allowed her the luxury of no longer needing her husband's money or the respect of her pompous peers.

Dear Orson's initial investment had made it all possible. But Pamela most appreciated his introducing her to Madelyn. She smiled. She loved Madelyn so. Now that Pamela was financially secure, the two of them were relocating to Thailand—a place where they could live the rest of their lives as they wished. But first they would need to ensure that any trouble from the past could not follow them. Madelyn's idea to frame Orson had been ingenious.

Before their plans were finalized, Orson discovered Pamela's secret files. Worse, he spoke to that fucking old hag who filed the lawsuit against her protégé, Dr. McLarty. In Pamela's darkest moment, Madelyn had again taken charge. Using Conway, she set in motion McLarty's fatal accident, neatly tying up that loose end. Under Madelyn's direction Conway abducted three young women, just as he had all those years ago. Every single piece of evidence, even Pamela's secret files, were arranged to point to Orson as the perpetrator of those evil deeds.

Her dear, oblivious husband would have been the perfect scapegoat. The plan would have worked beautifully, too, had Orson not killed himself before she was ready for him to die.

If only the old fool hadn't decided he couldn't live with what his discovery meant: his wife had committed these atrocities right under his nose. He would be dragged through the mud in the courts and the love of his life would be taken from him. So he'd killed himself.

Pamela could fix that problem. When she was ready, she would burn the contents of the safe room, save certain evidence and his suicide note, along with his body and then the house. His charred remains would be found, the only residual evidence would point to what he'd done and Pamela would be far away.

Then Conway had to go stupid. Madelyn had done all she could to cover any tracks he may have left. Men were such fools. He'd risked everything for sex. Idiot. Again, not an unsalvageable situation. Any videos the police were able to collect from Conway's apartment would only reinforce the theory that he was working with Orson.

Then Ima had come face-to-face with test subject #1. Joanna Guthrie was here and she had joined forces with the FBI agent. She could very well ruin everything. Time was running out.

Pamela stared at the monitor and the three women who were nearing the end of their young lives. Unlike all the other studies, this time no one would survive.

Now it was time for Pamela and Madelyn to go. As soon as she arrived, they were leaving. No more waiting. The risk was far too great at this point. The test subjects would die and that was that. All evidence would lead back to Orson. Since there was no time to burn the house as she'd planned, the police would determine that Conway had been doing Orson's dirty work for him and, upon finding his body, had decided to follow through with their latest venture without his partner.

Pamela shut down the monitors, set the system to erase all data and picked up her small briefcase that contained everything she needed for her and Madelyn to begin their new lives. She checked to see that her stun gun was there—just in case—then she left the small office behind, moving through the dark corridors by memory. The area had once been a disaster shelter for the patients housed in the building, but more than half a century ago it had been deemed unsafe. Pamela had turned the long forgotten space into a state-of-the-art lab.

At the end of the main corridor the old staircase brought her up to the tiny ramshackle place that had once been a guard shack. She closed the secret door that blended perfectly into the worn tile floor.

Madelyn's Jag was waiting outside in the darkness.

Anticipation making her pulse flutter, Pamela hurried around to the passenger side and slid into the seat. "Let's go."

"I was expecting a man."

The blonde woman who stared at her, a gun in her hand, was very young and the look in her eyes told Pamela she was more than a little mentally unstable. Pamela's first instinct was to run but the initial shock of the situation made her hesitate. "Who the hell are you? How did you get here?"

The woman shrugged. "It was easy. I just checked her navigation history and selected the most logical of her frequented locations."

"Where is Madelyn?"

"Dead. I killed her."

Pamela bit back the scream but she could not contain the moan. When she could breathe again, she demanded, "Who are you?"

"I'm Sylvia. You might remember my mother, Ellen Carson? She told me all the things you did to her...what you made her do. Now she's dead."

"I'm sorry for your loss but that is not my fault." Pamela filled her voice with uncertainty and adopted a pleading expression. "It was my husband who did all those things to your dear mother and the others. I learned of the evil he had done and—"

"No." Sylvia shook her head. "That's not true. You see, right after I killed him I watched the videos my father had on his computers. He recorded all the times that your friend Madelyn yelled at him. You're working with Madelyn, that makes you the one."

Stupid bastard. Miles Conway had raped many of the test subjects but Madelyn hadn't told Pamela until after he was dead.

Pamela should have killed him herself years ago.

She squared her shoulders and lifted her chin. "Your

mother volunteered to be a part of my program." With nothing but the car's dash putting off soft light, Pamela was able to inch her right hand into her case. "I really am sorry your mother died."

"She didn't just die," the girl shouted. "She killed herself because of what you did to her. And I know she didn't volunteer for anything. That piece of shit who raped her took her. Her friend Joanna figured out who he and the blonde woman who helped him were so it was easy for me to find them. I planned their murders for weeks. I made sure they both got exactly what they deserved."

*Joanna Guthrie.* That relentless bitch had spoiled everything. She had walked away with her life. What else did she want? Fury swelled inside Pamela. Madelyn was dead and it was Joanna's fault. She would pay for taking Madelyn from her.

"Wait," Pamela said suddenly. "Don't you want to rescue the missing girls first? If you kill me, they'll die. I'm the only one left who knows where they are. Your mother would never want you to do that."

Carson looked like a deer trapped in the headlights for a moment. "Show me where they are. Right now."

"You'll have to follow me."

"Just remember I've already killed two people," Carson warned. "I'll kill you, too. I don't care how many have to die before I'm finished."

"I'll do whatever you say," Pamela promised.

The girl didn't know it yet, but she was walking into her own grave.

Joanna Guthrie was going to die, too.

She had taken the one person Pamela truly loved—nothing else really mattered.

# *Forty-Seven*

*Day Twelve*
*Eighteen years ago...*

I don't know how many days have passed with no food. No water yesterday or today.

My skin burns like fire from the intense lights.

My brain refuses to shut down. I cannot sleep.

Ellen lies on the floor, not moving, not speaking, eyes closed.

Carrie doesn't move much either but she curses every now and then. He—whoever their captor is—has not spoken again.

Has he left us here to die?

It feels as if we are very close to death.

I think we've reached a place where we must choose to go on or to give up. I'm so tired and I hurt all over. I'm not really hungry anymore but I am very, very thirsty.

*Don't give up, Jo.*

Her brother, Ray, would shake her and say, you're no

quitter, Jo-Jo! You're just starting. We're a tough bunch. We don't give up. Look at what Dad accomplished in his life with nothing more than sheer determination.

Her brother would be right. Their father had no education, no money and no family to back him up when he aged out of the foster care system. But he didn't let that stop him. He worked hard doing any job he could find. No matter if it was digging ditches or washing cars or repairing cars, he did his very best. A few years later he was the top mechanic at the used car lot where he worked. Before long he was the shop foreman at a dealership. All with a sixth-grade education and pure determination.

I drag myself up. My daddy always says I'm like him. He says we have grit. Well, it's time I start acting like it.

"We have to get up." I open my eyes just enough to see. "We have to walk around." I reach for Ellen and start to pull her up. She doesn't look happy about it but she eventually stands. Her legs try to buckle.

"Get up, Carrie! We have to move around."

She groans and curses but she, too, struggles to her feet. I pull her to my side. With Ellen on one side of me and Carrie on the other, we walk around the room, holding on to each other for support.

We alternately laugh and cry but we keep going.

We aren't going to die today.

# Forty-Eight

The coroner with the help of a medical examiner from Macon had spent most of the night attempting to determine if Professor Orson Blume had committed suicide. The final conclusion was that he had, in fact, taken his own life.

At daybreak this morning Tony and Jo, along with Nick and Bobbie, had headed out to the Central State Hospital property. Their search had begun with the old cemetery. The idea that all those people were buried there with nothing more than numbered iron markers—most of which were now lost—was mind-boggling. They'd found no indication of new graves anywhere in the area so they'd moved on to join the other search teams.

Milledgeville PD had begun an investigation into Blume and his wife, who was still unreachable. Colleagues and neighbors insisted both were out of the country. Obviously that was not true. One friend of Pamela's suggested the two were rarely ever seen together anymore. Blume had retired and was busy writing a book on his life's work while his wife was still striving for the brass ring in her career.

Agent Johnson had checked with the Bureau and Pamela Blume hadn't left the country unless she'd done so using a passport other than her own. She was still here, somewhere. Tony suspected tying up loose ends before she disappeared.

He needed her to be here. He needed to find her. Otherwise Tiffany and the others might not be found in time. Wherever she was, a BOLO had been issued.

Tony needed to be back out there with Jo, Bobbie and Nick searching the hospital grounds. But Phelps had wanted him here for the morning briefing with the joint task force. This thing had grown far too big to be held in the small campus security conference room.

They'd gotten nothing on the BOLO for Sylvia Carson. She'd vanished the same way Tiffany and Vickie had. MPD had found her Honda Civic in Madelyn Houser's garage. Phelps had apologized profusely that his detective hadn't checked the license on the vehicle in Houser's garage. The vehicle had been backed in so the plate wasn't readily visible. The detective had assumed the car was Houser's. Carson had used the Jag to keep a step ahead of the police. There had been no sightings of the Jag either.

How the hell could they lose four women and one Jag in a town this small?

Volunteers from several counties had arrived to help

with the search. Tony was grateful for every pair of boots on the ground.

His cell vibrated and he fished it from his pocket. A number he didn't recognized flashed on the screen.

"LeDoux."

"Mr. Gates?"

Tony hesitated, then remembered giving that name at the walk-in clinic. "Speaking."

"Oh, good, hello. This is Renae from the walk-in clinic. I'm sorry to bother you. I know this is a terrible time for your family."

"No, hey, I'm glad you called." He stepped out of the conference room. The briefing was over and most had gone on their way. A few uniforms were still mulling over maps. "Do you have some news for me?"

"I don't know what difference it makes, but I think I do."

"You never know what might help," he offered.

"I guess you heard about Dr. Alexander. She was in a terrible car accident the same day you and your wife were here. Well, she died this morning."

Tony hadn't heard that news. "That's a shame. I'm sure she'll be missed."

"You know, I almost didn't call because it felt like I was going behind her back, but she's gone and there's no help for that. I want to do whatever I can to help your wife find her sister."

"I really appreciate that, Renae."

"I was looking through Tiffany Durand's and Vickie Parton's files and I saw where the office administrator had sent a copy to Dr. Blume. You might know him as the psychology professor at the college, though I think he's retired. Since neither woman was a patient of either one of the Doctors Blume, I found that odd. The report explained how both women were in good health and excellent mental condition. I asked our lead nurse but she's so upset right now she blew me off."

"You can't tell if the reports were sent to Orson Blume or Pamela Blume?"

"Sorry, it just says Blume."

"What about the address?"

"It's an address on Lands Drive."

They had found the two faxed reports at the Blume home but they still didn't know which Blume was the intended recipient. "Anything else?"

"That's all for now. I really hope you find your sister-in-law."

Tony did, too. "Thank you for calling me."

Tony moved back into the hall, headed for the lobby. The sooner he was back out there helping with the search the better. His nerves were jumping. His cell vibrated again. *Angie.* "Hey, sis. I'm just leaving the task force briefing."

"Oh God, Tony. Steve's had a heart attack."

"Is he okay?" Tony pushed through the front entrance doors and hustled to the parking area and his car.

"He's stable, but…" Her voice broke. "I'm scared, Tony."

"You're at the hospital here, in Milledgeville?"

"Yes."

"I'll be right there."

"No, please. They're talking about transferring him to Macon. I need to know you're out there trying to find Tif. Please, Tony, I can't leave but how can I stay with him if you're not out there trying to find my baby. Please, promise me."

"Don't worry, I'm heading back to the search now. You keep me posted."

"I will." Her voice rose on each syllable.

"Ang," he exhaled a big breath, "I love you."

"Love you, too."

He shoved the phone back into his pocket. "God-damn it." This was too much.

He fired up the BMW's engine and roared out of the parking slot. Today, he was going to find Tiffany. Her mom and dad couldn't take any more.

He didn't see any scenario that put Pamela Blume in the clear. She was somehow involved with the ab-ductions. There was no other explanation for her sud-den disappearance—unless she was dead, too. His gut clenched. Until he had a body, she was all he had in the way of a real lead. She had to be alive.

Maybe she and her husband were in it together. Her research in Cognitive Science could definitely be tied to the kind of treatment Jo and the others had endured. They were cautiously optimistic that she was still in the area, which could mean the victims were, as well.

All they had to do was find them.

Five minutes later he made the right onto the campus of Central State Hospital—the former Georgia Lunatic Asylum. He wound around the streets. Official vehi-cles and those of volunteers filled the parking lot of the Powell Building. He drove on until he located Nick's vehicle near the Ingram Building.

The search teams were going through each standing building, one by one. Tony walked through the gate of the twelve-foot wire fence as Nick, Bobbie and Jo were exiting the building.

"Any news?" Jo asked.

She looked so tired. Tony wished he could find Tiffany and the others and end this for all concerned. He shook his head. "Nothing really. Alexander's nurse called. She confirmed the reports we found at the Blume residence were faxed from Alexander's office. She also told me the doctor died this morning."

"You okay?" Bobbie asked. "You look like you need to sit down."

"My sister called. Her husband had a heart attack."

"Oh my God. Is he okay?" Jo took a step toward him, and then seemed to catch herself.

"Hope so." He suddenly felt as if an elephant had settled onto his shoulders. "Angie will keep me posted. She made me promise to stay here and keep looking for Tiffany. Anything new here?"

"We spoke to a group of squatters who call this building home," Nick spoke up. "Fewer and fewer are daring to seek shelter here. Too many have gone missing over the years. They think it's the ghosts of former patients haunting the place."

"I think," Jo said, "it's the third victim I've been telling you about. The throwaway victim no one will miss."

"The ones who die?" he asked.

She nodded. "The ones who die."

Tony clenched his jaw. How the hell could they know so much and not be able to find the goddamn hiding place?

"We should keep searching," Nick suggested, breaking the tense silence.

Since Tony was back they decided to divide up into pairs and take two buildings at a time instead of one.

Bobbie patted Tony's shoulder. "Come on. We haven't worked together in a while."

Jo gave him a nod and trudged on with Nick.

Bobbie started across the road to a low white block building. Security had gone through this morning and unlocked all the padlocks to help with the search. Most of the companies conducting business on the property had agreed to a search of their facilities. Phelps was working on the others.

"So what's going on with you?" Bobbie asked as she crossed into the dim interior of the building.

"You mean besides having a missing niece and a brother-in-law in the hospital hanging on for his life?"

"Ha ha." Bobbie shot him a look. "You know what I mean."

"I drink way too much. And…" He pulled out his flashlight and checked the corridor to the right before they moved in that direction. "I drink way too much."

Bobbie gave a somber nod. "You know the Bureau wants you back, right?"

"Oh yeah. I got really good vibes about that." He opened a door on the left and had a look inside.

"Nick talked to Jessup, his contact there. Jessup says you weren't fired. That you quit. Is that true?"

Tony moved on to the next door. He flashed the light onto a piece of concrete rubble on the floor. "Watch yourself there."

Bobbie waved her flashlight. "I got this. Answer the question."

"If I hadn't quit, my new boss would have fired me. I had no desire to give him the satisfaction."

Bobbie laughed. "You are such an idiot. All you have to do is get your ass in AA. Go to counseling and you can have your career back. If you don't want to go back to BAU, then don't. But drinking your life away is not the answer."

"Geez, you sound like my sister."

Bobbie moved to the next door. "I'll take that as a compliment." She opened the door and immediately stepped back, hand over her face. "Shit. We gotta ripe one in there."

Fortunately, it wasn't a human body. Tony and Bobbie peered at the carcass with the aid of their flashlights.

"Looks like a possum," Bobbie said.

"Think so." He scanned the room, spotted a hole in the wall that went clean through the backside of the building.

Moving around the decomposing animal, he leaned down and inspected the hole. A couple of squirrels scampered from the wall cavity. He jerked back, almost stepping on the possum.

"Whoa." Bobbie laughed. It was good to hear that sound, even under the circumstances. "We should move on. I think we've seen enough in here."

As they navigated from room to room, keeping an eye out as much for the wildlife as for another human, her earlier comment kept niggling at him.

"I'm not saying I want my job back." They reached the final door on the opposite end of the building. "How long is this offer good?"

Bobbie sighed. "Saw right through me, huh?"

"I did."

Final room was empty save for the trash of a former transient resident.

They headed back outside. "You have until the first of May to give them an answer and to prove you've secured the proper counseling and so forth." Bobbie hesitated at the door. "Don't throw away all you worked for just to prove you can. It might feel like you're getting the last word, but you're not."

"I'll think about it."

"Don't take too long," she warned.

May first. He had a couple of weeks. Plenty of time.

All that mattered to him right now was finding Tiffany alive.

# *Forty-Nine*

*Day Thirteen*
*Eighteen years ago...*

I open my eyes. The light is still blinding so I close them again.

I turn my head and look for the others. Ellen is near me. She is breathing. I see the faint rise and fall of her rib cage.

Forcing myself to move again, I roll my head until I'm looking the other way. Carrie is staring at me. At first I fear she's dead but then she blinks.

I smile. My lips crack painfully. "I thought you were dead."

"Maybe we all are and this is hell. Sure feels like it."

She has a point. Though my eyes are adjusting to the brighter light, they feel raw and my skin still burns.

My mouth and throat are so dry. It feels like I swallowed sand. No water today so far.

Of course I have no idea what time it is or what day it is.

I just want to go home.

Metal rattles and my gaze snaps to the steel cage-like door overhead in the center of the ceiling.

There's a clink. Then I see something fall. Another clink and then another falling object. Just a blur in my weary gaze.

Moving slowly, I crawl across the floor.

Shiny. Metal.

*Keys.*

Keys?

The gate suddenly opens and a box slowly descends downward. It isn't a large box. Slightly bigger than a shoe box. It comes down on a flat white shelf attached to metal things, not chains but wires of some sort.

The box settles on the floor. Carrie moves to my side. We sit on our knees and stare at the keys and the box that we now see holds three bottles of water.

I grab one and twist off the top and drink deeply.

"Put down the water!"

I almost drop my bottle of water.

Ellen has dragged herself to where we are. She reaches for the final bottle of water.

"If you wish to eat, each of you must swallow a key."

I stare at the keys on the floor. Insane, I think. Why would we swallow keys?

"Now."

We look at each other. We need to eat. I remember swallowing a quarter when I was a little girl. Didn't hurt me, just scared my mother half to death.

Carrie picks up a key and puts it in her mouth. She swallows big gulps of the water, and then she smiles. "Not bad. Goes down pretty easy."

I go next. Then Ellen. She has the most difficult time. She keeps gagging the key back up.

Finally she swallows the damned thing.

The box rises into the air again, the hydraulics of the lift whirring softly.

We stare upward as the box disappears.

We pray.

We are so hungry.

Then I smell something wonderful—maybe hamburgers.

The box lowers and sure enough there are three hamburgers inside. Just the meat and the bun but thankfully real food.

I grab a burger and take a big bite.

I gag.

The inside is completely raw. Only the outside is cooked.

I gag and heave but I force myself to eat it. I have to eat something and this is it. The others do the same.

The box disappears and the cage-like door slams into place once more.

I am thankful to have eaten.

No one wants to die on an empty stomach.

# *Fifty*

Jo didn't want to stop to eat but Tony insisted.

Bobbie picked at the food on her plate.

"Morning sickness?" Jo had read a post by her sister-in-law that said her morning sickness came every afternoon rather than in the mornings.

Seemed silly to call it morning sickness if it occurred at different times of the day. Jo figured she would never know how it felt to carry a child. You had to be able to connect with other humans on a deeper level to form that kind of bond and she couldn't quite accomplish the feat. Her gaze shifted to Tony and she cursed herself for being an idiot. They didn't have a bond; they shared a mutual need. Not the same thing.

"Every day, several times a day." Bobbie laughed softly. "But it'll pass."

Jo remembered that Bobbie had been pregnant before. Something else she couldn't imagine—the pain of losing a child. Losing her family had been hard enough. She wondered if her brother had given her message to her mom. Probably. Ray always stood by his word.

She'd made a promise to go home for a visit when this was over. Could she really do that? Go back and pretend to be that person again? She could try, couldn't she? There was much in this life that Jo was no longer capable of, but she could at least be as good as her word. When you had nothing else, you had that.

"How far along are you?" Since Tony and Nick were in deep conversation over a map, Jo figured she could at least be sociable. A totally novel concept for her. Bobbie and Nick had come a long way to help. They were nice. Tony was nice. She glanced at him again. He should stop beating up on himself.

If all the cops and these guys right here couldn't find those missing girls, no one could. For the first time in eighteen years, Jo felt some sense of hope that this might actually be over soon. She could close her eyes at night and know that the people who stole her life and the lives of so many others wouldn't be taking anyone else's.

"Three months," Bobbie said in answer to her question. "I only just started sharing the news. My uncle is over the moon. He's looking forward to playing the part of grandfather...again."

She lapsed into silence.

"I'm sorry. I shouldn't ask so many questions."

Bobbie smiled. She had the bluest eyes. So pale and bright. "It's okay. I'm getting used to touching the past without it hurting so much. I don't want to pretend my little boy never existed. Or his father. I love and miss them every day. I just realized that loving them didn't mean I couldn't love and be happy with Nick and the children we have together. Nick doesn't take the place of James any more than this baby will take Jamie's place. I never thought I'd reach this stage, but I'm glad I did."

Jo wondered if she would ever find that place. "I'm glad for you."

Bobbie reached across the table and put her hand on Jo's. "You can find it, too. You just have to open your eyes and your heart to the possibility."

Jo nodded. It was the best she could do without the risk of blurting out the emotions whirling inside her right now. The past few days had challenged her ability to stay indifferent.

Her cell vibrated.

She removed it from her pocket, expecting to see her boss's name on the screen. A frown furrowed her brow. She didn't recognize the number so she hit Decline and shoved the phone back into her pocket.

"Excuse me." She scooted back her chair. "Gotta hit the ladies' room."

Tony glanced at her as she turned toward the far end of the café.

Once she was in the ladies' room, she pulled out her cell and stared at the number of the missed caller. The phone started to vibrate again with a call from the same number. She jumped. Almost dropped it.

"Hello."

"Joanna Guthrie?"

Female.

"Yes." The only woman who had this number was Ellen. Wait… She'd written the number on the back of the card Tony had given Madelyn Houser.

"I have a proposal for you."

"Dr. Blume?" Had to be. Madelyn was dead. Who else could it be? Sounded way too mature to be Ellen's daughter.

"Where are you at this moment?" Blume, presumably, asked.

Jo laughed. "What do you want?"

"You tell me where you are and I'll tell you how to get here before I kill your new friend's niece."

Jo's heart slammed into her sternum. She didn't hesitate. "Aubri Lane's restaurant on Wayne Street."

"All right. You leave your friends right now," the voice instructed. "Go out the back of the restaurant, slip through the alley and loop to your right which will take you to a street just beyond where you are now. Two blocks to your left is Franklin. Take the next left and a car will be waiting in front of Memory Hill Cemetery. If you don't show up or you tell anyone else, they'll all die. Including Ellen's poor damaged daughter."

The call ended.

Jo's heart pounded faster and faster. She was familiar with the cemetery. Another of those haunted places new freshmen explored. First, she should tell Tony. No. She couldn't go back out there. She couldn't tell him and he would recognize something was wrong. Blume was right—had to be Blume—Jo had to go out the back. She had to do this.

But she couldn't leave without giving Tony something to go on. Ending up dead without leaving some idea of where to start searching for the others would be plain dumb.

Jo ducked out of the bathroom and into the kitchen.

She glanced around until she saw what she needed. She grabbed the pen from the counter and hurried back to the bathroom. Inside the first stall she considered carefully what to say before she wrote the message on the wall. If she told anyone or was too straightforward with her message he might catch up with her before she reached the car Blume was sending. Couldn't risk it.

Going to save Tif and the others. Sylvia is there, too. Lunch was too close to the dead. Look up and you'll see.

She shoved the pen into her back pocket and went to the door.

*Deep breath.*

She opened the door slowly and moved into the narrow hall. Bobbie, Tony and Nick were still at the table, hovering over the map.

Jo moved toward the back of the restaurant that had once been a historic home. This time when she reached the kitchen she moved on through as if she belonged there and out the door she went. She hurried along the alley until she found a narrow side alley leading back out to Wayne Street.

She moved fast from there. Not quite running, but close. She took the left at Franklin and spotted the cemetery immediately. Memory Hill was one of the oldest in the city. Students sneaked around the cemetery at night to see if the rumors that it was haunted were true.

A black car waited in front of the gate. Jo walked to the car. A man sat behind the wheel. He powered the window down. "Ms. Guthrie?"

She nodded.

"I'm here to take you to your meeting."

Jo looked around, spotted what she was looking for immediately so she climbed into the back seat.

As soon as the door closed he rolled away from the curb.

"Where are we going?"

"I'm sorry," he said, "I have orders not to discuss the destination with you. It's supposed to be a surprise." He smiled at her in the rearview mirror. "I pick you up. I drop you off."

"I get it. My friend likes surprises." She managed a smile back at him. "It's my birthday. I'm turning eighteen again." She prayed he would remember that when the police interviewed him.

The driver flashed her another smile before turning his attention back to the street.

Jo dug the pen from her back pocket. "You know," she said to the driver as she leaned forward pretending to peer out the front windshield, "this is my first visit to Milledgeville. I had no idea there was so much history here."

"Oh, you'd be surprised."

As he talked on and on about the city that had once been Georgia's capital, Jo kept her eyes on him in the rearview mirror while she wrote a message on the back of his leather seat.

Maybe she'd get lucky and the driver would see it when he cleaned the car this evening.

Or the next fare he picked up would take the message seriously and call the police.

Then she recognized the road they were taking and the pen slipped from her fingers.

She had known this was the place.

# *Fifty-One*

*Day Fourteen*
*Eighteen years ago...*

Carrie has a fever and she's sweating.

I hold her hand and say soothing things to her. She mostly groans and complains.

I don't know how many hours it has been since we ate the burgers. Maybe she has food poisoning or E. coli.

If only we had water.

We are all very weak today.

Ellen scoots next to me. "Is she dying?"

I elbow her. "Of course not. She'll be fine. The raw meat probably gave her a bellyache."

Ellen sits down beside me. "I feel kind of sick, too."

I feel the same but I keep it to myself. Maybe he or they poisoned us and now want to watch us die in agony.

What was the fucking point of the key?

At least we haven't been forced to fight again and the

horrible movies aren't playing anymore. That is something to be thankful for.

A loud clatter snaps my attention to the left just as something falls from the overhead door. It clatters and slides against the dirty floor. Then a second object falls.

What the hell?

A third one hits the floor, clattering and sliding into the others.

I release Carrie's hand and crawl to the pile and sit back on my knees.

Knives. Not just knives, butcher knives—the kind I remember from my grandmother's kitchen. She used one like this to chop up a chicken once.

"Oh my God." Ellen grabs my arm as if she needs something to hang on to.

The male voice commands, "Take a knife."

Fear twists in my belly along with the raw meat. "No!" I shake my head. I don't know what's coming but it can't be good. My instincts are screaming at me.

Ellen reaches out and picks one up. She turns it side to side, watching the shiny metal flash in the light. "Are we going to need these to protect ourselves?"

"Put it down," I whisper.

Carrie manages to sit up and scoot over to where we are. "What the hell?"

"Take a knife!" the voice repeats.

Carrie reaches for a knife.

I'm not doing it. I innately understand the knives are not for protection.

A grinding sound jerks my attention to the right. The hole we've been using for a toilet suddenly closes. There must be a hydraulic door I couldn't see, not that

I'd stuck my head inside the hole. It was too little to use as an escape route so I didn't bother.

A gushing sound came next. I glance around to see where it is coming from. Water pours down the walls in a thin sheet as if all four walls have suddenly turned into waterfalls. I remember seeing water walls like this in a restaurant once.

I look at the others and then at the walls again. I feel the water rising around my ankles. As if someone inside my head is speaking to me I hear the words: we are going to drown.

The male voice booms loud in the room. "All you need for your freedom is one thing…a single key."

We stare at each other. Carrie grabs her stomach and groans. Ellen clutches her knife and scoots away from us.

I pick up the final knife before the rising water can sweep it away and I turn to Carrie. Like Ellen, she scoots away.

The water rushes and rushes. The water is up to my knees now. I ignore it. They're trying to scare us. The water will stop. Or we'll just float up to the top and hang on to that metal gate-like door. Except the gate is even with the ceiling on our side. The wall around the opening goes up about another ten inches. The bottom drops out of my stomach. The water will rise above the metal gate by several inches.

Ellen and Carrie stare at me as if they, too, have reached this same conclusion.

I shake my head. "I'm not hurting anyone." I throw down the knife. It floats this way and that until it sinks to the bottom.

"Only two of you can survive," the voice roars. "One must die. Make a choice. Take a key before it's too late."

No way.

The water is at my waist now. I am really scared.

Carrie is clutching her stomach again. I want to go to her but I'm afraid. She has a knife in her hand.

The water brushes the tops of my thighs. I back away from the others. Against the wall where the water oozes forth.

I will not kill anyone. I will not.

Ellen and Carrie are staring at each other.

My heart pounds. I need to say something, to stop whatever is about to happen.

"No!" I shout. "Don't listen to him! He wants us to hurt each other."

Ellen rushes toward Carrie. Carrie starts forward but stumbles and falls face-first into the water. Ellen stabs at her with the knife.

I rush toward them.

Ellen and Carrie are fighting. I try to pull them apart. Can't. Water is at my waist now.

Carrie is under the water. Ellen kicks her in the stomach.

"Stop!" I scream and reach for Carrie.

Ellen holds her under the water. I pull at Ellen, first one of her arms and then the other but I can't move her.

"Stop!" I can't budge Ellen. How can she be so strong? Then it hits me, adrenaline. She is fighting to survive.

I grab her hair and yank her head back. She screams but won't let go of her hold on Carrie.

I push her head under the water. We struggle and

roll. Finally, she releases Carrie. I jerk loose from her and slug through the water to Carrie.

She isn't breathing. Her eyes are open, staring at me.

Oh shit. Oh shit. I try to help her but the water is so deep. I hold her head up out of the water and try to squeeze any water out of her lungs. But it's nearly impossible to keep her above the water level.

"She's dead!" Ellen snarls. She stands in front of us with a knife in her hand. "Now hold her up so I can get the key."

I stand there in a kind of shock, holding Carrie under her arms, her head sagging forward, while Ellen cuts into her. Blood rises up around us. Hot tears slide down my cheeks but there is nothing I can do.

It takes forever—the water is at our chins now. Blood swirls with Ellen's frantic movements. The water sloshes back and forth, hitting me in the face. I taste the saltiness of Carrie's blood. I stagger, almost fall. I don't care. I hope we all die.

"Got it!"

Ellen pulls Carrie's body away from me. I watch her sink to the bottom. Her insides floating all around her. Blood widening like a crimson cloud...

"Stand by the lock," Ellen orders.

Instinctively my head tilts back to keep the water out of my nose. We are going to die. It's too late to save ourselves. I don't care.

"Do it, Joanna!" Ellen screams.

I move to the spot beneath the lock we cannot reach. It hangs from the cage-style door eight feet off the floor. The door is flush with the ceiling.

Ellen climbs my back. I stumble, nearly fall over,

but I right myself and sputter water from my mouth and nose. She sits on my shoulders and works until she releases the lock. It splashes in the water next to me, sinking to the bottom with Carrie.

We should die, too. We don't deserve to live.

As if the lock released more than the cage-like door, the water stops running in and immediately starts to drain.

The sound is deafening. The pull of the water almost drags me down.

Ellen is jerking and pushing. I peer up. She's trying to push the cage-style door upward. Suddenly it starts to fall in on us.

We topple backward into the water.

When we surface again, the cage door is hanging from the ceiling like a ladder.

Ellen slogs through the water that is now only waist deep and grabs onto the ladder.

I rush after her and jerk her away from the ladder.

"Wait!" I put my face in hers. "We're taking Carrie with us."

"We have to get out of here!" Ellen cries.

I shake my head. "Not without Carrie."

Only two of us are alive, but all three of us will get out.

# Fifty-Two

Forty-nine minutes had passed since Jo walked out the back door of the restaurant. They had searched the restaurant from top to bottom, twice, and combed the surrounding blocks.

Tony had called Phelps for backup. He, Bobbie and Nick had searched the restaurant and expanded their search a full block around the building.

No one had seen her.

"What the hell is she thinking?"

Standing next to him on the sidewalk, Nick said, "She's thinking she had a lead or some plan she needs to do alone." He glanced at Tony. "We've all done it. At the time you think you know more than anyone about the plan or the lead or whatever it is you feel you have to do."

As badly as Tony did not want to admit Nick was right, he was. But that didn't stop him from being worried and pissed. Jo was an adult; she had the right to make a stupid decision. Tiffany was a kid. This move, he feared, would somehow impact her and maybe not for the best.

That wasn't fair. He didn't know Jo well, but he was certain she would never purposely hurt Tiffany or anyone else.

"Bobbie said her cell rang before she went to the restroom, but she didn't answer," Nick pointed out. "Maybe she got a call she couldn't ignore but needed privacy to take it."

Tony was pretty damned sure that was exactly what happened. "Son of a bitch."

Phelps joined them. "You know, LeDoux, it's always possible Ms. Guthrie decided she'd had enough. Or maybe she has something to hide. She was silent about what really happened for a very long time. Maybe there's more to the story than we know."

Tony resisted the impulse to punch the guy. "She came here to help set the past to rights. If she hadn't come back, we'd still be kicking around irrelevant scenarios."

Phelps turned his hands up. "Just saying. You never really know what a person is capable of and, the fact is, we don't know the full story about what happened eighteen years ago."

Tony bit his jaw, letting the pain distract his temper. Right now he needed this man's help. "But we do know what's happening right now and at least four lives are at stake."

"Hey," Bobbie called from the restaurant entrance. When they turned to her, she went on, "I went through the ladies' room again. Jo left a note."

Tony followed Bobbie to the ladies' room, the place Jo had claimed she was going before she took off. Nick was right behind him. Since witnesses in the kitchen had watched Jo walk out of her own volition there was no need to consider any part of the restaurant a crime scene.

In the first of two stalls a note had been written in red ink on the wall among half a dozen others of varying shades of black and blue.

Going to save Tif. Sylvia is there, too. Lunch was too close to the dead. Look up and you'll see me.

Tony looked from the note on the wall to the ceiling. "What does she mean *look up*?"

"One way to find out," Bobbie offered.

They moved through the entire restaurant scrutinizing the ceiling.

"Wait." Nick turned to Phelps. "Is there a cemetery nearby?"

Son of a bitch. Nick was right. She'd said this place was too close to the dead.

"Memory Hill is maybe two or three blocks away."

"Show us the way." Tony was already headed for the door as he said the words.

The cemetery was no more than a three-minute walk from the restaurant. Two and a half if you moved quickly and knew that every second you wasted could cost lives. Tony ran the entire distance. En route way behind him, Phelps called a couple of uniforms to help with the search of the cemetery.

Tony walked around the memorial to the thousands

buried at Central State Hospital several times. He'd expected that to be the first place she would go. Nothing. No messages, no clues. No bread crumbs.

Nothing.

They searched the entire cemetery and found not one damned thing that showed Jo had been there.

When they were at the front gate again, Phelps shook his head. "She said to look up and see her but I'm not finding anything in the trees."

Tony surveyed the street. His gaze lit on the traffic cam and he smiled. He pointed to the intersection of Greene and Wayne. "Traffic cams. She was talking about the traffic cams." He turned to Phelps. "If someone picked her up here, we might be able to see who it was and what kind of vehicle they were driving on the traffic cams."

Phelps gave a nod of agreement. "It's worth a try, but it'll take some time."

There was nothing else they could do.

*Milledgeville Public Safety Office, 4:15 p.m.*

Forty-five minutes were required to get the engineer on-site, and then for him to pull the traffic cam data. Phelps had relayed the latest turn of events to the rest of the task force. Bobbie and Nick had remained at the cemetery location to question anyone nearby who might have seen Jo. Tony had paced a hole in the carpet of the chief's office by the time the engineer scooted back from the screen and said, "There you go. That—" he pointed at the screen "—is about two this afternoon. Once you hit Play, it will move forward."

Phelps grabbed his phone from his utility belt. "Phelps."

Tony didn't wait for the chief, he hit Play and took the seat the engineer had abandoned.

"We're on our way out right now." Phelps snapped his phone back onto his belt. "One of my detectives is out front with a local cab driver. The cabbie says he's the one who picked up Guthrie and that she left a note on the back of his seat."

Tony hit Pause on the video and rushed after the chief. Outside, the cabbie's complexion revealed how worried he was.

"I picked up another fare and he told me about the message. I called 911 and came straight here."

Tony slid into the back seat and stared at the words written in the same red ink as the note on the bathroom stall.

Help me! Call the police!

"Yes, sir, that's her." The cabbie was pointing to the chief's cell phone and nodding.

Tony climbed out of the car. "Was anyone else with her?"

"No, sir," he insisted. "She was alone."

"Who hired you to pick her up?" the chief asked before Tony could.

"Dispatch received the call. When a third party hires a pickup they pay with a credit card. I called and verified that on the way here."

"What was the caller's name?" Tony asked.

"Orson Blume."

"You're sure the caller was a man?" Phelps asked.

They both knew Blume was dead.

The driver shrugged. "Dispatcher said his voice sounded kind of weird but it was definitely a man."

"Weird how?" Nick asked.

"You know," the man said, "like it was a computer speaking instead of a real person."

Probably because it was.

"Where did you drop her?" Phelps demanded.

"At one of those creepy old buildings out at the old asylum." He rattled off an address. "She said it was her birthday, that she was turning eighteen again."

Fear ignited inside Tony. He reached for the door. "Take me there. Now."

# Fifty-Three

Jo had begged Sylvia to listen to reason but she refused. Pamela Blume had evidently convinced Sylvia that Jo was responsible for her sister's—her mother's—problems. That if Ellen had not been covering for Jo all this time she wouldn't have slowly lost her mind.

The first thing Sylvia had done when the driver dropped Jo off was to take her cell phone. She'd tossed it into the woods, wagged her weapon and told Jo to move. Now as they walked through the dense woods toward wherever the hell they were going flashes of memory zoomed through Jo's mind. She and Ellen had managed to get Carrie out of the white box prison in which they'd been held. They'd carried her between them through dark corridor after corridor until they'd grown so exhausted they'd literally sat down on the floor and fallen asleep. Later Jo realized they had likely been drugged. Something in the air, she was certain. When they'd awakened they had been in the woods, lying on the ground with Carrie's cold, pale body between them.

At first fear and panic had them at each other's

throat. Then they'd realized they had no idea where they were or where they'd been. A dead woman they had murdered—Ellen had murdered—was with them. They had no proof of what really happened. No one to point to as responsible for what happened to them— nothing. How would they ever explain what happened? No one was going to believe such a bizarre story.

So they'd buried Carrie's body and they'd never told a soul what really happened.

Jo blinked away the memories. Sylvia ushered her from the tree line, across the road and through an opening in one of the tall fences that surrounded a decaying building she and Nick Shade had thoroughly searched. How could they have been so close and missed it?

Jo felt confident she could overtake Sylvia and wrestle the gun from her. But she wouldn't risk the girl getting hurt. The weapon could go off and one of them could end up dead. Jo needed to know where the others were so she cooperated. She would worry about clearing things up with Sylvia later.

If she was still alive.

To Jo's surprise Sylvia didn't go to the building; she went into the old guard shack that stood near the gated entrance to the compound. She raised a section of the cracked tile floor like a trap door and an old staircase lay before them, plunging into the darkness below.

"Go." Sylvia gestured to the stairs with the gun.

Jo took the first step down and automatic lights came on as if activated by her presence. As they moved downward, the trap door closed behind them. At the bottom of the long staircase Sylvia urged her forward, along a dimly lit corridor.

Fear slammed into Jo's gut.

She knew this place.

This had to be where she, Ellen and Carrie had been kept eighteen years ago.

Her heart pounded harder with each step.

Sylvia ushered her from the main corridor into a maze of narrower corridors, going through door after door. Jo couldn't get enough air into her lungs. The urge to turn around and run back to those stairs was nearly overwhelming.

Finally, Sylvia stopped and opened one last door. Inside, a row of monitors lined one wall. Televisions showing the news on three different channels hung on the wall above the monitors. A conference table stood in the center of the room. Four chairs surrounded it.

She recognized the dark corridors but she had never seen this place.

A door on the other side of the room opened and Pamela Blume walked in. She held yet another gun pointed at Jo.

"Very good, Sylvia. You may lay your weapon down now."

"I'm not stupid," the younger woman said. She shifted her aim from Jo to Pamela. "I want the whole truth. I want to hear it from her before I take your word for what happened."

"Dear, dear girl—" Pamela smiled "—did you really believe I would give you a loaded gun?"

Sylvia pulled the trigger on the .38. Nothing happened. She threw it aside and charged Pamela.

Jo screamed for her to stop a split second before the first of three shots rang out.

Sylvia crumpled to the floor.

Jo started toward her.

Pamela aimed her weapon back at Jo. "Do not move."

Fury roared through Jo. She wanted to kill Pamela Blume. She wanted to tear her apart with her bare hands. But she didn't move. If she got herself killed right now there would be no hope for Tiffany and the others. She owed it to Tony LeDoux to try and save his niece.

Blume said, "You should never have come back, Joanna. But—" she sighed "—you're here. Do you want to end this where you stand or do you want to join the others and die with them? Either way, my plane is waiting."

Jo stiffened her spine. "I'll die with the others."

"Very well. This way." Pamela gestured for Jo to precede her through the door on the other side of the room.

The door led into a room similar in size to the one they'd exited except there was a big square hole in the center. About a foot down from the top of the hole metal bars covered it. Inside the hole the light was so bright it hurt to look at it.

Something hardened inside Jo. The place where she had spent those fourteen days was directly below her. Her body trembled. The urge to vomit was so fierce her throat burned.

The smell, the tension, the undeniable sense of doom.

She was back.

The choking sensation had her breathing in unreasonably deep gasps.

Pamela used a key to unlock an almost-invisible control panel in the wall. She pushed a button and the bars rose upward. A white shelflike thing lowered from the ceiling.

Jo's gut clenched. This was the thing they'd used to lower food and water to the hostages—to her and Ellen and Carrie. To all the others imprisoned here after them.

"Hello?" one of the girls below called.

Suddenly, Jo knew exactly what she had to do. "Tiffany?"

"Yes? I'm Tiffany?"

The girl's hopeful voice was suddenly nearer the opening in the center of the room.

"My name is Joanna. I'm a friend of your uncle Tony's."

Pamela gestured to the lift with her weapon. "Move. You can continue your little get to know each other face-to-face."

Jo said, "Just one more thing." With her gaze fixed on Pamela, she shouted to those below, "No matter what you hear, stay away from the opening!"

Then Jo ran for the door.

One shot, then another exploded from Pamela's weapon, biting into the wall as Jo dodged and darted until she was out the door they'd only just entered. She slammed it shut. Two more shots pinged, the noise muffled behind the steel door.

She stabbed the lock button on the keypad.

Beyond the door Pamela screamed her name.

Jo moved away from the door. She hadn't wanted to leave the girls but she needed Pamela disarmed, and wrestling the gun away from her wouldn't have been a smart move. Jo did a quick count. Three shots fired at Sylvia. God, she hoped the girl wasn't dead. She rushed to where she lay. Checked her pulse.

"Oh my God," she breathed. There was a pulse. "Hang on, Sylvia."

She checked her wounds. There was blood but not as much as Jo had feared there would be.

Pamela was screaming at her to open the door.

Another shot and then another echoed in the room.

How many was that? Seven or eight? How many rounds did Pamela have left? She hadn't gotten a good look at the weapon she'd been wielding so she couldn't be sure.

She needed a phone.

Jo raced back into the room with the monitors. She awakened each one by touching a key on the keyboard. One showed the three women—all alive and huddling in one corner of their prison. Thank God! Another showed Pamela doing something at the door. The third showed the outside.

Okay. Phone. She needed a phone. Where the hell was a phone? Pamela surely had a cell phone. She checked the conference table. A cabinet that sat against one wall. No phone!

"Fuck!"

No time to try and find her way out of here. She wouldn't leave the others for that long. She prowled through the drawers. A flashlight, napkins, notepads. No phone. Pamela was still at that damned control panel. Just to play it safe Jo grabbed the flashlight from the top drawer.

The lights went out, including the monitors.

Jo decided she would take her quick thinking where the flashlight was concerned as a sign her luck was changing. Rather than use it for light, she opted to clutch it as a potential weapon.

She told her mind to settle. She listened.

It was way too quiet.

Had Pamela turned off the power somehow to disengage the auto locks?

Jo moved to the door that exited into that long corridor. Everything was pitch-black. Fear coiled in her chest. She remembered well all the days in utter darkness.

Don't think about it.

*Focus.*

She slipped into the corridor. No more gunshots or shouting. No sound at all.

She held her breath and pressed her body against the wall, the flashlight held at the ready. Eventually Pamela would come looking for her or simply to escape. She probably thought Jo had already taken off. She hoped that was what the other woman was thinking.

She dared to draw in a breath. Released it very slowly, careful not to make a sound.

The whisper of breathing brushed her ears.

Coming toward the corridor.

*Pamela.*

Jo couldn't see her but she could hear her.

She remained perfectly still and let the woman come to her. Slow, easy, silent breath.

Pamela was very close now. Her breathing was ragged. She was nervous. She had a good twenty-five or more years on Jo. This was far harder for her.

*Bitch.*

Sylvia cried out.

A weapon on Jo's left fired. A blast of light flared in the corridor.

Pamela stared at her during that momentary flash of light.

Jo ducked low and charged the woman, slammed the flashlight into the last place she'd seen her head. Missed. Hit her shoulder. Pamela screamed.

Another flare of bright light. Another explosion of a bullet from a muzzle.

Jo raised her weapon again. This time the flashlight connected with the other woman's head.

The blow sent the flashlight flying from Jo's hand and clattering to the floor.

Pamela went down.

Jo scrambled in the darkness for the gun.

Found it.

Pamela didn't move.

Jo felt around until she found the flashlight, turned it on. Pamela was out. Jo shoved the gun into her waistband, then grabbed the bitch by the arm. She dragged her into the room with the big square hole in the center. At the control box, Jo flipped switches until the lights came back on. She jiggled more switches until the lift lowered downward.

Dragging Pamela by the arm, Jo went to the edge of the hole. "Tiffany, send the other girls up one by one."

"Okay."

Jo figured if Tiffany was anything like her mother or her uncle she would be the strongest of the three.

First, the girl, Vickie Parton, rose to the top. She scrambled off the lift and into the nearest corner. Jo assured her everything was going to be fine as she sent the lift down again. This time a girl Jo didn't know came up. *The other girl.*

Finally, Tiffany Durand was on her way up.

Jo checked Pamela's pockets and found the key she'd

used as well as her cell phone. Damned battery was dead. Shit! She shoved both into the pocket of her jeans.

Pamela started to groan. Jo dragged her to the lift and lowered her down into the square prison where she had been kept for fourteen endless days. Then she looked to the girls. "Let's go."

Once they were in the short corridor, she locked the door, securing Pamela inside. When they reached the room with the computers, she said to Tiffany, "Look for anything to cover yourselves."

While they searched, Jo squatted next to Sylvia and lifted her into her arms. The girl was thin and petite, like her mother had been. She was still breathing and that was something.

There was nothing for the girls to use to cover themselves and they were out of time. Sylvia needed medical attention. Jo led the way into the first of the corridors.

When they reached a door, she said, "Take the key from my pocket. See if it unlocks the door." She hoped like hell since Pamela was no longer at the controls that the key would do the trick.

Tiffany fished out the key and shoved it into the lock. The door opened into another corridor. They moved toward the other end as quickly as possible. Warm, sticky blood was invading Jo's tee. *Don't you die on me, Sylvia.*

They reached another door. "Try the key again." Jo prayed.

Tiffany used the key again, the door opened into the wider, main corridor. Just a few more steps and that long staircase stood in front of them. Jo breathed a sigh of relief.

"Go ahead of me," she ordered. "There's a door at

the top. You have to push it upward. It opens into a guard shack."

The three young women huddled together as they climbed the seemingly endless stairs. It felt like hours instead of seconds before they reached the top. *Gotta get out of here. Gotta get out of here.*

Tiffany and the others cried out when they emerged into freedom. Jo hurried them out into the parking lot. Exhausted, the adrenaline receding, she dropped to her knees on the pavement and placed Sylvia carefully on the crumbling asphalt. She looked around. The girls were clustered close, sobbing.

She needed a damned phone.

Jo looked down at the injured woman. Wait…did Sylvia have a phone? Jo felt around in the pockets of her jeans. The feel of the thin bulge sent her pulse racing. Since she didn't know Tony's number by heart she called 911.

When the operator answered, she said, "This is Jo-anna Guthrie. I'm in the parking lot of the Ingram Build-ing at the old Central State Hospital in Milledgeville. I found the women the police have been looking for. One has been shot. Please send help."

Tiffany and the others came over and knelt down next to Jo. They thanked her over and over but she couldn't say a word. She was sobbing so hard she couldn't speak.

Within five minutes, sirens blaring and lights flash-ing, at least a dozen official vehicles showed up. When Jo saw Tony running toward them, she knew every-thing would be fine.

It was over.

# Fifty-Four

Tony pushed the wheelchair down the corridor toward the Cardiac Unit. A nurse followed close behind them.

Tiffany was alive. A little bruised, battered and plenty dehydrated but she was alive. As soon as she had been cleared to go by the ER physician back in Milledgeville, an ambulance had been ordered to bring her and Tony to Macon to be with her parents. Tony would forever be indebted to Chief Phelps for taking care of the details so there was no time delay. Tiffany needed to be with her parents.

When they reached the door to Steve's room, Tony said to the nurse, "Give us a moment."

She nodded. He came around to the front of the wheelchair and crouched down to Tif's eye level. "I might not have a chance to tell you this once your parents get their hands on you, but I'm very proud of you.

The other girls told the detectives how you helped hold them together. You're a hero, Tif. A real hero."

She managed a smile despite the tears slipping down her pale cheeks. Even the dark circles under her eyes and the bruises on her battered body didn't detract from how beautiful she was. "Thanks, Uncle Tony, but I'm not the hero. Joanna is the hero. That crazy old woman was going to kill us and Joanna saved us."

Tony blinked at the burn in his eyes. "That's right. She's a hero, too."

Tif's smile wobbled a little. "So are you. I knew you'd come."

She'd told him that over and over since the rescue. He kissed her on the forehead and stood. He swiped away a couple of tears he couldn't hold back and nodded for the nurse to open the door. Angie and Steve looked toward the open door as Tony pushed the wheelchair into the room.

His sister's eyes lit with joy. Steve cried like a baby. Tony stood back and watched the incredible reunion, his knees a little weak.

He needed to be with his family tonight, but tomorrow he was heading back to Milledgeville. There were statements to make and reports to sign.

And there was Jo.

# Fifty-Five

Jo picked up her bag and reached for the door of the Judge's Suite. The folks at the inn had insisted she have their best room for the rest of her stay. Chiefs of Police Phelps and Buckley had needed her to stay to sort out all the reports and for statements that would ensure Pamela Blume was sent away for the rest of her life.

She had told the parts of her story that she had never uttered to anyone. First to Tony. With his support, she had been able to repeat those awful details to Phelps, the two FBI agents and the GBI agent. They had all agreed that Ellen's actions would have easily fallen under an insanity defense. Since Ellen was dead, there was no reason to open any sort of investigation. Jo's statement would close the case.

Vickie Parton's parents had taken her home. Lexy Thackerson's aunt had shown up and insisted that Lexy was coming to live with her. Jo hoped Lexy would give her aunt a chance.

Thankfully Sylvia Carson came through surgery with flying colors. Mr. and Mrs. Carson had arrived early yesterday to be with her. Jo personally told them the story of what she and Ellen had survived. They cried together, but the Carsons were strong and determined. Sylvia had a difficult road ahead of her, but Ellen's parents were prepared to take care of her and to love her the way Ellen would have wanted. The Carsons promised to explain everything to Ellen's husband and to her children, when they were old enough. They needed to know how much their mother loved them and that what happened to her was not their fault or even Ellen's.

The local newspapers were calling Jo a hero. Even the cops were treating her like a VIP. It was strangely unsettling and comforting at the same time.

Angie and Steve had called to thank her. Steve's bypass surgery had gone well and he was doing great. They would be going home in a few days.

Something else to be grateful for.

Tiffany had asked to speak with Jo. She, too, had called her a hero.

Jo didn't feel like a hero. What she felt was exhausted and relieved and tremendously thankful.

She said her goodbyes to the innkeeper at breakfast that morning. Jo was ready to hit the road. There were things she had to do before she could go home.

*Home.*

It felt strange to think about going home but she was. She'd spoken to her mother and to Ray. They wanted her home. She wanted to be home. She wanted her family back—if they would have her. Ray assured her again that they had always wanted her. Deep down she had never stopped wanting them.

Bobbie Gentry and Nick Shade had dropped by yesterday afternoon to say goodbye. Nick told her to be kind to herself. She deserved good things. Bobbie had hugged her and made her promise to call if she ever needed anything or wanted to talk.

Jo's boss was fielding offers from publishers on her behalf. Suddenly the world wanted to write her story. At some point during all the conversations, interviews and interrogations, Tony had suggested that she should consider going back to college—anywhere but here, of course. Maybe she would.

She stepped out onto the porch and inhaled a deep breath of fresh air. This was the first day of a new beginning. Last night she had promised herself that she was never looking back after what she had to do today.

But today there was one final, very important matter she needed to take care of. She was going to Atlanta to see Carrie Cole's mother. She was still alive. Tony's friend at the Bureau had looked her up for Jo. After the disappearance of her daughter eighteen years ago Mrs. Cole had gone back to school, gotten her degree and was now a social worker who specialized in helping troubled teens. Jo had called and made an appointment to meet with her at one o'clock this afternoon.

Jo wanted the story of Carrie's final days to come from her before it ended up on the news. All involved had promised to keep Carrie's name from the press until after Jo spoke to Mrs. Cole personally. They would follow up with her tomorrow morning to verify that it was okay to proceed with the press release.

Mrs. Cole deserved to know that her daughter had sacrificed herself for Jo and Ellen. Jo had thought about that fourteenth day many times and Carrie had been far stronger than Ellen. Even physically ill, she could have stopped her but she had known that one of them had to die. Rather than fight, she had surrendered herself to save Jo and Ellen.

Jo tossed her bag into her Celica and walked around to the driver's side.

The sound of a car pulling into the parking area drew her attention toward it. The BMW came to a stop and Tony climbed out. She couldn't have slowed the smile that stretched across her lips if she'd tried. She was glad he'd come. No matter that he'd insisted on taking her to dinner last night so hardly a dozen hours had passed since she'd seen him, she was glad to see him now.

"I was thinking you could use a driver and some company on the trip to Atlanta." He reached around her and closed her car door. "I spoke to the innkeeper and he said you could leave your car here. Come on." His hand slid down her arm to grasp hers. "You don't need to do this alone."

At a loss for words yet again, Jo entwined her fingers with his and nodded. "Tiffany and her folks are doing okay this morning?"

He opened the passenger side door of his car. "They're doing great. They'll be going home on Friday."

"I'm really glad to hear that."

As she climbed in, he said, "I accepted a new assignment from the Bureau."

"Hey, that's great." Jo was happy for him. While she'd been confessing her deepest, darkest secrets, he'd shared a few of his own. They had a lot in common.

He rounded the hood and climbed into the driver's seat. When he'd backed onto the street, he turned to her. "The new assignment is in Birmingham, Alabama. If you're ever up that way, maybe we can have lunch."

Jo smiled. "Birmingham isn't that far from Atlanta. I was considering a university there. My brother thinks I can get a scholarship."

"Easy commute," he agreed. "We'll practically be neighbors."

She laughed and the true happiness in the sound was so foreign it startled her for a moment. Eighteen years was a long time to stay silent. No more secrets for her. No more hiding. No more allowing life to pass her by.

Time to live.

\* \* \* \* \*

*Dr. Rowan DuPont has returned to*
*Winchester, Tennessee, to take over the*
*family funeral home, but she is haunted by*
*the memories of her family members' murders.*
*Rowan is prepared to face her past in order to do*
*right by her father's wishes...and to wait out his*
*murderer, a serial killer who is obsessed with her.*

*Read on for a sneak preview of*
**The Secrets We Bury**
*by USA TODAY bestselling author*
*Debra Webb.*

# One

Mothers shouldn't die this close to Mother's Day.

Especially mothers whose daughters, despite being grown and having families of their own, still considered Mom to be their best friend. Rowan DuPont had spent the better part of last night consoling the daughters of Geneva Phillips. Geneva had failed to show at church on Sunday morning, and later that same afternoon she wasn't answering her cell. Her younger daughter entered her mother's home to check on her and found Geneva deceased in the bathtub.

Now the seventy-two-year-old woman's body waited in refrigeration for Rowan to begin the preparations for her final journey. The viewing wasn't until tomorrow evening, so there was no particular rush. The husband of one of the daughters was away on business in London and wouldn't arrive back home until late today. There was time for a short break, which turned into a morning drive that had taken Rowan across town and to a place she hadn't visited in better than two decades.

Like death, some things were inevitable. Coming back to this place was one of those things. Perhaps it was the hours spent with the sisters last night that had prompted memories of Rowan's own sister. She and her twin had once been inseparable. Wasn't that generally the way with identical twins?

The breeze shifted, lifting a wisp of hair across her face. Rowan swiped it away and stared out over Tims Ford Lake. The dark, murky waters spread like sprawling arms some thirty-odd miles upstream from the nearby dam, enveloping the treacherous Elk River in its embrace. The water was deep and unforgiving. Even standing on the bank, at least ten feet from the edge, a chill crept up Rowan's spine. She hated this place. Hated the water. The ripples that broke the shadowy surface…the smell of fish and rotting plant life. She hated every little thing about it.

This was the spot where her sister's body had been found.

July 6, twenty-seven years ago. Rowan and Raven had turned twelve years old that spring. Rowan's gaze lingered on the decaying tree trunk and the cluster of newer branches and overgrowth stretching from the bank into the hungry water where her sister's lifeless body had snagged. The current had dragged her pale, thin body a good distance before depositing her at this spot. It had taken eight hours and twenty-three minutes for the search teams to find her.

Rowan had known her sister was dead before the call had come that Raven had gone missing. Her parents had rushed to help with the search, leaving a neighbor with Rowan. She had stood at her bedroom window watching for their return. The house had felt completely empty and Rowan had understood that her life would never be the same after that day.

No matter that nearly three decades has passed since that sultry summer day, she could still recall the horrifying feel of the final tug, and then the ominous release of her sister's physical presence.

She shifted her gaze from the water to the sky. Last night the temperature had taken an unseasonable plunge. Blackberry winter, the locals called it. Whether it held some glimmer of basis in botany or was merely rooted in folklore, blackberry bushes all over the county were in full bloom. Rowan pulled her sweater tight around her. Though today was the first time she had come to this place since returning home from Nashville, the dark water was never far from her thoughts. How could it be? The lake swelled and withdrew around Winchester like the rhythmic breath of a sleeping giant, at once harmless and menacing.

Rowan had sneaked away to this spot dozens of times after her sister was buried. Other times she had ridden her bike to the cemetery and visited her there or simply sat in Raven's room and stared at the bed where she had once laid her head. But Rowan felt closest to her sister here, near the water that had snatched her life away like the merciless talons of a hawk descending on a fleeing field mouse.

"You should have stayed home," Rowan murmured to herself. The ache, no matter the many years that had passed, twisted in her chest.

She had begged Raven not to go to the party. Her sister had been convinced that Rowan's behavior was nothing more than jealousy since she hadn't been invited. The suggestion hadn't been entirely unjustified, but mostly Rowan had felt a smothering dread, a panic that had bordered on hysteria. She had needed her sister to stay home. Every adolescent instinct she possessed had been screaming and restless with that looming sense of trepidation.

But Raven had ignored her sister's pleas and attended the big barbecue and swim party with her best friend, Tessa Cardwell. Raven DuPont died that day, and Rowan had spent all the years since wondering what she could have done differently to change that outcome.

*Nothing.* She could not rewrite history any more than she was able to change her sister's mind.

Rowan exhaled a beleaguered breath. At moments like this she felt exactly as if her life was moving backward. She'd enjoyed a fulfilling career with the Metropolitan Nashville Police Department as an advisor for the Special Crimes Unit. As a psychiatrist, she had found her work immensely satisfying, and she had helped to solve numerous homicide cases. But then, not quite two months ago, everything had changed. The one case that Rowan didn't recognize had been happening right in front of her, shattering her life…and sending everything spiraling out of control.

The life she had built in Nashville had been comfortable, with enough intellectual challenge in her career to make it uniquely interesting. Though she had not possessed a gold shield, the detectives in the Special Crimes Unit had valued her opinion and treated her as if she was as much a member of the team as any of them. But that was before...*before* the man she admired and trusted proved to be a serial killer—a killer who murdered her father and an MNPD officer as well as more than a hundred other victims over the past several decades.

A mere one month, twenty-two days and about fourteen hours ago, esteemed psychiatrist Dr. Julian Addington emerged from his cloak of secrecy and changed the way the world viewed serial killers. He was the first of his kind: incredibly prolific, cognitively brilliant and innately chameleon-like—able to change his MO at will. Far too clever to hunt among his own patients or social set, he had chosen his victims carefully, always ensuring he or she could never be traced back to him or his life.

Julian had fooled Rowan for the past two decades and then he'd taken her father, her only remaining family, from her. He'd devastated and humiliated her both personally and professionally.

Anger and loathing churned inside her. He wanted her to suffer. He wanted her to be defeated...to give up. But she would not. Determination solidified inside her. She would not allow him that victory or that level of control over her.

Her gaze drifted out over the water once more. Since her father's death and moving back to Winchester, people had asked her dozens of times why she'd returned to take over the funeral home after all these years. She always gave the same answer: *I'm a DuPont, it's what we do.*

Her father, of course, had always hoped Rowan

would do so. It was the DuPont way. The funeral home had been in the family for a hundred fifty years. The legacy had been passed from one generation to the next time and time again. When she'd graduated from college and chosen to go to medical school and become a psychiatrist rather than to return home and take over the family business, Edward DuPont had been devastated. For more than a year after that decision, she and her father had been estranged. Now she mourned that lost year with an ache that was soul-deep.

They had reconciled, she reminded herself, and other than the perpetual guilt she felt over not visiting often enough, things had been good between her and her father. Like all else in her life until recently, their relationship had been comfortable. They'd spoken by phone regularly. She missed those chats. He kept her up to speed on who married or moved or passed, and she would tell him as much as she could about her latest case. He had loved hearing about her work with Metro. As much as he'd wanted her to take over the family legacy, he had wanted her to be happy more than anything else.

"I miss you, Daddy," she murmured.

Looking back, Rowan deeply regretted having allowed Julian to become a part of her life all those years ago. She had shared her deepest, darkest secrets with him, including her previously strained relationship with her father. She had purged years of pent-up frustrations and anxieties to the bastard, first as his patient and then, later, as a colleague and friend.

Though logic told her otherwise, a part of her would

always feel the weight of responsibility for her father's murder.

Due to her inability to see what Julian was, she could not possibly return to Metro, though they had assured her there would always be a place for her in the department. How could she dare to pretend some knowledge or insight the detectives themselves did not possess when she had unknowingly been a close friend to one of the most prolific serial killers the world had ever known?

She could not. *This* was her life now.

Would taking over the family business completely assuage the guilt she felt for letting her father down all those years ago? Certainly not. Never. But it was what she had to do. It was her destiny. In truth, she had started to regret her career decision well before her father's murder. Perhaps it was the approaching age milestone of forty or simply a midlife crisis. She had found herself pondering what might have been different if she'd made that choice and regretting, frankly, that she hadn't.

Since she and Raven were old enough to follow the simplest directions, they had been trained to prepare a body for its final journey. By the time they were twelve, they could carry out the necessary steps nearly as well as their father with little or no direction.

Growing up surrounded by death had, of course, left its mark. Her hyperawareness of death and all its ripples and aftershocks made putting so much stock into a relationship with another human being a less than attractive proposal. Why go out of her way to risk that level of pain in the event that person was lost? And with life came loss. To that end, she would likely never marry or have children. But she had her work and, like her father, she intended to do her very best. Both of them had always been workaholics. Taking care of the dead was a somber albeit important task, particularly for those left behind. The families of the loved ones who passed through the DuPont doors looked to her for support and guidance during their time of sorrow and emotional turmoil.

Speaking of which, she pulled her cell from her pocket and checked the time. She should get back to the funeral home. Mrs. Phillips was waiting. Rowan turned away from the part of her past that still felt fresh despite the passage of time.

Along this part of the shore, the landscape was thickly wooded and dense with undergrowth, which was the reason she'd worn her rubber boots and was slowly picking her way back to the road. As she attempted to slide her phone back into her hip pocket, a limb snagged her hair. Instinctively she reached up to pull it loose, dropping her cell phone in the process.

"Damn it." Rowan reached down and felt through the thatch beneath the underbrush. More of her long blond strands caught in the brush. She should have taken the time to pull her hair back in a ponytail as she usually did. She tugged the hair loose, bundled the thick mass into her left hand and then crouched down to dig around with her right in search of her phone. Like most people, she felt utterly lost without the damn thing.

Where the hell had it fallen?

She would have left it in the car except that she never wanted a family member to call the funeral home and reach a machine. With that in mind, she forwarded calls to her cell when she was away. Eventually she hoped to trust her father's new assistant director enough to allow him to handle all incoming calls. Wouldn't have helped this morning, though, since he was on vacation.

*New* assistant director? She almost laughed at the idea. Woody Holder had been with her father for two years, but Herman Carter had been with him a lifetime before that. She supposed in comparison, *new* was a reasonable way of looking at Woody's tenure thus far. Her father had still referred to him as the new guy. Maybe it was his lackadaisical attitude. At forty-five, Woody appeared to possess absolutely no ambition and very little motivation. Rowan really should consider finding a new, more dependable assistant director and letting Woody go.

Her fingers raked through the leaves and decaying groundcover until she encountered something cool and hard but not metal or plastic. Definitely not her phone. She stilled, frowned in concentration as her sense of touch attempted to identify the object she couldn't see without sticking her head into the bushes. Not happening. She might have chalked the object up to being a limb or a rock if not for the familiar, tingling sensation rushing along every single nerve ending in her body. Her instincts were humming fiercely.

*Assuredly not a rock.*

Holding her breath, she reached back to the same spot and touched the object again. Her fingers dug into the soft earth around the object and curled instinctively.

Long. Narrow. Cylindrical.

She pulled it from the rich, soft dirt, the thriving moss and the tangle of rotting leaves.

*Bone.*

She frowned, studied it closely. *Human* bone.

Her pulse tripped into a faster rhythm. She placed the bone aside, reached back in with both hands and carefully scratched away more of the leaves.

Another bone…and then another. Bones that, judging by their condition, had been here for a very long time.

Meticulously sifting through the layers of leaves and plant life, she discovered that her cell phone had fallen into the rib cage. The *human* rib cage. Her mind racing with questions and conclusions, she cautiously fished out the phone. She took a breath, hit her contacts list and tapped the name of Winchester's chief of police.

When he picked up, rather than hello, she said, "I'm at the lake. There's something here you need to see and it can't wait. Better call Burt and send him in this direction as well." Burt Johnston was a local veterinarian who had served as the county coroner for as long as Rowan could remember.

Chief of Police William "Billy" Brannigan's first response was, "Are *you* okay?"

Billy and Rowan had been friends since grade school. He had made her transition back to life in Winchester so much more bearable. And there was Herman. He was more like an uncle than a mere friend of the family. Eventually she hoped the two of them would stop worrying so about her. She wasn't that fragile young girl who had left Winchester twenty-odd years ago. Recent events had rocked her, that was true, but she was

completely capable of taking care of herself. She would
never again allow herself to be vulnerable to anyone.

"I'm fine, but someone's not. You should stop worrying about me and get over here, Billy."

"I'm on my way."

She ended the call. There had been no need for her to
tell him precisely where she was at the lake. He would
know. Rowan DuPont didn't swim, she never came near
the lake unless it was to visit her sister, and she hadn't
done that in a very, very long time.

Strange, all those times Rowan had come to visit
Raven, she'd never realized there was someone else
here, too.


Barely fifteen minutes passed before Chief of Police Billy—Bill to those who hadn't grown up with
him—Brannigan was tearing nosily through the woods.
Rowan pushed away from the tree she'd been leaning against and waved. He spotted her and altered his
course.

"Burt's on his way." Billy stopped next to her and
pushed his brown Stetson up his forehead. "You sure
you're okay?" He looked her up and down, his gaze
pausing on the boots she wore. Pink, dotted with blue-
and-yellow flowers. They were as old as dirt but she
loved them. She'd had them since she was a teenager.
Frankly, she couldn't believe her father had kept them
all those years.

Billy's lips spread into a grin. "I like the boots."

She rolled her eyes. "Thanks. And, yes, for the second time, I'm okay." She pointed to the throng of bushes

where she'd dropped her phone. "But the female hidden under those bushes is definitely not okay."

He moved in the direction she indicated and crouched down to take a closer look. "You sure this is a female?"

Rowan squatted next to him. "You can see the pelvis." She pointed to the exposed bones that were more or less in a pile. "Definitely female. I can't determine the age, probably over fourteen. I tried not to disturb the positioning of the bones—other than the couple I pulled up before I recognized they were human remains." She leaned in, studying the remains as best she could. "From what I see, it doesn't appear the bones have been damaged by any larger animals."

She indicated the smooth surfaces. "No visible teeth marks. Judging by the positioning, I'd say she was dumped here exactly the way you see. On her left side, knees bent toward her chest, arms flung forward. As tissue deteriorated, the bones settled into a sort of pile and the plant life swallowed them up."

Billy held out his arms in front of him. "Like she was carried to this spot, one arm behind her back, one under her legs—the way a man might carry a woman—and dumped or placed on the ground in that same position."

"That's the way it looks," Rowan agreed.

"You think she was dead when she was left here?"

She made a face, scrutinized what she could see of the skull. "It's difficult to say. There's no obvious indication of cause of death. No visible fractures to the skull or missing pieces, but there's a lot of it I can't see without disturbing the scene."

He hummed a note of indecision. "How long you think she's been here?"

"A while. Years." Rowan shrugged. "Maybe decades. There's a total lack of tissue. The bones I picked up are dry, almost flaky. If there was any clothing, it's gone. To disappear so completely, it would certainly have had to be an organic material of some sort. Maybe when they dig around they'll find a zipper or buttons—something to suggest what she was wearing." She looked to her old friend. "But I'm no medical examiner or anthropologist. I'm merely speculating based on a small amount of knowledge and a very preliminary examination."

"I appreciate your insights." Billy shook his head. "Damn. I can't believe she's been here that long and no one discovered her before now."

"It's a remote, overgrown area." Rowan looked around. "No reason for anyone to come through here." She kept the *except me* to herself. "I suppose it's a good thing I dropped my phone."

When she'd left the funeral home this morning, she'd tucked her phone into the pocket of her jeans. She hadn't bothered with her purse or even her driver's license. Just her phone and, of course, the pepper spray she carried everywhere. The drive to the lake was only a few miles. She had a handgun but she hadn't bothered with it this morning—not for coming here.

But then, she hadn't expected to stumble upon human remains.

In fact, she hadn't expected to see anyone. If she'd had any idea she would be running into Billy and the half a dozen other official folks who would now descend on what was in all likelihood a crime scene, she would have dressed more appropriately. She spent most of her free time in jeans and tees nowadays. The cotton material was breathable. Perfect for wearing under all that protective gear when working in the mortuary room and easy to launder afterward. She wouldn't be winning any awards for her fashion sense, but she was comfortable.

When working with the dead, it was always better to be as comfortable as possible.

Most of her time on the job in Nashville had been spent in heels and business suits. It was a nice perk not to have to dress up anymore. Since taking over the family business, she'd discovered that she preferred a ponytail to a French twist or a chignon any day of the week. And sneakers rather than heels were always a good thing.

Or maybe she'd grown lazy since returning home. She gave herself grace since she was still adjusting to the loss of her father. Of course, she dressed suitably for meeting the families of lost loved ones, for the viewings and the services. The business suits from her years with Metro came in handy for just those purposes. As her father always said, there were certain expectations when overseeing such a somber occasion.

"I'll need an official statement from you." Billy stood and offered his hand. "I can come by the funeral home later and take care of the statement if that works better for you."

She took his hand and pushed to her feet. "That would be my preference, yes." She glanced toward the road. "Does that mean I can go?" Rowan really did not want to be here when the media showed up. And the media would show up. As soon as word about finding human remains spread through the police department, someone would give the local newspaper a heads-up. It was the natural course of things. The possibility of a homicide was a secret hardly anyone could keep. Rowan had endured enough of the spotlight after the release of her book, *The Language of Death*, and then the very public unmasking of her friend and colleague, Julian Addington, as a new breed of prolific serial killer.

Not to mention this was the second set of human bones to be found in Winchester in as many months. The other bones had been identified and the old case solved. Still, a steady stream of homicide cases was never a good thing for the chief of police.

He glanced around. "I don't see any reason for you to stay." He studied her a moment, those dark brown eyes of his searching hers. "If you're sure you're okay?"

Billy Brannigan was a true hometown hero, always had been. First on the football field and in the local charity rodeo circuit, then for more than a decade and a half as a cop, and eventually as the chief of police in Winchester. Folks swore Billy was born wearing a Stetson and cowboy boots. He was a year older than Rowan and he'd made it his mission to take her under his wing after her sister's death. Rowan had been totally lost without her twin, and at twelve she'd had enough insanity in her life with adolescence anyway. Billy had watched over her, threatened to pound anyone who wasn't nice to her. And when her mother died only a few months after her sister, Billy had taken care of Rowan again. He was the only other person on the planet who knew her deepest, darkest secrets.

He and the bastard who murdered her father.

"I'm fine. Really. I'll see you later." The sound of traffic on the road warned that she needed to get moving.

"Hey." His fingers curled around her upper arm when she would have walked past him. "Next time you come out here, bring that big old dog of yours and your handgun or ask me to come. You shouldn't be in a remote area like this alone. We both know *he* is still out there."

*He.* Rowan pushed the image of Julian from her head. She patted her other pocket. "I have my pepper spray." She glanced around again. "And somewhere nearby there might even be a special agent from the FBI's special joint task force keeping an eye on me to make sure I don't aid and abet Julian."

Though at this point the FBI had stopped surveilling her, the very idea made her feel ill. But the Bureau had its reasons in the beginning for suspecting her—all of which were circumstantial and utterly misleading— but nothing she said or did was going to change their minds completely. Her name and the possibilities of her involvement with Julian on a sexual level as well as the suggestion that she might have been part of his extracurricular activities had been smeared across every news channel, every newspaper and online news source. How could she be so close to the man and not see what he was? Particularly considering her formal education and training?

The taint of suspicion would likely follow her the rest of her life. This ugly reality no doubt pleased Julian immensely. At least the folks in her hometown had ignored the rampant rumors for the most part. Business hadn't dropped off and no one looked at her any differently than they ever had. Then again, she'd always been considered strange.

Basically, not much had changed.

Billy nodded, a sad smile on his lips—lips she had fantasized about kissing when she was fourteen years old. So very long ago. A sigh slipped from her. Life would never again be that simple.

"The pepper spray is good, but you should bring your weapon next time," he said, "and Freud, okay?"

She drew in a big breath and let it out dramatically to show him that she was indulging his protective instincts. "*Okay*, Billy, I will not go to any other remote locations alone and without my dog and my handgun. No matter that I'm a grown woman and completely capable of taking care of myself."

For the past six weeks she had worked diligently at honing her self-defense skills. For the first time in her life she owned a handgun and, more important, she knew how to use it. Billy had insisted on giving her lessons. Maybe she was a fool, but she was not afraid of running into Julian. She was prepared for that encounter... looked forward to it, actually. Killing him wasn't her goal—at least not at first. She wanted answers. Then she wanted him to spend the rest of his days in solitary confinement being prodded and poked and tested by forensic psychiatrists.

Billy dipped his head in acknowledgment. "I'm aware, but do it for me."

She rolled her eyes. "For you. Okay."

She gave him a salute, then moved cautiously through the dense bushes until she reached the road, where she'd left her car. In truth, rather than acquiesce to his wishes, she would have loved to tell Billy he was overreacting, being overprotective. Overdoing the big brother thing. But that would be a lie. Julian had murdered all those people, some in ways so heinous that it shocked even seasoned homicide detectives. He had promised Rowan that before he was done, she would want to end the agony of living with all the guilt.

He wasn't the sort of man to make idle threats.

But Rowan intended to see that *he* was the one who wanted the agony to end. She wasn't the only one who had shared secrets during their lengthy friendship. It was true that she hadn't suspected for a moment that he was a killer, but she did know many, many of his most personal thoughts. He had worries just like any other person. He had hopes and dreams. Obviously it was possible he had made up much of what he had told her. Psychopaths oftentimes lied when the truth would serve them better. Still, he was a mere human with human frailties.

She climbed into her car, started the engine. Let him come.

The sooner, the better.

She was ready to show him all she'd learned.

*Don't miss*
The Secrets We Bury
*by Debra Webb,*
*available May 2019*
*wherever MIRA books and ebooks are sold.*

www.Harlequin.com

# THE BLACKEST CRIMSON

This story is dedicated to
my precious older daughter, Erica, whose
strength and courage continue to inspire me.

# One

*Ryan Ridge, Montgomery, Alabama*
*Friday, December 24, 6:30 p.m.*

"It's snowing!" Detective Bobbie Gentry smiled, her heart feeling glad for the first time in nearly a month. It rarely snowed for Christmas in Alabama. If they got snow at all, it usually showed up in January or February. She pressed her hand to the glass of the big bay window that overlooked their front yard. All the houses in the cul-de-sac, including theirs, were decorated with twinkling lights and garland, chasing away the darkness of the cold winter night. She needed this Christmas to be peaceful. She yearned for the normalness of family, for the roar and crackle of a fire as they gathered around the tree they had spent the day decorating.

A contented sigh slipped past her lips. The way those big flakes were falling the neighborhood would look like a classic Christmas card within the hour. Maybe tonight would make up for the endless hours of overtime and weekends away from her family she'd put in this month.

Her husband moved up behind her and circled her waist with his arms. "Man, it's really coming down out there. The weatherman said we're on the lower edge of the storm, but we could get several inches. Maybe more. Wouldn't that be nice?"

"Very nice." Bobbie leaned into him and covered his forearms with hers. A snowstorm bringing more than an inch or two was nearly unheard of this far south. Suited her just fine. In fact, the timing couldn't be better. Today was her first day off this month. She'd slept late and she'd been wearing her husband's Alabama sweatshirt and a pair of lounge pants all day. She might not bother with real clothes until after the holidays. She was so damned glad just to be home. "I really needed this."

James nuzzled her neck. "I'm glad it's over."

Would it ever really be over? The killer was still out there. God only knew where.

For the last three weeks Bobbie and her partner had been working with the FBI on a serial murder case. *The Storyteller.* If she lived ten lifetimes she wouldn't be able to adequately clear the horrors she had seen and heard from her mind. The images of his victims... The endless reports and profiles about the unknown subject's—the killer's—methodology and psychopathy. The Storyteller was the sickest bastard Bobbie had encountered during her career with law enforcement. If she were lucky, she would never encounter that level of pure evil again.

As rough as the past twenty or so days had been,

she was home tonight. She could stand right here for hours and watch the beauty of nature turn the landscape white. When she was a little girl her mother used to tell her that snow was a gift from God to brighten the long, dark winters. Those words had never been truer than they were at this moment.

Bobbie turned in her husband's arms and smiled. "Thank you for taking care of everything while—" she shook her head "—while I was so involved in the case. I was afraid Jamie wouldn't even remember who I was."

James pressed his forehead to hers. "No need to thank me." His arms tightened around her waist. "And, for your information, our son thinks you're a superhero."

She searched his eyes, so very grateful for this wonderful man. "Really?"

James nodded. "I told him Mommy was keeping the monsters away."

How in the world had she gotten so lucky?

"Mommy!"

Jamie slammed into Bobbie's legs. She leaned down and scooped up her little boy. "Look at all the snow. Tomorrow we can make a snowman with Daddy."

"Santa help, too?"

Bobbie kissed his soft cheek, deeply inhaled his baby shampoo scent. He was growing up so fast. In just four months he would be three years old. She wished time would slow down just a little. "I don't know about Santa, sweetie. Tomorrow's Christmas and he'll be very busy."

Her precious little boy had blond hair and gray eyes exactly like his father. Jamie had made her life complete. As much as she valued her career as a homicide detective, this—she smiled at her husband and then at their child—was her world. Maybe one of these days Jamie would have a little brother or sister. She and James had discussed the possibility after making love this morning. They were both ready.

Jamie pressed his forehead against her cheek. "Wu-dolph."

She grinned. "Is it time for Rudolph?"

Her son nodded, those big gray eyes twinkling with anticipation.

"Start the movie." James ushered them toward the sofa. "I'll put the cookies for Santa in the oven."

"Santa! Santa!" Jamie bounced in Bobbie's arms.

"Thanks." She gave her handsome husband a kiss on the jaw.

He smiled. "Love you."

"Love you more."

"Wuv you!" Jamie shouted in his sweet little-boy voice.

"Wuv you, buddy." James backed toward the kitchen. "Save me a seat."

"You got it," Bobbie promised.

As she curled up on the sofa, Jamie snuggled in next to her. She picked up the remote, found the movie they had recorded on the DVR and saved just for tonight, and then hit play. As the credits rolled and the celebrated Christmas song began to play, Bobbie sang along. "Rudolph, the red-nosed reindeer…"

Jamie burst into his own rendition of the tune and her heart swelled with happiness. She kissed the top of his blond head and hugged him tight.

A crash in the kitchen had her twisting around toward the entry hall that led from the front door, past the living room and dining room, and into the kitchen. Their home was a traditional, center-hall Southern colonial and she loved it. It wasn't the popular open concept, but the entire downstairs flowed from one room to the next.

"You having trouble with those cookies, James?" she teased.

Burl Ives's deep baritone filled the room. Jamie was mesmerized by the classic animation. But it was the silence in the kitchen that held Bobbie in an ever-tightening grip. The fine hair on the back of her neck stood on end while her pulse bumped into a faster rhythm. She eased away from Jamie and moved around the sofa. "James?"

Another clang echoed from the kitchen.

For one endless moment time seemed to stop, even as denial and a hundred explanations that didn't include what she understood was happening whirled in her head. Her gaze settled on the stairs. Her service weapon was in the lockbox on her bedside table. Seventeen steps up and then ten yards to the end of the hall, the door was on the left.

No time to go for it.

Adrenaline fired in her blood, jolting her into action. Bobbie reached across the back of the sofa and grabbed Jamie. Ignoring his protests, she ran to the front door. As she twisted the lock, her heart slamming mercilessly against her sternum, she heard the *clump-clump-clump* of rushing footfalls behind her. She jerked the door open and thrust her child onto the porch.

"Run, Jamie!" she screamed, frantic determination

and utter certainty of what was coming coalescing into
sheer terror.

Her little boy stared up at her, scared and confused,
with those precious, precious gray eyes.

"Run for help like Mommy showed you!"

Brutal fingers fisted in her hair and yanked her back.
She kicked at the door, sending it slamming closed. She
prayed her baby would run to the neighbor's house for
help the way she had taught him. Over and over they
had practiced what he was to do if she ever told him to
run because something bad happened.

*Please, please, please keep him safe.*

"Merry Christmas, Detective Gentry," a deep voice
announced.

A sweater-clad forearm looped around her throat and
dragged her backward. Her gaze zoomed in on the
bloody knife in the hand at the end of that arm.

*"James!"*

The sound of her husband's name echoing around her
snapped her from the strange frozen place she'd slipped
into. She clawed at the arm. Twisted hard to get free.

"I should be halfway across Mississippi by now," the
voice—male—said with a snarl. "But I simply couldn't
leave without coming back for you. I've done nothing
but fantasize about you for weeks."

Bobbie tried to dig her heels into the floor to slow
down his momentum, but he was too strong. She gasped
for air as his arm tightened on her throat.

*Think, Bobbie!*

*Relax. Let him believe he's won.* She stopped struggling. Just let him drag her limp body as if she'd lost

consciousness. The hardwood floor turned to tile. He was taking her into the kitchen.

James was in the kitchen.

*Please, please, please let him be okay.*

The bastard yanked her upright, pulling her around to face him, and pinned her against the island with his body. The bloody blade of the knife pressed against her throat. "I've never had a detective before. I can't wait to write your story, Bobbie."

*Oh dear God.* This couldn't be happening. The Storyteller never struck twice in the same place. No one knew his name...or had seen his face.

"You are so beautiful," he whispered roughly. "Even more beautiful than Alyssa or any of the others."

Bobbie bit back the rage she wanted to hurl at him. Alyssa Powell had been his last victim. The one he'd brought from Georgia and dumped in the Montgomery Police Department's jurisdiction.

"We're going to have so much fun together."

*Look at him, Bobbie! Commit his features to memory.* Brown hair and eyes. Soft jaw, narrow nose. Five-ten or -eleven. One-seventy or -eighty pounds. Late thirties. No noticeable facial scars or moles.

"We should go," the bastard said. "That kid of yours has probably alerted the neighbors, who will no doubt call the police. They'll surround your lovely home and make our escape problematic. Can't have that."

This was it. He was taking her.

Wait...where was James? Her heart threatened to burst. *Please, please don't let him be dead.*

"Be a good girl now."

The blade moved a fraction of an inch from her

throat and she snapped into action, ramming her knee upward. He pivoted. She nailed his hip instead of his groin. *Damn it!* She clawed at his eyes. The blade slid across her forearm, slicing through the sweatshirt and her skin. She screamed and punched him in the face with all her might.

He grabbed a handful of her hair before she could twist away and slammed her head against the island's unforgiving granite countertop. Pain split her skull. Her muscles went lax. The warmth of urine spread down her thighs.

She was falling…falling. Her body crumpled to the tile. She blinked, her vision narrowing.

Suddenly she was moving again. He was dragging her by her arm…moving toward the side exit to the garage.

Leaving.

*James*…where was James?

Her lids drooped lower, almost closing, but not before she saw her husband on the floor…his beautiful gray eyes wide open, frozen in fear…his mouth slack.

The tile around him was no longer white. It was the blackest crimson.

# Two

Pain.

Bobbie's eyelids tried to flutter open, but she couldn't bear the pain of opening her eyes.

Where was she?

*Think!* It was snowing. Her lips tried to smile. A hot sting tore at her mouth. Her tongue darted out. *Busted lip.*

What was wrong with her?

Was it Christmas yet?

*Jamie.*

A frown furrowed her brow, making her head throb and sparking little pinpoints of light behind her lids. What was wrong with her head?

Had James put out the presents from Santa yet?

Jagged images of white tile and black, flowing crimson flashed in her head. Unblinking gray eyes staring at her.

Desolate screams echoed in her ears, burned her throat.

Bobbie snapped her eyes open and listened. She was the one screaming.

*James was dead.*

Sobs thickened in her throat. Her husband was dead. The bastard had killed him. She tried to move. Couldn't. Where the hell was she?

The memory of her body sliding on the cold tile floor, her head hanging like the last pearl on a broken strand, and her arm feeling as if it was being pulled from its socket bobbed to the surface of her confusion.

*The Storyteller.*

Bobbie yanked at her restraints. More of those screams that welled up from deep, deep inside her reverberated in the air. This couldn't be happening. *Nooooo!* Agonizing sobs shuddered through her for long minutes. When she could cry no more, she struggled to pull herself together.

*Think!* She licked her dry and damaged lips.

What about her baby? A wail rose up from the farthest recesses of her heart. Was her baby okay? Hot tears slid down her face. She had sent him to the neighbor's house for help. *That kid of yours has probably alerted the neighbors, who will no doubt call the police.*

*Focus, Bobbie.* She had to get out of here. Her baby needed her.

Carefully, she moved each limb, tugging and pulling in all directions. She was tied to a flat surface that was not completely rigid. She rocked her body as best she could. The squeak of metal against metal accompanied her movements and the cold, crisscross pattern of it dug into her skin. A minute was required for her sluggish brain to analyze and determine that her restraints confined her to a narrow, probably portable bed, like a cot.

*Look around the room and get your bearings.* Dim lights. Wait. No. There was no light fixture on the ceiling. There was no ceiling, really, just wood beams and boards. Log walls, too. Rustic. Cobwebs hung here and there as if no one had lived here for a very long time. There was one window. Small. Feeble light filtered through the grimy panes. A hunting cabin, she decided. Deep in the woods probably. Met the criteria of the Storyteller's MO. She squeezed her eyes shut and thought of all the briefings she had attended, all the crime scene reports, the medical examiner files.

Not one of the Storyteller's fourteen known victims had survived.

*She was going to die.*

Her body started to shake. Who would take care of her baby? James was dead. Another sob quaked through her trembling body. Her parents were gone. She had no siblings. James was an only child as well. He'd been adopted at five by an older couple who were retired and spent the better part of the year in a senior community in Arizona.

Jamie needed her. There was no one else.

She could not die.

Renewed determination expanded inside her. She knew this bastard's MO frontward and backward. He would spend the next three to four weeks torturing her. Images of the other women—battered, raped and mutilated—flashed before her eyes. She squeezed them shut. *No looking back.* Near the end of his ritual, he would begin what he referred to as his victim's story. He tattooed their responses to his torture and their pleas for mercy on their backs before strangling them to death.

The nylon rope around her neck abruptly filtered into Bobbie's consciousness. Like the others, she would wear it like a too-tight, braided necklace until he was ready to finish her off. And then, in order to preserve his prized masterpiece for all to see, he would dump her body in a public place where she would be found quickly.

Except Bobbie wasn't going to die. She would not allow him to win. Fury simmered low in her belly. She closed her eyes and shut out all stimuli. *Ignore the pain and the fear, Bobbie. Just listen.*

Something—a branch, maybe—rubbed at the cabin. Definitely in the woods, she decided. The wind whistled softly, building to a weak howl now and again. The cabin wasn't insulated, allowing the wind to whip through any cracks. Quiet splats told her snow was still falling. The meteorologist had warned they might get several inches. James had mentioned they were on the edge of the storm. If what she heard was snow falling, that could mean she was not far from home.

Was the rope binding her wrists and ankles the same as the yellow nylon currently fitted around her neck— the same rope he'd used on the other victims? According to the ME reports the abrasion patterns were similar. All she had to do was get one hand loose and she could free herself. While she worked at the ropes, she concentrated on the scents around her. The place smelled old and a little like piss. A deserted property helped give the psychopath the privacy he needed.

*I've never had a detective before.*

"Biggest mistake of your life, you piece of shit." She would make him pay for what he had done.

All she had to do was get these damned ropes loose. Her head throbbed. It felt swollen, as if it was filled with cotton balls. She probably had a concussion from when he'd banged her head against the counter. The pain seemed to radiate from the right side of her skull. Her arm ached. The memory of the slice of the knife blade through her flesh made her flinch. A piece of cloth was tied tight around her forearm in a makeshift bandage. She couldn't tell if he'd stitched the wound as he usually did those of his victims. The dark curl of fear began again deep in her chest.

*You will not be like the others, Bobbie.*

*Focus on the details.* How long had she been here? If it was still snowing, it couldn't be more than a few hours to a day. Was it Christmas? Light filtered past the grimy window. Had to be mid-morning or later. How had she slept so many hours?

Drugs. The Storyteller drugged his victims, presumably to control them when he was away. It was doubtful he would do so when he was with the victim. He wouldn't want to numb her to his torture.

*Victim.* She was the victim now. No way to deny that cold hard fact. Agony welled inside her. She did not want to die. Her baby needed her.

*Stay in control, Bobbie. Think like a cop, not like a victim.*

She inhaled deeply. No scent of a fire, not even the ashes of an extinguished one. Judging by how cold it was, she doubted he'd built a fire. He wouldn't want to draw attention with the smoke. She shivered as if her body had only just recognized the lack of heat in the primitive shelter.

There was no way to gauge how long he would be gone. Ignoring the pain, she worked her hands harder, straining against the nylon in hopes of stretching it. She listened intently for any new sound. The gentle rustle of the tree limbs, the whisper of the wind and the occasional soft slaps of snow were the only sounds. The gentle pats of snow were fewer and farther between now. Maybe the snow had stopped and the noise was nothing more than the accumulated drifts falling from the tree limbs when the wind blew.

If she was in the woods, was there a road? Had to be. The snow would have covered his tracks even if the search for her had expanded far enough. Pinpointing her location would be difficult. No wonder he hadn't been caught.

The Storyteller was an unknown subject, or *unsub*— at least that was what the FBI called him. They had no name or physical description. The profile they had built based on his victimology suggested he was mid to late thirties, white, ritualistic and a true psychopath. He'd likely been abused by a family member as a child. He was methodical and meticulous in his work. The profile concluded that he held a quiet, unassuming job that drew little or no attention to him. He had friends, but kept his social life low-key. One theory was that he stalked his victims via the internet or other media. All his victims had public Facebook pages except her. Wait, there was the department's page. She and her partner had been spotlighted on the Montgomery PD page a few times.

Newt would be looking for her. Her heart swelled into

her throat. Howard Newton had been her partner since she made detective. He and her uncle Teddy, the chief of police, would be doing everything possible to find her.

"You gotta help them out, Bobbie." She jerked at the ropes restraining her hands. Her right abruptly pulled free. Her heart thundered into a faster rhythm. She reached across her torso and worked on the left. Her fingers fumbled. They were stiff and numb from the cold. She gritted her teeth and forced her fingers to cooperate.

At last her left hand slid free. Bobbie sat up. The room spun. "Shit." She closed her eyes until the spinning stopped.

When she'd regained her equilibrium, she slowly bent forward and worked to free her ankles. There was a chair and a table in the center of the room, along with what looked like a kerosene lamp. She spotted a kerosene heater as well. So that was how he kept himself warm when he was here. Kerosene heaters didn't smoke so there were no worries about drawing attention. Kerosene could be bought at most gas stations, allowing for untraceable purchases.

The ropes fell away from her ankles. Her hands and feet were a little swollen. Didn't matter. She had to get out of here. She swung her bare feet onto the cold wood floor. There were cracks between the floorboards. Icy air floated up around her legs. Had she been wearing shoes? No. She hadn't. *Damn it.*

Taking it slow, she stood. A little spinning accompanied the move, but she rode it out. It wasn't until she got up that she realized her lounge pants were damp where she had relieved herself. The cold, wet fabric made her shiver. When she could move without falling, she staggered to the window. Beyond the dirty panes of glass a blanket of white covered the earth. Bare trees sprouted up from that vast winter wonderland, making it impossible to see anything beyond the small clearing around the cabin. Definitely deep in the woods. No sign of tracks or a vehicle.

Okay. She needed a coat and shoes…and a weapon.

She surveyed the one-room cabin again. Where she stood was the cot and its bare rusty springs. Next to the rustic table and chair in the middle of the room was the portable kerosene heater. To her left and in the far corner was the only door. The single window was straight across the small space on the opposite wall. Against the rear wall of the cabin, opposite the door, stood a primitive cabinet. The cabinet looked really old, like something found in an antiques shop except it was covered with dust and cobwebs.

She padded over to the cabinet and reached for a wooden knob. The purr of an engine hauled her attention to the window. She rushed across the room, stumbling in her haste. Peering through the soiled glass, she watched an old, black SUV roll into the clearing. All she could see was one side of the front end with its dented fender and the driver's door. She stood to the side of the window so whoever was behind the wheel wouldn't see her.

The driver's door opened and a black boot planted in the snow. A man wearing a dark coat and skullcap emerged. He turned his face toward the cabin.

Bobbie drew back.

*It was him.*

# *Three*

Bobbie turned all the way around, frantically scanning the room. She needed a weapon. *Anything.* She grabbed the kerosene lantern and moved to the door. The lantern wasn't much of a weapon, but she had the element of surprise on her side. He expected her to be tied to the bed. She had a shot here. *Disorient him and get out the door. Run like hell.*

She tried to slow her heart, tried to quiet the blood roaring through her veins. *Stay steady.*

*Be strong.* This might be her only chance to make a run for it.

*He will kill me and I cannot die. Jamie needs me!*

She tightened her grip on the lantern's handle and prepared to swing it. *Come on, you bastard!*

Chains rattled. The door opened with a slow groan, creating a barrier between them.

*Wait...wait...wait. Let him get all the way inside. Then strike!*

Without moving past the open door he stamped his

boots on the floor, and then he scrubbed them back and forth to clear away the packed snow.

The door blocking his view of her and the empty cot, she braced to swing.

He stilled.

Fear exploded in her chest, rushed icy cold through her muscles.

*He knows!*

He shoved the door into her. She stumbled back and he rushed her. She swung the lantern at him. Glass crashed. The distinct odor of kerosene filled the air.

He jammed his elbow into her chest, knocking her off balance before throwing his body on top of hers. She kicked, scratched, latched onto his ear with her teeth and pulled for all she was worth.

He howled and punched her over and over in the stomach. She released his ear, gasping for breath. He wrapped his fingers around her throat and squeezed until her vision faded.

When she came to herself again, pain exploding in her head, he was dragging her by the hair toward the cot. The rough-hewn wood floor ripped at her skin anywhere it was bare. She clutched his leg and yanked with all her might. He fell forward. His fingers tugged free of her hair, tearing a handful of strands from her scalp.

She scrambled away from him and rushed toward the door on all fours. He grabbed her by the ankles and jerked her back.

He was suddenly on his feet. She tried to move away, but he was too quick. He kicked her hard in the side.

She curled into a ball.

"Did you think it would be that easy?" He kicked her again.

She grunted, the air discharging from her lungs.

"Now you get to find out what happens when you make me angry."

He raised his booted foot. She twisted, tried to roll away…too late. He slammed his heel down on her right leg. She felt the bone snap. More screams burst from her aching throat. Her body shuddered and bile, hot and bitter, surged into her mouth.

His fingers were in her hair again, dragging her. She clawed desperately at his leg. The new sources of pain stole her breath, but she couldn't give up. He flung her aching body onto the cot.

"I thought I'd wait until tomorrow. Until I was better prepared." He clutched her throat again, holding her against the rusty metal springs. "But I guess we'll begin now. It appears you can't wait."

Her vision faded from the lack of oxygen. She needed air. He kept the pressure on until she blacked out.

Minutes later—she didn't know how many—she regained consciousness once more. Her hands were tied so tightly to the cot they had gone numb. She couldn't feel her feet either. Her side hurt badly. Maybe a cracked rib or two. But it was her leg that throbbed so hard she could scarcely breathe.

The door slammed. She twisted her head in an effort to see what he was doing now. He'd been outside. Bastard. She wanted to poke his eyes out and twist his balls off his body. She wanted to watch him bleed nearly to death, and then, in those final moments, she wanted to put a bullet between his eyes. In her mind, she saw herself doing those things. For James…and for Jamie.

He dropped a bag, something like a canvas tote, and took off his coat, tossed it aside. He picked up the bag and stalked toward her. The scrape of wood against wood echoed as he dragged the table closer. When the table was positioned just so, he deposited the bag there.

Images of the Storyteller's victims, accompanied by the horrific details of each report she had read, sifted through her mind. The bag would hold his tools. Knives, scissors, needles and thread—all the instruments he would need to inflict days and weeks of torture. The reports concluded that he often stitched up the larger wounds to ensure no unnecessary complications cropped up before he was finished. Pain and suffering, as well as death, would come to the victim at his discretion.

He pulled the chair closer to the cot and sat down before settling his dispassionate gaze on her. "We'll see how your story goes, Detective. As I told you, you're my first member of law enforcement. I'm quite excited."

He picked up the scissors and grabbed the hem of her sweatshirt. She shuddered.

"You've already given me more trouble than the others." He paused in his work and smiled at her. "It'll be quite exhilarating to have a true challenge for a change. The same old same old at times grows boring." He made a face. "'Don't hurt me,'" he mocked. "'Please. I'll do anything!'"

He laughed, the sound grotesque. "No matter how dumb or smart or rich or poor, they all cried and begged the same way in the end. Is that what you're going to do, Detective Gentry?"

More ways to kill him rolled through her mind. She could stab him with those scissors. The knives he had in that bag would make perfect tools for whittling away at his body while he writhed and screamed. Then she would gut him like a deer being prepped for processing. She would do it slowly, making sure he felt every moment of fierce pain before she allowed him to escape into death. *For James.* The memory of her husband's motionless body burned through her.

*Don't look back. Focus, Bobbie.* She wasn't going to survive this monster unless she stayed smart and focused. *Turn the tables on him.*

"You killed fourteen women," she accused, her voice trembling with a new sense of rage. "And…my husband. You won't get away with it forever. You'll get caught eventually."

He smiled. It turned her stomach. "The brilliant FBI is way behind, Detective. They have no idea of all the stories I've told. They only know the ones I've wanted to share."

Her stomach roiled with the meaning of his words. "How many?"

He lifted an eyebrow at her. "Do you really want to know the answer to that question, Detective? I would hate for you to be more scared than you already are."

"I'm not scared." Bobbie banished the voice whispering *liar, liar* in her head.

A sadistic grin split his face. "Maybe you aren't, but you will be. I'm going to make you wish you were dead so many times that before I'm done you'll beg me to kill you."

"What if I kill you first?" She tried to swallow, wished her throat wasn't so dry.

He removed a knife from his tool bag. "We both know that isn't going to happen."

He pushed away the unattached sides of the sweatshirt and revealed her naked breasts. The first prick of the knife made her breath catch.

The tip of the blade trailed downward between her breasts. "So far, twenty-one."

She stared at him, willing him to look at her. "You've killed twenty-one women?"

Another of those sick grins twisted his lips. "Only eighteen. The others were male, including your pansy-ass husband. I certainly didn't choose him. He was simply in the way of getting to you."

She tugged at her restraints. She wanted to tear him apart. "He had a name. James. James Gentry." *Use the hurt and anger to your advantage!* "You have a name— what is it? If we're going to spend so much time together, you can at least tell me that."

"I walked in the back door of your lovely home like I owned the place," he said, ignoring her demands. "I'd been there many times fantasizing about you."

Fury burst inside her. She jerked at her restraints. "I've fantasized about you, too," she snarled. "I swear to God I'm going to watch you die."

"He was just putting the cookies in the oven," he continued as if she'd said nothing. The bastard made an annoying tsk-tsk sound. "Too bad he dropped the pan, alerting you to my presence."

She closed her eyes against his words. *Don't look.* Still those final images of James lying on the floor, blood spreading across the white tile in a river of crimson, overwhelmed her. *This is what he wants, Bobbie. To keep you off balance.*

"He looked so surprised. He didn't even have time to blink. I slammed him over the head with my tire iron. I hit him so hard it made my arm hurt. To tell the truth I think he was dead before I gutted him. Can't be sure if his heart was pumping out all that blood or if it was just gravity."

"Why?" The voice, though hers, wasn't even familiar. She sounded like a wounded animal, lost and alone and hopeless.

"You know how I love long, brown hair, but it was your eyes that did me in. You have the palest blue eyes I've ever seen. I had to have you."

Rage roared anew inside her. "I am going to kill you," she promised.

He chuckled as if he knew something she didn't. "You'll dream of killing me many times before I'm finished, I promise."

The knife pierced her skin near one nipple, slid beneath the surface as if he planned to lift the skin right off her breast. Bobbie gritted her teeth. She refused to scream for him.

"My name is Gaylon Perry, but you can call me Perry. I want to hear you cry out my name when I'm rutting into you, over and over." He leaned close. She recoiled. "I'm going to hurt you in every imaginable way until the moment you draw your last, weary breath."

Bobbie focused on her son's face. *No matter what this monster does, I'm coming back to you, Jamie. I promise.*

# Four

A drop of water plopped on her left cheek. Bobbie's eye twitched. She should open her eyes. *Don't want to.*

It was quiet. He was gone. She should try to escape. *Hopeless.*

Another splat of water. The roof of this godforsaken place leaked. Must be raining.

She didn't care.

She was dying. She *hoped* she was dying.

She wanted to die.

Her head didn't hurt anymore, but the rest of her body ached and burned as if gasoline had been poured down her throat followed by a lit match. He had broken her leg. She supposed it had started to heal, but she wasn't sure she could stand on her own. He dragged her off the cot twice a day to use the bucket in the corner. If she allowed her body to relieve itself in between, he made her lick it up.

*Why didn't she die?*

She told her heart to stop beating. She even held her breath in hopes of dying. As soon as she lost consciousness her lungs would draw in the stale, nasty air, forcing her to live a little longer. Her insides hurt. Cracked ribs, among other injuries. She had been raped so many times and ways, she felt hollow inside. At some point she had stopped caring what happened next. She simply lay there like an empty carcass while he banged into her over and over and over.

Lying on her back on the rusty springs, she turned her face to the ceiling. Her neck muscles protested the move. Her muscles were atrophying. As a twelve-year-old she'd broken her wrist. She remembered what her lower arm and hand had looked like when the cast came off. Shrunken and scrawny. The body that no longer belonged to her likely looked that way now. Didn't matter. It wasn't her anymore.

Mostly, she was gone.

One by one she counted the beams that held up the roof. She wished it would fall in or break open so the rain would drown her. It had been raining for days. She'd lost count of the number of days she had been here. She'd tried to keep a tally, but without any reliable cues she'd lost the rhythm. Weeks for sure. Maybe a month. Her time should be coming soon.

She had reconciled herself with the realization that she could not be brave enough to survive. Not even for her son. She was too weak. Each day the Storyteller allowed her a small bottle of water and a little prepackaged lunch—the kind kindergarten kids took to school in their backpacks. According to the monster's calculations, that was sufficient to sustain her. To prolong the agony.

Soon he would kill her. He'd brought the new tools, bottles of black ink and an odd tattoo instrument. He'd said it was more than a century old. The solid-brass tattoo needle that looked more like an iron stake made her stomach roil. Something else to look forward to in the coming days.

The rope around her throat had abraded her skin to the point that it felt like an oozing sore.

She was filthy and weak.

Why didn't she just die?

In the beginning she had been strong and determined. She memorized every detail of his face as he taunted her. After he'd raped her three or four times she tuned out the shock and horror and studied him. She wanted to remember it all. His torso was covered with scars. Words were carved amid the waffle-pattern scars. *Evil. Devil.* Who had marked him a monster? His father? Mother? Another intimate?

Then she stopped caring.

She was going to die. She wanted to die. She needed this nightmare to end.

*I'm so sorry, Jamie.*

The familiar rattle of chains and groan of the door opening signaled he was back. She didn't have to look to know for sure. She recognized the routine of his movements, the smell of his cheap aftershave. The way he walked, how he breathed. Bile rose in her throat. It was feeding time. Did she have the energy to chew, much less swallow? Didn't matter.

"Today is a special day," he said as he came closer.

She didn't bother to open her eyes. Who cared what today was? There was only one thing she wanted. *Please forgive me, Jamie. Mommy couldn't be strong enough.*

A heavy object plunked on the floor by the cot. She opened one eye just enough to have a look. Big, plastic ice chest. She licked her dry, cracked lips. Maybe he was going to chop her up and put her in there.

Not his MO. He had to tattoo his goddamned story first. She would be left in a park or other public place to ensure she was found before decomp had done too much damage. Preserving the story was, after all, the most important step in his MO.

Sick son of a bitch.

Changing the way he disposed of her wouldn't be the first time he'd deviated from his MO, she suddenly remembered. For the first time in all the years the FBI had been tracking him, he'd changed his pattern when he abducted and murdered Alyssa Powell. He had never, to the FBI's knowledge, taken two victims in one year, much less three.

"Why did you take her…and me?" Her voice sounded rusty and alien to her ears. The answer didn't really matter. Nothing mattered anymore. She was already dead in every way that mattered.

He stared at her for a long moment. "I've already answered that question, Detective. It was those lovely eyes of yours."

The tiniest spark of anger fueled her. "No," she argued, the single word coming out in a growl. "You took Alyssa Powell and then me after you'd already carried out your annual hunt."

Another of those endless moments elapsed with him

staring at her with those empty eyes. "That's precisely where the FBI screws up. They forget that the monsters they seek are only human. You see, Detective, I lost someone this year, too. For a time I was quite beside myself. We all seek solace in our own way. Sweet little Alyssa was like a healing balm to my tortured soul." A sickening smile spread across his face. "You, however, were for pure pleasure."

Whatever flicker of emotion she had experienced vanished. *Don't give him the satisfaction of a reaction.* She lay still and silent, and waited for what came next.

He removed the top from the ice chest and steam rose in the cold air. Somehow her other eye opened. After the last beating she wasn't sure if that eye would work again. The pungent scent of bleach permeated the room. He reached in and pulled out a white wad of cloth and then he replaced the lid.

"It's time for a little housekeeping, Detective." He smirked. "We wouldn't want the FBI to find any trace evidence. I prefer to keep my DNA to myself." He sniggered. "And, of course, I want you to look nice for release day."

He started to wipe her face with the cloth. Heat melted into her skin. She couldn't move or resist. It felt...*good* even if the bleach smell stole her breath.

"Feels good, doesn't it?" He laughed, and taunted, "So good."

She ignored his voice and allowed herself to cling to the promise of the warm cloths. Again and again he removed a hot cloth from the chest and washed her. The smell of bleach burned her nose and her eyes. Every inch of her body was carefully cleansed and left sting-

ing by the harsh chemical. The FBI profile said this was
his final step before tattooing the story. The Storyteller
always cleaned the bodies with bleach before disposing
of them. He never left evidence.

Yes, death was near.

Bobbie closed her eyes. The bleach smell no longer
bothered her. Soon she would be out of her misery. She
was so tired. All she wanted was for the pain to stop.
She didn't want to remember anymore.

She had failed her husband and her son. If she hadn't
been so gung ho to be a part of the investigation, this
piece of shit would never have laid eyes on her.

This was her fault—all of it. Her husband's murder,
her son becoming an orphan. She didn't deserve to live.

He untied her hands and her feet and lifted her up.

"Time for a potty break."

She didn't argue or struggle. She couldn't. The ability to fight had deserted her days ago. He carried her to
the five-gallon bucket and set her down on top of it. Her
body instinctively relieved itself. He cleaned those parts
of her again and dragged her back to the cot.

"Almost finished with this step."

From the chest, he pulled a large rubber thing with
a small hose attached. An old-fashioned douche bottle,
she realized. He wasn't leaving anything to chance even
though he'd used condoms all the times he'd stuck his
dick inside her. He bragged to her about how he kept
his body free of hair, except his head. He couldn't walk
around bald. His father was bald; he was nothing like
his father.

The bleach stung. She closed her eyes again and tried
to go someplace else. A place far away by the water

where it was warm and sunny. James would be sitting next to her. Jamie would be playing in the sand a few feet away, his blond hair gleaming in the sun. His bright gray eyes would be dancing with excitement and that beautiful little-boy smile would be wide on his face.

"Jamie," she murmured. She missed him so.

The bastard stuck a water bottle to her lips. Her mouth instinctively sipped at the cool wetness. She tried to stop herself, but her body was too desperate for water.

He poked food into her mouth. She chewed, and then swallowed. Why did her body keep gasping for the next breath, reaching toward the next sip of water or bite of food? All she wanted was to die.

As if the God who had forsaken her suddenly felt pity on her, her mind and body seemed to float away from the rusty springs and the tight ropes. The pain disappeared.

Jamie's sweet face swam before her eyes. "Mommy's so sorry, baby."

"You don't mind if I use that, do you? It'll make a great line in your story."

The ugly voice shattered her fantasy.

"Over you go."

Brutal hands flipped her facedown on the scratchy, rusty springs.

A needle pierced her hip. Something hot singed the muscle there.

"Sweet dreams, Detective."

# *Five*

It was daylight again. More sun than usual penetrated the film on the window. The sky must be clear. No more rain.

Her cot was in a different location. Farther from the wall. More in the center of the room, away from the place where the roof leaked. He probably didn't want to risk his masterpiece getting wet if the rain started again.

She wished she had the strength to get up and look out the window. It had been days or maybe a week since she had allowed herself to wonder if the FBI and her partner were still looking for her. They wouldn't find her. The Storyteller's victims were never found until he was ready for the reveal.

Didn't matter. She was going to die, like the others. She had resigned herself to that fate. Maybe her partner would take Jamie in. Tears burned her eyes. She found it amazing given her numerous injuries and the level of pain she continued to endure that she still noticed the sting of tears. Yet, somehow she did.

She wished she could hold her baby one last time, give him a kiss and promise him that he would be okay.

How could he be okay? His father had been murdered.

Had they buried James already?

Her chest tightened. She hadn't gotten to say goodbye.

*Don't think about it. Focus on the pain and the promise of death.* It was the only relief she could trust.

Today she had new pain. Her back was raw and burning from the hundreds of tiny pricks of the needle. The rest of her wasn't much better. The rusty springs had scratched and rubbed at the front of her body, inflaming the old as well as the new cuts and scrapes. The bleach had irritated her skin and her insides.

She quieted her thoughts and listened. When had he left? A frown drew her eyebrows together. Her hands felt different. Ever so carefully she moved her right hand. It wasn't restrained. With much effort she lifted her head. It felt as heavy as a bowling ball. The room spun a little. Her left hand wasn't restrained either. He couldn't have gone far. Out to that black SUV he drove, maybe. He would never leave her unrestrained like this if he was going far.

Moving slowly, she drew her hand to her face and touched it. The small rectangles of the springs had imprinted on her cheek. She thought of all the times he had sliced and split her skin, and then sutured or glued the lacerations. She hurt in so many places. Yet, it was inside that hurt the worst. The things he had done to her where no one would see had finished her off, stolen her desire to go on.

Though she was still breathing, she felt dead. Jamie needed a better mother than she could ever be after this. He would be safer and happier if she died. She was too broken to be reliable.

Unable to keep holding her head up any longer, she lowered her cheek to the bedsprings. She closed her eyes and thought of her precious little boy. He would grow up to be smart and kind like his father. She hoped they would tell him stories about his parents. Maybe keep pictures in his room so he would remember her and his father. Would he remember her as he graduated high school or married one day? When he had children of his own, would he wish his mother could meet them?

A plaque with her name on it would be added to the long line of others commemorating fallen officers at the Montgomery Police Department. Years from now when Jamie was in the fifth grade, his class—like all the fifth-grade classes across the city—would take a tour of the department. Would he point to the plaque and tell his friends that one was for his mom?

More tears welled and she closed her eyes. She was so tired. It was time to die. Perry would be back soon to finish her story. Then it would be over.

Bobbie dozed off. She had no idea for how long. The sound of her little boy calling for his mommy awakened her.

"Jamie?"

She blinked. Reminded herself that she was still here in this hellhole. No one was coming to save her because no one knew how to find her. They never found the Storyteller's victims until he was ready.

She had been dreaming.

It was still daytime. Sunlight filtered in through the grimy window. She needed to pee. It was so cold. Her aching body shivered. If she peed on the floor, he would make her lick it up. She wasn't sure she had it in her to do that again.

Could she get up and make it to the bucket? Were her feet unrestrained as her hands were? Why would he leave her this way? Was it a trick? Was he watching from some hiding place she couldn't see?

Moving slowly, she worked her way into an upright position. The dull ache in her right leg made her cry out. Her ribs were better but still sore. The only thing good about the new pain on her back was that he hadn't touched her in those other horrible ways since he started his twisted tattooed story.

Once she was sitting with her feet on the floor, she grabbed hold of the table and attempted to pull herself to a standing position.

"Oh God." She flopped back down onto the cot. The springs bounced and squeaked. She panted to ride out the wave of nausea and the intense pain. Slowly, the worst of the pain subsided and she tried again. She pulled to her feet. Her legs wobbled and the room spun, but she stayed upright. After a few deep breaths, she tried to walk. The pain in her leg was nearly unbearable, but she refused to give up.

The bucket was nearly full of urine and feces. The smell as well as the sight had her retching. Didn't matter. She had no dignity left—who cared where she peed or puked as long as it hit the damned bucket? After she'd relieved herself, she stood for a few moments, testing her weight. Wherever he had gone, he'd taken his bag of tools. Had he really left her here untethered for this length of time? Hope dared to register. She hobbled to the window and peered outside. The snow was long gone as was the rain. The woods looked denser without all the snow; the tree limbs were bare and desolate. She could see the narrow dirt road now. It was muddy and rutted. No sign of his SUV or of him.

Maybe he was dead. Maybe he'd been in a car accident. What if he'd been arrested? He could have left evidence at her house. The decision to take her had been a hasty one, the act not as well planned as his usual ones. Was there some reason he'd acted so carelessly? Oh yes, he'd told her he lost someone.

The hope that had registered minutes ago dared to expand. She needed clothes to protect her from the cold. Shoes. Could she escape before he came back?

Maybe he wasn't coming back. The bastard could be dead or incarcerated.

She laughed, the sound as rusty as the bedsprings she had lain on for weeks.

She could run. What did it matter if she died in the woods or here? Dead was dead. At least if she ran she had a chance…*to get back to Jamie.*

Agony flooded her. How could she dare to hope? Giving up all hope had been her only escape from this hell. If all she wanted was to die, nothing else mattered.

But she didn't want to die.

Sobs rose in her frail body and shook her. She dropped to her knees and cried so hard she couldn't breathe. Her baby's face filled her mind. All she wanted was her little boy. She wanted to keep him safe, to take him to his first day of school, to watch him graduate and get married one day. She wanted to hold his children...

*She didn't want to die.*

The realization roared through her like a train bursting from a dark tunnel. She wanted to live. By God, she had to get out of this damned place and back to her baby.

Even if she died tomorrow, today she had to try.

She struggled to her feet. Where were the lounge pants she'd been wearing? He'd cut the sweatshirt off her body. She searched the cabin. Nothing.

*Damn it.* She'd been barefoot when he dragged her out of her house. She'd just have to make it without shoes or clothes. Freezing to death was as good an option as having him strangle her.

She touched the rope around her neck, tried to loosen it but couldn't. All she succeeded in doing was breaking the scabs beneath and causing blood to seep from the damaged skin. The rope could wait. The lead to the noose was only two or three feet long. It wouldn't get in her way.

*You can do this.*

She was making a run for it. Adrenaline lit inside her. She was getting out of here right now.

She tried the door. It wouldn't budge.

*Shit!* She'd forgotten it was chained on the outside. The window. She could shatter it with the chair and then climb out.

The roar of an engine broke the silence and snapped her attention to the door.

Fear detonated in her heart.

*He's back!*

She glanced around the room. Like before, there was nothing she could use for a weapon. Her gaze landed on the bottles of ink on the table. Between the bottles lay the Asian tattoo needle. It was bigger around than her thumb, save the pointy needle tip, and at least twelve inches long. Her heart kicked into a faster rhythm. That could work.

He was at the door. Chains rattled. *Oh, hell!*

She grabbed the needle and quietly settled facedown on the cot. With the weapon hidden by her hand and forearm, she laid her right cheek against the springs, closed her eyes and waited.

The door opened with its too familiar, weary groan. Fabric rustled as he removed his coat and tossed it aside. His footfalls echoed around her as he came nearer. She held her breath. He sat down in the chair next to the cot.

"Beautiful." He sighed. "This might be my best work yet."

The rip of Velcro echoed in the cold air, and then there was a soft splat on the floor. She cracked her eye open just enough to see what he was doing. He had withdrawn a hypodermic needle and was about to plunge it into her hip.

She screamed bloody murder.

His attention snapped to her face.

Bobbie lunged upward, the tattoo instrument held like a stake, and stabbed it deep into his chest.

The hypodermic needle hit the floor as he tried too late to jump back.

The chair overturned. He sprawled across the floor.

Bobbie grabbed the chair and slammed it down on

his head. She hit him again and again. "Die you son of a bitch! Die!"

When he stopped flailing his arms, she stumbled back, the air surging in and out of her lungs. A crimson stain spread from the brass tool she had jammed in his chest. Shuddering at the charge of adrenaline, she wished she had matches so she could burn the place down and send him to hell where he belonged.

She rushed to the door, grabbed his coat and ran. In her haste, she stumbled down the steps, falling flat on her face on the cold wet ground. Pain screaming through her, she staggered to her feet and dragged on the coat. She felt in the pockets and found the keys. *Thank God.*

Shaking so hard she could hardly hold on to the keys, she climbed into the vehicle that was at least as old as she was and turned the ignition. When the engine roared to life, she cried out in relief.

She shoved the gearshift into reverse, turned the SUV around, and took off along the narrow dirt road.

"I'm coming, Jamie!"

Bobbie Gentry was not going to die today.

# *Six*

*Hurry! Hurry!*

She had to get away. The last vestige of good sense she possessed restrained the urgency. She drove as fast as she dared. Though it was daylight, the narrow and crooked road was hard to navigate.

She fought the steering wheel, taking the curves with the SUV's back end fishtailing.

*He's dead. He's dead.*

Uncertainty trickled into her thoughts. Had she killed him? If she hadn't killed him, she had come damned close.

*I'm free!* Bobbie glanced around the gloom of the woods. She had escaped. She'd stabbed him. He'd been bleeding.

Tears rolled down her cheeks. Her breath came in big, rushing gulps. She was free. She was going home!

She needed a phone. She glanced around the interior of the SUV.

The steering wheel jerked to the right as the passenger-side tires bumped off the shoulder of the narrow road. She corrected, pulling the vehicle back in line.

"Pay attention." She had to get as far away from that cabin as possible—as far away from *him* as possible.

"Find the main road. Drive to the nearest town." She drew in a deep breath and let it go slowly. "Good plan, Bobbie."

Did she have enough fuel?

She glanced at the gauge. Three-quarters of a tank. Of course the monster wouldn't take any chances. He was too careful, too organized. He would never be so incompetent as to run out of gas.

There was no way to know where she was. Another state, for sure. The Storyteller always selected a victim from one state and then disposed of that victim in another.

Would he be coming after her? She checked the rearview mirror. Even if he wasn't injured, he couldn't run this fast.

She had stabbed him in the chest...close to the center. She'd seen the blood. She'd beaten the hell out of him with that rickety old chair.

Was he dead?

She should have checked his pulse. Maybe injected him with whatever he'd intended to shoot into her veins. She shook her head. No way would she have gotten that close to him. She had to get away. Her son was waiting for her. She could only imagine how much he had cried the past few weeks. Had he attended his daddy's funeral?

Bobbie swiped at her tears with the back of her hand. "We'll be okay, baby." Her lips trembled. Would she ever really be okay again? Could she be a good mother after what Perry had done to her?

Would Jamie be safe with her?

A deer leaped across the road.

Bobbie hit the brakes. The SUV slid on the muddy road. The rear end fishtailed. She tried to straighten out. Couldn't. The vehicle bulldozed into a tree.

Her head hit the steering wheel.

Bobbie felt paralyzed for a moment. She blinked.

Her head ached. She touched her forehead. No blood. *Thank God.*

She assessed the rest of her body. No worse than when she'd climbed into the vehicle. She scanned the area. Nothing but trees and that narrow road. She twisted around and looked back the way she had come. No sign of Perry.

"Okay." She moistened her dry, damaged lips. "Just get out of here." The engine had died. She tried restarting it. When she turned the key there was nothing but a *click click click*.

"Shit!"

She had to get moving. She looked around again. If he had survived, could she walk without him catching up? Her muscles were weak and her leg was broken for sure, but adrenaline made her stronger than she had a right to be.

What she really needed was a phone. She searched the vehicle. In the back floorboard she found a tire iron covered in blood. He'd bragged about hitting James with his tire iron. A moan tore out of her. He'd used this to kill her husband. She grabbed the heavy tool. The urge to run back to that cabin and bash his head in with the damned thing was nearly overwhelming.

*No.* She threw it down. She had to get to Jamie. The tire iron would only weigh her down.

The boots he'd worn in the snow stood in the passenger-side floorboard. She grabbed them and tugged them on. No weapons. No flashlight or communication device.

She climbed out of the vehicle and listened. Silence swallowed her up. She zipped the coat and followed the road. "If this is as good as it gets, so be it."

Pain vibrated up her right leg with every step. She ignored it. She tried to judge the time of day. How much light did she have left? The sun was high in the sky. Noon or one o'clock, maybe. Which meant she only had three or four hours before dark. She had to move faster. There could be miles between her and civilization.

Bobbie lost count of the number of times she fell. She tried to pinpoint a part of her body that didn't hurt. Everything hurt. The pain in her leg steadily worsened. Didn't matter. She had to keep going. She *would* keep going.

The sun had dropped considerably. She could scarcely see a slice of it hovering above the treetops now. She was cold as hell. How long before hypothermia set in? *You're okay as long as you're moving. Keep going.* The sky was clear. No worry about snow or rain, but the temperature would drop dramatically as night fell.

Surely she'd find a road before dark.

The adrenaline was receding now and her body trembled. Her muscles didn't want to work right. She felt uncoordinated and as weak as a kitten. Over and over she looked back, but there was nothing but the encroaching gloom.

She was so tired. Could she risk sitting down just for a moment to catch her breath?

*No.* She had to keep moving. Her feet were numb. She thought of all the people Gaylon Perry had murdered and she kept walking.

Her son's sweet laughter and her husband's sexy smile urged her onward. She missed them so much. Her life would have so many empty places without James. But she had Jamie. Her baby would fill her life with happiness. She and James had promised each other that if one of them died, the other would make sure Jamie had the best life possible. He would always come first.

"I'm coming, Jamie."

She felt guilty for having given up for a while. Giving herself grace—maybe that had been the only way to survive the horrors she had endured.

By the time dusk crept through the trees, the cold had seeped deep into her bones. The road seemed to go on and on. She walked in one of the ruts to ensure she didn't veer off and hit another tree.

How much farther?

Nausea had begun to churn in her belly. She had tuned out much of the pain, but it was there, pulsing and radiating beneath her skin. Her right leg was numb. By now whatever bone he had broken would be on the way to mending, not necessarily the way it was supposed to.

A sound hummed in the distance. Bobbie staggered to a stop.

A vehicle…? She had to be close to a road.

She hobbled faster. The too-big boots made her stumble again, but she dragged herself up and kept going. Her heart pounded so hard she worried it would burst.

She was going to make it. Soon she would hold her baby.

A surge of strength filled her and she moved a little faster. The road took a sharp turn and the trees gave away to a broad expanse of asphalt that split through the woods in either direction like an endless black river.

She cried out with relief.

Her body trembled so violently she could hardly stay vertical.

She picked a direction and started walking. Another vehicle would come along eventually. All she had to do was keep moving and try to maintain her body heat. She hugged the coat tighter around her. The disgusting smell of the monster she'd left bleeding on the floor made her sick. She comforted herself with the knowledge that she had beaten him.

She could scarcely walk by the time twin beams of light topped the rise in the distance. Bobbie perked up. She couldn't really feel her lower body anymore. Her bare legs and sockless feet were freezing.

This was the first vehicle to come along since she found the road.

As the headlights neared she moved into the center of the road and forced her arms over her head. She started to wave.

The car would either stop or it would run her over.

# Seven

Paramedics had arrived first. They'd patched Bobbie up as best they could under the circumstances. The noose around her neck had been removed, the wound cleaned and bandaged. One of the paramedics had rounded up an extra uniform for her to put on, along with long johns, thick socks and sneakers. It felt good to be warm again. The Mississippi State Police were on the scene within half an hour of Bobbie's call. An agent from the Meridian FBI field office had arrived minutes later along with the Lauderdale County Sheriff's Department. Bobbie's partner and chief, as well as the FBI agents who had been working the Storyteller case, were en route. All personnel on site were preparing to move in on the cabin, save one deputy who would stay behind to escort the late arrivals.

"Detective Gentry, you really should be at the hospital," the paramedic named Thad insisted. "You're dehydrated and your blood pressure is way low. That leg is in bad shape. You have numerous lacerations that appear to be infected and at least one toe that's frostbitten."

She shook her head. "Not until this is done."

Thad exhaled a big breath. "I wish I could give you something for the pain. It has to be bad."

She waved him off and headed toward the sheriff's SUV. The plan was to go in via the county's four-wheel-drive vehicles. Before they reached the cabin, a group would unload, continue through the woods on foot and surround the cabin. If Perry was still alive and heard them coming, he would make a run for it. She had not seen a firearm and she hadn't found one in the SUV. Still, she couldn't confirm that he was unarmed.

Bobbie had him figured for dead. He would have come after her if he'd survived. With her bum leg, she felt confident he could have caught up with her even with the meager head start she'd managed with the SUV.

*He was dead.* She repeated those words over and over in her head as she loaded into the passenger seat. She wanted him to be dead.

As soon as she had identified his body—since she was the only person who could ID him—she was going home to her baby. The hospital could wait until she was home.

"You're sure you're up to this, Detective?" Sheriff Dorning asked, his face reflecting the same concerns the paramedic had voiced.

Bobbie lifted her chin and met his assessing gaze with lead in her own. "I'm not going anywhere until this is done."

Dorning nodded. "Can't say as I blame you."

Two other SUVs moved ahead of the sheriff's. Bobbie's heart rate picked up with every mile they drove. She couldn't wait to see that son of a bitch's face, pale

with death and twisted in surprise. She hoped he had
felt every drop of warm blood draining from his body,
leaving him cold and dying. She hoped he had shit his
pants while the last moments of life drifted from him.

When they reached the SUV she'd wrecked, getting
around it proved a challenge. The Lauderdale County
SUVs barely squeaked between its rear bumper and the
trees on the other side of the road.

The cabin wasn't far now.

She pushed aside the uncertainty that threatened to
resurrect during the final mile or so of the dark journey.
Under no circumstances was she going to allow the fear
to best her. She hadn't survived the bowels of hell to fall
apart now. As the headlights bounced against the log
exterior of her prison, her heart thudded harder. Uniforms had already fanned out around the small building.

"You should stay in the vehicle until it's safe to get
out," Dorning offered.

"Not a chance, Sheriff."

When they'd both emerged and rounded the hood,
he put a hand on her arm. "At least stay behind me."

Bobbie acquiesced. He was armed and she wasn't.
No point putting herself in unnecessary danger. She
wanted to see that this guy was dead, and then she
wanted to get home to her baby.

Her chest hurt with the renewed realization that
home would never be the same. James was gone.

"Clear!" The single word echoed through the darkness.

Uniforms had entered the cabin.

She hurried to keep up with the sheriff. Her heart
started that fierce rush as if she were running a mara-

thon. She needed to see the body, to confirm that the stake she'd wielded had hit its mark.

She wanted him in hell where he belonged.

The sheriff walked through the door; she was right on his heels. The smell of urine and feces instantly hit her.

When the sheriff stalled a few feet inside the cabin, Bobbie moved around him.

There was no body.

*The Storyteller was gone.*

Her heart plummeted to her stomach. "He was right there." She pointed to the blood on the floor and the shattered chair.

Sheriff Dorning moved closer. "Judging by the amount of blood he lost, he likely didn't make it far."

Bobbie drifted into a trance of disbelief and despair as the sheriff barked orders to his men. They were calling in the search dogs. The FBI agent was on the phone relaying the news.

She heard someone say that the Montgomery chief of police had arrived. The pain she had been ignoring abruptly roared back to life. The room started to spin and Bobbie crashed to the floor.

Someone called her name. She tried to focus on the face. Newt, her partner, was coming toward her…or was she imagining him?

"We've got you now, Bobbie," Newt's voice said.

She couldn't see his face anymore. Her eyes refused to stay open.

"We're getting you out of here."

*Yes… I'm ready.* The words trapped inside her.

"Don't worry about anything else," he said gently.

"We'll find that son of a bitch. You're going to be fine, Bobbie. Just fine."

Her partner was right. She stopped fighting and let go, drifting into the darkness. She was going to be fine.

She was going home to her baby.

\* \* \* \* \*

# Get 4 FREE REWARDS!

**We'll send you 2 FREE Books plus 2 FREE Mystery Gifts.**

**FREE**
Value Over
**$20**

Both the **Romance** and **Suspense** collections feature compelling novels written by many of today's best-selling authors.